the princess and the paparazzi

a modern fairytale retelling of the Prince and the Pauper

Lit Lovers

ciara blume

COPYRIGHT PAGE

The Princess and the Paparazzi by Ciara Blume

Published by Dolce Villa Press

www.ciarablume.com

This is a work of fiction. All characters, businesses, events, and situations
portrayed in this book are fictional and not intended to represent any real
person, business, event, or situation. Names, characters, businesses, events,
and incidents are the products of the author's imagination. Any resemblance
to actual persons, living or dead, or actual events is purely coincidental.

The views and opinions expressed in this book are those of the characters
and do not necessarily reflect the views or opinions of the author or
publisher.

To all the Princesses in my life, past and present, who take the dares, crash the parties, get on boats and planes, and sometimes get in over their heads. Life is too short to sit around, staring at the grass on the other side of the fence, wondering.

"I am a princess. All girls are. Even if they live in tiny old attics. Even if they dress in rags, even if they aren't pretty, or smart, or young. They're still princesses."

- Frances Hodgson Burnett, A Little Princess

"So we grew together, Like to a double cherry, seeming parted, But yet a union in partition, Two lovely berries moulded on one stem."

- Helena, from A Midsummer Night's Dream by William Shakespeare

prologue: kenna

. . .

 podcast, we're talking about all things summer. Summer romances ... beach reads ... summer stock theater!"

I'm listening to my friends' podcast while I take photos of a fluffy Pomeranian stray that's just been groomed. I take the beauty shots for the shelter's website. Today, like most days, I'm doing the pictures in the Celestial Pets boutique owned by my best friend, Georgia. But I'm alone in the colorful shop today because, for the first time in years, Georgia has taken a few days off.

This mutt has a delightful underbite and shining, bug-like eyes. I suspect there's some chihuahua in the mix. She's standing on a carpeted platform, in front of the star-and-constellation-themed photo wall, panting placidly and staring regally at me. She seems unperturbed by the gleaming, bejeweled tiara that is balanced precariously on her head and the cloud-like, white-tulle tutu that she is practically engulfed in. Her pink tongue is dangling out of her mouth, just slightly off center. Her expression seems to say, "Well? Are you going to get on with it?"

As I lift my battered, old camera back up to my eye, the battery dies. Again. I pop in my only spare, an off-brand one that barely holds half a charge.

"We'll have to make this quick, your highness," I tell the dog. She wags her tail expectantly, and I am prepared to pounce in order to catch the tiara, but somehow she manages to keep it on herself. She lifts her furry chin and resumes her regal pose.

"To the manner born!" I laugh. I snap a few more shots.

"We're all pretty excited about the celebrities coming to Ephron for the summer stock theater season," says Alexis. "I cannot believe Lorelei Dupont and Rafe Barzilay will be here in town! I wonder if Rafe likes to shop local? I wouldn't mind bumping into him in the produce aisle."

Alexis always likes to lay it on thick, gushing about sexy celebrities. But then again, haven't I thought the same on occasion? Who hasn't had a fantasy or seven about the chiseled, Israeli actor who plays the title character in the *Titanium Man* superhero trilogy?

"He *is* pretty hot," I explain to the dog. "He's got that amazing, long, dark hair and those dark, mysterious eyes. He's gorgeous. He's perfect. Nobody messes with Titanium Man." Even thinking about him right now makes me feel a little swoony. Oof. What if I did run into him at the supermarket? I probably wouldn't be able to speak.

The dog gives me a look that's dripping with pity. "Don't you judge," I say to her. "If you ever met Rafe Barzilay, you'd be drooling all over him, too."

She sniffs and turns to chew on her butt. Now the tiara does fall off. I catch it with my free hand and wait a moment for her to settle before placing the decoration back on her head.

"I have to say, things really are changing here in Ephron," says Chelsea, another one of the podcast hosts. "Do you think it's becoming just like one of those small towns that romance novels are set in?"

"You're too much with the rose-colored glasses, sis," groans Jackson, Chelsea's cynical brother who is the main host and founder of the podcast. "You're only saying that because you're so in lurve with the theater owner, Dean Riley."

Chelsea might have a point about the romance novel effect. In the last year, three of my local friends have managed to meet their "perfect" mates and fall in love. I, meanwhile, have remained single.

I pause the podcast.

I'm so sick of third-wheeling it. Why am I still alone? I don't know why I resist so hard when people try to set me up with "nice" guys. How many times have Georgia and her boyfriend tried to fix me up with Jackson? Men like him look down their noses at me. Maybe if I hadn't moved in with Cody right out of high school I would have gone to college. But I didn't go to college. Instead, I wasted five years of my life on a toxic, stoner loser.

And now I still live at home with my uncles, who are the closest thing to parents that I have.

I'm a lowly barista who takes photos of dogs. It's not so glamorous, but it's better than being with a gaslighter. Cody's limited life skills include packing bongs, setting up "sick" gaming systems, doing dirtbike donuts, and making me doubt myself.

I'm glad I got out when I did, but I wish I had those years back. It doesn't feel like I've moved on. My friends are all getting married. Georgia is having a baby. A child! She's going to be a parent, and I'm still living like a teenager. I'm being lapped.

The bootleg spare battery dies before I even have a chance to review my shots.

"Crap." I set the camera back into my backpack. "I guess we'll just have to hang out together for a while, Princess Von Floofy," I christen the canine. She just looks like a princess.

Since no one's coming for the dog just yet, and there aren't any customers in the shop, there's not much else to do besides chill.

I take the costume off the mutt and scoop her up, carrying her to the back of the shop where a worn and faded wingback armchair has always had pride of place near the counter. *My* chair. Georgia and I both call it that because I spend all my spare time hanging here.

Except, my chair isn't here. It's missing. In its place is a brand-new bassinet. Still wrapped in plastic and only partially assembled. What the hell? Where is my chair? Peeking into the back room, I locate it ... shoved behind a clothing rack.

"Let's go for a ride, Princess." I plop the dog onto the chair and slide it back out into the shop.

I'm so tired. Princess makes room for me on the seat and snuggles right into me. I close my eyes. I worked a double shift yesterday and opened the diner this morning.

I am just starting to drift off when my phone bursts into song. "Mama Mia" by Abba. It's the ringtone I have set for my uncles, who are presently on their annual trip to the Greek Islands.

I swipe my uncle Nick's face on the screen. It's only been a week, but I miss him and Stavros being at the diner every day when I clock in for my shifts.

"Kenna!" Nick is sitting outside, on their rental's patio, which during the daytime has spectacular views of the Mediterranean. His salt-and-pepper, hipster mustache and beard are perfectly groomed, as usual. But his nose and forehead look a little sunburned. He's wearing a blue, linen, button-down shirt, and his smile is more relaxed than I've seen it in ages. Vacation smile. He looks a little drunk, and very happy. "How's my girl?"

"I'm good. It's late there, no?"

"Yes, almost 2 a.m. Wow! We had some friends over and lost track of the time. I've got some big news, and I wanted to share it with you. Uncle Stavros and I are thinking about buying a place on the island!"

"Like a timeshare? For your annual visits?" I ask, getting the distinct feeling that I'm about to get some shit delivered in sparkly wrapping paper.

"No, Kenna." Uncle Nick is beaming. "Like a semi-permanent thing. We're considering opening a little café here and slowing things down. We're not getting any younger."

"But ... what about the diner? Will you get Carlos to manage it full time?" I lean forward in the chair. *I will not hyperventilate. I will not vomit.* Princess Von Floofy licks the underside of my chin.

"No. Carlos is even older than me and Stavros. We've spoken to a realtor, and we're going to try and see what we can get for the diner. You, me, and Stavros. Three-way split." Uncle Nick grins, and I can see Uncle Stavros in the background, clearing dishes from the table. "It's a great time to sell. The place is doing well, and with all that's been going on in Ephron, I'm sure we can find a buyer."

"You would sell the diner?" It's unthinkable! The Ephron Diner has been run by Papadopoulos family members since the 1950s.

"Nothing lasts forever, sweetie. Think of what a great fresh start this could be for all of us. Anyway, Stavros and I wouldn't move here full time till September, so nothing's happening tonight. I just wanted to give you a heads-up that we've listed the diner and the house with Hearth and Holm Realty. Let's just see if there are any bites."

"The house, too?" *The house with the apartment over the garage, where I currently live, rent-free?*

September is only three months away.

"It's going to be okay, Kenna." Uncle Stavros grabs the phone and chastises Uncle Nick. "Why do you have to tell her like this? We're still here for you, honey. Maybe you want to come to Greece and stay with us here. You should see how many cats there are living on this island. I bet you would take the best photos of them! Maybe you could make a calendar. We could sell it to tourists in our café!"

For a moment, I actually consider this. Living on a Greek Island, taking photos of cats, does not sound terrible. It definitely beats 5 a.m. shifts that start with me sleepily schlepping forty-pound bags of beans and coaxing coffee out the world's crankiest espresso machine. Snapping photos of lazy, feral felines catnapping on blue benches, shaded by bunches of fuchsia-colored bougainvillea is way sexier than wiping crusty food off the laminated menus and scraping gum off the undersides of tables at 1 a.m. But then I pan back and observe the bigger picture.

Sponging off my elderly gay uncles, as I turn the big 3-0, is hardly aspirational, even for me.

I know how much both of them have dreamed of retiring to Mykonos someday. I just hadn't expected that day to come so soon. Somehow, I thought I'd just keep living in the apartment above the garage and working at the diner indefinitely. At least until I figure out what I really want to do with my life.

"I understand." I swallow and force a smile onto my face. "Sounds like a great plan. You two deserve this."

The pity party commences the moment I end the call. Why isn't Georgia here to talk with me about this? I really need her to be here, not off glamping in a yurt with her handsome, wealthy fiancé.

My friends are all falling in love, getting married, and having children. My beloved uncles are jetting off to Greece and selling the family biz. Meanwhile, I'm a twenty-eight-year-old orphan with no man in my life, no real career, a semi-functional camera, and a lapful of dog fur. I am the poster child for arrested development. I'm still wearing the friendship bracelet Georgia made for me in high school.

I haven't felt this alone since my mom died when I was fourteen. Honestly, what do I have going for me besides making a decent cup of coffee and taking okayish photos of dogs?

"What am I going to do?" I ask Princess. But she's fallen asleep and she merely snuffles and snores, wiggling closer to my belly.

Hey Kenna! I stopped in the diner earlier, but they told me you were photographing some strays today.

Got a min?

My phone lights up with a message from Dean Riley, the owner of the same theater that was being discussed on the *Lit Lovers'* podcast episode.

Just finished the shoot. What's up?
Everything going well with the show?

Yes! That's what I'm texting about. Can I get you to take some photos for the playbill?

I sit up straighter in the chair. Princess grunts her displeasure at this.

Like what ... photos of the sets?

No, you dork, photos of the talent.

Dean includes a LOL emoji.

Everyone is arriving this weekend. They'll be getting settled, and rehearsals start the following week.

You want me to take photos of celebrities?

I pet the sleeping dog absentmindedly as I text.

You do know I'm a pet photographer?

We want to work with locals. Pets are way harder to capture than people. It's just headshots. It'll be a piece of cake for a pro like you!

I eye my old Canon DSLR dubiously. It's flattering that Dean thinks I can handle this. But even if I can, I'm pretty sure my camera can't.

Can I think about it for a day or two?

There's nothing to think about. Can't wait to introduce you to Lorelei Dupont. You two look so much alike, it'll be a trip. Let's discuss more on Monday.

I'll get back to you.

Great, as long as you say yes. I'm counting on your help!

There's no way I can take photos of actual celebrities with this camera. And there is no way I can afford to buy a new one. My heart sinks with the certain knowledge that I'm going to have to let him down.

kenna

· · ·

I'M in the middle of remaking a drink, for the fourth time, when the cute cop with the whiskey-colored eyes and buzz-cut hair skips to the front of the line, leaves cash and a generous tip for his cinnamon bun, and winks at me before leaving. He looks so familiar, but I can't put my finger on it. Did I see him at The Onion or The Grumpy Stump? There are only so many places that people my age can socialize here in Ephron.

My phone, sitting beside the register, lights up with a burst of animated hearts and flames on the notification screen. One new match on the dating app. I can't resist tapping the screen to see who I matched with.

That's why the cop looked so familiar. I saw him on the dating app.

"Hey, are you going to gimme my drink, or what?" The disgruntled customer demands my attention.

"Okay." I set the phone down. "That's a four-shot, half-caf, soy milk latte ... no foam." I push the drink across the counter. "Did you need me to take its temperature this time?"

The man in the black beanie fixes me with an exasperated stare. "If you don't mind, honey." He taps his fingers on the counter impatiently. I can't help but notice the dirt under his nails. Gross.

"You got it!" I chirp with mock cheer. I plop the glass food thermometer into his drink. We both wait while the mercury rises. I'm sick of remaking this drink. The other attempts were all unacceptable to him. Too foamy. Too milky. Too hot. The Starbucks mermaid herself couldn't please this dude. He even had the nerve to ask if there was anyone else who knows their way around the espresso maker better than me.

"Nice camera," I comment, looking longingly at the Sony camera with the superzoom lens slung on his hip. He glances down at it, stroking it proudly and preening a bit.

"Yeah, she's a beaut." His face softens slightly.

I remove the thermometer, reading off the number. "It's 195 degrees, exactly."

"You sure? Maybe you didn't leave it in there long enough. I don't wanna get burned."

"If you wait much longer, it's going to get cold," I say, pushing the paper cup toward him. "And you look like you could really use it. Just take it. It's on the house, same as the other ones."

And if he doesn't like it, there's a Circle K down the street with a coffee machine that I'd be happy to direct him to.

"Okay, okay. No need to get snippy," he remarks, digging in his pocket for a tip. He waves the five-dollar bill around show-ily, making sure everyone else in the diner gets a gander at his generosity before shoving it in the tip jar. "I was kind of hoping you and I could be friends. You from this town?"

"Why? Who wants to know?"

"America wants to know, sweetie." His voice is gravelly, with a hint of East Coast. He takes a sip and raises his eyebrows, nodding at the cup that has finally passed muster. "Eh, what do you know? This isn't half bad."

"You should try it with almond milk and one less shot next time." The suggestion just spills out of me, unbidden. I hold out a packet of raw sugar. I cannot help it. I'm a coffee witch. It's a blessing and a curse. Particularly when I know people are ordering the wrong drink. Their whole day would go better if they'd just take my advice.

He eyes me skeptically. "You think I don't know how I take my own coffee?" But he takes the sugar and tears it open with his teeth, spitting paper out on the floor.

"Anyway, sweetheart," the man says, still eyeing me cannily, "I was hoping you could help me out." He reaches into his back pocket and fishes out his cell phone, swipes it a couple of times, and turns it to face me. "You seen this guy around here lately?"

If only.

"Isn't that the actor who plays Titanium Man?" I feign wide-eyed surprise at his photo of Rafe Barzilay.

"You recognize him?"

That explains the giant lens and expensive camera. It figures that the paparazzi would arrive just ahead of the celebrities. *If only I had a camera as nice as this guy's to shoot on. It isn't fair.*

"I mean, doesn't everyone know Titanium Man?" I answer.

Over the man's shoulder, I notice Noah Greenberg, a local high school teacher limping into the diner with his laptop. *Saved by the bell.*

I wave hello at Noah, greeting him extra enthusiastically in order to make my point that I'm done with the pushy photographer. "Hey Noah! So great to see you here! What can I make for you? The usual?"

Before he turns to go, the photographer slaps his card on the counter. "You'll let me know if you see any celebrity types? Text me any time. I pay a sweet finder's fee." He does the thing where he points to his eyes with two fingers, then points at mine, and back at his own.

"Mm-hmm, sure! You betcha! Have a nice day." I slide the card into my apron pocket and turn my back on him, busying myself with cleaning up my area. Finally, he gets the message and slinks away, heading out the door toward Holm Square.

As soon as his back is turned, I drop his card into the trash. Is it wrong for me to wish a fly finds its way into his cup?

"What was all that about?" Noah asks as he gets settled with his laptop at the counter. "What was with the mafia eye-finger thing? Was he threatening you?"

"Not really." I make him his usual mocha macchiato. "Mostly annoying me." I notice now that Noah's got his cast off, and he doesn't have the crutches anymore. He's graduated to a walking stick. Wonder when that happened? Noah is definitely an under-the-radar kind of guy. Regular brown hair. Medium tall. His eyes are nice. Sort of puppy dog-like. He reminds me a little of Chandler from *Friends*.

"Looks like he's not going anywhere." Noah tilts his head toward the park. Through the diner window, I can see our new friend slouched on a park bench, holding up a newspaper in a pathetic attempt to camouflage the giant camera in his lap.

"That's not conspicuous," I joke.

I hand Noah his drink. "We should probably get used to his type hanging around here," he says. "There's bound to be at least a few of them, given the all-star cast Dean Riley has lined up for his theater."

"Yeah, you're right," I agree. "I just wish they weren't so predatory."

"Not much we can do about it." Noah sips his coffee. "This is great, as usual." He studies me for a moment. "Is there anything else bugging you, Kenna? Anything you need to talk about?"

When I don't respond immediately, he sets down the coffee and folds his hands together. Just waiting and gazing at me patiently.

Maybe it's his understanding-English-teacher tone of voice, or maybe it's because I really have nobody else to talk to, or maybe it's the fact that I know I've got to get back to Dean Riley today.

"Dean Riley asked me to take photos of the cast, and I don't think I can do it," I blurt.

"Don't be silly, Kenna. Dean wouldn't have asked if he didn't think you were up to the task."

I retrieve my backpack from under the counter and pull out my camera. I plonk it down in front of him. The flash is completely missing—it looks like an empty eye socket—and there is duct tape holding on the cover to the battery compartment. There's a strawberry, scratch-and-sniff sticker on the strap that lost its scent seven years ago, but there's still some sticky stuff on the part I tried to peel off. Bits of lint and several strands of my hair are stuck in the residual goo.

"It's one thing when I'm taking photos of dogs. But how can I show up to take photos of celebrities with *this*?" I wave a hand over the camera, presenting it in all its flawed glory. "I mean, I can't. It's too embarrassing."

"You know, I'd be happy to check a few blogs and see what *Consumer Reports* recommends if you're in the market for a new one," Noah offers. "I have a subscription."

"Thanks, but there's no point." I politely turn him down and pack my camera. "Excuse me. I think it's time for my break."

I already know exactly what model camera I want. And I know there's no way I can afford it. Not even in my wildest dreams. I might as well dream about dating Rafe Barzilay and hanging out poolside with Lorelei Dupont, braiding each other's hair and snapping selfies.

"I'm taking my break," I call out to Carlos, who is sanitizing menus in the back room. Carlos is normally our delivery guy, but he's been filling in a lot since my uncles went on vacation. He sets down the spray bottle and his rag and wipes a forearm across his leathery, wrinkled brow.

"No problem, Kenna. I'll take over. Take your time."

I need to figure out what I'm going to tell Dean. As if on autopilot, I fill a bag with muffins and exit the diner. First, I'll do a loop around Holm Square to stretch my legs, then I'll head over to Celestial Pets to sit in my chair and think.

Will I regret turning down the offer to photograph the cast?

I pull a coin from my apron as I pass the fountain at the center of the square. What to wish for? New camera? Boyfriend? Vacation? I don't even know what to wish for. Kissing the coin, I toss it in with a more general request. *I just wish something good would happen for me, for a change.*

The idea of meeting Rafe Barzilay in the flesh is thrilling. Scary, but thrilling. He is iconic. As nervous as I am to even potentially meet Rafe, the thought of meeting Lorelei Dupont gives me butterflies. For totally different reasons. Dean Riley wasn't the first person to tell me I look like her.

I've been hearing how much I look like Lorelei since I was eight and she was America's darling, starring in a top sitcom on the leading kid's network. Everyone was always commenting how much I looked like "Moxie McAllister," the sassy, freckled, redheaded kid detective. Except with blonde hair and fewer freckles. I'd loved hearing it, too ... until Moxie and her show both jumped the shark.

After the show was canceled, Lorelei dyed her hair black, hit the party circuit, and was at the center of a number of unfortunate tabloid scandals. "Poxy Moxie" became a meme when someone suggested she was spreading STDs. When that shithead Bryce Holm called me that at a house party our freshman year, Georgia had nearly beaten the shit out of him.

That episode had really cemented my friendship with Georgia. She is a badass force that is not to be messed with.

Lorelei Dupont dropped out of the mainstream media for a while, mostly acting in indie films, but she'd come back as a supervillain—the Ember Enchantress—in the two final Titanium Man films.

I'm surprised that Dean made the connection between us. Grown-up Lorelei 2.0 looks nothing like Moxie, or me. As the Ember, she is pale and severe, with long, glossy, black hair and a vaguely Russian accent.

My phone buzzes. There's another notification from the dating app. The cute cop has sent me a message. I pause to perch on a park bench while I open the app to read it. First, I look back over the cop's profile. He's no Rafe Barzilay, but he's cute. Medium height, obviously into bodybuilding and working out. His photos show him lifting weights, hunting, and fishing. No dirt bikes, bongs, or gaming consoles. A good sign.

Tentatively, I open his message.

> Hi, Kenna. Would you be open to a throuple? My wife and I are looking to spice things up. We'd love for you to be our cinnamon bun.

Ummmm ... no. No. No! And why? Why does this happen to me? The last guy I dated off this app asked me to go in on a cosmetic surgery groupon with him. I'm done. I'm going to be alone forever.

> No thanks!

Immediately, he unmatches and blocks me, leaving me to wonder how many people he's propositioned with pastry references. Yeuch!

"Hi, Angie, I've come bearing muffins," I announce myself as I walk in the pet shop.

"Well hello, dear." The kind-eyed, older woman in a tie-dyed "Man's Best Friend" tee greets me as I march into the shop and seat myself into the comfy, wingback chair. It's still sitting in the middle of the store, and it just doesn't feel right there. I drag it back toward the register, shoving it awkwardly in the corner. It's a little cramped behind the bassinet, but I can still sort of fit. I fling myself in my seat properly, sitting sideways with my legs draped over the arms, legs swinging rhythmically as I think.

Angie sets aside her romance novel and pushes her reading glasses down her nose to look at me. "Oh, dear. Is it that bad?" Absentmindedly, she jiggles a pink stroller parked beside her, as if to keep a baby asleep. An elderly pug pokes its head up, and I cannot help but notice the dog's pirate costume. I raise an eyebrow.

"It's not International Talk Like a Pirate Day till September, but Daisy Bones here was feeling saucy," the woman explains. Angie is one of the local shelter's biggest benefactors. When she is not working there or filling in here at the boutique, she can be found dressing up her rescue mutts. She was the natural choice to mind the shop in Georgia's absence.

"I need some advice, Angie," I say. Perhaps Angie has some sage wisdom to share.

"Advice? From me?" She looks flattered and stands up straighter, brushing pet hair from her shirt. "I'd be honored. What's this about? Boy trouble ... again? You know, if I were you, I would spend more time volunteering at the pet shelter. You never know what kind of man you might meet there. We get some real super heroes passing through. You know, serious alpha males? Abs of Steel. Top dogs? You catch my drift?" She winks and wiggles her eyebrows at me like she is performing a vaudeville act.

I let it go. Clearly Angie, like everyone in Ephron, still associates me with my big, bad breakup with Cody, even though it's been over five years. It's like my bio reads: *Poor Kenna, she has the worst taste in men. Once a doormat, always a doormat.*

"Nope, it's not about a boy." I open the bag and take out a muffin, pausing to offer one to Angie before stuffing my face. She waves the bag away.

"It's about the theater—" I start to say, but my phone rings, interrupting me. I check the screen. It's Carlos.

"One sec." I hold up a finger and answer the phone.

"I'm so sorry, Kenna," Carlos apologizes. "I don't want to steal your break, but we have a big delivery order that needs to go to the theater, ASAP. They were going to pick it up, but they just called back to ask us if we'd bring it to them instead."

"Okay, I'll be back in fifteen minutes," I say. "Can you wait till I get back to take it?"

"Okay, but everything is ready now. Also, my car is getting detailed. I can't do the delivery. They want it right now. I don't know what to do."

"Fine. I'll deliver it then. Can I just take five minutes to pee?" I ask.

"Well, that's the other thing," Carlos says. "Hurry. That guy from earlier is back. The one with the Brooklyn accent? He said he found a fly in his coffee, and he needs you to make him a fresh one."

lorelei

. . .

"SERIOUSLY," Rafe says to the local actor playing the part of Puck, "next time, you have to let Lorelei pick out your lunch. It's freaky how she always knows just what to order, for anyone."

"Thanks a lot, Rafe." I roll my eyes at him. He's correct, of course. Ordering the perfect items for people is my superpower, but it's a large group, and I don't really know them all that well yet. Now everyone is going to be coming to me like I'm the DoorDash oracle.

Rafe whispers in my ear as he pecks me on the cheek. "That's what you get for calling my new dog an ugly pug. Have fun choosing everyone's side orders all summer."

To the group he says, "Sorry, I gotta run, guys. Great read through. Great meeting everyone. I can't wait to do this show with you all!"

People start clapping, they adore him so much. He's so genuine, so charismatic, so real. I'd hate him if he wasn't my best friend.

We are all gathered in the covered seating area in front of the amphitheater's circular stage. The rear of the stage is flanked by a series of platforms, stairs, and ramps that will bring the action to multiple levels. Beyond that, a forest of tall, swaying pines stands silent and majestic.

Although the stage and the area where we are seated is covered, it still feels completely open. It feels more like a ship, floating in an ocean of trees.

All of the building materials have taken their cues from the landscape. They are either natural wood tones or shades of green. The only other colors come from the baskets hanging from the lampposts. These are bursting with clouds of purple, red, and orange blooms, spilling out of the bowls like fireworks.

To the left and right of the stage are grassy, terraced areas where theatergoers who want a less formal experience will be able to pack a picnic, spread out a blanket, and set up camp for the night. Dean has placed a couple dozen striped, green hammocks there for cast members to lounge in between scenes. When we break, half the group heads up the hill to a picnic area, and the other half slinks off to the hammocks.

"Are you sure you can't stay for lunch?" Dean Riley, the theater owner, asks Rafe.

"I wish, but duty calls," Rafe says.

By duty, he means his three-and-a-half-year-old daughter, Orly. And I really don't understand him being at her beck and call like this. What's the point of having a live-in nanny if you're going to be on call 24/7?

Rafe was a lot more fun before Orly came into his life. I mean, he wasn't exactly spontaneous, but I could still talk him into a spur-of-the-moment trip to New Zealand, or going to

Carnival in Venice on occasion. Now, he doesn't want to do anything or go anywhere with his friends. He just wants to hang out at home. With her. If I was into kids, I'd be impressed by the way Rafe is constantly dropping everything for that toddler. It's so twenty-first-century Super Dad.

"Rafe, wait." I follow him up to the gravel parking lot and ask, "Will I see you before you head to LA? Stop by the guesthouse and say goodbye at least?"

Rafe and I are both staying at a rented estate for the summer. Since he has Orly and family visiting, he's staying in the main house. I'm fine by myself in the guesthouse. The house sits on ten acres, with a pool, gardens, and a state-of-the-art security system with twenty-four-hour monitoring.

"Don't worry, Lorelei," Rafe says. "I'm not leaving for another day. You could still do Disneyland with us this weekend. I'm sure my mom would love to see you."

Rafe has been trying to get me to do Disney with him, Orly, and his mother, but that's a hard pass. Titanium Man and the Ember Enchantress go for a spin together on the Tea Cups ride? I can just imagine the feeding frenzy. Then again, I can't. Rafe doesn't go on any rides that involve speed or spinning. Even if we hired a VIP tour guide and somehow managed to steer clear of psycho fans and paparazzi, between him and the toddler, I wouldn't get to ride any of the good rides.

Plus, I don't think his mom actually likes me.

"Your mom hates me," I say. "And I don't want to go to Disney. I just want to chill."

I'm lying, of course. I don't want to chill. I want to go on the Matterhorn and Space Mountain! I just don't want to do it as *me*, the former kid star of the *Moxie McAllister* show. And I certainly don't want to ride the kitschy kid rides as Ember.

It must be nice to go to theme parks and park your car in the far back of the Goofy lot, never worrying about what you'd do if someone in a car recognizes you. I'd gladly stand in line with everyone else for two hours to ride the new Star Wars-themed rides, if I could just have a day at a theme park, pigging out and taking pointless selfies like a normal, non-famous person.

Hell, I'd be happy just moseying through Target, pushing a red cart in a pair of pajama pants. Unnoticed. Undisturbed. Just me and forty aisles of mediocre retail products. Leave me alone. In public.

Once I start with this fantasy, I cannot stop. It takes on a life of its own. Maybe a bookstore. When was the last time I went into a bookstore?

What if I could walk into a bar and order a drink, or sit in the window of a café, writing poetry? Maybe I could drop in on a *DND* session at a local gaming store. Do people still do that?

I'd really been hoping I'd be able to let my hair down here this summer, but so far, I haven't even been able to take off my wig. It's not as bad as LA. But people still know who I am.

"Okay, well, drive safe. Look out for the vultures!" I tell Dean, while he's pulling on his motorcycle helmet. He rode here on a ridiculous, vintage motorbike. The kind with a side car. Zero chance that we'll be carpooling to rehearsals in that thing.

"Do you really think the paparazzi are already here?" he asks.

"Probably," I say.

"Not a problem, I got this." Rafe lowers the mirrored visor down on his helmet. "Nobody's going to suspect it's me. This helmet is awesome. It even has Bluetooth." He revs his engine and speeds off, going only slightly faster than a cautious toddler on a tricycle.

"What do you think, Lorelei?" one of the local actors asks me shyly when I come back down the hill. "Should I have gone with the Reuben or the BLT?" I consider him for a minute before telling him to get the fish and chips next time.

"Really?" he asks incredulously. "I haven't had that since I was a kid. But now that you mention it ..."

"It's so cool how you can do that!" Tabitha, my latest PA, scurries after me as I make my way toward a free hammock. She's pale and uptight, and very overdressed in a navy blue, polyester pants suit that feels a little like a costume or a uniform. She reminds me of an agency nanny. For adults. "Have you always had this amazing talent?" Her solicitousness borders on patronizing, but I prefer it to the checked-out PAs I've had to fire in the past. It's so hard to find a decent PA.

"I guess," I shrug. "We ate out for pretty much every meal when I was growing up. I got good at menus." I don't tell her that my momager was always too busy taking calls and reading scripts to talk to me. Or that I would have been too exhausted to hold up my end of a conversation, even if she'd tried. So I read the menus. I memorized every last item. I could tell you the sides available at all the diners, cafés, burger, and sushi joints in a ten-mile radius of the studio where we filmed *Moxie*. I could tell you what the average prices of the entrées were, and whether they offered fries, onion rings—or both— with their burgers. Not that the momager ever let me order fries. I was on a strict diet of side salads, protein shakes, and the occasional scrambled egg. Moxie McAllister was the kind of kid people liked to call "string bean," not "butterball."

I climb into the striped hammock and cocoon myself.

"Do you need more water? Sunscreen? Bug repellant? Handi Wipes? Snack?" Tabitha buzzes over me in the hammock like a pesky beetle. "Are you sure you're going to be able to manage without me this week? I just hate the idea of leaving you alone. If my sister wasn't getting married … Maybe I should tell her I can't come."

"Aren't you a bridesmaid? I'll be fine, Tabitha," I assure her. "Stop worrying about me. I'm going to be working your ass off all summer. Enjoy the week off."

"I'm just going to go sit in the shade while we wait for the food. Text me if you need anything else from me, Lorelei."

"I'm fine!" I say, closing my eyes. The sun is shining, and it feels so good. Not too hot. The air smells piney and fresh with underlying notes of newly mown grass and sunscreen. Someone's been hitting the classic Coppertone. I listen to the pleasant buzz of the cast and crew around me. It reminds me of my acting camp summers at Idyllwild, the closest thing to a normal childhood I ever experienced. Snippets of conversation. The hum of bees. Laughter.

I snake a finger under my jet-black wig to scratch my scalp, wishing I could take it off altogether. But only my PA, Rafe, and my stylists have seen my natural hair since I started growing it out a year ago. I was surprised to discover that I'm a curly girl and a natural blonde. When you dye your hair every three weeks from the time you are ten till you are well into your twenties, you lose track of your roots.

My natural hair color and texture also could not be further from the stick-straight, black hair that's been my signature look for the last decade. It would be so much easier, not to mention more comfortable, to take the wig off. But of course, I can't just do that. I'm not a real person. I'm a brand. Normal people can change it up any time. People like me need to consult their manager and their agent and a life coach, aka the "advisory board," first. It feels like every little change has to be run by a team of professionals and a focus group.

On the plus side, the wigs are easy. I don't have to spend hours blowing my hair dry or styling it. I just pop on a wig and go. As long as it doesn't get too hot here, I should be fine.

More laughter drifts up from the stage. A group of local teenage girls, one of whom was cast as Helena, are standing center stage and giggling. I open one eye to peek to see they are clustered in a group, making silly faces at a phone that one of them is holding aloft. I'm jealous of these normal girls. Acting in this show is probably a dream come true for them.

"Hey! Ladies! Watch where you're pointing that thing!" I hear my PA chastising the girls. "Don't forget the NDA you signed."

"Leave them alone, Tabitha," I call out. Not that I want to appear in their photos. But I also don't want to spend the whole summer being roasted for acting like a bitchy diva. "They're fine."

kenna

. . .

THE PAPARAZZO IS WAITING for me when I get back to the diner. This time, when I remake his drink, he takes it without comment. And he insists on paying. He pushes another generous tip into the tip jar before settling himself on a stool at the counter.

"Kenna, is it?" He uses my name. "Or do you prefer to be called the 'coffee witch'?" He gestures at the embroidered legend on my barista apron.

I smile at him and nod, without really answering. He makes me uneasy. I suddenly feel incredibly sorry for the celebrities he must habitually stalk.

"Do you ever take pictures of other stuff besides celebs with that camera?" I ask him, pointing at it. His camera is clearly his baby. He doesn't even set it on the counter. He cradles it.

"What, you mean like puppies and kitty cats?" He laughs disdainfully and wrinkles his nose. "That doesn't pay my bills, sweetheart."

His clothes are shabby. I notice the hem of his jeans are frayed and his cuffs are worn. It makes me wonder if he's actually a very good paparazzo.

"Well, you must have started out wanting to take pictures of something besides celebrities," I prod, because now I'm curious. "You didn't pop out of the womb with a lens like that and a penchant for catching pop stars picking their nose, did you?"

The paparazzo laughs. "Nose-picking shots aren't paying what they used to back in the day when using coke was a scandal."

"Shame." I shake my head in mock sympathy.

"You're telling me." He swivels and fidgets in his stool at the counter as he sips his coffee. "But no, you're right. Sort of. I started out doing wildlife photography. Whales mostly. But the seasons are short, and the only whales most folks care about seeing are pregnant supermodels on beach holidays."

"Delivery order up!" the cook yells from the back. He and Carlos carry two large boxes out from the back and set them down on the counter.

Carlos counts the bags of fries and matches the sandwiches against the order that was phoned in earlier as he loads it all into insulated bags. "Are you sure you don't mind doing the delivery to the theater?" he asks me.

"Of course not! It's not far. I think I'll take the bike, actually," I say. Last summer, the uncles bought a custom-painted, three-wheeled cruiser trike for making deliveries here in town. "Think it will all fit in the basket?"

"Just barely," Carlos says. "Let me help you get it loaded."

"Thanks, Carlos," I say, picking up one of the bags. When I turn to say goodbye to the photographer, he's already gone. There's just an empty cup sitting on the counter.

———

Today is the first day that has really felt like summer. As I pedal back across Holm Square, I'm so glad I took the bike.

There are quite a few people enjoying the sunshine in the central town square. The park benches are full, and it's not just the usual seniors who like to sit and feed the pigeons. Moms watch their toddlers splashing in the fountain, and a gaggle of giggling tweens is gathered near the gazebo. I recognize a tall, blonde girl showing off a trick on her skateboard. She's the little sister of Georgia's fiancé, Hudson Holm.

Things have really changed in Ephron since Hudson came back. He renovated his family's old warehouses into live/work spaces, and then he turned his attention to sprucing up the area around Holm Square, including the building that houses the diner and Georgia's shop.

But more importantly, and significantly for me, Hudson fell in love with my best friend.

Georgia deserves to be loved. Worshipped. As tough as I've had it, losing my mom as a teenager, Georgia has had it tougher.

Maybe it was because we both got to Ephron at the beginning of high school. Maybe it was because we'd both been orphans. Or maybe it was the forced proximity of the diner and the pet store, side-by-side neighbors. But Georgia and I bonded fast— and hard. She's more than a best friend. She's family. From heartache to fashion disasters, true love to true loss, she's always been there for me and vice versa. We've done it all, toasted the toasts, and held each other's hair.

But lately, less so.

Lately, Georgia's life has revolved around her booming business and blossoming relationship with Hudson. It's only natural. It's not like she's deliberately ditched me or anything. It's just that I feel like I've gone from being her costar to being a bit player. Maybe if I had my shit more together—if I had a boyfriend, too, and a solid career—this wouldn't be the case.

I notice an unfamiliar, old man in overalls strolling along Main Street. He waves at me as I pedal toward him and points toward an old car with tinted windows and California plates that is crawling slowly down the street behind me. I look back over my shoulder, doing a double take.

Is that the same paparazzo who was just talking to me in the diner?

The old man is waving me over with his cane. He looks super familiar, but I don't think I've seen him in the diner. He's wearing a flannel shirt with overalls, and he has on an old-fashioned, wool-brimmed cap that's shading his face. It looks like there's a pipe in his front pocket. As I slow to a stop, I catch a whiff of cherry tobacco.

"Can I help you, sir?" I ask.

"Is that car following you, young lady?" he asks, shaking his cane in the direction of the car.

I look back over my shoulder again. The car is stopped now, but I can make out the paparazzo through the windshield. It's definitely him.

"Ugh," I groan. "Actually, yes, I think he might be following me."

"Huh," the old man says. "Well, that's not right."

"It's not me he's interested in," I reassure the old man. "He's stalking some celebrities that I'm delivering food to. I was just headed over to the amphitheater now. He must have overheard when the order came in."

"Celebrities, you say?" The old man looks tickled by this news. "Here in Ephron?"

"They're part of the cast for *A Midsummer Night's Dream*," I say. "You ever heard of Titanium Man?"

"Can't say that I have," the old man laughs. "Sounds like a great name for an old guy like me with a hip replacement, though."

I snort. "Something like that. Except, nothing like that. Oh, well. Thanks for letting me know I have a tail," I say.

"Just you leave him to me." The old guy nods and steps into the street, waving his cane wildly as he strides toward the car. I have to wonder if he has a titanium hip himself. He's awfully spry and quick on his feet. The cane seems to be there mostly for show.

"Go on! Git!" he shouts sideways at me as he continues to advance toward the vehicle. "If you cut behind the apartments there and take the footpath to the community center, there's no way he'll catch up."

"Thanks!" I say, smiling and pumping the pedals hard. As I turn the corner, I look back over my shoulder. The old guy is poking his cane in through the paparazzo's open window. A funny, old motorcycle with a side car zooms by them, but neither of them seem to notice it as they argue. The shocked-looking paparazzo has his hands up in a gesture of complete and total surrender.

"Woo-hoo!" I let out a small whoop as I roll down the hill toward the gated entrance to the amphitheater.

There's no way the paparazzo would have made it past security. But it still feels great to have shaken him like that.

It isn't till I reach the gate that I realize there's a fairly good chance Dean will be here, and I am going to have to give him an answer about taking the cast photos. I glance down at my stained apron, then use it up to wipe some sweat from my forehead. A glance in the rearview mirror confirms what a hot, sweaty mess I am.

Not at all how I pictured looking and feeling if I ever got the chance to meet Rafe Barzilay and Lorelei Dupont.

lorelei

. . .

I'M HOLDING *on to a precious bundle, and someone—my momager—is trying to take it from me. I feel so weak and powerless to fend her off. But then I am morphing into Ember, sending flames from my fingertips, blasting the momager into the ether. Then I am sitting on the church steps, unwrapping the bundle. Layer after layer of faded fabric, and then, nothing. There's nothing. I am alone. I curse in Kyrgyz, shouting one of the epithets from the movie. Rafe shows up with Orly and his mom, and the momager. They are all wearing Mickey hats. When I glance down, Rafe's feet are covered with fur.*

Tabitha's face is hovering six inches above mine. She is spraying a fine mist of ice water over me. I startle hard and wrestle with the hammock fabric as I bolt upright, almost flipping over onto the grass.

"Jesus fucking Christ, Tabitha!" I admonish her. "Are you trying to give me a heart attack?"

I can't believe I fell asleep. And not just a slight snooze. We're talking full-on snoring, no clue where I am, coma.

"I was afraid you were getting overheated. I wanted to wake you up before they started passing out the food," she hiss-whispers, looking a little wounded. "You were out pretty hard." She gestures at a trail of drool on my cheek and looks over her shoulder, stepping closer to block me from view. From the depths of her old-lady blazer pocket, she retrieves a plastic-wrapped packet of tissues.

"Sorry," I mutter, wiping the spittle off my cheek. "I never sleep well the first few nights in a new place." Tabitha hands me the monogrammed water bottle that came with the cast gift bags. I take a swig. "Was I talking in my sleep?"

"A little." She confirms my fears.

"Oh, shit. Did I say anything incriminating?" I ask.

"I don't think anyone noticed. And even if they did, I doubt anyone understood you. You were muttering in another language. I think it was Russian. And you said something about troll toe?"

"Kyrgyz," I say. "I learned a bunch of proverbs for my role. I practiced them so much, I could literally recite them in my sleep." *Apparently, now I do.*

"Oh. What's a troll toe?" Tabitha asks.

"No clue," I lie. Rafe Barzilay's secret is safe with me. Titanium Man is very self-conscious about his feet. He has super-hairy big toes.

"Who's hungry?" Dean Riley calls out. The handsome, auburn-haired, blue-eyed owner of the theater cuts a striking figure as he heads down the hill from the gate, followed by a delivery girl walking alongside a heavily laden adult tricycle. The red-faced girl is wearing a pink apron that says "Coffee Witch," and her curly, blonde hair is sticking out all over her head. She's shyly looking around as she rolls her ride down the hill, chatting with Dean. Probably another local hoping to catch a glance at Rafe. It's almost embarrassing how the man draws admirers. They swarm like flies.

Not that I don't have my own share of fans. They just tend to be a little less mainstream than Rafe's. Mine fall into two camps—fans of the character I played as a kid, or Ember fans who are mostly goth girls and guys who like to cosplay as the villain. The Ember camp also includes many foreign fans. Learning all those proverbs paid off. I have a standing invitation to the Nomad Games in Central Asia.

A couple of the stagehands rush up the hill to unburden the delivery girl of her load, parking the bike and pulling bags out of the insulated containers in the oversize back basket. My stomach growls, and I stand to join the cue that's forming.

"Want me to go wait in line for you?" Tabitha offers.

The sun is high, and it's gotten a lot warmer. I consider this for a moment—risk a sunburn and get all sweaty making awkward conversation with the locals, or park myself in the shade and get labeled as an entitled princess?

"Hey! Lorelei!"

Before I can make a decision one way or the other, I hear Dean Riley calling my name. He's headed toward me with a couple bags of food and the delivery girl in tow. Uh-oh. I sigh and snap for Tabitha to fetch my tote. I usually carry a few photos or Titanium Man items to sign in order to satisfy fans. A cheap price to send them off quickly on their way.

Which will it be? Moxie McAllister or Ember? She doesn't seem the goth type. So maybe she's an OG? To be honest, I like the Moxie fans much better. They're smarter, and they've always had my back. Most of the original fans scattered when the show was canceled. But the ones who stuck elevated both me and my character to cult status.

It all started when I carelessly told an interviewer that I always thought that Moxie might be on the spectrum. And queer. I was fifteen. I'd thought I was being super progressive. The network thought otherwise.

The social media campaigns that kicked off were the beginning of the end. Conservative picketers protesting outside the studio nearly came to blows with LGBTQ fans gathering signatures. They wanted the writers to end the season with Moxie asking her (female) bff to the eighth grade spring fling dance.

The funny thing about this girl, I notice as she gets closer, is that she looks a lot like Moxie. There's something about her unadorned and fresh-scrubbed, freckled look. Of course, her hair is more of a strawberry-ish blonde than Moxie's flaming red, but she's got the corkscrews framing her sweaty face.

"Hey Lorelei! This is Kenna!" Dean is shouting. "Remember I told you about her? I sent you a photo when we were going over the contracts? Stay there, I have your order!"

I think back, trying to recall. Dean *had* texted me a photo a few months ago of a girl in a diner. This must be that girl. Complete with pigtails and an apron. She's the small town, low budget version of me.

The girl stumbles as he pulls her forward. She slides the rest of the way down the grassy slope on her butt, coming to a stop a couple of yards in front of me and my PA, who's just returned with my bag.

Wide-eyed and open-mouthed, Tabitha glances from me to the girl, back to me, back to the girl, back to ...

"What are you gawking at, Tabitha?" I ask her.

"Are you kidding me? She looks just like—"

"Just go get your lunch."

"Oh my God, Kenna!" Dean catches up to his charge and helps her up. "I'm so sorry, I didn't mean to pull you over!"

"That's okay. Really, I'm okay." Kenna springs up quickly, brushing herself off. Aside from a massive grass stain on her baggy, jeans shorts-clad butt, she doesn't seem worse for wear.

Kid's got moxie!

The old tagline from the show pops into my head unbidden.

"Do you see it?" Dean asks. "Isn't it crazy? She's a dead ringer for you."

"I don't know about that, Dean." Kenna rolls her eyes. "I think you might be overselling it." And then she turns to me, all earnest-eyed and open-faced. "I did get called Moxie all the time as a kid, though."

There's probably a word in German for the disorientation you experience when unexpectedly encountering your own doppelgänger. A vortex opens in the time space continuum, sucking both of you in and spitting you out somewhere else entirely in the multiverse. But of course, the whole time, it's still Tuesday.

"Really?" I ask casually. "That's adorable. I don't see it, but I'll have to take your word for it," I say while digging in my tote. "I'm sorry I don't have any items to give you from the show. I think I have some Ember trading cards. Or I could sign a take-out menu for you if you have one?"

"You don't see it?" Dean splutters. "Have you had your eyes checked lately, Lorelei? Same nose. Same chin. Same eye shape."

"Lorelei's right," Kenna agrees amiably. "Totally different hair color, and look at Lorelei's eyebrows. They're perfect! I've always wanted eyebrows. Mine are practically invisible."

As would be mine, if I hadn't had them microbladed. Beats dying them constantly. And as for the hair color? I'm not sure, but I do suspect that if I took off my wig in the sunshine, it would be pretty darn close to Kenna's color.

Realizing all of this makes me uncomfortable. Extremely uncomfortable. Who is this girl, and how dare she look so much like me? It's unnerving. Is it bothering her, too? She seems to be having trouble looking at me. She won't even meet my eye.

Determined not to show how much it's freaking me out, I continue to feign disinterest, all the while taking stock. I think she's around my age. Maybe a little younger, but it's hard to tell. Same high cheekbones and wide-set eyes.

"I don't care what you say, Lorelei. If you ask me, you two could be twins!" Dean insists.

The odds of this stranger being my blood relative are insanely low. But it doesn't take much to set my wondering wheels in motion. Could we somehow be related? I know less about my biological parents than most international adoptees because I was not given up by a birth parent. I was found on the steps of a church in Siberia almost thirty years ago.

"There is another reason I wanted to introduce you to Kenna Papadopoulos," Dean says, interrupting my train of thought.

"Papadopoulos?" I ask. "Is that Greek?"

"My family is Greek," Kenna nods. "I know. It's a cliché. Greek people owning a diner. My uncles are actually the ones who own it, though. I just help them out."

She's talking too fast. Clearly, she's nervous.

"Your uncles?" I ask. "So, your family is from Ephron?"

"Actually, I grew up in Bellingham until I was fourteen." Kenna kicks at a tuft of grass. "Um ... my mom died, and I came to live with her brother and his partner—the uncles."

"Jesus, Kenna." Dean's eyes grow wide. "I didn't know that about you. I guess I was already in college when you moved here. I'm so sorry. That must have been so hard for you."

"It was, at first. But my uncles have always made me feel welcome. My mom and her brother were super close. He actually traveled with her to pick me up when she adopted me. I was still a baby, so he's been really involved in my life right from the start."

My heart starts racing, and there is a lump in my throat threatening to choke me. My goose bumps have goose bumps. I take a big gulp of water before I speak.

"You were adopted?" I ask. Casual. Keep it casual. *Be cool.* "Where from?"

"Oh, I'm terrible with geography," Kenna laughs. "I always forget the name of the town. Somewhere in Russia."

I wonder if she's ever done a DNA test.

I signed up for one of those DNA sites several years ago, hoping to find relatives who might be able to help me fill in my backstory. I want to know why my birth mother abandoned me. And who I get my freckles and acting abilities from. In the first few months after I signed up with the service, every time I got a "You have a DNA Match!" message in my inbox, my heart would stop beating for a moment.

But of course, every time I clicked, it was a terribly distant relation. Nothing traceable. I have a fifth cousin in France. A sixth cousin in Ireland. The closest match I've found thus far is a possible third cousin living just outside the Arctic Circle in Finland.

"So, Russia? Wow! Have you been back?" Dean asks. "Do you remember any Russian? Aren't you curious about your real parents?"

I grind my nails into the palms of my hands. Dean's managed to hit the trifecta of idiotic things to ask an international adoptee in one fell swoop. I feel the hairs on the back of my neck starting to stand on end, and my wig feels way too tight. I'm on the verge of launching into a lecture when Kenna laughs.

"Don't be silly, Dean. I don't speak Russian! I was six months old when my mom adopted me. I wasn't even speaking yet. And no, I haven't been back. I kind of won the lottery with my mom and the uncles. They *are* my REAL parents. I have no idea who my biological parents are. I mean, I wish them well, but aside from collecting some genetic info from them, I've never really wanted to seek them out. I know not all adoptees feel the same way as me, but my feeling is that it's best to leave well enough alone. Who knows what kind of nut jobs I came down from, right?" Kenna gives a little self-deprecating laugh.

"Well, their loss. They must have been crazy to abandon you," Dean agrees, squarely stepping in it again. He's clearly ignorant about the many complex socioeconomic and cultural issues that led to a wave of Eastern European adoptions in the 1990s. But Kenna lets this misstep slide as well.

"Obviously," Kenna joshes, unperturbed. "Crazies!"

Her attitude almost reminds me of the momager. Every time I wanted to search for my bio parents, she would say, "Lorelei, we don't know what kind of folks you came from. They must have been desperate. They might still be desperate. Do you really want to open that can of worms? Why can't you just be happy with the life you have? Why isn't *my* love enough?"

Maybe the momager should have adopted this girl instead of me.

"So what's the other reason you wanted to introduce us?"

"Well, I was really hoping to introduce you and Rafe to Kenna today." He turns back to Kenna and says, "I'm so sorry you didn't get to meet Rafe. He had to leave early, but he's a great guy. You'll see."

"She will?" I ask, raising my eyebrows.

"Yes, she will. Kenna is shooting the cast photos. She's an amazing local photographer."

"Excuse me, Dean," Kenna interjects. "I haven't said yes. I said I would tell you my answer today."

"So you're a food delivery person and a photographer?" I say, narrowing my eyes. "I hope you're not planning to become a member of the paparazzi this summer." I've seen it happen before. A little access and a long lens are an enticing and lucrative combo for some ambitious amateurs.

"Never!" Kenna looks shocked and insulted. "Some of them are here, though. A man tried to follow me on my way to the theater today."

"Really?" Dean looks concerned. "Thanks for mentioning it. We'll have to let security know. I'm glad that you and Rafe are staying together at that estate," Dean says. "It makes me feel better that you're not alone and the place is gated."

"Not to mention the security cameras all over the property," I comment. "It's like *Better Homes & Gardens* meets *Orange Is the New Black*."

"Oh, please," Dean scoffs. "It's a gorgeous estate. Beautiful gardens. They do wedding shoots there. Actually, now that I think about it, we should get Kenna over there. She should do the cast photos there."

"Listen, Dean," Kenna says. She looks completely dejected, staring at and talking to her shoes rather than facing the man she was joking with a moment ago.

"I'm sorry to let you down, but I need to get my camera serviced. So I don't think I can do the shots after all."

"Don't be silly. We'll just rent you something." Dean puts a hand on her shoulder and flaps his other one, waving her concerns away. "I'll have my team set something up for next week. In the meantime, maybe you want to scout locations for the shoot? Check out the gardens at the estate? What do you say, Lorelei?"

"When are you free?" I ask Kenna. She looks like a deer caught in the headlights.

"Free for what?" she asks distractedly, still looking at Dean in the manner of someone who is trying to do complex restaurant bill math in their head.

"To scout out locations for the shoot on the property where I'm staying?" I restate the question, speaking a little slowly. She blushes.

"Um ... right. Of course. I dunno, whenever? My schedule is pretty flexible. My uncles are away, but I've got a lot of help at the diner. I could do any day really." Kenna shrugs as she gives her laid-back answer to my question, causing my "normal girl" jealousy to flare like one of Ember's smoking fireballs.

Her schedule is "flexible." She can get away "whenever." Must be nice. The last time my schedule was truly flexible and I could "do any day" was ... I think back as far as my memory allows. Oh, yeah—never!

There's no way I'm going to be able to relax until I can ask her more questions about her adoption.

"What are you doing tomorrow?" I check the schedule on the clipboard in my bag. I have a three-hour block in the afternoon that I've set aside for practicing my *Midsummer Night* lines, checking in with the advisory board, and scheduling my social media. I can rearrange that a little. I already know the entire play by heart.

"Nothing too serious," she shrugs.

"Why don't you stop by the property after lunch." I smile cordially at her, attempting to be friendly and professional now. Like I'm not some kind of weirdo who's toying with the idea of requesting a DNA sample from her. Like I'm not scared she'll say no. And most of all, I'm doing my best to act like it's not completely freaking me out that looking at her face is like looking in the mirror.

If this was a *Moxie McAllister* episode, I'd be scheming a way to steal her hairbrush right now so I could send strands of her hair in for analysis.

And what would the results show? What am I even hoping for here?

"Sure, what time?" She smiles at me shyly, and I see a flicker of the same recognition in the mirror of her eyes. This has got to be a little freaky for her, too.

"Just pop by after you eat lunch, and we'll scout out some locations for those pictures."

"Awesome!" Kenna grins.

"Perfect," I say, before tossing my water bottle and take-out order into my tote bag. "Dean can give you the address and my phone number. See you tomorrow!" I can't get out of here fast enough and get to googling everything about Kenna Papadopoulos.

kenna

· · ·

I HAVE to use an aux cord to connect my phone to my car's sound system so I can listen to the new episode of the *Lit Lovers'* podcast. I'm on my way over to the compound where Lorelei Dupont is staying.

"Sometimes," Chelsea says, "people get a little too caught up in 'grass is greener' type thinking."

I laugh ruefully to myself. The hosts are discussing rom-coms with "across the tracks" themes. And, rather fittingly, the grass really is greener in the neighborhood I'm driving through. This enclave of homes actually *is* on the other side of the tracks from where I, and the majority of Ephron residents, live.

Judging by the acres and acres of perfectly manicured lawns here, the homeowners must all own tractors. Or herds of pure-bred goats. There's no way anyone is using a push mower on lawns this large.

The homes are spread out over miles, separated by small forests, affording each resident plenty of privacy. Many of these houses aren't even visible from the street. They are set back on private, gated roads off the main drag. I know the area pretty well. Back in high school, this was where the best parties always happened when someone's family was out of town. The Holm family, Ephron's founders, have an estate here.

It must be nice.

Of course, Lorelei Dupont and Rafe Barzilay are staying up here. A high-security haven with gardens and grounds and its own system of paths and trails. According to my research, the house had been used in at least two films and several weddings. It can be rented with or without staff, which includes a butler, a chef, a gardener, two full-time housekeepers, a groundskeeper, a pool boy, and three maids.

Like freaking *Downton Abbey*.

I try to imagine what it's like to live on the other side of the gate, with pool boys to clean your pool, housekeepers to load the dishwasher, and a personal chef to make your truffle toast. Of course, living with my uncles, I've got nothing to complain about on the toast front, other than the shocking lack of truffles. Then again, Uncle Stavros is weirdly obsessed with cheese. All I'd have to do is say the word, and he would find me an imported cheese—with truffles.

The home where Lorelei and Rafe are staying is newer construction, built to resemble a Spanish Mission, more like what you'd find in Napa or Sonoma than the Pacific Northwest. The website showed drone video of sprawling, covered patios and wisteria-covered arbors. Apart from the main house, there is a one-bedroom guesthouse and a poolside cabana with its own outdoor kitchen. Everything on the property boasts high-tech security and perimeter surveillance, making it "the perfect rental for high-profile individuals looking for a safe, private retreat."

"Maybe the grass is greener when you can afford staff," Jackson says, "but wealth is not a good indicator of happiness. Study after study shows—"

"Shut up," Alexis interrupts him. "Just shut up."

"Honestly! It's a fact!" Jackson argues.

"You're telling me you're not happier now that you're a tech mogul than when you were struggling?" Alexis sounds annoyed.

"I'm not happier. I mean, I'm less worried about my mom, and it's nice to be able to order whatever I want off the menu for dinner, but trust me, it's not everything. The everyday issues are still there," Jackson says.

"I think what my brother means to say is that he still spends his Saturday nights alone," Chelsea teases.

"By choice!" Jackson defends himself. "I'm not interested in being anyone's sugar daddy, and frankly, I'm not really even sure that monogamy is for me."

"Forgive me if I don't fetch my violin and play a solo for you and your 'everyday issues,'"

Alexis replies in a voice dripping with sarcasm. I can practically hear the air quotes. "Why are rich dudes like you always so unhappy? Go hot air ballooning with Richard Branson or something. Maybe you'll meet someone, or find the meaning of life. I can house-sit if you need someone."

"No can do!" Jackson laughs. "But there is a bit of travel news in my future. I'll be sharing that in the next episode of Lit Lovers. But for now, I just want to remind everyone that every Wednesday Night is Happy Hour at—"

I turn off the podcast as I pull up by the kiosk outside the elaborately scrolled and detailed wrought iron gate.

A security system prompts me to type out my name on a flatscreen console prior to entering the code that Lorelei texted to me earlier. All sevens. Lucky number. I also have to pose for a photo, presumably so they'll know if someone else tries to use my code. Finally, almost anticlimactically, I am granted access. The gate slides open, slowly and silently.

A part of me is vaguely disappointed the system did not ask to scan my eyeball.

The private street leading up to the house is flanked by cypress trees. It almost looks like Tuscany. I can see why people want to get married here.

As I turn into the circular driveway in front of the house, I notice a flash of motion through the trees. Bouncing, jumping, flesh-toned motion. Then I realize what that motion is. Or rather who.

The movement belongs to a shirtless, nearly naked Rafe Barzilay in a pair of running shorts. He is doing stretches on the side of the house. His long, lean, bronzed body is shimmering in the sunlight, like some sort of sparkly vampire, but with an enviable tan. His lean muscles ripple as he lunges and then stands, bouncing off his heels and rolling his neck. He's like a piece of art, come to life.

How can he be real? How can he be so perfect? Even from this distance, I can see his thick eyelashes and the way his long, dark, wavy hair cascades almost to his shoulders, catching the light. What kind of shampoo do you use to have hair that shiny? His hair is being held back from his face with a pink headband. Is that terry cloth? With a strawberry on it? I like it. I bet it's from some start-up fashion brand started by a rap star ...

And now he's waving. At me? At me! Rafe Barzilay is waving at me.

A second too late, I realize I'm about to run off the drive. My wheels bump up against the stone curbing and I course-correct, veering to the other side of the driveway before centering myself again. I jerk to a halt, putting the car in park. I have no more than five seconds to gather myself as Rafe jogs over to the car. It's just Rafe Barzilay. This is normal. It's normal that Titanium Man is approaching my car, wearing the world's smallest set of running shorts. I'm not looking at his package. I'm just minding my own business.

I roll down the window.

"Hey," he says, a little crossly. "You should watch where you're going. There are kids living here. And pets. You could have killed someone."

"I was watching," I argue. "I could see there were no kids in the driveway. You just distracted me when you waved."

"I waved because you were driving way too fast," he chides. "Who are you, by the way? What are you doing here?"

There's a drop of sweat in the divot of his collarbone. I cannot look away. The breeze picks up and I can smell him. He doesn't smell sweaty. Of course he doesn't. He smells like cardamom cake and cedar trees. Like clean air and a warm bed. Why is it that his clean smell makes me think dirty thoughts? His scowl doesn't even do much to cool me off. If anything, it does the opposite.

Just then, Lorelei throws the front door open and steps out onto the covered porch. She's wearing a flowing, black, linen caftan with striking tribal embroidery and an oversize pair of dark sunglasses. "Back off, Rafe. This is Kenna. She's doing our headshots for the playbill. I asked her to come by today. Didn't Dean text you?"

"I can't do headshots today. Why didn't anyone check with me?" he complains.

"I wasn't planning on taking the photos today," I explain. "I just want to scout out some good places to do them."

As I'm speaking, a small, furry dog barrels past Lorelei, racing out into the driveway and making a break for it.

"See!" Rafe gestures at the dog. "What if she ran out a minute earlier? Lorelei, you need to be more careful." He makes a clucking noise at the dog, but she ignores him, running rings around him.

"Princess!" he calls. "Heel! Get over here!" He chases after her, unsuccessfully lunging and missing her. She barks excitedly and wags her tail, clearly enjoying this game.

"Princess!" he calls exasperatedly, again, and I can hear the slightest remnant of his Israeli accent. The dog runs in large circles, taunting him, leaping in the air and dancing on her hind legs. I can't help but laugh.

"You think this is funny?" he says, narrowing his eyes at me. "This dog is a runner. I only just rescued her from a shelter this past weekend. If we don't catch her, who knows what could happen!"

The dog sits down in the middle of the gravel driveway, daring him to chase after her. Her little, pink tongue is dangling off center as she pants excitedly.

That's when I recognize her. I realize that I know this dog. Princess! Princess Von Floofy! She's the same Pomeranian that I photographed at the shelter. How on earth?

"Come here, Princess Von Floofy!" I throw open the door of my car and reach into the glove compartment for the dog treats I bring to photo shoots. "Come on, girl! You remember me, don't you? We're besties!"

Princess raises her nose to sniff the air. I shake the bag of treats. "Come here, Princess! Wanna go for a ride?"

That's all it takes. The dog makes a beeline for me, leaping into my car and up into my lap, where she smothers me with kisses.

"Awww. You remember me, too! How did you end up here, sweetheart?" I dig in the bag for some treats, which she eats out of my hand while I speak soothingly to her. "What a good girl. Why are you trying to run away?" With my free hand, I pull the car door shut.

A moment later, Rafe is back at my window, shaking his head in disbelief. "How did you know to do that?"

"It usually works with the runners. You might want to try luring her into a car instead of chasing her next time," I suggest, still petting the dog and not minding one bit having my face licked. "She's a sweetheart."

"Thank you." Rafe breathes a sigh of relief as I hand the dog back to him through the window.

"Is she really your dog?" I ask, still trying to puzzle out how this happened. I swear Princess is staring smugly at me. What a lucky little bitch. Literally.

"She's my daughter's dog." He frowns sternly at the Pomeranian. "Shame on you, *Hamuda*! You nearly gave me a heart attack, running away from me like that—again."

The little dog seems unfazed by his reproach. She licks his face enthusiastically, wagging her entire, little body. And who could blame her?

"Oh, please, that is totally *your* dog, Rafe." Lorelei rolls her eyes as she comes down the steps toward me. "You're not fooling anyone. You're like a mother hen with that smelly, little beast."

"Princess doesn't smell!" I argue. "She was just groomed."

Rafe looks at me suspiciously. "How would you know?"

"I volunteer at the shelter," I explain as I get out of the car. "I take photos of the dogs for their website. By the way, you should put a tracker on Princess. I know she's chipped, but you don't want it to get to that point. Super important with the runners."

"Wait, what?" Lorelei does a double take, looking from me to Rafe. "You know Rafe's dog? This really is a small town. And more to the point, you're a dog photographer? Is this another one of Dean Riley's jokes? Getting a pet photographer to do our headshots?"

It's a good thing she hasn't seen my camera.

"I don't know," Rafe argues with Lorelei as he snuggles the dog. "If it wasn't for that photo of Princess on the website, I never would have stopped at the shelter. Clearly, this girl"—he pauses, looking me over and making eye contact as if he is seeing, truly seeing me for the first time—"what's your name again?"

"Kenna." I furnish my name, trying not to get lost in the depths of his dark-brown eyes.

"Kenna," he repeats. My name sounds cooler in his mouth. More exotic. He puts the accent on the end. Ken-NA. "Clearly, Kenna knows how to take a compelling photo."

"So maybe she can make it look like you're actually housebroken," Lorelei says archly.

Rafe smirks, visually acknowledging the ribbing, but doesn't respond.

He's still staring at me with those famous eyes. Still half naked. Still holding the little dog, who is looking at me like butter wouldn't melt in her mouth.

Well played, Princess Von Floofy.

"Is that your daughter's headband?" Lorelei skips down the stairs and pulls me out of my car. She loops her arm through mine. "And Kenna's not a girl, Rafe. She's a grown-ass woman. Have a little more respect."

With this, Lorelei drags me off toward the guesthouse.

———

It takes an hour to tour the property. Since I want to take the photos outdoors, Lorelei shows me the rose garden and the dahlia beds full of dinner plate-size blooms. There's a small Japanese garden with stone benches, a koi pond, and a firepit. And at the far end of the property, there's even a small vineyard.

Closer to the big house, there are pergolas covered in wisteria and trumpet vines. We swing by the pool area, which has a full outdoor kitchen and bar outside a cabana that houses a home office. Fluffy, blue-and-white-striped towels that have been rolled into chubby cylinders fill the cubbies outside the restrooms. On top of the shelves, assorted sunscreens, body wash, shampoos, and conditioners are grouped in clusters, like you would see at a spa.

I'm too embarrassed to ask if they are for sale or freebies that come with the house. They are not the sort of brands you see at Target or the supermarket, and I'm dying to sniff them to see what they smell like.

"Have you tried the outdoor shower?" I ask Lorelei, pointing at the teak-lined shower with a view of the mountains. It's surrounded by lush foliage.

"Not yet." She shakes her head. "It seems like it might be a little buggy. Why? Is that the sort of thing you like? Are you into nature?" She's staring at me so intensely, like she's taking stock of my reactions and has been throughout the tour. At least I think she has. It's hard to know for certain with her giant, black sunglasses.

I'm still unnerved by how much she looks like me, but not like me. Lorelei is like a china doll version of me with paler skin, fewer freckles, and higher contrast. Everything about her is groomed to perfection. Her long, glossy, black hair looks a lot like Barbie-doll hair, and her nails are painted a dark red—probably acrylic or gels, neither of which I have ever tried. She's narrower than me and has possibly had lip injections. I can't tell for sure. I'm trying not to stare, which is difficult. I am mesmerized by her exquisitely shaped brows.

Those brows command attention, animating her entire face when she speaks and adding so much drama. I never realized what a difference brows make. Like exclamation points and question marks. Without them, a face is unpunctuated. Wishy-washy. Like me.

For the first time in my life, I wonder if a salon procedure could change my life. Maybe if I had some fierce-looking eyebrows, I wouldn't attract so many losers, like Cody and that cop. The new-and-improved version of me with perfectly shaped brows wouldn't be panicking about a lack of career, impending homelessness, and being left behind by her friends and family. Kenna-with-brows would be a girl boss. She'd run pop-up pet photography events at coffee shops. She'd call it Hotshots. She'd be profiled in magazines. People would say her name like Rafe said it—Ken-NA!

I wish I could be that girl.

Finally, we head to the guesthouse where Lorelei is staying. She shows me into the kitchen, which is small but luxurious. Shiny, glass-fronted cabinets and sleek, granite countertops.

"Give me a minute. I just want to jot some notes," I say.

I perch with one butt cheek propped on a leather barstool at the bar-height table and make a quick list of the areas I'm thinking might work, noting what equipment I'll need to shoot in full sun vs. shade.

"Have a drink with me?" Lorelei asks, opening a cabinet door that is cleverly disguising a small refrigerator. When she pushes up her sunglasses, I see she has dark circles under her eyes. So she is human after all!

She takes out a glass pitcher. "I'm addicted to iced-tea lemonade, but I have some other stuff in the mini bar." She points at a glass-fronted second fridge under the counter that is filled with a hotel room worthy assortment of beverages and snacks.

"Is that green tea?" I ask.

"Yeah," she nods.

"Try it with a squeeze of lime and some strawberries in it sometime," I suggest.

"Really?" She looks at me curiously. "What makes you say that?"

"It's how I like it," I admit. "But it just occurred to me that you might like it, too."

"Interesting," she says, turning back to the fridge. She rummages around and pulls out a lime and a basket of strawberries. "So you're a tea witch as well as a coffee one?"

"Let me help you with that." I look around for a cutting board while she washes the fruit. "Got a cutting board?"

"Over there." Lorelei gestures at a drawer. "And the knives are right there on the counter. Don't stab me." She laughs nervously, and I'm not entirely sure she's joking. "Sorry, terrible joke. I have stalker anxiety. Comes with the kid-star territory. I really need to put that knife block in a cabinet. I've just watched too many true crime documentaries."

"Ugh, I know," I commiserate. "Those shows will mess with your head. I mean, nobody gives a damn about me, but I still get the willies when I'm home alone. Maybe that's why I still live with my uncles at twenty-seven."

"Oh, is that how old you are?" Lorelei pauses for a moment, patting the berries dry.

"Yeah," I smile. "Sort of pathetic. But it's not like I live with them, live with them. I have my own apartment over their garage."

"Sounds nice," Lorelei says. "I haven't lived with anyone since I was sixteen."

"Shit!" I exclaim. "I can't imagine living on my own at sixteen." It sounds so lonely.

"I was pretty used to it. We filmed on location a lot for *Moxie*, and I spent half of my life in hotels anyway." Lorelei hands the limes to me. "How much do you put in?"

"Just a squeeze." I quickly quarter the lime and squeeze two halves into glasses, reserving the other two for garnish. "And maybe two berries?" I suggest. "Sometimes I muddle them, but I also like to eat them, in which case I leave them whole."

"Sounds good to me." Lorelei tosses two berries into each glass and pours the tea. She hands me my cup and directs me back out to the egg-shaped, hanging chairs on her sunny patio.

"Great view," I comment. The patio has a spectacular view of the mountains, near and far, like a torn paper illustration—the closer ones in shades of green, layered on top of more distant and taller silhouettes in shadowy purples and gray tones. It's such a perfect spot to relax. Like something out of a magazine.

"Yeah, I guess it doesn't suck," she agrees, looking at the scenery as if she's only just noticing it now. Then she leans back in her seat, closing her eyes. She looks so tired. Maybe she isn't sleeping well. I wonder if I'm going to have to touch up her photos. I guess we'll cross that bridge when we come to it.

"So," Lorelei speaks without opening her eyes, "you mentioned you were adopted? What was that like for you?"

Her chair sways, and her words hang in the air for a moment as I consider my answer. Lots of people are curious about my adoption and want to know more about it. The truth is, I don't think about it all that much. I think about my mom, and what things were like before I lost her. But I don't think much about what happened before she adopted me. I don't really wonder about my birth parents or feel like there's stuff I need to know.

"Being adopted was normal, I guess? I've always known I was adopted, and it isn't a big deal," I say. "I mean, I don't remember anything before it happened. I was only six months old when my mom came for me."

"And you mentioned your uncle traveled, too?"

"Yeah, she didn't want to make the trip alone. At least it wasn't cold when they went. It was summertime, so they didn't have to freeze." I stretch out in my seat and take a sip of the iced tea.

"This tastes perfect," I say.

Lorelei reaches out her glass and clinks it to mine. "To new friendships," she says and takes a sip. "Damn! That *is* good." She takes another sip and licks her lips before continuing. "So when did your mom go to Russia for you then? I'm guessing it was twenty-seven years ago?"

"Almost exactly," I nod. "My 'gotcha day' is coming up. We used to celebrate it when I was a kid," I backtrack immediately to explain. "A gotcha day is kind of like a birthday for adoptees. It's the day your family adopted you."

"Oh, I know what it is," Lorelei says quietly, rattling the ice cubes in her glass. "Mine's in June, too, but we never really celebrated."

"Really?" I sit up in my seat. "You're adopted, too? Why don't I know that? I had no idea!" I sift through the *Moxie McAllister* trivia that's still filed away in my brain, alongside the lyrics to every song Miley Cyrus and Taylor Swift ever recorded. I can remember the type of waffles Moxie liked— round, not square—and that Lorelei was rumored to have had a crush on a Jonas brother.

I don't recall anything about Lorelei being adopted. I would have remembered that. I didn't have many adopted peers growing up, and I can practically recite every celebrity I know who was adopted, along with the ones who were dyslexic, like me. One of the main reasons I loved Moxie's show so much was that the main character was supposed to be dyslexic. But instead of her dyslexia being a disability, it gave Moxie superpowers that she used to solve crimes. She had highly tuned visual abilities. I could relate. Nobody can find Waldo faster than me.

"My momager didn't really want me to talk about being adopted. In fact, she didn't really tell me until I was eleven, which is stupid because I still had some memories of the orphanage, even if I just thought they were nightmares."

"You were in an orphanage?" I ask. "Where?"

"Siberia," Lorelei says. "That's why I asked you where *you* were adopted from." She turns to give me a significant look, and I get chills all the way down my spine, to my fingertips and toes. My hand shakes. I have to set down my drink.

"What do you mean?" I attempt to laugh off that feeling. My mom used to say it was like someone dancing on your grave. "You don't actually think ... I mean, there's no way. And you even said it yourself. We don't look *that* much alike."

"Are you kidding me?" Lorelei sits up straight now and places a hand on top of her head. I'm not even sure what she's doing until she pulls the wig off, exposing a head full of thick, strawberry-blonde curls.

Just like mine. With her sunglasses off, and no makeup on her face, the resemblance is startling. Irrefutable.

"See?" she says.

I am stunned, speechless. And when I do finally regain the ability to speak, what I say is, "But ... you have brown hair!"

"Ha!" Lorelei laughs and swigs her tea. "I thought it was brown, too, but it's been so many years since I let my own color grow out, I really had no idea. I decided to do a little experiment when we were filming the last Titanium Man film. I had to wear a wig for my Ember character, and it was a much easier process in hair and makeup without my own hair being in the way. I got a buzz cut while we were filming, and afterward, I just let it grow. My agent and my manager didn't want me going out in public bald, so they insisted I continue to wear a brown-haired wig. And they still want me in it because —branding. But honestly, I'm pretty over it."

She tosses the wig onto the side table and runs her hands through the messy curls.

"My God, that feels better. I was suffocating under that thing."

I don't know what to say. My brain feels like I just shoved a fork into an outlet.

"You okay? Say something." Lorelei pokes me.

"I'm just ... surprised," I say.

"Yeah, that was a real drama move, whipping off the wig like that," Lorelei concedes. "But aren't you curious? Have you ever done a DNA test?"

"No," I say. "I mean, I did get my blood type tested one time, in case I had to give Uncle Stavros blood when he had his appendix out. Apparently, I'm a universal donor. But he didn't need my blood. Good thing. I hate needles."

I'm rambling.

"You don't need to give blood to get your DNA tested," Lorelei says. "It's just a cheek swab."

"Huh?" I swallow. "Interesting."

"Would you consider doing a DNA test, Kenna? I signed up with one of those services years ago, but all they ever turn up are super-distant cousins. Wouldn't it be wild if we were somehow related?"

"I guess ..." I say. "It seems like a long shot, though. I mean, what are the odds?"

"I don't know," Lorelei says. She suddenly looks younger. Much more like her Moxie McAllister self. Much more like me. "Think about it. Both of our moms went to Russia around the same time. Maybe they went to the same region. I've heard stranger stories."

I ponder the possibility. "I'm not sure where in Russia my mom went," I say. "I have to ask the uncles."

But in the back of my head, I'm replaying the stories they told and remembering the significance of it being summer. It wasn't cold because it was summer. And if it hadn't been summer, it would have been really cold. Siberia?

"It can't hurt to do the DNA test. I mean, you also find out a bunch of health-related stuff, so it's a good idea for adoptees. It's not just about finding family." Lorelei lobbies for the test again. "I can have my PA set it up."

"I guess it would be nice to know that stuff." I nod my head. "But I'm not really looking for relatives, and it seems like a total long shot that we could be related."

"Of course." Lorelei sits back in her chair. She seems more relaxed now that I've agreed to do the DNA test. "I'll just text Tabitha to take care of getting us the kits."

She taps out a series of messages into her phone and then sets it aside, satisfied. Having a PA must be a little like having magical powers. You just make a wish and *poof!* Tabitha takes care of it.

"Okay," she says. "It really would be something if we were sisters, wouldn't it?"

"I guess?" I say. I want to share her enthusiasm, but it's all coming at me way too fast, and it seems so preposterous.

"Well, I mean, I'd be thrilled, but maybe you don't want to be the butt of any more Poxy Moxie jokes," she says, raising her eloquent eyebrows at me.

"Ugh, how did you know?" I groan.

"I AM Poxy Moxie," she says. "The OG. And I'm willing to bet with how much you look like me, you caught some of the flak when I decided to ditch the good-girl act."

I can feel the blush creeping over me. "Well ... yeah," I shrug. "Maybe I got teased a little."

"I'm so sorry, Kenna," she says. And then she gets a mischievous look on her face. The eyebrows are in motion. She's got an idea. I can tell. It's just like when she was playing Moxie. The thinking face followed by—

"I just had an idea!" Lorelei announces. She picks up the wig and twirls it on one finger. The long, dark strands spin out into a swirling vortex. "Want to play dress-up with me?"

lorelei

. . .

KENNA and I are standing in front of the mirrored wardrobe in my bedroom, trying on each other's clothing. She's got on my shiny, black, latex catsuit and a pair of platform stilettos that I wear to events when I'm working the Ember vibe. The catsuit is cut in a deep V, almost all the way to the navel, and if I'm being honest, it looks better on her. She's a little curvier, with a more dramatic hip-to-waist ratio. I finish penciling on some brows and tug on the wig.

"Voilà!" I exclaim, as we both stand back to admire my handiwork.

"Holy shit!" Kenna gasps. Then she totters a bit. "And how do you walk in these?" She lifts a foot.

"Oh, you get the hang of it. The important thing to remember with the latex suits is that baby powder is your friend. Also, it's a good idea to take the suit off in the shower because the sweat pools." It feels good to have someone to pass down this wisdom to.

I flop sideways in the upholstered chair by my bed, legs flung over one arm. I've got Kenna's tank top and jeans shorts on, and my hair is down, and I have to admit, it's pretty comfy and carefree. I feel like a kid again. Kenna turns right and left, looking over her shoulder to admire herself from different angles in the mirror, while I scroll through old social posts, trying to find a photo of myself in the same suit.

It gives me an idea.

"Let me take your picture." I toss her my sunglasses. "Put these on." I point at the friendship bracelet on her wrist. It's the one thing that's wrong with the photo.

"Does that come off? Give it here."

"You can look at it, but don't lose it!" Kenna slips the bracelet off over her wrist. "My best friend, Georgia, made this for me in high school."

"And you still wear it?" I ask incredulously, sliding it onto my wrist.

"Sometimes. I really like the colors." The blue strings are faded, stretched, and worn, and the ends of the cotton thread are curling. There's a little, red heart bead in the middle. It's so incredibly cute. And sweet. I feel a stab of jealousy, wondering what this friendship bracelet-making buddy of hers is like. Probably just as apple-pie wholesome as Kenna.

Nobody has ever made a friendship bracelet for me. Ever.

"Okay," I say, leaning precariously sideways to line up the phone at ground level. This angle makes Kenna look extra tall. Her legs are a little longer than mine, which only adds to the overall effect. "Nice, nice ... bend forward a little. Snarl ..."

I snap away from this awkward position, clinging to the chair with my knees. Finally, I sit myself up, turn to face forward, and go back over the shots.

"So good!" I flip the phone around to show her the results of our little shoot.

We're both on our third iced tea, and we've been adding generous splashes of vodka into the mix for the last two. It's strange how comfortable I feel around her. Two hours have passed, and it feels like we've known each other forever.

I, for instance, now know all about the guy Kenna dated for five years right out of high school. Some dirtbag named Cody. He sounds like a total piece of shit. I know that she has a penchant for Taco Bell drive-thru and that she really hates letting people down, especially her uncles.

She's way into her photography and loves helping homeless pets at the local shelter. So much so that she does it for free. But she's starting to make a little money taking pictures. A few of the pet owners who found their pets at the shelter have commissioned portraits.

And what have I told her? I told her about emancipating myself from the momager when I was sixteen. That I've dated a lot of men, but nobody serious. I let her know that I haven't ever dated a Jonas brother ... the rumors aren't true. But a certain other kid celebrity still sends me dick pics.

And then she won my respect, admitting she has a gallery of unsolicited dick pics that includes one with freckles on it in the shape of a penguin. She called it the "penguinis," and I laughed harder than I have in ages.

It's not the first time I've bonded with another woman fast and hard. It's happened a few times when I was filming in remote locations. It's a fish-out-of-water phenomenon. A whole "since we're stuck on this desert island together, we may as well be besties" effect. But these friendships rarely last. Six months later, we're on to the next thing.

We swear we'll stay in touch, but after all the closeness, confessions, and inside jokes, it never happens. We barely stay in touch. It sucks. That's why I'm grateful for Rafe. He's not exactly the same as having a close girlfriend, but we've known each other since we were kids, and I can tell him anything.

I wonder if I will stay in touch with Kenna after this summer.

"I can't believe you walked around in public in this." Kenna pulls at the latex suit to hitch it up, and it doesn't budge. She frowns.

I frown.

I've been studying her for the last hour, mirroring her expressions. There's a thing she does where she bites her lip and flares one nostril. It's taken me a bunch of tries to get it right, but once I do, it's filed away in my catalog. On average, it takes me ten minutes to learn a new facial expression. Once I've got it down, it's almost like muscle memory. I don't have to think about doing it. I just picture it, and my face just *does* it.

That's what a lifetime of acting gets you. That, and the ability to lie convincingly. These are actually important life skills. I'm fully prepared to take up a life of crime or international espionage, should the opportunity arise.

"I have to admit, you're freaking me out with the way you're mimicking me. Are you making plans to wear my personality like a skin suit?" She crosses her eyes and sticks out her tongue.

"That's pretty funny, considering the fact that you are essentially wearing my skin suit right now." I hold up the photo of her snarling next to my face and copy it.

Then I swipe to the next one, a more natural face for her, and zoom in. I hold it up and imitate that one as well.

"Cut it out. I don't actually make that face, do I?" Kenna looks a bit alarmed.

"Only all the time," I say.

I relax my face back into its natural state. Which is a sort of blank slate I've learned to adopt. It doesn't give much away, but it also doesn't give anyone the warm fuzzies. People are constantly saying I have resting bitch face. I'm okay with that.

"I cannot do that face." Kenna points and shakes her head vigorously, knocking the wig askew. "And I can't see how you can stand wearing this suit. I'm already starting to sweat. I look ridiculous. I could never pull this off. I could never be you."

"Of course you could!" I roll my eyes and pull up my Instagram account. I select the photo of Kenna snarling and quickly post it to my account with the caption: *"Can't wait to switch it up a little this summer."*

The likes start pouring in immediately ... followed by the comments:

"OMG! Classic Lorelei."

"You look hawt."

"Nobody wears that catsuit like Lorelei Dupont."

"U wanna be my baby mama?"

"What did you do?" Kenna asks, looking horrified.

"Nothing. I just posted a photo of *me* hanging out here in Ephron." I stand to show her the feed. The like count is climbing fast. Every time I hit refresh, there are several dozen more.

"But that's not you!" Kenna's mouth is hanging open.

"I know that, and you know that, but apparently, nobody else does. So when you say you could never be me? Clearly, not true." I point a finger at her. "You ARE Lorelei Dupont!"

I am slurring a little bit. Too much vodka, too fast, and I hadn't eaten much for lunch. What I am craving right now is a big, juicy burger. But it's not like I can just pop out and get one. Especially now that I know the paparazzi are prowling.

Kenna totters over to the chair and lowers herself gingerly into it.

"Kenna?" she says, calling me by her name. "I think I am a little bit tipsy."

"S'okay." I pat her shoulder and sit on the bed next to her. "We should get burgers. Where do we like to get burgers from around here?"

"The Onion," Kenna says. "They have the best burgers. And even better chili fries. I love their chili fries. I could marry them."

"I wish I could just go to The Onion and order a plate of chili fries." I hug my pillow. "Do you have any idea how lucky you are?"

"Yeah, well, I wish I could have my personal chef whip up a salad for me, while I lay poolside and read messages from my sixteen bazillion adoring fans." Kenna glances sideways at me.

"I wish I could ... do a grocery run!" We're playing my favorite game now.

"I wish someone would clean my apartment and do all my laundry," she says as she twirls the boot laces around her fingers.

My turn.

"I wish I could pump my own gas at the gas station."

Hers.

"I wish I had a driver."

"I wish I could be you." We both say it at the same time. And then we both clap a hand over our mouths at the same time, in perfect, mirror-image fashion. My old improv teacher would have given us a standing ovation for this.

I'm bouncing on the bed as the idea comes to me. "What if—"

"No." Kenna is shaking her head. "I know that Moxie McAllister look. You are about to have a REALLY BAD IDEA and try to suck your stupid sidekick in." She unzips a boot. I reach out and zip it back up. Then I stand on the bed, bouncing slowly, like it's a trampoline.

"It's not a bad idea!" I hold out the phone. Six hundred likes and counting. "It's a totally awesome idea!"

I drop back down onto my butt beside her. "You can absolutely be me. It'd just be for a few days—one week—then we can swap back."

"Why would you even want to be me?" She wrinkles her nose.

"Hello? Burgers? Shopping? Taco Bell drive-thru?" I am getting excited. I'm not even joking. I think this could work! It could be just the hint of freedom I need.

"But what would I do? How could I pull it off?" Kenna attempts to cross her legs but thinks better of it when the catsuit creaks.

"Picture this." I stand up for my pitch. *Jazz hands.* "You spend the week at a private, luxury estate. Your every need is attended to. Private chefs, lavish buffets, laundry service, maids. Sleep in. Lie by the saltwater pool. Relax in the award-winning gardens. Oh, and treat yourself to an immersive day spa experience at the Arbors. It's an exclusive spa/vineyard experience. I almost forgot that I have an appointment there. Have you been?"

"No," Kenna snorts. "They charge three hundred dollars just for lunch!"

"Well, your day of luxurious pampering would be on me. And ..."—I hold up a finger, sweetening the pot—"you can get the groundskeeper to drive you, or you can drive there yourself in my brand-new Porsche. It has all the bells and whistles, plus the extra new-car smell."

"What would you drive?"

"Your car!" I grin. I saw her car out front. It's seen better years, but it's a perfect vehicle to drive if you want to blend in around here.

"What about Rafe?" Kenna folds her arms across her chest, watching me pace.

"Rafe and his daughter won't be around. They are heading down to LA for the week. Come on. All you have to do is drive my Porsche to the spa, show up, and pretend you're me. Or skip it. It's okay if you want to spend the whole time lounging around by the pool here, if you want. The point is, it's not like anyone you're encountering will have met me. You don't have to even talk to anyone. Just wear a pair of huge sunglasses, smile, and nod. Like this ..."

I locate the discarded, oversize sunglasses on my nightstand and slide them on. Then I affect a vanilla smile and blander-than-bland tone as I slowly say, "Thank you. Thank you very much."

"Who are you, Elvis?" Kenna raises her eyebrows at me, still unconvinced. "Honestly, I still don't know why you want to do this. Hanging around here and going to the day spa sounds like a better way to spend a week off. Why would you want to work at the diner and do my job? It's not all that easy, you know."

"Making coffee?" *Please.* "I'm sure I can figure it out."

"The espresso machine is very temperamental. And there's more to it than just making coffee." Kenna chews her lip.

"So you'll teach me." I wave her concerns away. "Come on, it's just one week. It can't be harder than learning Kyrgyz or climbing a glacier with an ice pick."

"I can't believe you do your own stunts," she says.

"Look, you deserve some time off." I take another tack, speaking soothingly. "You said it yourself ... you never get any time off to think about the future and your photography." *She said something like that.* "Sometimes you have to put on your own oxygen mask, no?"

This seems to work. I see her shoulders relaxing.

"The uncles did arrange for extra help at the diner this week," Kenna muses. "I don't technically have to be there all the time. But I was kind of hoping to put my tips toward a new camera."

"Do this swap, and I'll buy you whatever camera you want. And I'll toss in a laptop. Pleeeease?" I cajole.

"Why?" She is still shaking her head incredulously at me. "What if the paparazzo sees you?"

"He's not looking for this." I gesture to my clean-scrubbed face and natural hair. "He's looking for that," I say, pointing at her.

"Let me see your phone." I hold out my hand. "We should probably switch cases."

"Like now ... you want to do this now?" Kenna is starting to squirm in the catsuit. That was fast. We should have put more baby powder in.

"No time like the present!" I clap. "How's about we pick up some burgers and head to the diner after closing, and you show me how stuff works. Starting tomorrow, I'm you, and you're me."

"I still can't believe you're serious about this," Kenna says.

"What's the worst that can happen?" I ask. "You'll get new photography equipment and a great story to tell your grandkids."

"I'm going to need you to make me some cheat sheets or—"

"Hey Lorelei!" Tabitha calls out from the front door, followed by brisk knocking. "You in there? I saw the Porsche in the lot!"

Shit. I forgot Tabitha was coming by.

Kenna is sitting bolt upright, staring at me with wide eyes.

"Okay, so that's Tabitha, my PA. But this is perfect timing. Why don't you go answer the door as me?" I grab Kenna by the hand and hoist her up. In the platform boots, she stands a good five inches taller than me next to her barefoot. She does look fierce, if I do say so myself. I wonder if this is what it's like to visit a wax museum and see a statue of yourself.

Like a statue, Kenna isn't moving. She looks like she might panic. "And say what? I don't know what to say to her!"

"Ask her when the DNA tests are coming. I texted her earlier to order them. I'll just duck into the powder room here and hide." I drag her into the hallway, toward the front door.

"What if she figures out I'm not you?" Kenna hisses.

"So what? She's on my payroll, and she signed an NDA. She's not saying anything. If anything, she'll be able to help you get settled before she takes off for the week."

Tabitha knocks again a little louder and calls out, "Lorelei! Everything okay? I just wanted to check in and go over the schedule for the next week."

"Go!" I tug the wig back into place on her head and shove her gently toward the door.

"Hi, Tabitha," I hear Kenna say when she answers the door. I crack the powder room door open so I can spy on them. I've got the perfect vantage point from where I am hiding. I can see the entire foyer, kitchenette, and living room.

"Hi, Lorelei." Tabitha breezes in with her clipboard. "I have your schedule for the week here. There's a list of all the numbers and contacts in case you need to call anyone to change anything."

"Thank you," Kenna says stiffly. Too stiff. She can do better than that.

"Do you need me to pick up anything from the grocery store before I leave tomorrow? More iced tea? Fruit? More vodka?" Is that a note of judgment in her voice?

"So about those DNA tests," Kenna says. "Did you pick them up for me?"

"Noooo ..." Tabitha narrows her eyes. "I told you they have to be mailed. They're overnighting them, though. Should be here by tomorrow. What do you need them for anyway?"

"Oh, ummmmm ... research," Kenna says.

Just at that moment, there's another knock on the door. *Uh-oh.*

"Lorelei, you decent?" Rafe calls out before walking in. Typical Rafe. Just lets himself in. Although, I had asked him to stop by and say goodbye before he left for LA.

He's freshly showered and wearing a pair of jeans, trainers, and an old, faded hoodie. Pretty casual for travel on a commercial airline, but whatever floats his boat. Rafe does whatever Rafe pleases, and Rafe gets away with it.

"Hi, Rafe," Tabitha says. "Can I offer you anything to eat or drink?" *What is she, his mom? She's supposed to be my PA, not his.* "Maybe you'd like me to pack a picnic basket for your trip?" *Is she batting her lashes at him?*

"No thanks." Rafe sounds a little cagey. "I hope I'm not interrupting anything here."

"Oh, no. Lorelei and I were just going over the schedule for the week. I was about to tell her that I checked in with the security company about posting someone here." She turns back to Kenna. "I hate to say it, but after hearing about the paparazzi hanging around, I'm worried about you staying alone here all week, Lorelei."

"Okay, thanks?" she says. I cringe at the uptick in her voice. She sounds so unsure of herself.

"That's it? No argument from you?" Rafe asks. He knows I hate having a bodyguard. It seems a little extreme.

"Well, you know, better safe than sorry." Kenna nods.

"Uh-huh." Rafe looks at her, unconvinced. She's not ribbing him or meeting his eye. This is not good. When she casts a panicked look toward the bathroom, it takes all my self-control not to burst out and rescue her.

"Why are you wearing that?" Rafe points at the catsuit and boots. His eyes pan over her and don't even linger on her rack for a moment, which is a crime. Her rack looks magnificent in that suit. But Rafe and I aren't like that. So interesting to observe it from this angle.

"Oh, you know, for old time's sake," Kenna says. She takes a step and wobbles, then over-corrects, practically careening into the sink.

"So you're totally fine with us posting an extra guard here while I'm away?" Rafe asks again. His jaw is set.

"I mean, if you think it's necessary." Kenna, having regained her balance, bravely takes a step toward the table. She whisks the empty iced-tea cups and cutting board into the sink and commences tidying up. First, she attempts to put away the vodka, opening the cabinet where I keep my Fruity Pebbles stash. *That is not the vodka cabinet, Kenna! The vodka goes in the cabinet over the toaster.*

I smack my forehead.

"You forget where you keep that?" Rafe asks. I can *hear* the raised eyebrow.

"Oh yeah, you know, moving around so much," Kenna says. She opens and closes three more cabinets before finding where I keep the alcohol.

"How much have you had to drink?" Tabitha asks. *She is definitely judging.*

"Ummmmm ..."

Kenna looks imploringly toward the bathroom door.

In a blur, Rafe lunges across the kitchen, pulling a plastic whisk from the canister of utensils by the stove. He grabs Kenna's wrists in one hand and twists them behind her back.

With the other hand, he holds up the whisk in front of her face.

Tabitha screams.

To Kenna's credit, she doesn't pee herself. At least, I don't think she peed. Hard to tell with latex.

"Ohmygod. Ohmygod. What is happening?" Tabitha is backing away with her arms up.

"Who are you?" Rafe is asking. "Where are Lorelei and the dog photographer? What have you done with them?" Rafe glances around, peeking into the living room. He looks like he'd like to slap my PA. "Tabitha! Get it together, check the bathroom." Rafe is speaking with a full-on, menacing-sounding, Middle Eastern accent now. I have to wonder if he's using it to sound more intimidating, or if he's genuinely emotional at the thought of me being tied up in the bathroom.

Kenna is staring cross-eyed at the whisk, cringing.

"Do I have to check?" Tabitha asks.

"Lorelei!" Kenna squeals. "Get your ass out here—now!"

"Is that a wig?" Rafe asks. I'm riveted to the scene as he uses the tines of the plastic whisk to twirl her hair and lifts the wig off Kenna's head. With a dramatic, Expelliarmus-esque flick, he flings it across the kitchen. It lands in the sink. I'm praying that the kitchen security camera got all that. Not that I plan to share the footage. I plan to rewatch the hell out of it, though.

"Let go of me, you asshole!" Kenna growls, and stomps on his foot with the spiky heel of the platform boot. There it is. *Now* she sounds like me.

"You're not Lorelei!" Tabitha gasps. I have to admit, I'm a little disappointed in her. I would have bet good money that my uber-attentive PA would notice the impostor faster than my colleague.

Slow clapping, I come out of the bathroom.

"Let the poor girl go already," I say to Rafe. "Honestly, what was your plan with that whisk there? Were you going to whip her with it till she formed hard peaks?"

I'm not sure who blushes more, Kenna or Rafe. He releases Kenna with a little push and tosses the whisk into the sink, on top of the wig. He looks pretty pissed off.

"Kenna?" Tabitha stares warily at me.

"Try again," I say to her. She looks from me to Kenna, to me to Kenna and finally back to me as the lights come on. The only thing that would improve on her muddled reaction would be a full-on comic faint. Sadly, she remains conscious as I reopen the cabinet to offer her a stiff drink.

"No thanks," she refuses me, primly. "I'm just going to hit the road. I'll stop by and check in with whichever one of you is wearing the wig before I leave tomorrow."

kenna

. . .

I REALLY WASN'T EXPECTING this day to culminate with me borrowing Lorelei Dupont's shampoo. And using it in her shower. I feel worse than foolish. Mortified. Lorelei had to come into the tiled shower stall to help peel the catsuit off me. It's a two-man job getting out of those things.

Now I listen to Rafe and Lorelei arguing as I change into Lorelei's black, silk pajamas that she's left out for me. No sleeping in a grubby, old tee for her. I don't think I've ever worn anything this luxurious in my life. I don't know why I've agreed to go along with any of this. The rational part of me wants to run away. But the day spa-curious part of me is rallying to stay.

"No," Rafe objects. "No way. I am not going to be a part of this ridiculous exchange. Have you lost your mind? And have you forgotten that I have a small child? You expect me to be fine with a complete stranger staying on the property with me and my child?"

"And your little dog, too!" Lorelei imitates the witch in *The Wizard of Oz.*

"You think this is funny?" Rafe summons thunderclouds.

"It's a little funny," Lorelei giggles. "When you did that thing with the whisk and flung her wig. And when you were all 'who are you' with the accent?" She wipes a tear from her eye. "God, I hope the security cam footage has sound."

I slip into the kitchen quietly, my feet clad in Lorelei's plush socks. My hair is wrapped in a towel, but I can still smell the delicious scent of orange-blossom conditioner. It left my hair completely tangle free without weighing it down. I don't know how I'm going to live without it now.

"For the record, I didn't think it was fun being threatened with kitchen implements," I say. I can't even look at Rafe. Lorelei's hand waves back in his direction as if to say, *Take it up with him.*

"I don't see what your problem is anyway, Rafe." Lorelei pours two cups of hot tea and hands one to me and one to Rafe. "You're not even going to be here. Lock up the mansion. Kenna will stay here in the guesthouse. She's just going to hang out and chill. Nobody's going to be any the wiser."

"Actually"—Rafe folds his arms across his broad chest and leans back against the counter

—"there's been a change of plans. That's what I was coming over to tell you."

"Change of plans?" Lorelei asks.

"I'm not going to LA. My mom decided she'd rather spend the week with me and Orly here. We'll all fly down this weekend to visit Disney and see my sister."

"Your mom is coming to visit you *here*?" Lorelei asks.

"Why not? She's never been to the Pacific Northwest, and she wants to spend some one-on-one time with Orly." Rafe stirs some honey into his tea. "So you can see why all this is impossible."

By this, he means me. He waves a dismissive hand in my direction.

"Wrong!" Lorelei disagrees with Rafe. Then she turns to me to explain. "His mom hates me," she says, turning this into an argument *for* the switch. "All the more reason why it's better for everyone if I'm not here this week."

"Lorelei, are you even listening to me?" Rafe is getting frustrated. "My mother doesn't hate you. She just hates how you won't listen to anyone."

"Well, I hate how she's always trying to tell me what to do and guilt-tripping me about the momager. She has four kids of her own. She needs to back off. I am a grown-ass woman. I don't need any more parenting." Rafe and I both watch as Lorelei stirs a pile of colorful marshmallows into her cocoa.

"She means well, Lorelei," he says. "She cares about you."

"You need to listen to me, Rafe. I need some time off! I'm going to lose my mind if I don't get some downtime in between projects."

"So take some time. Sleep in. Go to a spa. What was that wine spa place Zara recommended we try?" Rafe asks.

"The Arbors. I booked it but—" Lorelei stares off into the middle distance, sadly.

"But what?" Rafe interrupts. "What's the problem?"

Rafe turns to look at me now, but it's like he's looking right through me, like I'm not really here. Like I'm an extra. A prop. "I can't even wrap my head around the reason why this dog photographer is still here and wearing your clothes, Lorelei. You have to admit, it's all a little weird, even for you."

Lorelei's nostrils flare, and she squares her shoulders as she steps closer to Rafe. Her eyes are all Ember-ified. The only things missing are the CGI fireballs. "Kenna's not 'just a dog photographer,' and I'm the one who insisted we swap clothes. Did you not notice that we look *exactly like each other*?"

Rafe looks from me to Lorelei and back again. "Okay, there's a resemblance, but it's superficial. Anyone who knows you will see right through the ruse."

"Tabitha didn't," Lorelei argues. "And neither did you, right away."

"Of course I did," Rafe says. "I knew immediately. She wasn't standing like you, or speaking like you. She wasn't even breathing like you."

"Okay, Sherlock. You're extraordinarily observant," Lorelei fawns sarcastically.

Suddenly, all I want to do is go home and sleep off this fever dream.

"Rafe's right, Lorelei," I say. "People are going to figure it out. I told you I couldn't pull off being you. I'm no actress." I sort of hate conceding Rafe's point. Especially since it means I'm not going to get the chance to stay here after all. *So long, truffle toast.*

"People are not going to figure it out, Kenna. Rafe's known me for years. The receptionist at the spa and the household staff here have never met me in person before and aren't as critical as he is." She pulls up the Instagram post and shows it to Rafe. "Here's what 'people' think."

"So this photo isn't you?" Rafe squints at the photo.

"Nope," Lorelei grins smugly.

"Well, it's just a photo." He hands her phone back. "It's not like a public appearance. She's not speaking."

"And she wouldn't have to. She'll just be here for the most part."

And the spa. I haven't ever been to a spa. I wouldn't know how to act even if I was just going as me. I start to back out of the room.

"Don't you go anywhere!" Lorelei commands. To Rafe she says, "Don't you see how uncomfortable you're making my guest feel? It's not enough that you threatened to make a meringue out of her!"

The corner of his mouth twitches up and he shifts uncomfortably against the counter, staring at us both and sipping his tea.

Lorelei points to a barstool and invites me to sit. She speaks less brashly this time. "Have a seat, Kenna. Please? I promise we'll work all this out. More tea?" She opens a drawer with about twenty varieties of imported tea.

"No thanks, I'm good." I shake my head and sniff my Darjeeling. The embossed, gold-foil packets confirm what I already suspected—nothing but the good stuff for Lorelei.

"I still don't understand the *why*," Rafe says. "It's like you're going all 'method actor' on me, except there's no role you're actually prepping for."

I steal glances at him through lowered lids as I pretend to sip my tea. I can see he has tiny laugh lines around his eyes and a small scar under his chin where there's no stubble. One of his knuckles is scraped—looks like dog claws—and he has a purple hairband around his wrist. He's a person. A real person. They both are.

Rafe sets his cup in the sink. Someone has removed the wig. He squeezes Lorelei's shoulder as he passes her. There's real affection in his eyes, I see. Affection and confusion. "Tell me what this is," he says.

"I just need a little break from being me." Lorelei runs her hand through her natural hair. "Whoever that is. I'm not sure I know anymore. Maybe I never knew. I never had the chance to find out. I mean, look at me!" She tugs on her hair. "This is my natural hair color. Who knew I was a blonde all along? I didn't!"

Lorelei pulls up a barstool at the kitchen counter beside me, laying a hand on my shoulder now. "I want to be a regular person like her. I want to go shopping at a strip mall and go out to dinner alone without anyone writing about it on *TMZ*. I really want to get carded at a bar!"

"Look, Lorelei, if anyone gets it, you know I do. And if that's what floats your boat, impersonating this person"—he waves his hand in my direction—"then, fine. I just am not OKAY with having her here on the property at the same time, imper-sonating you."

Whatever happened to him calling me Ken-NA? Perhaps I shouldn't have scrubbed the penciled-in brows off just yet.

"Where else would she go? Someone's gotta be me while I'm being her. I need a seat filler!"

"I should probably go," I say, sick of being spoken about instead of being spoken to. I've had all I can take. "Can I get my bracelet back?" I hold out my hand. I don't care about the shorts and tank, but I need the bracelet.

"No. No one's going anywhere yet," Lorelei insists, popping up and pulling her phone, still wrapped in my case, from the pocket of my shorts that she is still wearing. "I'm calling Dean Riley."

"Look, it's probably best if I don't do this swap OR the photos," I stammer and stand again. "This ... was a mistake."

"What has this got to do with Dean?" Rafe asks.

"Sit!" Lorelei commands us both. Rafe narrows his eyes at me, but deigns to pull up a stool beside me. Lorelei lays her phone faceup on the counter between us.

"Hey, Lorelei, what's up?" Dean answers on the second ring. "Everything okay?"

"Yeah, Dean, I'm here with Rafe. Rafe's a little nervous about Kenna spending time on the property. Maybe you could put his mind at ease?"

"What's the problem?" Dean asks.

"There's no *problem*," Rafe says. "We just haven't run a background check on her, and we don't know much about her."

"I'm still here," I mouth at Lorelei, and she holds a finger over her lips to silence me.

Dean laughs. "Are you kidding me, Rafe? My girlfriend, Chelsea, has known Kenna since high school. She's beloved around here. Aside from being famous as the town's best barista, she spends her weekends volunteering at a pet shelter. And just to let you know, she shook off a paparazzo on her way to deliver lunch to the cast yesterday. What else do you need to know? Her uncles own the local diner, she's sweet and funny, if a little quirky, and it's rumored she has terrible taste in men. Must be why she's such a huge fan of yours."

I rest my head in my hands at the 'terrible taste in men' part. This? This is what everyone thinks of me? I knew it.

"So this Kenna is a big fan of mine?" Rafe is smiling a little now, one eyebrow raised as he makes eye contact with me. Ken-NA. He said my name. God, it sounds so much cooler that way.

"Oh, come on, man, who isn't? No need to get all conceited about it. I mean, she's a fan of the franchise. Not some creepy stalker type. I can't think of a more loyal, dependable person. I'd hire her to babysit my kids, if I had any. In fact, I think my brother, Eli, has hired her to babysit his son, Braden, on a couple of occasions."

Lorelei raises her eyebrows at Rafe and smiles victoriously at me. "Okay. That's all we needed. That and a rec where we can get some good burgers."

"The Onion, although it's a little gritty. You might want to send someone else in there to pick up your order. Not sure they deliver all the way out to where you're staying."

Lorelei makes an impressed face when Dean tells her the same place I did.

"Thanks, Dean."

"Anytime, Lorelei. I still can't get over how much Kenna looks like you."

"Neither can we," she says. "Thanks again, and see you next week, Dean!" Lorelei spins the phone triumphantly on the counter after hanging up and looks at the two of us. "There! You feel better now, Rafe?"

"Maybe ..." He stares at the phone until it stops. Then he sighs and turns to me resignedly. "Any chance you could help me find a trainer for Princess while you're here?"

"OMG. This is perfect!" Lorelei snaps her fingers. "Rafe can give you acting lessons and coach you on being me if you have to appear in public."

"No. That is not a good idea. I strongly advise against her appearing in public dressed as you," Rafe says.

"But you'll do it!" Lorelei does a little victory hop that reminds me of an excited child, and I'm surprised to see her joy.

"What's there to do?" Rafe sheepishly shrugs her off when she attempts to hug him from behind. "If what you mean is I won't rat you out, fine. I'll go along with it. But I don't approve. And I really don't get what's in it for you." He surveys me again. He still seems a little doubtful, despite Dean's glowing reference.

"She's getting a much-needed break," Lorelei says. "Kenna here works like a dog. Plus, she had to put up with being called Poxy Moxie in high school. It's payback time. She deserves a little R & R and star treatment." She winks charismatically at me. I'm grateful she isn't mentioning the camera and laptop that she offered as payment.

I look at Rafe. "I can help you find a local trainer. I'm sure Angie from the shelter, or Xander, the groomer who groomed her when she came in, can recommend someone."

"Perfect!" Lorelei squeals. "Now you just need to teach me the secret handshake that you and your butler do, Kenna."

"Pardon?" I look at Rafe for help, but he just shrugs.

"You know." Lorelei rolls her eyes. "The handshake thingy ... *da da da da da-DA, da da da da da-DA.*" She sings the tune from *The Parent Trap.* "What was the butler's name? Martin?"

"Ha!" I laugh. "I hardly have a butler. If anyone had a butler, it would be you."

"Rafe can play the butler," Lorelei laughs.

"No, Rafe can be going home now." He pushes back his chair as he stands to go. "I still don't approve of this, but I'm not going to get in the way." He looks at me. "Call me if you need anything. The food deliveries come to the main house, and you're welcome to use the big kitchen there. Just shoot me a text so I don't get surprised and attack you again."

"It could be more serious next time," Lorelei nods gravely. "He might grab a silicon spatula."

"Right." Rafe stands to go. "On that note, I'm out of here."

"Are you sure you don't want to bring the whisk with you, when you beat it?" Lorelei quips, cracking herself up. Who knew Lorelei Dupont was so punny?

After he leaves, Lorelei turns back to me, still smiling. "We have a lot of territory to cover, but I'm starving."

"Well then," I say, "let me call in our order to The Onion. It's going to be a late night. I can teach you how to use the espresso machine after the diner closes.

lorelei

· · ·

KENNA WASN'T KIDDING about this stupid coffeemaker.

"Who's the diva here?" I grumble at the giant, imported coffee machine. It replies with a fart of steam, spewing hot droplets of liquid that threaten to scar me for life. "Fine, fine. Nice coffee machine. Good girl," I speak soothingly to it, as Kenna suggested I do during our training session last night. The session that lasted till 3 a.m.

I barely got two hours of sleep on Kenna's lumpy futon before dragging my ass back to this place. But that's fine. As a working actress, I'm used to early call times and faking it on little to no sleep. I can do this. It's a small price to pay to experience what it's like to be a regular person.

The smell of coffee and pastries, bacon, and fresh-squeezed oranges helps. It's comforting and familiar. This, if anything, is the real smell of my childhood kitchens. The actual kitchens in whatever apartment near the studio the momager rented smelled like cleaning products and old Formica. But there was always a diner nearby where we would stop on our way to work.

By 8 a.m., there's a line snaking out the front door of the diner, and I am fascinated by the people coming in. None of them recognize me. Well, none of them recognize who I really am. Several of them seem to recognize "Kenna." It's working!

"Hey, Kenna. The usual," a pretty, brown-haired woman says absentmindedly to me. "Actually, make it extra strong? I'm on deadline for an article and need all the caffeine I can get." She tosses her curls and digs around in her massive satchel before pulling out a pen and a notebook. "Just got an idea. I don't want to forget it!" she says, rapidly scrawling something in her moleskin notebook.

"Are you sure you don't want a mocha macchiato?" I say hopefully, suggesting the one drink I've mastered, which happens to be the only coffee drink I really enjoy. It's basically cocoa with a shot of espresso. I point at the chalkboard sign by the register on which I've written:

Switch it up! Swap your regular coffee drink for a mocha macchiato today! Only $2!

I'm pretty proud of myself for coming up with this idea. I figure I can just watch some YouTube tutorials to figure out how to make all the other ones.

"Mocha macchiato? For me? You think?" She eyes me suspiciously, then shrugs. "Okay, sure, why not. If you're suggesting it, it's probably the right way to go. Got any interesting pastries today?" She glances sideways at the pastry case that I filled earlier with a variety of goodies from the local artisanal bakery. I consider her carefully. This part is easy.

"You should try the carrot cake donuts," I suggest. "They're new."

"Okay, sure. Add it to my order," she says.

The next three customers order plain, old, drip coffee, but when they overhear me suggesting items from the pastry case, they groggily ask me for recommendations. Carlos, the old guy who seems to do pretty much everything around here, rings them up, and the line starts to move faster.

There's a pretty even mix of men and women, most of them in casual clothes. A police officer comes in, oozing authority and self-importance. His eyes do a sweep of the surroundings like he's looking for a perp. But then they settle on me. "Morning, Kenna," he smirks. "Late night last night?"

Something clicks. Kenna mentioned something about a married cop messaging her on a dating app, wanting a three-way.

"Oh, you know ..." I shrug. "Things got really interesting with this girl I met." I lower my lashes and conjure a blush onto my face, knowing that the real Kenna would probably never wind this jerk up. But how can I resist?

"What?" His eyes pop wide, and his face explodes into an expression of hungry delight. Bingo! "You and another *girl*? Who is it? Anyone I know?" He leans in closer and speaks in a lower tone. "Anyone I'd like to get to know? You know I'm open ..."

He's handsome-ish, if you like the short, brawny types, but I can't help but notice his morning breath and the stray hairs between his eyebrows. But more than that, it's the dullness behind his eyes. He's not the brightest bulb.

"Sorry, Jed," I say, pushing a cup of coffee at him. "I don't think she'd be into you. You're not her type."

"But you and me matched." He juts his chin out, staring at my boobs.

"Yeah, there must have been a glitch in the app," I say. "Oh hey, you should try the strawberry tartlets, by the way. They are really good. The strawberries are super juicy this season."

His eyes light up, and I can practically hear his stomach rumbling. Such a simple creature, this one. I can't help him with his carnal appetites, but at least I can send him off satisfied with something.

I'm feeling pretty confident once I've got the line shortened down enough that it no longer snakes out the front door. The rush slows a bit, and the short-order cook and the waitress settle into a sort of dance between the tables and the kitchen. If Carlos suspects anything, he doesn't say so. He chats up each customer patiently as he rings them up, and I file away the tidbits that I overhear for future use.

Just when I think I'm done with the morning rush, the bell on the door rings, and a tall, wolfish, floppy-haired man with a trekking stick in one hand and a briefcase in the other limps in.

"Morning, everyone!" He waves, taking a seat on a swiveling stool at the counter.

"Morning, Noah!" the waitress announces. "Be right with you!"

"No hurry." He waves her off, then reaches into the briefcase and pulls out a padded laptop case. He takes out the laptop slowly and carefully polishes the screen with a microfiber cloth.

"Can I get you anything to drink, Noah?" I ask, thanking the waitress for inadvertently giving me his name.

"I'll just have a regular cup of coffee for now. Thanks, Kenna." He smiles warmly and familiarly at me. Those medium-brown eyes of his are just like melted chocolate, and I love how swoopy his upper lip is. His brows could use a quick cleanup, but nothing so serious as the cop earlier.

"Oh, and I have something for you." He reaches into his bag and pulls out a folder. Long, strong fingers, clean nails. No ring. I have to wonder why Kenna didn't mention this guy in her briefing. He seems really nice.

"I know you said you had it covered, but I was curious for myself, too. I did a little research on the latest DSLR cameras. There are several new ones on the market that aren't prohibitively expensive. But if your heart is set on the Sony, I think you should just rent it. I'd hate to see you give up a great opportunity just because you're embarrassed by your equipment."

"Thanks for doing this research for me, Noah." I smile at him and take the folder. The contents are bound, and flipping through it, I can see he's highlighted a few cameras and made notes. "Very thoughtful."

"Again, I hope I wasn't overstepping. I've been researching cameras for myself, and I have the *Consumer Reports* account, and well ... you know. I don't need anything nearly as fancy as you, but I was thinking I would get something full frame. I'd like to take more bird photos," he says, blushing a little when he says this. As if he didn't mean for that to slip out.

"I didn't know you take bird photos, Noah." I set the folder down on the counter and lean in conspiratorially. "So you're into birds?"

"Well, yeah. I know. I'm such a dork, right? It started when I was a kid. My mom and I kept birding journals, and we did a lot of hiking. It's always been my dream to do a Big Year."

"Like the Owen Wilson movie?" I ask.

"Yes!" he says, smiling. "I can't believe you watched that!"

I grin. "I liked it. Birds are cool. Isn't this area famous for being part of a migratory path?"

A birdwatching tour was one of the best options Tabitha had run by me for my week off, but I hadn't wanted to become the bird in everyone's sights.

"Yes!" Noah enthuses. "That was part of the appeal when I moved here. Birdwatching is best in the spring here, but it involves hiking to remote areas. Sadly, these days, I'm a bit more stationary. Can't hike as far because of the leg, but my PT says I'll probably be back almost to normal by this fall. There's always next year, I suppose."

"Tough break." I nod sympathetically.

"You're telling me," he says. "I still can't believe I fell off the stage like that."

This is a story I am going to need to hear, but obviously, I cannot ask him about it because I am supposed to already know it. I wish I could call Kenna right now. She is probably still snuggled up in my bed, in the lap of luxury, sleeping in.

"I like the Panasonics," Noah comments. "Great glass, and they have an exceptional selection of long-range lenses."

Seriously, this guy appears made for Kenna. Not married. Seems straight. Loves cameras. Why isn't she dating him? He's smiling shyly at me. At Kenna, I remind myself.

Suddenly, he leans forward, like he's got a secret. He beckons me closer and folds down his laptop screen halfway.

"Speaking of long-range lenses, your 'friend' is back," he speaks in low tones.

"My friend?" I ask.

"The photographer, paparazzo. Whatever. I saw him parked out there before I came in this morning."

"That guy is not my friend." I stand up straighter and turn to fetch the coffee for him. I pull a mug from the stand by the percolator. "Cream and sugar?" I ask.

"Yes, please," Noah nods. "And I didn't mean anything by that. I know he's not your friend. He was pretty obnoxious, making you remake that drink so many times and quizzing you about the actors."

"Well, he was probably just trying to get me flustered so I'd give something up." I pour the coffee.

"Exactly!" Noah nods. "Very misogynistic of him, if you ask me."

"At least he didn't try to explain cameras to a photographer." I wink at Noah. I'm being a little mean, and possibly totally out of character for Kenna, but it pops out before I can stop myself.

Noah looks horrified.

"I didn't do that! Did I do that? Oh my God. Was I mansplaining?"

"More like camerasplaining," I laugh. "But your heart was in the right place, and this is actually helpful. I'm keeping it." I tuck the folder onto a shelf behind the counter. "As for that photographer ..."

"Can you ban him from the diner?" Noah asks. "Not for nothing, but I find it a little off-putting having the guy hanging around like a vulture."

"We can ban photos inside the diner." I consider this. "It's private property, and a lot of places in LA and Vegas have a 'no paparazzi' policy."

But if he's got a long-range lens, he can probably shoot through the glass window. And there's nothing stopping him from sitting in the public park opposite this place with his camera.

"I know Dean's theater is good for Ephron, and everything," Noah says, "but I can't help but wonder if he really needed to get celebrities in for his production. It changes the nature of the place, you know? Next thing you know, there'll be a *Real Housewives of Ephron* franchise."

"What?" I'm not sure I follow him.

"I just mean, it changes the culture of our town having so many celebrities around. I've always liked how simple and straightforward people are here. That's part of Ephron's charm. I hate that people are acting stupid about celebs like Rafe Barzilay and Lorelei Dupont being here, just because they were in a few blockbuster superhero movies. And I gotta wonder whether Dean was thinking about the quality of the performances, or was his decision to involve them really about the bottom line?"

I set the metal coffeepot down with a thunk, grateful that my back is to this man while I consider my response.

"You don't think Rafe and Lorelei can act?" I spin around. I want to hate him, but instead, I'm struck again by how cute he is.

"Who knows?" Noah peels back the lids on three plastic creamers and dumps the contents into his coffee, one at a time. He stacks the empties neatly. He's a stacker. Such nice hands. He also doesn't stir his cream in right away. We both watch the patterns in the swirling liquid. Why was I mad at him again?

"I mean, who knows how many takes those two are used to burning before they get their lines right," he says. "I'd have to watch one of them live or in a live streaming format before I felt confident saying they could really act," Noah says.

Oh yeah. That's why he sucks. He thinks I can't act. I take in a quick breath and bite down on my lip. What would Kenna say? Kenna. I'm Kenna. But I barely know Kenna.

"Yeah, well, I'm sure they both know how to act," I say. "Dean knows them well. And what's wrong with wanting the theater to make money? Most people are pretty excited to have celebs here in town."

That's a WAG. A wild-assed guess. I have no clue how the locals feel about having us here. I can only go by what Dean has told me. Which might have been a little fluffed.

"Ugh. Okay. I get it. You're a Titanium Man fan." Noah dunks his spoon in the coffee and gives it a rough stir. The belly of the spoon hits the interior of the mug like a warning bell.

"Guilty." I shrug. Again, wagging it, but judging by the breathless way Kenna reacted to Rafe yesterday, I wouldn't put her above being a member of the Pedal to the Metal Titanium Man Fan Club. Too bad his fans have no idea how slow he actually drives.

"So, who would you rather see playing Titania and Oberon?" I can't help myself.

"I don't know," Noah replies a little defensively. "Maybe someone with a little more experience on the stage?"

"You know most actors start out doing stage productions, right?" I argue.

"I guess. Maybe I'm being unfair. Rafe's probably fine." He pauses to pour some raw sugar into his mug. "It's more Lorelei who has the rep for stirring things up. She's the poster child for teenaged rebellion. Poxy Moxie and all that. She's cool again since she started playing Ember. My students worship her and emulate her every move." He sighs. "They don't need to see her brand of bad behavior up close and personal. She could really use someone to rein her in."

Old news. Old, old, old news. I bristle at the way I'm still being characterized by things that happened nearly a decade ago. I'm never shaking that rep, am I? *Rein me in?*

I don't get a chance to defend myself because the bell on the door chimes, and a little man in a black beanie, with a face as pockmarked as an unshelled almond, swaggers in.

"You!" He shakes an accusatory finger at me as he strides toward the counter, cradling his big lens like a baby.

He's staring at me with fire in his eyes, and for a moment, I freeze. Does he recognize me?

"Kenna, is it? Nice job throwing me off yesterday. But I've got my eye on you. I knew that you knew more than you were saying. You and me are gonna be besties this summer, girlie."

I square up my stance and smile at him. He wants to play? Fine.

"You know the cast is off this week"—I smile at the paparazzo —"but I heard Rafe and Lorelei talking about how they were taking a road trip to Vancouver, BC in Canada."

"Vancouver?" The paparazzo pulls a tiny notebook and pencil from his pocket and makes a note. "You get anything else more specific?"

"Nope." I shrug. "But they definitely seemed excited about checking the city out. Something about a night market and Whistler?"

"Thanks for the tip!" The paparazzo grins excitedly, tucks the pencil behind his ear, and turns to go.

Noah watches the exchange and waits till the door closes to comment. He looks thoroughly impressed with me. "Tell me that wasn't total BS. You wouldn't really tip that jerk off, would you? Did you just make that up?"

"Yep." I smile, basking in Noah's warm, intelligent, chocolatey gaze. I'm starving because I haven't eaten yet, but it's better than breakfast.

"Damn! Very convincing." He grins back at me and lifts his mug in tribute. "You, Kenna ... now *you* are a natural actress."

kenna

. . .

I HAVE no idea where I am or what time it is when Tabitha bangs on the bedroom door in the guesthouse.

"Kenna, aren't you up yet?" she projects. "It's me, Tabitha. I have the DNA test kits."

I feel the unfamiliar slip of satiny, cotton sheets against my skin and open one eye. Instead of the familiar sight of dust motes flickering through beams of sunlight in my garage apartment, I'm greeted by near darkness and treated air. A diffuser in the corner emits a faint, blue light and makes a light hissing sound as it emits a quick burst of carefully calibrated lavender and eucalyptus scented mist.

"Kenna? Are you there?" Tabitha calls out again.

"Just a minute!" I croak. *What time is it?* I look at my phone. It's 10 a.m.! When was the last time I slept in till 10 a.m.? I can't recall.

I fumble my way to the door and let Tabitha in, excusing myself immediately to go pee. Worry about the diner trails me into the bathroom. How did Lorelei manage the morning rush? She seemed to get the hang of the coffee machine last night in our practice session, pulling out a half-decent mocha macchiato, but there's more to making coffee than just pushing buttons. You have to set your intent. I'm not sure she understood that part.

And what about the regulars? I made her a list of all the people and drink orders that I could remember, but now I'm remembering people I left off it. I should probably text her with those.

"Have you heard anything from Lorelei?" I join Tabitha in the kitchen. "She hasn't texted me." I hold up my phone.

In fact, nobody has texted me in the last ten hours. Not Lorelei, not Georgia, not Carlos, or Angie, and not the uncles. No texts. Nada. No wonder I slept so hard. I should be grateful, but instead, it makes me uneasy. Being on everyone's fast dial is kind of my thing.

"Can I make you some coffee?" I ask Tabitha, looking through the cabinets and locating pods.

Pods. Ugh.

"Oh, yes," Tabitha says. "I would love it if you would make my coffee. I buy whatever flavors are on sale. Make me salted caramel, please. Make sure the machine is set to extra dark." She pauses. "Oh, and make sure the reservoir is filled with fresh spring water. That's what I prefer." She settles into a chair at the counter, primly crossing her legs at the ankle."

I pull out a mug and a "Salted Caramel Latte" pod and try not to shudder as I smell the artificial flavoring. I'm going to have to scare up a frother and a French press at the very least if I'm going to survive the week here.

"Not that mug," she corrects me pertly. "I prefer the white one, to the right." I return the pink mug in my hand. I reach for the mug she's indicated, an oversize, white mug with a golden handle and a large, loopy letter "L."

"Cream and sugar?" I ask, her coffee on the table.

"Just cream. There's some in the fridge, I think." Tabitha is opening the package with the kits. "So these DNA tests are pretty self-explanatory. Even *you* should be able to figure them out. I spoke to the lab, and they will put a rush on them. You just have to swab your cheek for one, and spit for the other. You should wait for a few hours after eating and drinking or brushing your teeth, though." She pauses, considering before she asks her question. "So what do you think? Honestly. Do you really think you and Lorelei are actually related?"

She asks me this like she's asking me if I believe in Bigfoot.

"Who knows?" I set the creamer on the table. French vanilla. More artificial flavoring. Yuck. "Hope this is okay," I say.

"It's my fave!" Tabitha licks her lips. "Lorelei doesn't drink coffee. So I mostly stocked stuff I like. Hope you're okay with it."

"I'll manage," I say. "Thanks for bringing the kits by, I really appreciate it. This is all pretty weird."

"What's on tap for today?" Tabitha asks.

"I don't know," I say, feeling a slight sense of panic. I have no plans for the day. Nothing. No drinks to make, no photos to take, no friends to meet, no aging uncles to assist. I have no idea what I'll do with myself!

"Where's that schedule?" I ask Tabitha.

She stands and retrieves the clipboard from the kitchen counter. "It's here. But there's nothing on here for *you* to do."

"Nothing?" I ask. "What would Lorelei normally do on a day with nothing planned?" If I was home, I would clean my kitchen or organize my closet. But there's staff to clean here. The kitchen is immaculate, and every sock and bobby pin in Lorelei's closet is thoroughly organized.

"Lorelei doesn't have idle days with nothing planned. She's always prepping for a role, doing research, strategizing with her team, or meeting with her stylists and aestheticians." Tabitha is speaking to me like I should already know this. *I don't like Tabitha.*

"Okay, so what does she do when she has a few hours off?"

"She's a big reader. She averages two to three books per week. I can pull her TBR list up on Kindle if you think you're up to it." Tabitha looks down doubtfully.

I don't even know what a TBR list is. I only know what a Kindle is because Uncle Nick likes to read his space operas on his. I saw all the books on Lorelei's nightstand, but dyslexia has always made reading a chore for me. I'd rather listen to books or, better yet, see a movie.

"Anything else?" I ask.

"She's always working out. Never misses a day. And she likes to hike."

None of this is convincing me that we share any of the same DNA.

"Maybe I'll go for a swim," I say. I wish I'd packed up more of my things last night after we stopped by my apartment. I forgot to grab a swimsuit. I'll just have to wear one of Lorelei's.

"So, before I go," Tabitha says, checking her watch, "all the reservation info for the spa tomorrow is here." She taps a finger on the clipboard. "As well as my number. You can call or text me in a pinch. I haven't been Lorelei's PA for very long, but I was a huuugge fan for years before I landed this gig. I was prepping for it my whole life. It's kind of my dream job."

"What about Lorelei's family and friends?" I ask. "Should I be concerned that someone might just stop by?" And then another thought occurs to me. "And what about Rafe's mom? Does she really hate Lorelei?"

Tabitha sighs heavily and sits back down on a barstool. "Okay, I can see that you're clueless and that you're going to need the entire Wikipedia debriefing." She checks her watch again.

"Am I?" I wonder how long this information-gathering session is going to take that she needs to check her watch. I've learned it's best to let officious and annoying people say their peace. If you argue with them or interrupt them, they'll just drone on forever.

"Yeah, if you've got a prayer of not screwing this up. I can't believe Lorelei has entrusted her whole life to someone who knows so little about her. It's a big chance she's taking, leaving her reputation in your hands like this."

Tabitha doesn't seem at all concerned that Lorelei is currently mucking about in my life, and that my reputation is in her hands.

"Here's what you need to know about family. Lorelei doesn't have any besides her mom, and they haven't spoken in years. They're estranged." Tabitha drags out the "strange" part of the word, making me think that she herself is very strange.

"She mentioned to me that she was emancipated at sixteen?" I confirm.

"That's what I said. Estranged." Tabitha repeats the word.

"Okay," I nod. "Got that."

"I personally think what happened was that they had a big falling out after *Moxie* was canceled. Lorelei doesn't talk about it publicly or privately. But I know that her mom still sends her birthday cards, and she runs the OG Moxie fan site. She's spoken out a few times on podcasts and stuff that she'd love to reconcile with Lorelei someday," Tabitha continues.

"Sounds complicated," I say, wondering how much of Lorelei's actual Wikipedia entry has been contributed by Tabitha.

"Well, if you ask me," Tabitha says, without being asked, "I think it's super sad. I blame the network. They never should have canceled *Moxie*. I just think it's a miracle she's not a drug addict or totally screwed up like so many other former kid stars."

"Yeah," I nod dumbly, like I know what she's talking about. Of course I know the trope, who doesn't? But having met Lorelei, it's hard to picture her as anyone's victim.

"And Rafe's mom ..." Tabitha shakes her head. "I don't know this for sure, but from what intel I have been able to gather, it all goes back to something that happened when they were kids."

"Rafe and Lorelei knew each other as kids?" I ask incredulously.

"Oh yeah! Totally. You didn't know that?" Tabitha looks at me like this is Titanium Man fandom 101 content, and I'm some kind of idiot who couldn't even be bothered to read the syllabus.

"No," I admit. *Whatever. I have a life.* "I didn't know."

"Huh," Tabitha says, clearly pondering a universe where this information is not taught in kindergarten. "Well, let me dumb it down for you then. You know how they were both child actors?"

"Rafe was a child actor?" I ask, bracing for the inevitable get-with-the-program comeback from the PA.

"Oh yeah, well, not many people know about Rafe's early acting career. He was on a really popular Israeli TV show when he was a teenager."

"He was?"

"Yeah, but that's not how he met Lorelei." Tabitha speaks faster and more animatedly, enjoying her moment on the podium.

"Okay," I say. Just when I thought I was starting to follow.

"He met her because he was also, very briefly, in a boy band. It wasn't long after *Moxie* took off and *his* show was canceled. Rafe came to LA with the band and attended the Kids' Choice Awards. Somehow, their moms met at the awards ceremony and became friends, and he and Lorelei ended up hanging out together."

"Okay," I say. "What a bizarre coincidence. They met as kids and then again as adults on a blockbuster film."

"There are no coincidences in Hollywood," Tabitha scoffs while shaking her head and rolling her eyes. "Rafe was the one who insisted they cast Lorelei as Ember. They've stayed in touch all these years. He pulled her career out of the indie toilet."

"But they're not, you know ..." I blush, thinking again of Rafe in the driveway. And then I blush more, thinking about his hand against my bare chest in the catsuit, fist wedged against my cleavage. *Fist that was holding a plastic whisk.*

"I mean, the rumors would suggest they are, and have always been, a couple, but I haven't seen any evidence to support that. I've kind of been rooting for them to finally hook up this summer. I mean, who else could be more perfect for Lorelei than her childhood friend Rafe Barzilay?" She gets a dreamy, faraway look that has me wondering if she is planning their wedding in her mind. I raise my brows at her, and she finishes her thought. "Ideally, I would be working for both of them."

"Okay," I say. "But what about Rafe's mom?" *Is she the reason Rafe and Lorelei haven't ever hooked up?*

"Oh, this is the juicy part!" Tabitha's eyes get wide, and then she glances around nervously, as if she's afraid she's on the nanny cam. "Is it warm in here? Let's go sit outside, shall we?"

"Sure," I say, following her onto the patio. I'm going to have to seek out a viable caffeine source soon, or I'll get a headache.

"Okay." Tabitha settles into one of the hanging, egg-shaped chairs on the patio behind the guesthouse. The view in the morning is even more spectacular than it was yesterday after-noon, if that's even possible.

"Mind if I play some tunes?" She swipes her phone and pulls up a pop playlist, and it takes me a moment to realize why. She's trying to cover what we're saying from any prying ears, electronic or otherwise.

"Now I can talk." Tabitha leans toward me. "This is just between us, okay? This is off the record."

"Okay." As if I've ever had a record, or would know what to do with a record. I have no record.

I climb into the other egg and lean back, giving myself a solid push before tucking my legs under me.

"So the rumor is, she got him stoned," Tabitha says with a face of pure scandal.

"Who got who stoned?" I ask, wondering if I should have eaten something before coming out here.

"Are you even listening to me?" She looks incredulous.

"Yes," I nod. "I'm sorry. I'm just easily distracted."

"You're as bad as Lorelei," Tabitha chides. "Well, listen up, because I am not going to repeat this again. I was just saying that the rumors were that Lorelei gave Rafe drugs. She got him stoned. At some point during or after the Kids' Choice Awards. And it wouldn't have been such a big deal, but it was Passover, and I guess his dad is some kind of Rabbi or something? Rafe was supposed to sing with him at a big LA temple, but he showed up wasted, and I don't know exactly what went down. All I know is that his family was mortified, and the boy band broke up." Tabitha pauses dramatically, taking a moment to gauge my reaction.

"Okay," I say. "Thanks for sharing. That was interesting." Whatever went down, it would be nice if Lorelei had given me the scoop. But maybe these were details she didn't think I needed to know. I almost wish Tabitha hadn't dragged me out here to dish.

"Yeah, you should definitely ask her all about what happened with Rafe and his family," Tabitha says. "And then you should tell me what she says."

Now I get it.

"That's not going to happen, Tabitha," I say. "If you want to know more, why don't you just ask her yourself?"

"Oh, I couldn't!" she gasps, as if I'm the one who's breached professional standards and not her.

"You could also just ask me," a low, measured voice somewhere behind us says.

Tabitha goes pale and rigid in her chair.

Using one toe on the ground to rotate myself in the swinging chair, I confirm the source of her horror and mortification. Rafe Barzilay is standing on the patio behind us, holding a box of farm-fresh produce. He's wearing workout clothes again, although sadly, not the same shorts as yesterday. Today, he has on a close-fitting, black tracksuit and running shoes. His hair is loose, curling around the collar.

He meets my gaze. He doesn't look angry. If anything, his dark-brown eyes are lit up with honey-gold sparks of amusement, like we're sharing a joke. The warmth in his eyes takes me by surprise, causing me to lose my toehold, which has me spinning out again.

He takes a step forward and catches the edge of my chair, steadying it. Then he sets the produce on a side table.

"Sorry to sneak up on you," he apologizes.

"Are you a human being or a panther?" I ask.

"I thought I'd bring over your stuff from the farm share box. There are fresh eggs and a few other items up at the house for you, too."

"Is there coffee?" I ask, hoping against hope.

"None that came for Lorelei, but I've got some whole beans and a moka pot."

"French press?" I ask.

"Probably one in the pantry. You're welcome to check."

"I'm so sorry, Rafe," Tabitha shudders. "I shouldn't have been gossiping like that. It's just that Kenna was asking me leading questions, and I wasn't sure how to answer them."

Is that the wheels of the bus I'm getting thrown under that I hear roaring in my ears?

"Kenna was asking you questions?" Rafe repeats.

"Yes, about you and Lorelei," Tabitha nods, earnestly.

Rafe throws his head back and laughs. "You want to know the sad thing, Tabitha? It's a funny story, actually. You should have asked her about it. I'm sure she would have loved to tell you about it."

"Maybe ..." Tabitha says nervously. "Maybe we can ask her next week." She jumps up and grabs the farm box. "How about I put all this stuff away for you before I get going, Kenna?"

"Not so fast," Rafe says. "How about you apologize to Kenna for lying and throwing her under the bus first? And then you can put the groceries away. And after that, you can call your agency and tell them you're not coming back next week. They'll need to send someone else for Lorelei. You're done."

"But—"

"Uh-uh. Apologies first," Rafe says, cutting her off.

"But you don't understand. It's not what you think. She—" Tabitha scrambles for excuses, but Rafe doesn't respond. He just stands there, staring stone-faced at her with his arms folded and his eyebrows raised in the universal "I smell bull-shit" position.

Finally, she realizes the worm has turned and her face gets red and angry. She is glaring at me.

"She is not worthy of trying on, let alone walking in, Lorelei's shoes!" Tabitha looks at me like she might spit. "She's not a *true fan!*"

"Did you need me to call the agency and tell them why you're getting fired instead then?" Rafe asks.

"No. Fine. Sorry, Kenna. Whatever." Tabitha is red and twitchy, but she turns her wrath back at Rafe, nonetheless. "For what it's worth, Rafe? I think Lorelei can do much better than a stoner like you."

"That much is probably true," Rafe concedes. "Make sure you put the celery in the crisper and the parsley in a cup of water. Don't try anything funny … there are cameras. And you can show yourself out. I'll take the key now." He takes the farm box from her so she can search for it in her bag. "Good girl," he says as he pockets it. He shoves the farm box back at her. "And goodbye."

Tabitha scurries back toward the house, leaving me alone on the patio with my own personal superhero. If that was the audition for the part, he nailed it. I haven't felt this vindicated by anyone since Georgia decked Bryce Holm for calling me Poxy.

"Can you believe her?" he asks, still staring warmly at me. "And this is someone who's been thoroughly vetted, no less."

"I can't imagine what it's like to have people prying constantly," I say, honestly unable to imagine it. My life isn't interesting enough to inspire anyone to snoop.

I brace myself for some kind of "let this be a lesson" lecture from him, but he's speaking to me like we're on the same side. Like we have the same problems.

"That wasn't the real problem," Rafe says. "She was a kook and a liar, but what I really couldn't stand was how rude she was to you. She had no right to be speaking to you the way she was. Lorelei's probably going to kill me for firing her PA, but I'm sure the agency will send another. In the meantime, feel free to call on me."

He didn't just fire her PA for me, did he? She was a crappy stalker. That's why he did it. It really isn't about me.

"Thank you," I say. And then because I can't think of anything else to say, I throw in, "Lorelei is lucky to have a friend like you."

"Mind if I sit a minute?" Rafe lowers himself into the seat Tabitha recently vacated without waiting for my answer. He sticks out his leg and rocks himself, smiling, clearly lost in a memory. Then he turns to look at me again. This is when I remember I'm still in my pajamas, I have bedhead, and haven't even brushed my teeth. Perfect.

"She did do it, you know," he says.

"Who did what?" I ask.

"Lorelei. She got me stoned." Rafe makes a face like a guilty teenager.

"Oh. Wow." I raise my eyebrows.

"I was sixteen, and it was my first time smoking pot. I was what you'd call a 'goody-goody,' and Lorelei was only thirteen. For whatever reason, her agent and mine introduced our moms to each other at the Kids' Choice Awards, and we ended up hanging out together at an afterparty. I think Lorelei was trying to impress me, and she gave me a joint. I smoked it the next day, before going to synagogue with my parents."

"Uh-oh," I say.

"Big uh-oh," Rafe nods. "Because my dad was a cantor. You know what that is?"

"No." I shake my head, no clue.

"A cantor is like a special singer who sings the prayers and songs in the temple. My sister was living in LA, and she had arranged for my dad and me to sing in her synagogue that night."

"Oh no ..."

"Oh yes." Rafe runs a hand through his hair. "I was too stoned to perform. I forgot the words and started laughing."

"Your dad must have been so mad," I say.

"Actually, no," he smiles wryly. "He was pretty cool. My mom was pissed, though."

"Yikes," I say. "Is that why she hates Lorelei?"

"No," he laughs. "This story gets worse."

"Really?" I can't imagine the next part, but I'm all ears. "She forgave Lorelei for getting you stoned?"

"Shh ... she still doesn't know that it was Lorelei who got me the joint." Rafe shakes his head. "But she did know Lorelei got drunk on kosher wine at my family's Passover Seder the next night. She puked all over my sister's brand-new, white carpet."

"Wait, what's a Passover Seder?" I ask.

"Oh, sorry," Rafe apologizes. "I should have said. A seder is like a special dinner Jewish families have on Passover, when they retell the story of Exodus. It's customary to drink four glasses of wine, but I think Lorelei put away a bit more than that. Poor girl. She was a skinny, little thing. I can only imagine the hangover."

"Wow," I say. "Celebrity kids ... they're just like us."

I can still recall the first time I drank too much. I'd been fifteen, and Georgia and I had gotten into Uncle Stavros's ouzo. Her mom and my uncles decided our epic hangover was probably the best punishment, but we'd both been grounded for three months. Rafe is looking at me expectantly, waiting for me to share my story. But I change the subject instead.

"So, you were in a boy band?" I ask.

"Let's never speak of it again." He reaches out to shove my chair and stands up, leaving me swinging.

"Anyway, my mom is getting in late tonight, and all things considered, I was going to suggest a spa day for her tomorrow. How would you feel about the three of us all going together?"

"I thought you said your mom hates me." I dangle a leg to steady myself, but nothing feels steady right now. There is no solid ground here.

"That's an exaggeration. My mom might not have been Lorelei's biggest fan when we were kids, but she's fine with Lorelei now. And she's still good friends with Lorelei's mom."

Interesting. Lorelei doesn't speak to her own mom, but Rafe's mom does?

"Look, we'll probably all be in our own treatments, so it's not like you have to interact with her. But I thought we might drive over together. I can handle checking us all in, and you won't have to worry as much about anyone figuring out that you're not Lorelei."

"Wait a minute. Are you just doing this to keep an eye on me?" I ask, suddenly suspicious of all this solicitousness.

"Maybe." Rafe gives my chair another shove before turning to go. "And maybe not. Maybe I just want to get to know you, Ken-NA," he says. Again with the low, intimate tones. Again with the way he says my name. Again with the way my whole body melts when that happens. Caramel core.

We pause the conversation when we hear the blip-blip sound of Tabitha's remote unlocking her car. A minute later, we hear tires spinning out on the gravel.

"Oh, thank goodness she's gone," Rafe says. He leans forward, surprising me with a kiss on my cheek. Feather light, smoking hot, and spicy as hell, if you describe hell as a look-but-don't-touch kind of environment. It leaves me dizzy with the impossibility of even wanting more.

"Don't forget to ask around for a trainer for Princess," he calls over his shoulder as he jogs back toward the main house.

lorelei

· · ·

"ORDER UP!"

The cook passes a bagged order through the galley window.

"It's for Georgia," he says. "She should be here in about twenty minutes."

"Okay," I answer. I feel like this name should mean something to me. But I'm too tired to remember it. I'm operating on two hours of sleep, nearing the end of my shift, and there's just so many people in this dang town. Who can keep track of them all?

Not one person has sussed out the switch. Sure, they might privately be thinking that Kenna's having an off day. She's quieter than usual. Her coffee isn't quite as on point. But so far, nobody is out there wondering if she's been body-snatched. I'm going to call that a win.

I shift my weight from side to side to minimize the throbbing. My neck is stiff from staring down at the register and the coffee machine controls. The skin on my hands is all dried out from washing and sanitizing them so many times, and I've had the song "Harvest Moon" stuck in my head ever since the diner's playlist looped for the third time. But the point is, I've gone the whole day working here without anyone calling me Lorelei, Moxie, or Ember.

The diner is quiet, so I open YouTube, seeking my favorite guilty pleasure channel—Max Mercury's *Dice of Destiny*. Not even Rafe knows I'm a Max Mercury subscriber. Five years running now. I almost never miss a session with Dungeon Master Max.

Nobody knows who the DM with the sonorous, compelling voice really is. I listen to the show while I'm working out and every night when I go to bed. Most nights, it's Max's voice telling me bedtime stories while I'm drifting off to sleep. Max is so adept at seizing the reins of my imagination, painting vivid images that I swear I can feel with my entire body.

His storytelling skills are pretty good, too. But then again, Max's voice is so damn hot, he could probably get me off reading an End User License Agreement in my ear.

Another thing about Max—he never takes off his dragon masque. Never shows his face. It's part of his mystery.

And that's just so fucking hot.

I don't believe the rumors that he's disfigured or that he's not even really one person. I believe he's a real guy who's actually out there. And one of these days, I'm going to find a way to meet him, and then I'm going to ...

The little bell on the diner's door clatters against the frame as a short, dark-haired woman walks in. She's wearing a long, baggy raincoat over a pair of overalls, but I can see she has some really interesting ink snaking out onto her collarbone and wrist.

"I'm back!" she announces.

"Welcome back!" I wave. I have no idea who she is, but I'll play along.

Halfway into the diner, she freezes and tilts her head sideways. She looks me up, and then looks me down, and her face suddenly goes blank, suspiciously blank.

"Hey, Georgia, what are you doing back already?" Carlos comes in the door behind her, carrying a small bunch of flowers. "I thought you and Hudson were camping up in the hills for another week?"

"Glamping," Georgia replies. "Hudson caught a cold, and we decided to come home. I'm here to grab some soup."

"There are some nasty bugs out there. Let me put these flowers in water, and I'll ring you right up. My wife is a sucker for tulips."

"No rush, Carlos, you take your time. I wanted to have a word with Kenna here." Georgia is talking to Carlos, but her eyes do not leave my face, and I have to give her credit ... my expressionless, resting bitch face hardly holds a candle to hers. Some people are just born looking fierce.

"What's up, Geo—" I try to act carefree and unaffected, but she cuts me off.

"Outside." And then she spins on her heel, lithe and catlike. "After you ..."

"Where are we going?" I ask once we're outside.

"You know, our secret place behind the building where we like to talk?" Georgia leads me into an alley. And like an idiot, I follow her.

Georgia stops abruptly just after we pass a dumpster, where the alley narrows. "Who the hell are you, and what have you done with my best friend, Kenna?" she demands to know.

"I don't know what you're talking about. It's me, Georgia!" I try to defend myself.

"Tell me what color dress you wore when you went to prom with Bryce Holm?" she asks like an unfazed, Cold War-era interrogator.

"Yellow?" I guess a quirky color, based on what I know of Kenna's personality.

Next thing I know, the rough brick of the alley wall is smooshed against my cheek. I'm pinned to the wall with my arm twisted behind me.

"Wrong. Kenna would rather have gouged out her own eyeball with a spoon than go to prom with Bryce Holm," she says icily in my ear.

Does this little bird seriously think she can take me? I've got six inches and at least twenty pounds on her, and I do a lot of my own stunts!

I take a cleansing breath while recalling that cool, evasive maneuver the stunt coach taught me in the stage-fighting class. Do I shift my weight to the front foot or the back? Lean into the twist? I manage to spin free.

Georgia steps out of my way, her raincoat billowing open. This is when I notice she has a small baby bump. Great. I'm going to have to fight a pregnant chick.

"This is silly! I really don't want to fight you, Georgia," I say. "Think of the baby!"

She snorts. "I'm not worried about the baby. The baby is probably going to sleep through the whole thing. Because the only person who's going to be crying three seconds from now is you."

Three, two, one ... ouch!

I have no freaking clue how she did it. For a second, I thought she was giving up, stepping away from me. But then she did something with one hand, spun around, stuck out a foot, and bam! I was down. Flat on my back on the pavement, flopping like a fish.

Before I can catch my breath, she puts her foot on my right hand. Not enough weight to break it, just enough to keep me there. It feels like all the available air is hovering just above me, slightly out of my reach. Like I'd need a straw to suck it in from all the way down here.

I cough and splutter.

"Kenna's a lefty, by the way. She'd never wave hello with her right hand," Georgia says, still glaring. I can't help but notice she's got kittens and puppies and sparkly pawprints on her talonlike nails. "So let me ask you again: who the hell are you, and what have you done with my best friend?"

"OMG. You're the secret handshake," I manage to choke out.

"What are you talking about?"

I am an idiot. I hadn't paid attention when Kenna was talking about her *best friend, Georgia,* because Georgia wasn't going to be a factor in our ruse. Georgia was out of town. Camping off the grid with her boyfriend. I just kind of tuned it out.

"Never mind," I say.

This is the girl who made the friendship bracelet? Her foot is still pressing down on my hand, and I'm starting to get the feeling that I will suffer permanent damage if I don't start explaining.

"Look, Kenna is fine. She's at my place, pretending to be me. We traded places for the week."

"Bullshit. She didn't tell me anything about this," Georgia says.

"That's because you were supposed to be out of town, off the grid, all week, right?"

"Keep talking." Georgia nods calmly at me. God, I love her. But I also hate her. I kind of want to be her. She is so cool.

"Shit, can I please sit up?" I ask. "I promise I won't fight back. We can call Kenna and clear this whole thing up. Her number's in my phone. It's in the apron pocket."

"Hand me the phone with your other hand," she says, foot still firmly planted on my right hand.

"Here you go." I pass her the phone.

"Code?" she asks.

I say, "1234."

"Really?" She looks disdainfully down at me.

"I used to change it all the time, but I kept forgetting and it was just easier," I babble.

She shakes her head and opens my settings. "You should be more careful ... Lorelei." Then she scrolls down to my photos, does a quick sweep through my roll, looks down at me again, and comments cooly, "Shut the fuck up. You're Poxy fucking Moxie. You really do look a lot like Kenna."

"Yep, that's me. Can I please get up now?" I beg.

Georgia nods and steps back, still staring at me warily.

I push myself to my feet, brush off my hands, and hold one out. "Lorelei Dupont. And may I say, what a pleasure to meet you, Georgia. That was some serious, badass shit. I think you may be my new girl crush. *'Though she be but little, she is fierce.*'" Hermia's line from *Midsummer Night* pops into my head.

But Georgia ignores my outstretched hand and scrolls through my contacts till she gets to Kenna's number and hits the call button.

"Hey, Lorelei. Everything okay at the diner?" Kenna sounds a little too worried. *Why wouldn't things be okay? Everything has been great. Barring this Georgia incident.*

"Hey, Kenna, how's it going?" Georgia asks in a falsely cheerful tone, like a telemarketer.

"Oh my God, Georgia! What happened? Are you back? Are you okay? What's going on?" Kenna's words tumble out in a rapid-fire heap.

"I am back. I am fine. Hudson caught a cold. What the fuck is going on here? I didn't realize it was *Freaky Friday.*"

"More like *The Parent Trap.* We didn't swap brains," I point out. Georgia fixes me with her deadpan stare.

"So I take it you and Lorelei have met. Where are you guys right now?" Kenna asks.

I answer, "In the alley, where she mugged me."

Georgia asks, "So does anyone want to explain what's going on?"

"Well, Kenna and I—" I start to speak.

"Not you." Georgia cuts me off.

Kenna groans. "Ugggh ... I know this is going to sound weird, but we discovered how much we look alike, and we both thought it might be fun to trade places for a few days."

"Fun? Trade places? That is not a real life thing, Kenna. That is something people only do in movies," Georgia says.

"Movies are kinda my thing," I volunteer.

Georgia looks both surprised and annoyed. "Why didn't you call me? Why didn't you even tell me about this."

"You were unreachable," Kenna pouts. "There's been a lot of stuff I need to talk to you about, but you've been kinda busy."

"Getting a body double seems like a bit of a dramatic overreaction to me leaving town for a few days," Georgia says. "Anyway, gig's up. Time to switch back."

I object. "The hell we are. I'm just getting the hang of this barista gig."

"Really?" Georgia raises her eyebrows at me. "On my way in, I heard two people talking about how shitty their coffee was this morning."

"It's just for a few more days, Georgia," Kenna says. "I'm having fun. I'm going to the Arbors Day Spa tomorrow."

"Oh, wow. Good for you. But how much longer were you two planning to keep this up?" Georgia's brow is furrowed.

"Just through the weekend. We're planning to swap back on Monday," I say.

"You don't honestly think you can pull off pretending to be Kenna till then, do you?" Georgia looks unconvinced.

"Maybe, with your help?" Kenna says. "Please, Georgia? I haven't had a vacation in years. I really need this."

Georgia's entire demeanor softens when she hears Kenna's request. She's suddenly a shelled egg. "I don't know how either one of you thought you could pull this swap off without my help," Georgia says.

"So you'll help?" I grin and bat my eyelashes at this marvelous human.

"I'm still not sure I understand why this is happening, and it's probably the stupidest thing I've ever volunteered for. And mind you, I met my fiancé while impersonating a dog online. But if it's something Kenna wants, then I'm here to help. Kenna, I'll call you when I get back to the loft. Give me a bit. I have to get Hudson settled with his soup. Men are such babies when they get sick," Georgia says. She turns to me next. "Stop by my shop tomorrow, and we'll talk some more."

"Deal!" I hold out my hand, and this time, she takes it, shaking it firmly.

kenna

. . .

I POUR myself a big bowl of Fruity Pebbles for breakfast. Eating them makes me nostalgic for my early childhood. My mom used to sprinkle them into pancakes when I was little. She'd call them fairy cakes. I'd been convinced she got the recipe from a real fairy—or at the very least, my fairy godmother—but it was actually Uncle Nick's concoction. Fairy pancakes are still on the menu at the Ephron Diner and remain a town favorite.

Where are people going to get their fairy pancakes if the diner closes? I understand why the uncles want to sell, but a part of me is hurt that they didn't consult me first. Or even ask me if I wanted to try and take it over.

There's a soft knock on my door.

"It's just me," Rafe says. "And I brought you some coffee." He's standing at the door with two travel mugs—one with a donut, and the other with a big, old salmon on it. I will never understand why anyone would want to put a fish on a coffee mug. Who wants to imagine eating fish when they're drinking coffee? Of course, it's not Rafe's mug.

I invite him to join me at the counter, and he sets the donut mug down in front of me.

"Thanks." I reach out for the cup. "That was thoughtful of you." I take a tentative sip, bracing myself for the coffee to be bitter and overly strong. It's still caffeine, and I don't want to be ungrateful. But instead of an assault on my senses, this coffee is good. So good. Smooth, and not bitter in the least. There's a slight hint of sweetness ... and some spice. Cinnamon? No. Cardamom. Maybe both.

"Wow," I say. "You made this? Where did you get the beans?"

"They're from a small roaster in Jerusalem," Rafe says. "My mom imports them for her restaurant in Toronto. She brings me some every time she visits. I'm addicted."

"So good." I close my eyes and inhale the aroma, forgetting all about the salmon. I wonder if I could get my hands on these beans for the diner ...

"I put in some cream, but I didn't know about sugar," Rafe says.

"It's perfect," I say. "You could put me out of a job with this stuff."

"I don't know about that"—Rafe grins bashfully—"but my mother is a chef, and my father was a night owl. Learning how to make good coffee was a prioritized skill in our family." He fiddles with a pen that's sitting on the counter.

"Your dad *was* a night owl?" I ask.

"He passed away a little over ten years ago," Rafe says. "Sudden heart attack."

"I'm so sorry," I say. And then I just blurt out, "I lost my mom when I was a teenager, too."

Awkward. And here I was, ten seconds ago, just drinking coffee and shooting the breeze at my breakfast bar with Rafe Barzilay, like that was a normal turn of events in my life.

"I'm so sorry, Kenna." Rafe looks at me with so much unfiltered kindness that I can feel the tears springing to my eyes. How many times have I dated guys whose eyes glazed over if and when I mention losing my mom. It's the "check please" moment of a hundred failed first dates. "That must have been awful for you," he says.

"Well, it was tough, but I was lucky I had my uncles. They really stepped up." I notice the time on the microwave clock. "Oh, wow. We should really get going! It's about twenty minutes to get to the Arbors," I say, looking around for the car keys. "Is your mom ready to go?"

"She's not coming." Rafe strides to the sink and takes the lid off his empty coffee cup. He gives the cup a quick rinse and sets it on my dish rack. "She said she's too tired. Jet lag. She wants to sleep in and spend the day with my daughter, Orly."

Thank God I no longer have to deal with the mom who hates "me."

"You don't have to come with me," I say. "I'm sure you have better things to do. Maybe spend some time with your family?" But even as I say this, I feel the wiry tendrils of panic vining in. I don't want to go to the spa alone. As much as I hate to admit it, it would be nice to have some backup. If Rafe does the talking, it will be much easier to impersonate Lorelei.

"My neck's actually been pretty stiff." Rafe rolls his shoulders, then rotates his neck slowly, eyes half-closed. I can't take my eyes off his Adam's apple. His skin is so smooth, and he smells almost … buttery? Like a croissant on a picnic blanket in a field of—

He is staring at me, staring at him.

"Kenna," he interrupts my reverie, "I'd ask if you minded my coming, but the fact of the matter is, I'm coming whether you want me to or not."

"You are? Why?" I ask.

"Because I want to come." He smiles dazzlingly at me. It's not fair. It's blinding. That smile is a lethal weapon. But I've seen it before, in the movies. This isn't a genuine smile, a smile for me.

"You know what, Rafe? It isn't necessary." I scrabble around in the bag I've packed for the day, looking for the huge sunglasses that Lorelei suggested I wear and pop them on. They are big and round and perfect for hiding behind. "I'll be fine. I don't need a babysitter."

I do need a babysitter. A super-hot, six-foot-three bronzed god of a superhero babysitter. But I don't want to admit it.

"I disagree." Rafe shakes his head. "I think it's entirely necessary. There's no way you're passing for Lorelei. I need to make sure you don't crash and burn. I don't want the press descending." His charming smile is gone now, replaced with a look of grim determination. "Either we both go, or nobody goes."

I weigh my options, playing out different scenarios while looking around for the car keys.

"I have the car keys," Rafe says, somehow sensing what I was looking for. He reaches in his pocket and produces a shiny fob emblazoned with the Porsche logo. "We keep them all at the main house in case the staff needs to move them."

"Thanks!" I reach for the keys. "I've never driven a Porsche before. Should be fun!"

Rafe pivots, holding the keys out of my reach. "Both of us, or neither of us," he repeats, staring me down.

"Fine," I say, holding out my hand for the key. "But I'm driving."

Thirty-five minutes later, Rafe backs the Porsche into a spot in the small lot behind the Arbors Day Spa.

"I can't believe you don't know how to drive a manual!" he laughs. "What is it with all you American women? I can teach you if you want."

We were supposed to be here fifteen minutes ago, but Rafe drives slowly. Like, really slow. Grandpa slow. It's sort of funny given the number of high-speed chases his superhero character has been involved in.

"Will you teach me how to use *all* the gears?" I ask.

"Of course," he smirks. "Why wouldn't I?"

"Because you barely made it past third the entire way here," I point out.

"I was driving the speed limit." Rafe looks wounded.

"You and nobody else! A tractor passed us."

"That's only because I slowed down to give him the right of way," he says.

"Rafe, nobody gives tractors the right of way."

"It's farm country," Rafe argues. "Farmers should definitely have the right of way."

"Sure, whatever." Still chuckling, I step out of the Porsche and swing the door shut. It doesn't slam but closes slowly and firmly with a luxurious ka-chunk. I can still smell the leather and new-car smell of it clinging to my hair as I'm walking in.

"You should keep arguing with me. By the way, don't let me win," Rafe leans to whisper in my ear.

"What? Why?" I rub at my neck, trying to erase the telltale goose bumps arising from his nearness.

"Because Lorelei would never let me win. She'd keep giving me shit all the way in."

"Okay ... Grandpa!" I do my best sarcastic Lorelei impression.

"Perfect," he mouths and winks at me before sliding on his own dark aviators. They aren't doing anything to conceal his identity. If anything, they're just highlighting his hot mysteriousness.

"Sorry we're a few minutes late." Rafe lowers his glasses to look at the desk clerk, and there's that blinding smile again.

The poor thing isn't prepared for the full-charm assault. She turns beet red.

"Welcome to the Arbors. Hello, my name is Heather. And it is not a problem, Mr. Bar ... I mean, *Mr. Adams*," she says.

"Call me Doug." Rafe dials the dimmer down on his smile from supernova to mere sunny day.

"And this is my wife, Morticia."

"Riiiiight." The desk clerk tries not to giggle. "Can I offer you some fruit-infused water before I escort you back to the changing area?"

"Thank you," I say as I accept the proffered drink. "Thank you very much."

Rafe raises his eyebrows at me, but Heather just keeps talking.

"We've reserved the Chardonnay Suite for your exclusive use. There are private changing areas and your own sauna, steam room, and oak-barrel hot tub. I hope you are both ready for a day of sybaritic delight?"

"So ready, Heather." Rafe leans forward. Heather blushes again.

"Just to review the schedule for today, Ms. Du ... I mean, *Morticia*, we have you booked with our estheticians for a facial, microblading, waxing, mani-pedi, and deep conditioner treatment—our Full Day of Beauty Package! We're going to start with the mani-pedi and the facial right away, followed by a massage and detoxifying salt scrub. We'll leave you to relax for a bit, and then rinse you off in the Swiss showers. And, *Doug*, I have you down for a sound bath and our signature sports massage?"

"Sounds dreamy," Rafe grins.

"After that, we'll serve the two of you a light lunch out on the patio of your suite." Heather checks the computer. "No food allergies? Oh, and should I arrange for a wine tasting in the oak barrel hot tub?"

"Is all this written down anywhere?" I ask. I feel like I felt on the first day of high school at Ephron High—lost. Like I'm bound to show up in the wrong classroom at the wrong time, and forget where my locker is when it's time to change out of my gym gear.

"Well, no," Heather frowns. "But don't worry. Our staff will be on hand to escort you and answer any questions. Shall I show you to the suite now?"

"Thanks, Heather," Rafe nods. "It all sounds so delightful, right *Morticia*, darling?"

"Right *Doug*," I say.

As I turn to follow Heather, Rafe walks behind me, massaging my neck and shoulders. "Try to relax," he whispers in my ear. "You're here already, so you may as well enjoy it." *And I do. So much that I wish he wouldn't stop.*

"So this is the Chardonnay Suite." Heather gives us a quick tour of what is essentially a mini-apartment, complete with a living room, two changing areas with bathrooms, and the aforementioned sauna and steam room. Out past the patio, I spy a hot tub framed to resemble a wine barrel. It occupies pride of place on a covered deck that is shaded by grape-laden vines. I don't even have to venture outside to see that it has a great view of the vineyard.

"There are robes for you in the closet. Make yourselves completely comfortable. You are our most special guests. You won't have to worry about encountering any of our other guests during your stay today." With this last bit of information, Heather slips obsequiously out of the room, leaving me alone again with Rafe ... aka Doug.

"Doug?" I splutter. "Doug and Morticia Adams? Shouldn't you at least have been Gomez?"

"What can I say? I'm a fan of the *Hitchhiker's Guide to the Galaxy*," Rafe says with a playful smile.

"And Morticia?"

"Come on, you've met Lorelei." Rafe chuckles.

"Yeah, but she's more Wednesday than Morticia," I argue.

"Fine, fine. Next time, we'll make the reservations for Doug and Wednesday," he concedes.

"Aren't you afraid of feeding the rumor mill about you and Lorelei?" I ask.

"Not really. If we give them something tame to speculate about, they're less likely to dig around for a juicier story."

"Oh," I say. I hadn't considered that angle.

"Guess we better slip into something a little more comfortable now." Rafe crosses to the closet. The clean scent of fresh lemons and eucalyptus wafts out as he swings the door open and pulls out two snowy-white, waffle-weave bathrobes.

"Here, take the smaller one." He hands the robe to me and turns toward one of the changing areas.

"Rafe, wait!" I stop him. "Are you going to ... um ..." I swallow at the thought of him stripping naked on the other side of the pocket door.

"Take it all off?" he says, eyes flashing at me.

"Um ... yeah?" I say, willing my toes to uncurl.

"Probably," he says. "But you should just do whatever is comfortable for you. If it makes you feel any better, I like to leave my socks on."

———

"You were totally snoring." Rafe does an imitation of me passed out on the chaise lounges, post-massage. We're sitting on the patio, eating our lunch.

"I was not!" I pull my robe tighter and smooth the oversize napkin on my lap, admiring my newly polished nails. I hope the gel polish lasts, though it's hard to imagine myself serving drinks and washing dishes with these glittery, glamorous hands.

"Yes, you were. And talking in your sleep, too." Rafe raises an eyebrow at me.

Oh, shit! I don't usually snore, but I *am* famous for talking in my sleep.

"Lorelei talks in her sleep, too." Rafe dips his fork in the cruet of artisanal honey mustard dressing and spears a strawberry slice with his lettuce. I can see the pleasure crossing his face as he tastes the flavorful combo. "Wow, these strawberries are so tart and sweet! Almost as good as the ones in Finland. Must be local."

"Pretty sure it's all grown on the premises," I say. "Most of the local vineyards serve farm to table. A few of them even make their own cheeses. I'm pretty sure they have goats here." I slice a lump of chèvre and drizzle it with honey before popping it in my mouth. Bliss.

"Try it with a Marcona almond," Rafe says, scooping another slightly larger chunk and spooning more honey. He places a nut on top and holds it out for me. The honey is dripping down the sides of his fingers, and when I hesitate before taking it, he says, "Sorry, I'm making a mess. May I?" He raises the bundle toward my lips, as if he means to feed it to me.

When Titanium Man is offering to hand-feed you mouthwatering snacks, you don't question it. You just go with it. Quick, before you wake up.

Obediently, I part my lips, and Rafe pops it in, catching a drip of honey with one long and slightly sticky finger that lingers on my lower lip for a delicious moment longer than it needs to. Long enough to have me crossing and uncrossing my legs. *I want to lick the honey off his fingers.*

Rafe licks off the honey, then wipes his hands off on his napkin and resumes eating, like nothing happened.

"How do you know about the cheese?" he asks.

"There are local orgs for the restaurateurs. My uncles' diner may be less fancy, but we source our supplies from a lot of the same places. It's kind of cool seeing how they present things here. I've never eaten here or been to the spa."

Or any spa. Not that he needs to know.

Rafe gives me a curious look.

"You know what?" I say, gazing over at the bubbling tub. "I think I'm ready to go in that thing." I push back from the table.

"Okay." Rafe drains his wineglass, stands up, and says, "Let's do it!"

"You don't have to do *everything* I do, *Doug*," I say.

"Oh, but I do, *Morticia*. I can't leave you alone for a minute." His eyes are dancing mischievously.

"What do you think is going to happen? We're the only ones here," I say, rolling my eyes.

"I'd rather not let you out of my sight." Rafe is staring at my robe, which is still tightly closed.

I lean forward, feeling bold. "Rafe, what if I'm not wearing anything under this robe?"

"All the more reason not to let you go in the hot tub alone," he deadpans. "Can I help you with that?" He reaches out and tugs the sash gently between two fingers.

Our eyes lock, and he raises his eyebrows at me, then shrugs semi-apologetically. "Last one in's a rotten Zin." He drops the sash and throws off his own robe.

For a hot second, I hold my breath, hovering between hope and fear about what I'll see when the fabric falls.

Board shorts. Dammit.

He lowers himself into the steaming, oak barrel-style hot tub and groans in delight. "Get in here, Morty," he calls out. "It's practically a religious experience."

"I know nothing about your religion, Doug."

"Come on. I'm closing my eyes. I'm like a blind man. Don't leave me in here alone." He closes his eyes and makes splashing motions, as if he's feeling for me. "Is that you, Morty?"

"Fine," I say, undoing the sash.

"Marco!" he calls out, still splashing and flailing with his eyes closed.

"Polo," I say. I drop the robe on the railing by the tub's deck and slide into the water opposite him.

Rafe opens one eye.

"Are you peeking?" I ask him.

"Busted," he grins. "I had to see if it was safe."

"And?" I ask.

"The jury is still out on that."

From out of nowhere, Heather appears with a tray full of small wineglasses that she holds up and sets on the deck beside us.

"Complimentary wine tasting," she says. "All of these are produced from local grapes and are available in our gift shop. Let me know if you have any questions."

"Thanks, Heather," Rafe says.

We both sit silently till she's gone. I glance at the wineglasses, noting the charms at the base of each glass, identifying the varieties.

"Nice bikini," Rafe says.

"Thanks, it's Lorelei's," I say, grateful that I packed it. Not that it offers much coverage, but it's something.

"Well, you wear it well." Rafe bobs in the water, watching me. This would normally stress me out, but it's impossible to feel stressed with the warm water pulsing all the tension out of my body.

"Is that your way of saying I can pass for Lorelei after all?" I ask him.

Rafe sends a splash of water my way. "Stop. There's nothing lacking about your body," he says. "In fact, I think—"

"Yeah, yeah," I interrupt him. "But this," I say, gesturing to myself, "is not like *your* body."

"Thanks for noticing my sparkling personality." Rafe rolls his eyes.

"I'm sorry," I say. "I could pretend that you aren't drop-dead gorgeous, but we both know you are, so what's the point? You're like freaking *perfect*. It's intimidating."

"I assure you, I am not perfect," Rafe grumbles. He dunks himself under the water and comes to sit next to me.

"Check this out," he says, then sticks out his foot.

"What?" I ask. "It's a foot."

"Look closer," he says, still holding the foot aloft. I run my eyes along his muscled calf, pretending it's my hand, over his ankle, down to his instep and his arch, up to his toes ...

Oh.

"You see?" he says, reading the surprise on my face. "Troll foot. All the men in my family have hairy toes. Lorelei loves to tease me about it, and so do my sisters. I'm getting them waxed later."

He lowers his foot with a splash.

"So, as you can see, I am not perfect." Rafe leans back, positioning himself in front of a jet. He is sitting so close to me now. Our hips are just inches apart.

"Okay fine, you win. You are not perfect. But you're as close as it gets. I know it's part of your job to look good, and that's why you work out so much and all that."

Who the hell cares about toe hair, anyway?

"My acting job isn't why I work out." Rafe dunks himself again. He blows out a stream of bubbles while he is underwater. When he comes up, he grabs one of the glasses of wine from the tray sitting on the deck beside us, and drinks it down in three sips.

"Mmm ... not bad," he says. He picks up another and hands it back toward me.

"Pinot Noir. Thanks. My fave." I sip the wine.

"Want to know why I work out so much?" he asks, picking up a second glass. "It's because I'm afraid I'll drop dead in my forties like my dad did."

"I feel that so much. I'm only twenty-seven, but I pay out of pocket to go and get a mammogram every year," I admit.

"Huh," he says. "You know what you said when you were sleeping?"

I have no idea what I said, and I'm not sure I want to know.

"It's usually just gibberish," I say. "It doesn't mean anything. It's not like in the movies when people confess their deepest, darkest secrets."

"I dunno," Rafe says. "You just said one word. You almost shouted it. You said 'Mom!'"

I want to duck under the water and stay there.

"Oh, come on. Don't be embarrassed. Massages release all kinds of crazy, pent-up emotions," Rafe chides me. "It's only natural to miss our parents ... and to worry that we might be like them. It's actually worse for me now that I'm a dad." He swigs from his second glass and floats in the water beside me. "God, this feels good. Orly wanted to ride on my shoulders all day yesterday, and my back was killing me. I needed that massage."

So he wasn't lying when he said he needed a massage.

"She's lucky to have you," I say.

"It goes both ways," he says. "I didn't expect to be a dad in my early thirties. When Orly's mom asked me to be her daughter's godfather, it didn't even occur to me that something like this might happen. And while I hate how it happened, I can't imagine not having her in my life now."

I can't *not* ask.

"How did it happen?" I flip onto my stomach and place my hands on the bench, stretching my shoulders and back as I float.

"Her mom died in a freak accident when Orly was a little under a year old. Allergic reaction to a medication."

"Were you in love with her?" I stare down into the pool when I ask this question.

"She was a great girl, but no," Rafe says. "Really beautiful soul, inside and out. She emigrated to Israel from Ethiopia as a teenager, and somehow she landed a regular role on the same TV show I was on. We were good friends, sometimes with benefits. And before you ask, no, Orly isn't mine."

"No judgment," I say, flipping onto my back to float. I study the patterns made by the dappled sun coming through the vines.

"I wish she was," he sighs.

"Well, she really is," I say, speaking with authority. "She's your daughter and you're her father. Even though it took something tragic to make that happen, you're still family." I turn to look at him now. His face is impassive.

"I just hope I can live up to the challenge."

"What do you mean?" I finish my Pinot and reach for a dark cab. "You're rich, you're famous, you're successful ..."

"I'm an actor," Rafe says, picking up glass number three. "It's hardly rocket science. Which, by the way, is what my brother-in-law does for a living. My sister, whom he's married to, is a neurosurgeon. And that's just the tip of the iceberg. In my family, I am not the success story. Trust me. You're looking at the black sheep loser of the Barzilay clan."

"Except, I'm not admiring you for your sparkling personality, right?" I splash him.

"Right." Rafe laughs. "So you *were* looking."

"Well of course I was looking, you idiot. I have a pulse."

"Me, too," Rafe says, scooting back toward me, just close enough that I can feel the tension of the water between us moving every time he shifts. Much to my surprise, he reaches out and takes my hand. "For the record, I really liked it when you looked."

When he squeezes my hand, I don't want him to let go. But he does. He stands and kisses me on the forehead before reaching for his towel.

"It's time for my next treatment," he says. "So long troll toes, hello fairy feet."

"Thank goodness." I stand and reach for my own towel. "The next time I see you, you really will be perfect."

———

Rafe knocks on the changing room door. "Meet me in the lobby in five? I'll just go settle the bill."

I have to sit down on the bench. I don't recognize myself.

With my hair blown out, makeup done, and new, fierce brows, I don't look like me. I'm too shiny. Too smooth. It's like every rough edge has been buffed away. Every stray hair plucked and every part perfected. My skin is glowing and my toes are shooting glitter sparks as the polish catches the light.

I drop my robe in the hamper and toss my tote over my shoulder as I head out to reception. I can't help but stand a little taller and walk a little swishier. My hair is swishing. I feel like a million bucks.

Heather glances up from the desk and does a double take. "It's been an honor having you here today," she says. "And I love the blonde hair."

"I'm trying something new," I say, patting it and smiling.

And then I notice Rafe is staring at me. But something is different. All the warmth is gone from his gaze. Did I say something wrong? Was I not supposed to mention the hair? What? I thought we had a moment in the hot tub. I thought …

Stupid, stupid Kenna. You actually thought a celebrity like Rafe Barzilay would be into a Plain Jane like you? The voice in my head isn't mine. It's Cody's. But it makes perfect sense.

"Let's get going?" Rafe takes my bag and heads out the door, walking briskly toward the lot.

Neither of us speak till we're both in the car.

"Did I do something wrong?" I ask.

"No." He starts the car and backs out.

"Then what's wrong?" I ask.

"Nothing's wrong."

"Is it how I look? Because I mentioned the hair?" I ask, racking my brain for a reason why he's suddenly giving me the cold shoulder.

"No, your hair looks great"—he reaches out and touches it— "and it feels great, too," Rafe smiles wryly and indicates before exiting the lot. He waits to let several cars pass before turning onto the road. "You also smell great," he says.

Then what the fuck?

"Thanks for telling me about Orly earlier," I say.

"About that …" Rafe tenses up again. I can see it in the way he's gripping the steering wheel and the set of his jaw. He keeps his eyes on the road as he speaks.

"I'm really protective of my daughter, as you've probably already noticed. There was this incident last fall. A bunch of us were in Cabo, including a woman I'd just started dating."

He glances sideways at me for a second, and I nod for him to go on. The sun is setting, and it's nearing the twilight hour where everything goes from orange to purple in an instant. Hot to cold. Rafe turns on his headlights before continuing.

"The woman, my date, was practically treating Orly like an accessory. Picking her up when the paparazzi were around and then dumping her when they weren't. It was really hard on Orly. She was confused. She started pulling her hair out ..." Rafe looks upset as he stares at the oncoming road.

"Who knows if it was related, but ever since then, I've had a strict policy about introducing new people to Orly. I really try to limit her interactions to close friends and family. She's had enough loss in her life."

"I get it," I say.

Rafe shifts gears. "Anyway, you'll meet Orly when we go back to the house. My mom insisted on making us all dinner. But it's probably best if you say you have a headache or something and beg out. Obviously, Orly knows Lorelei, but you're not really her. I'm honoring my promise to Lorelei to help you out with your scheme, but I really don't want things to get messy."

"Of course," I say, hearing all the echoes of self-doubt and voices of reason at once. *Real people don't trade places with celebrities, Kenna ... Poxy Moxie Wannabe ... You wouldn't have to be out till September.*

What am I doing here? I should be job hunting and looking for a new place to live. This has been fun, a dream, but Rafe is right. I should probably switch back with Lorelei sooner than we said. There's no way I can keep this up for a whole week. Things might get messy.

"Thanks for understanding," Rafe nods.

And then we drive the rest of the way home in silence. Slowly.

lorelei

. . .

ON MY SECOND day in the diner, everything is so much easier. Word has gotten out about the half-price mocha macchiatos, and people are into it. It's such a great deal that everyone and their sister starts ordering them.

Noah Greenberg comes in again at about 8:30, with his laptop. I find myself admiring his dimples and the endearing way he wedges the walking stick in the door before shimmying in sideways. He has nice, thick hair and such an adorable ass. It's too bad he's just getting over an injury. Two weeks of booty camp, and that cute, little butt of his would be next-level delicious. Like the gorgeous, round buns I put in the front part of the bakery case this morning.

Noah collapses his trekking pole and hangs it from a hook under the counter that presumably was put there for purses, but whatever ... it works. He opens the laptop and cleans the screen, then twists side to side on the stool, stretching and flexing. Then he interlaces his fingers and cracks his knuckles. Finally, he dives into his work. It's the same as yesterday.

His little morning ritual is captivating. I wait till the line dies down to approach him.

"What are you working on?" I ask him, topping off his coffee. The cup is still full, but I'm curious.

He blinks a few times, as if hearing my voice from a great distance, and holds up the pointer finger of his left hand while he finishes typing with the right. Finally, he notices me standing there with the coffeepot. I smile.

"Thanks, Kenna." He smiles and takes a sip of the coffee. "Sorry, I was deep in it. Did you say something?"

"Yeah." I lean closer, trying to see his screen. "I was asking what you were working on."

He angles the screen down toward himself, trying to hide it.

"It's not ... porn, is it?" I gaze sideways at him and flutter my eyelashes in mock horror.

I'm expecting him to blush brighter than a Jersey tomato, but he seems entirely unfazed by my ribbing.

"That would be difficult." He pushes the screen upright again and studies me for a moment, like he's making a decision. "I'm not even online. See?" He rotates the screen toward me to show me. I lean in to look. It's obviously a word document. A play? There's some sort of character names and dialogue.

"Let me guess," I say. "You're working on your screenplay. The next great blockbuster ..." I hadn't pegged him as the type, but it wouldn't shock me. Thank goodness he doesn't know who I really am. He'd probably want me to read the thing. Pass it along to my "people."

"No, nothing that ambitious." Noah shakes his head. "Do you know anything about *Dungeons and Dragons*? It's a *DND* Campaign Module for an adventure based on *A Midsummer*

Night's Dream. I've always loved the play so much. Big fan of the bard. I'm sad I can't be more involved with the production here this summer, but maybe next year." He fiddles with the Velcro on his leg brace. "Although, maybe I should stay away from the theater altogether, considering what happened."

"Right." I pop the coffeepot back on the stand and come around the counter to sit next to him. *I just gotta hear this story. And then I want to read the campaign module. OMG.*

"Tell me the story again about your leg?"

"Oh, come on, Kenna, don't play dumb. I know the whole town was talking about what a pathetic klutz I am."

"Not true. Nobody told me a thing."

"Chelsea didn't tell you?" Noah looks doubtful.

"Chelsea's not much of a gossip," I say. This much I'm pretty confident about. Chelsea is Dean Riley's girlfriend, and I've met her a few times at the theater. She's an arty type. A little aloof, and kind. But not the sort to idly spill the tea.

"There's not much to tell," Noah says. "I was helping Chelsea drag out all the props in the high school theater. To be honest, I was kind of trying to impress her. But that was silly, of course. She only has eyes for Dean Riley."

"They go way back," I nod knowingly. This much I know. Dean's talked about Chelsea a lot. Like he kind of won't shut up about his childhood sweetheart and how ridiculously small-town-romance happy they are. It's like the *Hallmark* channel. *Gag.*

"Anyway, I was carrying this really heavy set and not watching where I was going, and next thing I knew, I fell off the stage. Broke a leg. In the theater. Go me!" Noah raises his hand in a halfhearted cheer. "Really put a lid on all my summer plans."

"Right," I nod sympathetically. "Tell me a little more about the campaign module you're working on? Who's it for? Is it just your students, or do you have, like, people you meet up with regularly or something?"

I'm feeling a little excited. My heart is racing, like I've had too much coffee. But of course, I haven't had any. I avoid the stuff because it gives me palpitations and makes me sweat. Apparently, Noah also has that effect on me.

Noah studies me for a moment. "I didn't know you were into *DND*, Kenna. How am I just hearing about it now?"

"Oh, you know," I say, fanning myself with a menu. "I dabble. I watch stuff on YouTube."

"Really." Noah smiles conspiratorially, and his voice drops an octave. "Which channels are you into, Kenna. You can tell me."

There is something about Noah's voice when he says "you can tell me" that sends a heatwave through me. Now I'm blushing, and I can't make it stop.

"I dunno," I lie. "Just stuff. Nothing specific." I busy myself with a rag, wiping down the already clean counter.

"Well, I am hoping to use this campaign module in my classroom next year. But we'll see. I'm really focusing on introducing world-building to my students. They're all into the whole fae thing right now. In my version, Titania is super badass. Like you wouldn't want to mess with her."

"Do tell." He has my attention now. I've been rallying to make my version of Titania a little more Ember and empowered.

"Who do you picture playing your version of Titania, then?" I ask.

"I hadn't thought about it," he says smiling, "but you know, that's a really good question. I guess subconsciously, I might have been thinking about Lorelei Dupont's Ember character in the Titanium Man films, knowing that she's playing the role of Shakespeare's Titania this summer. I do wonder what she's going to do with the role."

Yasssss!

"I thought you were worried she couldn't act." I smirk.

"Oh, she can act," Noah says. "I just don't know if she can act on the stage."

"Can I read your campaign module?" I ask. "I'm into emerging genres, and a lot of my fans are gamers."

Oops. Shitsticks.

"Your fans?" Noah raises an eyebrow.

Jesus. Did I just break character? What the hell is the matter with me?

"Ugh, did I say fans?" I giggle nervously. "I meant friends. Friends. Man friends. Like a lot of the dudes I've dated have been big gamers."

Nice save.

"Your friends are big gamers? Which ones?" He looks doubtful.

"You know, like guys. Guys I've dated." This seems like it might track. Kenna mentioned that she tends to pick losers. And not to typecast, but losers are prone to spending a lot of time getting stoned and playing video games.

Immediately, I see the flaw in this. Those kinds of guys are not into these kinds of games. Too lazy to come up with their own narratives. They just gotta blow up the things other people dream up for them.

"I mean, I'm not really writing this for the first person shooter crowd." Noah smirks. "It's still Shakespeare. I've met some of the guys you've dated ..."

Poor Kenna. She really can't catch a break. All the more reason I should encourage this friendship with Noah. She needs more good guys in her life.

"Come on, Noah. Give me a chance? I'm into fairies, and I don't see anyone else in here beating a path to your barstool."

"You really want to read my stuff?" He's starting to look intrigued.

"I would love to roll the dice," I say, smiling my sweetest Kenna smile.

"Okay then." Noah's face takes on a new seriousness, and he looks at me with a different level of respect. "I'll print something out and bring it back. And hey, Kenna? Wanna grab dinner sometime? Even if you change your mind about reading the campaign module, I'd love to take you to dinner. You've been so kind to me during my recovery."

"Of course. I'd love that." I twist side to side on the seat, releasing the nervous energy that's building up in me. This whole swap is going so well! Who knows, it could be life-changing for Kenna.

"Great chat, Noah," I pop up. "I can't wait to read what you've written."

"I can't wait to hear what you think," he beams. "And think about where you want to go for dinner?"

"Will do!" I excuse myself back to the kitchen. Best to exit on a high note.

"You did NOT say Kenna would read Noah's *DND* crap!" Georgia is looking at me with a look of sheer horror. I wonder if she would mind if I snapped a photo? I'd love to preserve the expression.

"I did!" I fling myself sideways into the frumpy, old armchair in the back corner of her shop, causing her to do a double take.

"What?" I ask, kicking off my shoes and rubbing my feet.

"It's just … just then, you really reminded me of Kenna. She's always sitting sideways in that chair, too. Always has."

"Well, obviously"—I scooch back a little, making myself comfortable—"it's the correct way to sit in a chair like this."

"That's what she would say, too." Georgia narrows her eyes at me. "Are you two related or something?"

"Who knows?" I shrug breezily. No point in speculating. The DNA tests will come back soon enough.

I hear my momager's voice in my head. *Do you really want to open that can of worms, Lorelei?"*

"You gotta back off on Noah Greenberg." Georgia rearranges a rack of leashes, trying different combinations of colors and materials. "Tell him you changed your mind."

"I will not!" I argue. "I think he's perfect for Kenna!"

And I have to admit to myself, I'm more than a little curious about his campaign module myself.

"Oh, man. Kenna is seriously gonna kill you," Georgia snort laughs.

"Why? What's the big deal? How could she have a problem with Noah? He's so nice."

"Oh, she doesn't have a problem with Noah," Georgia says.

"So what's the issue?" I stand up and pad over to the leash rack, taking the leashes out of her hands. "Let me do it."

"Really? Thanks." She hands me the leashes and goes to sit in the chair I've vacated. Facing forward. Weirdo. "Ahh," she sighs, propping her feet up on a box. "Pregnancy really is exhausting. They weren't lying. I'm either dying to inhale a pizza or dying to take a nap. If only I could do both at once. But of course, then I'd have to get up because I'd have to pee. Again."

I consider the rack and separate out the leather leashes from the paracord ones, grouping them by type.

"That sounds really horrible." I try to be sympathetic, but honestly, this is another reason why I never want to have kids. She chose this for herself?

"It's not all that bad. My fiancé has been awesome. And my brother keeps buying us super weird baby gifts."

"Back to Kenna ..." I set aside a few leashes from each group, and then I start braiding.

"What are you doing?" Georgia sits up and peers suspiciously at my handiwork.

"Sit back, mama," I say. "I know what I'm doing. Organizing shit is my jam."

"Shit jam doesn't sound very appetizing," Georgia says, wrinkling her nose.

"You know what I mean. Now, spill about what the issue is with Kenna reading Noah's thing."

Georgia sighs and leans back again.

"Okay, so she's a little touchy about this, but there's no getting around it now. The problem is that she's dyslexic. Kenna *hates* doing anything that requires a lot of reading."

"Oh, shit." I groan. "I had no idea."

"How could you have known?"

"Why didn't she tell me?" I shove the loosely braided leather leashes back on the rack, arranging the three loose ones in front. Then I get to work on the paracord ones.

"That looks pretty good," Georgia says. "I wouldn't have thought of braiding them."

"This way, they won't get tangled," I explain. It's a trick I use when I hang my wigs and extensions. "Just keep the braids loose so nothing gets kinked."

"Got it," Georgia says. "So, Kenna probably didn't mention it because she's so sensitive about it. It's one of the reasons she never went to college. She's so afraid of being judged and having people call her stupid. But honestly, she's one of the smartest people I know. About people and other stuff, too. She's an incredible photographer. She's always just had this amazing eye."

"A lot of dyslexic people are really visual," I say. I happen to know a lot about it—not because I am dyslexic, but because my character Moxie was. "It's what made Moxie McAllister such a great detective. Visual recall." I bite my lip.

"Oh my God, I totally forgot about that," Georgia says. "No offense, but I wasn't really much of a fan."

"None taken." I grin and step back to admire my handiwork. "I didn't watch it, either. Still can't."

The phone rings, and Georgia drags herself up to retrieve it from the counter.

"Hey, we were just talking about you," she says. Then she pauses. "Yes, she's here. Hang on. Let me lock the door and put you on speaker."

Georgia places the phone on the counter and then goes to lock the door, placing a "Back in fifteen minutes" sign in the window.

"Go ahead and talk. It's safe now," she says.

"Hi, Kenna!" I say. "How was the spa? Did Rafe and his mom end up going?"

"I'll get to that," Kenna replies, "but first—Georgia, can you ask Xander if he can rec a dog trainer for Rafe Barzilay's dog? He needs to be discreet."

"That is not the first word that comes to mind when I think of my brother." Georgia inspects her nails.

"Is this for Rafe's dog?" I ask. "Good call. That mutt needs to learn some manners. She's a humper."

"Yeah," Kenna answers. "Rafe is worried about her tendency to bolt, and frankly, so am I. Xander is familiar with her. He groomed her when the shelter brought her in."

Georgia looks shocked. "Wait, Rafe Barzilay adopted a dog from the Ephron Shelter and I'm just hearing about it now? How is it possible that Angie hasn't shouted this from the rooftops?"

"You were *off the grid*," Kenna says, accusatorially.

Georgia shakes her head in disbelief. "That'll teach me to go anywhere."

"Speaking of going anywhere," Kenna says, "Lorelei, you failed to mention your car is manual."

"What's the problem with that?" I ask.

"I don't know how to drive a stick shift!" Kenna sounds exasperated.

"No problem," I say. "I'll have another car sent over. I'll just tell them I didn't like this one and request an automatic. Want me to get you a Maserati?"

"You can do that?" Georgia looks impressed.

"Anything is possible," I say, smiling. I feel my phone buzzing in my pocket and dig to see who's calling. Rafe. I decline the call and search my phone for the car rental company.

Kenna sighs. "I don't know, Lorelei. Honestly, I'm feeling a little overwhelmed. It's clear that Rafe doesn't really want me around his mom and his kid. Don't bother with the car. I think it would be better if we could switch back sooner. Rafe was right in saying this could get messy."

Dammit, Rafe. I'm going to throttle him. Later.

At just this moment, I spy Noah hobbling briskly by the pet boutique, presumably on his way back to the diner. I wave but he doesn't see me. He is so intent on getting back. To me. And is that what I think it is? It is!

It's a printout of his whole adventure!

"Let's table this for a bit?" I say. "Something important just came up. I'll text you later tonight."

"But Lorelei!"

"Later, I promise!" I shove my feet back into my shoes, crushing down the heels and not even bothering to do the laces. Turning the lock, I let myself out and scuffle-dash down the street, trying to catch up.

"Hey Noah! Hang on a minute!"

kenna

. . .

UNCLE NICK'S text wakes me from a deep sleep.

Sorry to bug you, sweetie.

I check my phone. It's 7 a.m. Normally, I'd be up by now, but the blackout curtains, Duxiana mattress, and bazillion thread count sheets, not to mention the ambient mister thingy, are all very sleep inducing. At least I know where I am this time when I wake.

Heads up. The realtor wants to stop by the diner tomorrow with a potential buyer.
They're interested in the house, too.

Ok. What time?

I wipe the sleep from my eyes.

In the afternoon, but you really don't have to be there, Kenna.

I'd like for someone to be at the house, if it's ok with you. It just feels weird. We haven't prepped it.

Ok, sweetie, if you're not doing anything special. It's just an informal visit. We haven't finalized our listing yet.

If I'm not doing anything special. I can't believe that Uncle Nick has forgotten that tomorrow is gotcha day. We usually have cake and go through my album. But I'm not a little girl anymore. I reread the message. They haven't finalized anything yet. A part of me wishes this means they might still change their minds. But the next text dashes any hope.

Good news, though! The house is worth more than we suspected! Ephron just got named as a top 10 destination in WA State. Lots of interest in established biz like ours.

That's great, Uncle Nick.

Take a day off, won't you? Carlos says
you've been in the diner every day.

I like to stay busy.

Well, he's on strict orders to send you home
if you try to work today.

I wonder what Lorelei will do to amuse herself. I still haven't
heard back from her about switching back early.

How's it going in Mykonos?

Uncle Stavros made a new friend.

Nick texts a photo of Uncle Stavros asleep in a lounge chair.
His straw Panama hat is tipped down over his face. There's a
big, fat ginger cat splayed out in the shade under the seat. The
whole scene looks so perfectly sunny and Mediterranean. I
"like" the picture, sending back hearts.

When was the last time I left Washington State? I really need a
vacation. But where would I go? And with whom? Traveling
alone would be better than third-wheeling it. But it's not what

I dream of. I'd really love to share the experience of travel with someone else.

My stomach is growling. I'm officially awake. I pull on some dark, denim shorts and a loose, flowy, Indian print top and pad into the kitchen in search of coffee. And then I remember. There is none. Nothing potable anyway. I don't even have any milk for my cereal.

Oh, well, Rafe had to come over to the main house to stock up and use the kitchen any time. He hadn't forbid me from coming over. He just didn't want me *hanging out* around his mom and his kid.

Just to be on the safe side, I shoot Rafe a text to warn him that I am coming over. Once again, it strikes me. I have Rafe Barzilay's number. In *my phone*. Is that ever going to feel normal?

I wonder what will happen to my contact info in his phone after we swap back. Will he block me? Or maybe he'll just delete my info and forget he ever knew me, until one day when I accidentally butt-dial him, and he's all, "Who the hell is this? How did you get my number?"

Shit. I'm going to have to delete his number the minute we switch back, which I really hope is sooner rather than later. I can't live with that kind of fear. I've got to speak to Lorelei already. Just as soon as I have some coffee in me.

• • •

I slip on a pair of platform flip-flops, still admiring my sparkly toes, and grab the Fruity Pebbles from the cabinet. *Be grateful for small mercies.* Lorelei and I share the same taste in cereal.

My feet sink into the pea gravel, crunch-crunching across the long driveway in front of the main house. There's a farm delivery van parked out front, and the man getting into it looks like the old man from the street the other day. Same overalls. He sticks an arm out the window and waves as he pulls away.

I pause to grab the wire crate full of old-fashioned glass milk jugs and the basket of farm-fresh eggs from the front porch. Maybe I'll make myself an omelet? There's got to be at least two dozen eggs here. Tucking the cereal box under my arm, I skip back down the front steps and take the path around to the back. Rafe told me to head into the house directly through the kitchen, so I let myself into the sunroom/kitchen through the oversize sliding glass doors.

The kitchen is spectacular. Everything new and state of the art. There's a twelve-foot-long, quartz-topped island with seating for seven. Restaurant quality appliances and a glass-fronted fridge. But the most stunning feature is the colorful, Moroccan-tile backsplash. It's a spicy punch of color in an otherwise neutral space, which I am sure keeps it feeling warm and sunny even in the depths of a Washington winter.

There are no signs of gray weather today. The sun is shining brightly, and the view out the wall of glass is all bright verdant green and bursting blooms. I note the peony bushes and wonder if anyone would mind if I cut a few. But then again, why bother? I really need to switch back with Lorelei ASAP.

Carefully, I set the jugs of milk and eggs on the counter and think about enlisting Rafe's help. Surely, he'd agree with me. He never thought this was a good idea to begin with.

"Who are you?" a little voice says, startling me.

I spin around toward the adjacent sunroom. There's a large, green sectional sofa in here and some upholstered chairs, gathered around an oversize, round coffee table. The coffee table is strewn with Barbie dolls and action figures. The voice is coming from a large wingback chair that's got its back to me.

Ruh-roh!

Slowly, I approach.

"Hi, Orly," I say, tentatively. "It's me, Lorelei ..."

As I come around the side of the chair, I see her, and she nearly takes my breath away. She's so tiny and perfect. And beautiful. But not at all what I expected. Although honestly, I don't know what I expected. I've seen a couple of blurry shots of Orly in the tabloids that customers leave at the diner, but they didn't do her justice.

· · ·

She's wrapped up in a blankie surrounded by pillows. Her hair is half naughty and half nice, like a schoolyard of ruffians squared up against the good girls. There are a few curls clustered in perfect, delicious coils, but the rest is a fuzzy, tawny halo. Her eyes are large and hazel, speckled with brown and green, and her skin is so perfectly smooth and tanned, it puts the organic eggs to shame. She lowers her head and squints at me.

"Lie? Why's your hair lello?"

One of the pillows wriggles, and I hear a soft "yip" as Princess pops her head out from under the blankie and rushes at me.

"Pincess! No!" Orly chastises, holding up a tiny finger with a pink, sparkly fingernail.

She glares at me. "I was bushing her!"

I'm not sure I follow what she is saying till a second later when a wooden hairbrush clatters to the floor.

"Oh good," I say. "She really needs someone to brush her."

"Yes." The child nods gravely at me. "Her hair's all messy. I fix it!"

. . .

Given the state of the toddler's hair, it's impossible not to smile at the image.

"I hungy!" she announces, suddenly throwing off her blankets and jumping to grab my hand. "You make me breakfast?"

"Well, I ..." I stand there, frozen, not sure what to say. I reach in my pocket and pat my phone, ready to pull it out and text Rafe again. But before I can get it out, I hear footsteps, and a very hungover girl with an Australian accent pokes her head in the room.

"Oh, thank God," she says, holding her head with one hand. "I'm so sorry. You're Lorelei, right?"

"Yes," I answer, "and you are?"

"I'm Rainey, the 'nanny.'" She makes air quotes with her fingers. "Actually, I'm not normally a nanny. I'm doing my post doc on child psych. Rafe told me his mom was going to be spending the day with Orly today, so I didn't set an alarm or anything. She wasn't in her room when I checked her bed after the back door motion sensor alarm went off on my phone. Ow." She leans forward, steadying herself against the counter.

"Rainey! I hungy!" Orly stomps over to the nanny.

. . .

"Can I make you a cup of coffee or something?" I offer.

"Actually, I think I'm just going to grab a bottle of electrolyte water and head back to bed, if you don't mind. I was out till closing time at this place called The Onion."

"Ah …" I smile knowingly. "Was there a good band there last night?"

"No." She slugs the water. "They were terrible. As were the cocktails. But I had too much of all of it. And a really great time." She smiles sheepishly.

"Hungy?" Orly pouts. It's impossible to be annoyed. She's so stinkin cute. The dog barks again, as if to say, "You better feed her!" Rainey looks stricken.

"Ugh. I think Rafe is out for his run. And his mom is still asleep. Shit." She slaps a hand over her mouth. "I mean … ship!"

"I can make her breakfast," I offer sympathetically. "Is she allergic to anything?"

"No. No allergies," Rainey says. She squats down and takes Orly's hands in hers. "Orly, darling? Lorelei here is going to make you breakfast, okay?"

. . .

"That's not Lie Lie!" says Orly.

Rainey looks confused and squints up at me.

"It's my hair," I shrug. "She's not used to seeing me without the wig."

"Right," says Rainey, clearly satisfied with this explanation. "And thanks."

"Come back later, and I'll make you some coffee," I call after her.

"Me coffee, too?" asks the child.

"Sure." I smile, hoping there's some chocolate in the house, or at the very least, some sugar, vanilla, and cinnamon I can stir into some warm, frothed milk.

"And Pincess?"

"I'll get her something to drink, too," I promise. "Now, why don't you introduce me to your Barbies while I make some fairy pancakes?"

· · ·

Orly holds up a Tiana doll. "I'm going to meet all the pincesses at Disneyland," she says.

"You're a lucky girl," I answer. "I've never been."

lorelei

. . .

"NOPE. You aren't working today. Go home." Carlos pushes me out the door. "Nick and Stavros texted to tell me to tell you that you're supposed to take some 'you time' today." He pauses and wrinkles up his face as he considers the message he's just passed along. "Whatever that means. Do you know what that means? Can you explain the difference between 'me time' and 'you time?'"

"'Me time' is about me, and 'you time' is about you," I say. *Obviously.*

"But if I use my 'me time' to think about you, then is my 'me time' really 'you time?'" Carlos strokes his chin as he steps away from the diner.

"Cut it out, Carlos," I say. "I'm onto you."

"What?" He feigns innocence.

"You're trying to lead me away."

"Okay, but it's only because your uncles told me to. Come back later, and I'll make you a Cuban sandwich for lunch."

"Thanks, Carlos. We really gotta talk to the uncles about getting them on the menu." His sandwiches are epic. If matzoh ball soup and gyros can be on the menu, why can't a perfect Cubano?

"What are you talking about?" He looks scandalized. "They are on the secret VIP menu. That's the whole point. I gotta like you to make one for you."

With this, Carlos winks and disappears back into the diner.

I check my watch. It's now 8:15 a.m. Celestial Pets is not due to open for another forty-five minutes, but it's clear that someone's in there. The bells on the door jingle as I let myself in.

"Hey, oops! Sorry! We're not actually open yet!" a male voice calls out.

A man with hot-pink hair, wearing a tie-dyed hoodie and some sick trainers is kneeling in the corner, packing some dog treats, costumes, and other items into a box.

"Hey Xander!" I say. This has got to be Georgia's brother. I've heard so much and checked out his grooming videos on TikTok. He seems almost as cool as his sister. Huge personality. I really can't wait to meet him.

"Kenna! What's—" He freezes midsentence, eyes wide. He barks and leaps to his feet, making a crazy, dramatic face that's straight out of a Fellini film. "You're not Kenna. Freeze. Stay where you are." He leaps to his feet and swings a leash slowly over his head like a lasso. I am stunned speechless. *What the hell is up with Georgia's family?*

The leash is making whirring noises that any sound engineer would swoon over. But not me. Is he shitting me? Is Groomer Van Man actually going to come after me?

Just as abruptly as he jumped up, he stops swirling the leash, drops it to the floor, and bends over, laughing.

"Oh, shit. Your face. I am so sorry. Give me a minute." He pats his eyes with his hoodie. "I don't know where that came from. That was some seriously misguided superhero improv bs. I just can't believe I'm standing here with the Ember Enchantress!" he squeals, and then he seems to remember he wasn't supposed to say that out loud, bites his lips, and looks around guiltily.

"Sorry! That just popped out because nobody else is in here with us. I swear your secret is safe with me. Promise. OMG. I can't believe it's really you! Squeeeeeee!"

"So, Georgia told you." I breathe a sigh of relief.

Xander nods and picks up the leash to put it away. "Yeah, G suspected I might figure it out when you didn't know how to work Kenna's camera to take photos of the dogs. But damn, you are pretty convincing. You might have fooled me. Except, Kenna's a lefty."

"Who notices these things?" I sigh and flop into the comfy chair.

"Other lefties?" Xander mentions. "Kenna likes to borrow my left-handed shears to trim her bangs."

"Kenna trims her bangs with *dog shears*?" The look of horror on my face must show because Xander suddenly looks defensive.

"I'll have you know my shears cost fifteen hundred dollars, and I sterilize them after every customer," he huffs. "I might not play a superhero like you, but I have higher standards than most barbers."

"Okay," I shrug. "Whatever. I'm sorry. For what it's worth, I can totally see you as a colorful superhero sidekick. Ember could use someone like you to give her regular trims and tips."

"Honestly?" Xander clutches his chest. "That's the nicest thing anyone's ever said to me." He holds out his arms and says, "Bring it in," and for some reason, I feel compelled to give him a hug. Resistance seems futile.

"So, uh ..." Xander releases me from his bearhug and looks at his phone. "I don't mean to be rude, but I wasn't joking about the shop not being open yet. I was just picking up a few things for the grooming van. Georgia probably won't be here for at least another half hour, and I gotta run."

"That's okay, I can wait for her," I shrug. "I've got stuff to read." I reach into my bag and pull out the campaign module.

"What's that you're reading?" Xander asks. "A new script? Is the franchise coming back?"

I tuck Noah's manuscript under my arm. "Sorry, top secret," I say. "I am not at liberty to share."

"I knew it!" Xander crows victoriously. Then he sighs. "As much as I'd like to, I can't just leave you here alone with the keys. I have to get going. I told my partner, Mac, I would pick up some coffee for him before I head out for the day. I'm gonna have to ask you to leave."

"Seriously?" I sit up straight and give him the Ember eye. "I just got comfortable, and I really want to talk to Georgia." I'm hoping she can think of some fun "regular folk" things for me to do today. Plus, I thought I might help her stage the pet costumes better.

"Seriously." He puts a hand over his face.

"What if ... I recommend you to Rafe Barzilay as his dog trainer?" I ask.

Xander freezes. "Rafe Barzilay has a dog?"

"Yes," I nod, "and it's very poorly behaved."

"But I'm not really a trainer. I'm a groomer." I can see how much admitting this pains him.

"But you've trained dogs?" I ask.

"Technically? Yes. I ran a dog-walking service in high school and did a lot of training with the dogs." He nods, a little breathless.

"Trust me," I smile imploringly. "I've already got the keys to the diner and Kenna's place. If anything goes wrong, you know where to find me, and I'm insured out the wazoo."

He still looks a trifle dubious. I hold up my phone.

"And I'll call Rafe right now to make the rec."

"Well, then, I suppose I could wait with you till Georgia gets in."

kenna

. . .

"YOUR FAIRY PANCAKES and unicorn coffee are served," I announce, bringing the silver tray to the

coffee table.

I kind of hate interrupting Orly's drama-in-progress. The plot involves a headless Barbie, a Batman figurine, and a stuffed dog and what appears to be some seriously high stakes.

"Yayyyy!"

She looks up from her toys, sees the food, and sweeps them out of the way. The Barbie head bounces when it hits the floor.

"I'm telling Abba you let me have coffee." Orly smiles wickedly, reaching first for the mug.

"Special unicorn coffee," I say, grinning. It's just warm chocolate milk with a little whipped cream and crushed, fruity pebble dust.

Then she sees the pancakes, and her eyes light up. She picks up a pretend cell phone and proceeds to take a photo. "Cama eats first!" she says.

I laugh. "Who taught you that?"

"Savta taught her that!" A tall, graceful, middle-aged woman saunters into the room. "Right, Orly?"

I can only assume that Savta means grandma in Hebrew, given the striking resemblance between this beautiful woman and Rafe.

"Good morning, Lorelei. Do my eyes deceive me, or did you make breakfast for my granddaughter?" She seems shocked as she looks warily from me to the tray and back to me.

"I did," I nod, feeling nervous. There's something about this woman that is so intimidating. She just oozes charisma, self-assurance, and having-your-shit-togetherness. I can picture her employees standing at attention, shouting, "Yes, chef!" in response to her every request. Her linen dress doesn't have a single wrinkle. Her hair is perfectly cut, and the streaks of gray are dramatically gorgeous. They don't look like the kind of gray you get when you run out of time to get to the salon. They look curated and intentional, like war ribbon warrior grays.

She lowers herself to sit beside her grandchild, dropping with the grace and flexibility of a yogi. Her eyes crinkle with warmth as she looks at Orly. And then un-crinkle as she stares cooly back up at me.

"So tell us, chef, what have you prepared for Orly today?"

Fudgesicles. She's an actual chef, and she's just toying with me now, like a cat with a mouse it doesn't intend to bother eating. It's just having fun batting it around and torturing it. I take a deep breath. This isn't personal. It's not me she has the issues with. And surely, Lorelei isn't afraid of her. Lorelei doesn't seem to be afraid of anyone.

"Fairy pancakes," I say, turning back to the kitchen to clean up after myself. "And unicorn coffee."

"You made coffee for a three-year-old?" She takes the mug from Orly's hands.

"Magical unicorn coffee with special imported *cacao* beans," I say, attempting to wink at her while Orly is not looking.

Rafe's mother merely blinks back at me. Unimpressed. She lifts the mug and sniffs the contents before handing it back to the child.

"Interesting," she says.

"Speaking of coffee, I was about to make some. Can I make you a cup?" I scrutinize her, before guessing. She'd take her coffee straight up. Black. Maybe a touch of raw honey. No milk. But I don't want to presume.

I open a cabinet and pull out the French press, coffee grinder, and beans. I'm gasping for a decent cup of coffee myself at this point. I sniff the beans, closing my eyes. When I open them, Rafe's mom is staring at me.

"I didn't think you drank coffee, Lorelei?"

"Well," I vamp, "lately I've been drinking it more. And these beans just smell so great."

"They do, don't they? My friends roast them in a little shop just outside the Machane Yehuda Market in Jerusalem. They are very special. I'd love a cup of French press if you are already brewing some. Make it strong?" Then she takes the utensils from Orly. "Let me cut them up for you."

"Oooooooo! Rainbows!" Orly wiggles with delight at the colorful centers of her pancakes.

"Interesting. So colorful."

I realize I don't know Rafe's mother's name or whether Lorelei even calls her by her first name. Perhaps I can excuse myself to go to the bathroom to text Lorelei to ask?

But first, I busy myself with grinding the beans and making the coffee. I'm glad the press is oversize, big enough for two or even three cups.

Rafe lets himself in through the sliding glass door. *Good Lord, he is glistening.* He's all sweaty, and he's stripped off his shirt and his running shoes, which he's carrying in one hand. His tank is draped over one arm, and he uses it to mop his face, which is somehow radiating a golden, bronzed glow. I, on the other hand, would be glowing like a boiled beet root if I'd gone for a run before my morning coffee.

"Abba!" Orly jumps to her feet and flings herself at Rafe. Abba must mean papa, I realize, filing away another new word.

"Ugh, Bean, I'm all sweaty," Rafe laughs, holding her away. "Let me take a shower before I hug you."

"Ewww gwooss!" Orly freezes in her tracks.

"What is that deliciousness I smell?" Rafe asks. "Did Savta make you a special breakfast?"

"No!" Orly points at me. "Lie Lie did! She made me fairy pancakes and corn coffee!"

"Lie Lie?" Rafe looks surprised, and wary.

I shrug and shake my head, holding up my hands, a sign of my innocence.

"Is that why the kitchen is so messy?" Rafe asks, shooting me a warning look. What is he even talking about? I've already washed most of the dishes. Messy? What mess?

Messy. Then I recall it's the same word he used yesterday when talking about me possibly meeting and interacting with his daughter. He doesn't want things to get *messy.* But is it my fault that she was playing alone in here when I arrived? And that she was hungry? Wasn't I just doing what any decent human being would do under those circumstances?

Rafe's phone rings, and he picks it up on his watch, speaking via his EarPods.

"Rafe here."

He glances at the small dog that has begun to chase him as he paces, nipping at his heels. The dog is ostensibly the reason why he doesn't want to open the door to go back outside. He paces by the glass doors like a caged lion as he speaks.

I pour his mom some coffee and hand it to her, along with some organic honey I found in the pantry.

"You might like it with a little honey," I say.

"Good call." She takes the coffee, sniffs it, and nods appreciatively. "And thanks. This smells wonderful."

We both look over at Rafe, who has stopped pacing now.

"Great. Oh, thank God. When can he come over? Today?"

He pauses and bends to stroke Princess. I can see some of the tension melting off him.

"Great. We'll be here all day. Tell him thank you. And also, no video or photos. I'll need him to sign the standard NDA."

Rafe hangs up the phone.

"Who was that?" his mom asks.

"It was a volunteer from the shelter," he says, looking pointedly at me. "Girl by the name of Kenna. Said she found a trainer who could work with Princess. His name is Xander. He's going to come over later today."

Oh, shit. What has my evil twin done now?

"That's great," says his mom. "Why don't you go take a shower and get dressed. And then you have to try these pancakes Lorelei made." She helps herself to a little piece of pancake from Orly's plate. "They're oddly delicious. Lorelei, you wouldn't mind whipping up some more for us, would you? I'm suddenly famished."

lorelei

. . .

"GOOD LORD, Lorelei, what have you done?" Georgia moans, looking at the row of dressed-up stuffed animals on top of the pet clothing rounder. "This is a pet boutique, not Build-a-Bear."

"Well, I thought it would be cute if people could see how the costumes looked on actual animals," I huff, undressing the stuffed unicorn I put in the pirate costume. Talk about looking a gift horse in the mouth. I was expecting her to be delighted when she got here, and I'd already spiffed up her boring display. I'd had the stuffies shipped priority, early morning delivery.

"Look, Lorelei. I know your heart is in the right place, but I'd prefer not to use random, stuffed animals to represent people's actual pets."

She speaks to me simply, like I'm the slow student in class. Not that I'd know, being homeschooled. But it was how the teacher on *Moxie* spoke to my idiot sidekick. I feel my face flush and take a deep breath to control it. I'm an actress. I don't wear my feelings on my face.

But the deep breath doesn't help. In fact, I feel the sting of tears threatening. This is the second time in two days I've lost it like this. I probably need more sleep.

"Hey now, I do really, really love what you did with the leashes," Georgia says as she pats me on the shoulder. "And you're right. It would be better if people could see some of the outfits on a more generic animal. Maybe there's a mannequin or two I could order. That's a really good idea."

"It's fine," I say. "I'll just donate these to a shelter or something." *Except I'm totally keeping the walrus. I already named him Wally.*

"What do you have planned for today?" Georgia asks.

"I was hoping you'd help me out with that," I admit. "I've got the day off. I have no idea what Kenna would normally do."

"Kenna never takes days off. She can't stand sitting still."

"Does she belong to a gym?" I ask hopefully. Maybe I can get in a good workout and sauna.

"Ha!" Georgia snorts. "That's a good one. I didn't mean that kind of not sitting still. I mean, she's always doing stuff. Volunteering at the shelter, taking pet portraits, working at a food bank, taking food over to the senior center ..."

"She sounds like a saint. Does she ever do anything else?"

"She hangs out here a lot." Georgia casts a glance back at the chair that's still shoved in the corner.

"What else?" I ask.

"She likes listening to funny podcasts. *Lit Lovers* is one of her faves."

I sigh. I don't have to do everything Kenna would do, do I? "Is there a bookstore around here?" I ask.

"Yeah, I think there's one in the mall a couple of exits away." Georgia finishes wrestling the octopus she's stripping and hands him to me. "Just curious. What made you think cat clothes would look good on an octopus exactly?"

"It's whimsical!" I say. "And octopi are very intelligent creatures." I decide right then and there that I'm keeping Olly, too. Olly and Wally. They'll make great travel pillows.

"So what happened last night? Have you gotten back to Kenna yet?"

"I'll get back to her before I go to the bookstore. She needs to chill."

A short, older lady bursts into the shop. She is wearing a hot-pink sweatshirt with pawprints all over it. She's holding the ugliest one-eyed dog I've ever seen. Its one eye does the Mona Lisa thing. It seems to be following you, no matter where you or the dog are located in the shop.

"Georgia! Did you hear? Xander is headed to Rafe Barzilay's house to work with Princess! Can you believe our humble Princess has been adopted by such Hollywood royalty? Who knew?"

"I knew," I sigh, stuffing Wally and Olly in my bag. The one-eyed dog growls at them.

Georgia wide-eyes me, and I realize that I probably should be a little more careful talking to this woman. Who is she again? Angie? Pet shelter employee? It's only been a couple of days, but I've met so many new people.

"How did you find out, Kenna dear?"

"Kenna is doing the cast photos for *A Midsummer Night's Dream* and stopped by Rafe Barzilay's rental to scout some locations there." Georgia fills Angie in quickly.

"Right," I continue, "and I saw the mutt, I mean, Princess, while I was there."

"Oh my!" Angie beams. "Did she look happy? Does she have enough treats? I could run a care package by there—"

"She seemed just fine," I say. "Except for the bad behavior thing."

"Well, I'm sure Xander will have good advice," Angie says. "Life here in Ephron sure has gotten exciting lately!"

"You betcha!" I say, unconsciously reciting another one of my signature lines from *Moxie*. Why is it that whenever I try to do Kenna, it comes out like a half-baked version of my childhood role?

"You know what I just noticed?" Angie whistles. "You look just like that actress Lorelei Dupont. But not the grown-up version. What was that kid detective show she was in?"

"*Moxie McAllister*," Georgia says.

"That's it! You look just like Moxie, dear! All grown up, but same freckles."

———

The Barnes and Noble in the strip mall two towns over isn't the indie bookshop of my dreams, but it's still a little slice of heaven. All the necessary ingredients are here. Aisles and aisles of brand-new books just waiting to be read. I want to crack open all the spines. Breathing in the smell of so many new books makes me feel a little high. Like I'm huffing story. Inhaling info. Ink and paper, with undertones of coffee and pastries wafting in from the café. Hunchbacked and Gollum-like, I haul my bounty to a café table, a mere twenty-two titles split into three stacks.

But the best part of this whole experience is that I'm not wearing a costume of any sort.

Normally, I'd be sitting here in my wig, itching and twitching, afraid of being recognized as myself and equally afraid of being unmasked as a wig-wearing fraud. Not today.

Today, I am sitting at a table ... alone. Gloriously alone, in public. My hair—my real hair—is piled on top of my head in a messy bun. I've got on a pair of cargo shorts and a ridiculous, faded T-shirt from some kind of rural gas station rest area in Maryland that reads, "Guns, Ammo, Snow Cones" that I found among Kenna's many tees.

I park myself and my books at a table in the café and page through the novels, setting aside the ones I want to read first. Next, I tackle the books on *DND* I've selected. Mapmaking, characters, history, and lore. And there's a collection of Anime-style comics, including several retellings of Shakespeare Classics.

"Hey Kenna, you want to introduce me to your friends?" I look up from my notes, spying the familiar trekking stick. For the first time, I notice the sticker wrapped around the sturdy pole.

"Dungeon Masters do it better."

Noah is wearing jeans and a flannel and holding his own armload of books. He's smiling down at the tote bag on the chair at my table. Wally and Olly are peeking out over the rim.

"Mind if I sit down?" he asks. Then he looks from my stack of books to his own. We've got several of the same titles in our piles.

"Are you stalking me, Kenna Papadopoulos?" he asks.

Sweet irony.

"You know what they say." I attempt to play it cool. "There are no coincidences. But how do I know you're not the one stalking me?"

"Fair enough," Noah says. "If I'd have known you were going to be here today, I might have made a special trip. What a treat to run into you here, away from work."

His eyes are magnetic. Puppy-dog brown. Chocolatey and rich. Staring into them makes my heart somehow beat slower and harder. Like I'm being melted into them. I force myself to glance away, and then when I look back, all I can see is his swoopy upper lip. I'm dying to touch it and ... *uh-oh.*

Erotic images are tumbling through my mind, unbidden. I pinch my lower lip, hard, to distract myself. It works, for a moment.

"You look nice in that tee." His irresistible lips twist a little as he reads it out loud, "Guns, Ammo, Snow Cones?"

"What else could a girl need?" I look down at my chest. I should have worn a real bra. My dirty thoughts have loaded my guns.

"Someone to share it all with?" Noah says. He's flirting. Like, for-real flirting. And I don't want him to stop. He's also looking at my chest. Which is my bad. I looked first.

"I have someone. Someones, actually," I say in an attempt to defuse the situation.

"Oh really?" Noah raises an eyebrow. "Anyone I know?"

"I mean, you've just met them." I gesture at the stuffies in the bag that I've moved to the floor. "Wally and Olly are great company. But don't worry, they're not the jealous type of marine animals."

"Thank goodness for that. It would be dreadfully unfair if they wanted to keep you all to themselves." Noah smiles slowly, his face opening up like one of those timelapse videos of a flower blooming. First, one corner of his mouth. Then the lower lip, then the other corner, and one eye crinkling. Then his forehead, and suddenly, his whole face is lit up, like a thing of beauty. It feels like a deliberate release. Like we've just shared a secret, and he's showing me his hidden treasure.

What the hell is the matter with Kenna anyway? With this whole town? Thump. Thump. Thump. My heart is beating so slow. So hard. The eye contact goes on for longer than it should. But I cannot look away. I can feel the saliva in my mouth. I can feel the heartbeat throbbing … everywhere.

Noah licks his lips, and I want to taste them. My own tongue snakes out to lick my own. Monkey see, monkey— Noah raises an eyebrow and lays his hand on my arm without breaking contact.

It's warm. Bare skin on skin. Oh, God, how long has it been since I have had sex? Longer than it's been since I've been in a goddamn bookstore. There are only so many smut novels a girl can read before she can't take it anymore.

"Kenna," he says, hungrily. And then I remember who I am. Which is not Kenna.

"Noah." I blink and look away, yanking my arm away as I pretend to distractedly search through my bag for something. A pen? A phone? A notebook? All already on the table. Absent another excuse, I pull out Wally and hug him to my chest, attempting to discharge my tension by stroking his fur. *Ugh. It's no use!*

I'd rather be stroking Noah's fur. Would his chest be furry under that flannel? From the way he's staring at my hand, I think he might be thinking the same thing.

"I was just about to grab some tea." Noah exhales. "Can I get anything for you or your friend?" Noah asks, standing slowly and grabbing the walking stick.

"I'd love a hot cocoa," I say. "I was actually planning to read some more of your module next. I'm pretty much done looking through these." I gesture to the pile.

"In that case," Noah says, "let's get out of here. These chairs are not even a little bit comfy, and I've got some great Dutch cocoa at my place."

"That sounds like a line, Mr. Greenberg," I say.

"Oh, God, do not call me that. You sound like one of my students," he groans.

"Then what am I supposed to call you?"

"How about 'Master' Greenberg?" He leans forward, and his eyes crinkle and twinkle again, but this time, there's a little smolder there. A tiny spark, threatening to catch. All it would take is the slightest breeze. I'm tempted to blow on him. Gently.

"As in Dungeon Master Greenberg?"

"If that's what you're into." Oh, God, his voice just got all low and smoky again.

This is not good. But it's *so* good. I can't stop. It's like I've ripped into a big, old bag of chips.

"So just to be clear, you're attempting to lure me back to your dungeon with promises of hot beverages?"

"Just to be clear, Kenna"—his voice drops an octave and feathers in my ear—"if and when I invite you into my dungeon, it won't be for tea."

"Or cocoa?" I swallow.

Noah nods, smiles slowly again, and straightens up. He taps his walking stick and points at his stack of books.

"Honestly, I was just here to pick up a couple of these map books, but I was planning on working at home on the map for the *Midsummer Night's Dream* campaign module. I sure wouldn't mind the company, if you don't mind me working. My couch is a lot comfier than these chairs, and the cocoa's a lot cheaper."

I glance down at my phone. I still haven't replied to Kenna, and Georgia has texted me again as well, probably reminding me to call her.

Not now, Kenna. I am not switching back with you now!

"Well ... okay," I agree. "I just have to answer a text from my friend." Quickly, I type a message to Kenna.

> Sorry, it's been so busy, but everything is GREAT. Talk later today?

Kenna writes back immediately.

> Xander just got here. Not sure when I'll be free. You have some explaining to do on that.

I breathe a sigh of relief. She's not demanding an immediate switchback. I still have a little time as a free woman.

> No prob. Talk tonight?

> Sure.

"Okay, I'm good to go." I smile at Noah and toss the phone and Wally back into my bag.

"Was that a real friend you just texted or an imaginary one?" Noah looks from my phone to the stuffed animals.

"What do you mean?" I ask.

"I couldn't help but notice you were answering a lot of texts that were coming from someone named Kenna."

"Maybe I'm just leaving a trail, in case you try to lock me in your dungeon."

"Probably smart. It's always the nerdy English teachers," Noah says.

kenna

. . .

I FINALLY GET the chance to learn Rafe's mother's name when I mention I'd like to cut some of the peonies.

"Peonies!" she exclaims. "Oh, we must cut some! Give me a moment, let me grab my shoes!"

Rafe, who has just polished off two generous servings of my fairy pancakes, scoots closer to me at the kitchen counter and pushes back a curl to whisper in my ear.

"I'm sorry I doubted you. You're really doing great. I don't think she suspects anything. You should call my mom Naomi, by the way."

Then he nudges me with his shoulder and squeezes my leg before jumping up to watch a video on the couch with his daughter. It gives me a moment to sit there and recover from the effects of his unexpected affection. Such a little nothing, but it has me buzzing.

"You're doing great." He didn't have to say it. I'm not sure I believe it. But it sure was nice of him to toss me that bone. I keep expecting him to tell me I'm getting it wrong. That I

can't do this. To reprimand me for creating this unnecessary chaos in his life. This *mess*.

I keep expecting him to be Cody. Cody hadn't used the word mess. He'd used the word *complicated*. With Cody, everything was simple, or it was complicated. Black and white. Simple was good. Complicated was not. Simple was my decision that college was not for me. Simple was me hanging with him and his friends while they got stoned and played video games practically every night. Someone had to fetch the snacks.

Complicated was me wanting to take photos of the Milky Way in the desert, when Cody wanted to go dirt biking. Complicated was me wanting more support when I tried new things. And then there was *thirsty*. That was what he called it when I complained about how withholding he was with physical affection. By the time we broke up, I was like a twisted plant that had withstood a drought. Awkward. I didn't know how to get or give hugs anymore.

Five years later, and I'm still working on that. But I've realized how much I like physical affection. And I notice it. I appreciate the ability some people have. People like Xander, who are always saying "Bring it in" and summoning hugs. Xander who is coming here later! How ever did Lorelei engineer that one?

I'd put ten-buck odds on Xander getting Rafe to hug him by the end of this week.

Rafe is not withholding. This surprises me a little. Maybe because he's so famous. I just expected that he'd be more standoffish. But Rafe is a physical person. The sort of person who is always putting a hand on your shoulder or patting you on the back. He doesn't skimp on affection with his daughter, and though I haven't seen him in many social situations, I'm guessing he's not the sort who likes to keep the people in his orbit at arm's length. Including me.

That little knee squeeze may have left me buzzing, but I really can't read too much into it. It doesn't mean anything. It's just how he is.

If Naomi suspects anything is up, she's not saying it. When she gets back, she is wearing a pair of clogs. She hunts for some shears in the kitchen drawers, finally locating a pair in the junk drawer. "Ready?" she asks.

I'm starting to think Lorelei must be crazy. Naomi is intimidating, but she's not exactly a monster. Whatever happened when Rafe and Lorelei were kids is clearly ancient history now. Cautiously, I make small talk while we choose the best blooms to cut off the bushes.

Naomi seems delighted when I ask her about running her restaurants, emigrating to Canada, and what it was like to raise such a large family while building her own business. Not to mention, I add, managing her son's acting career.

"Oh, no. I really didn't have anything to do with Rafe's acting," she says, shaking her head vehemently. "You met Rafe's father, Lorelei. He could never say no to that boy. I wanted Rafe to pursue something more academic, but my husband, may his memory be a blessing, insisted that Rafe follow his heart. He said we have enough surgeons and lawyers in the family and that God had other plans for that one. But that was my Avi. He was a very spiritual man."

"You must miss him so much," I say, recalling the conversations I've had with Rafe. *He was so young.*

"I miss him every single day." Naomi twists the wide, platinum band on her ring finger. "But life is for the living, no? Avi always loved peonies. They didn't grow well in Tel Aviv. Come, let's not take too long getting them into water or they won't open properly."

"Ugh! The ants!" I drop the flower I'm holding and brush four angry ants off my forearm. The one thing that's always made me crazy about peonies. My mom used to tell me that the ants were our friends.

"They tickle the flowers and trick them into opening." My mom would love these peonies.

"Not a problem," Naomi says, grabbing a bucket off a nearby potting bench and filling it with cool water from the spigot on the side of the house. "Just give them a quick swirl."

"And they'll still open?" I ask.

"Of course. Faster if you use a little warm water in the vase," Naomi nods confidently.

When we get back to the house, Rafe and Orly are fast asleep. Orly is sprawled across Rafe's chest. Princess is snuggled happily beside them, belly up, paws in the air.

"I wish I had a photo of this," Naomi whispers to me. "My phone is up in my room. Do you have yours handy?"

Uh-oh. I freeze. I could lie, but the phone is on display in plain sight. Right in the palm of my hand. And I can't say it's dead because I just checked it.

"Are you sure Rafe wouldn't mind?"

Naomi makes a face. "Who cares? I'm his mother."

"I just don't want to, you know, violate his privacy?" I say.

"Give the phone here!" Before I can stop her, she reaches for the phone, snatching it, dancing away, and pulling up the camera. She zooms in and snaps happily away before smiling triumphantly at me. "There. You didn't take any photos. I did. Let me just send them to myself, and you can delete them."

My heart is in my throat. I can't wrestle Rafe's mom to the ground for my phone, but what if the real Lorelei finally texts me back now? Or anyone else, really.

Hurry up, hurry up, hurry up, I chant to myself as she types in her number, doing my best not to show the level of my discomfort. Thankfully, she is fast. With a whoosh, the photos she's sent to herself are off.

She gestures for me to help her bring in the rest of the cut flowers from the patio.

"You're pretty tech savvy for—" I start to say as she hands me the phone.

"For someone my age?" she raises her brows.

"No," I backtrack. Of course, that's what I'd been about to say, but not exactly what I meant. She isn't old. She's younger than my mom would have been.

"For a woman?" She looks even more dubious.

"For a non-native English speaker," I grasp.

She seems satisfied with this. "I have to be. I run my entire business myself, and I have to know how to use all the technology involved, in multiple languages."

"Everyone in your family is very smart," I say. Now I'm just kissing her ass. But I can't help myself. I really want her to like me.

"Well, not everyone," Naomi says, squinting back through the glass at Rafe. "But we can't all be super geniuses, can we?"

Excuse me?

I blink at her, a little confused and unsure how to navigate this sand trap. Am I supposed to ignore the fact that she basically just called her ultra famous, A-lister son the dimmest bulb in her bunch? *What the hell?* Just because he hasn't pursued a highly academic career like her other children? He still speaks multiple languages, and I can't even imagine how many zeros are at the end of his bank balance sheet. His net worth must be staggering, given the success of the films he's done.

But success is relative, apparently. Because Titanium Man's own mother just dissed him. Shame on her. How dare she? My desire to be liked by Naomi is at odds with my urge to defend Rafe.

"I'd say he does okay." I shove my phone back in my pocket and frown at her. "I can't believe you're not bursting with pride!"

"Okay, fine," Naomi says. "I realize he is handsome, and he makes a lot of money. But is he making the world a better place? Did his last movie save anyone's life? End a coup? Fix global warming? He didn't even finish college. Such a shame. I'm just saying."

"You don't expect much, do you?" I fold my arms across my chest. "You know I didn't go to college either, right? And since when does making excellent hummus qualify *you* for a Nobel Prize, Naomi?"

Too late, I realize that I actually have no idea whether Lorelei went to college. I don't think she did? And that comment about the hummus? Where did that even come from? I'm just so annoyed with her. Everything was going so well, and bam! Sometimes I don't know when to keep my mouth shut.

I brace myself for Naomi's wrath. But instead, she laughs. The criticism rolls right off her.

"Touché, darling. I deserved that, didn't I?" She sighs and tilts her face back to bask in the morning sun. "I guess it bothers me that Rafe didn't finish college because I never had the chance. And you know what? It bugs me that *you* didn't go, either. I blame your mother. She failed you there. I've told her as much."

"You have?" I find myself asking. I play back what Lorelei and the recently fired PA have told me about Lorelei's "momager" and cross-correlate this information with the story that Rafe told me on the patio. *Rafe and Lorelei's mothers are still friends.*

Naomi seems surprised that I'm asking. Encouraged. "Your mom has really changed. Mellowed out. I mean, she's still a little meshuggah, but she knows she made some mistakes with you. And she's dying to hear from you. She's not getting any younger, Lorelei."

Oh wow. This must be that famous Jewish mom guilt I've heard tell of.

"Right." I flip my phone over and back in my pocket, uncomfortably, feeling conflicted. What can I say?

On the one hand, I don't know everything that went down between Lorelei and her mom. But on the other, I'd love to have a mom who was dying to talk to me. Better yet, a mom who wasn't dying ... or dead.

"Anyway," Naomi is still speaking, "I'm sure *you* could have gone to any college you wanted to. If you were my daughter, I would have encouraged you to apply to Yale. They have an excellent drama department, and they like former child stars."

If I was *her* daughter? This cool, exotic powerhouse? It isn't even something I can begin to imagine. All I can think about now is how unfair it is that I've lost two mothers in two different countries. And here's Lorelei, rejecting two mother figures. Imperfect ones, perhaps. But certainly better than nothing?

Lorelei—who has all the money and resources to do whatever she wants, wherever she wants, with whomever she wants—and all she seems to want is to push people away. While I'm here clinging to the past, unable to make up my mind about anything, desperately afraid of being left alone. It's too much. Too unfair. I excuse myself abruptly and head back to the guesthouse with what now feels like pilfered peonies.

Back at the guesthouse, I change into a bikini and a cover-up. I have every intention of going for a swim, but instead, I curl up in the hanging egg chair with a podcast, gazing at the three fragrant peonies sitting in a glass milk jug on the end table. I watch them opening in slow motion. Unfurling. Revealing their secrets. Pillowy, pink centers and sticky, yellow-gold-dust-coated stamen. The scent and the motion of the swing lulls me into a stupor. And then I'm asleep. Fast asleep at noon on a summer Thursday. Nowhere to go. Nothing to do.

I wake with a start when a June bug dive-bombs me, landing in my hair and getting tangled. What the ...? Frantically, I shake out my hair, raking my hands through it till I am satisfied it's bug free. Then I check my phone. One o'clock already? I've been out for an hour!

I slip on my slides and head for the pool. *When did Rafe say Xander was coming? Two?* With a little luck, I'm hoping that I'll be able to spy on Xander and the dog-training session from there.

I'm a little surprised to find that I don't have the pool to myself when I get there. Rafe is lying on a lounge chair, eyes half-closed, an open beer sweating on the table next to him, and a bowl of chips and guac on his perfectly taut, firm belly. He seems to be engrossed in some sort of a podcast. I pause for a moment to listen.

"Is that ... *Lit Lovers*?" I ask, incredulous. There's no way that Rafe Barzilay is listening to *Lit Lovers*. No freaking way.

He sits up slightly, placing the chips on the side table.

"Yes!" he says. "You know this podcast?"

"Of course," I say. "It's an Ephron classic. I know the hosts—Jackson and Chelsea, Emily and Alexis."

"Right," he says. "I'm still learning who's who. Jackson and Chelsea are siblings, right?"

"Where is everyone else?" I sit down in the chair next to him and look around for the towels.

"My mom took Orly into town to get their nails done," Rafe reports. "We're on our own. There's snacks and drinks inside if you want." Rafe points in the direction of the cabana. "And I've got sunscreen here if you need it."

He turns his head to look at me and does a double take.

"Whoa! What happened to your hair?" he laughs.

"My hair?" I pat my head, shaking it. "What is it? Is there a bug in my hair?" I jump up and whip off my cover-up, shaking it vigorously just in case. Rafe tilts his head and watches me curiously.

"You okay, Kenna?"

"I'm fine. I just fell asleep on the patio before, and a June bug attacked me." I can't escape the urge to give my hair another shake and rake my hand through it, anxiously. "Are you sure there's not another bug in my hair?"

"No, no." Rafe pushes up on his elbows and lowers his sunglasses. "No bugs. It's just ..." He sits up and gestures for me to come closer. "Come here."

I step closer to his chair.

"Closer," he says, removing his sunglasses.

"Cut it out, Rafe. Just tell me already if there's a bug in my hair."

"Sit down." He takes my hand and pulls me to sit beside him. I can smell the suntan oil and pool water on his skin, and some of the water droplets from his wet hair fall onto my shoulders as he sits up next to me and starts to rub my neck with one hand. With the other, he hands me his mirrored sunglasses.

"Take a look at yourself," he says. "Your hair is wild. Like a lioness."

"Oh!" I say. "Yeah, it does that. It's a curly hair thing. That's why I usually wear it up." I relax slightly for a moment, until I remember who is rubbing my shoulders and neck so expertly. With two hands now.

"I like it." He pauses for a moment and rests his chin on my shoulder. "It's incredibly sexy, Kenna." Then he scoots even closer, positioning himself behind me, swiveling his hips and placing a thigh on either side of me.

"Jesus, you're tense," he mutters. "It's only been a day since the spa. Is this okay? More pressure?"

I'm dreaming, right? This is not actually happening, is it?

"Why are you being so nice to me?" I ask, biting back a moan as he digs into that spot behind my left shoulder blade that is always locking up after a long shift or session with a heavy lens.

"Why wouldn't someone be nice to you?" He sounds puzzled.

"Well, you weren't particularly nice when you tried to slay me with a whisk."

"I thought you were an intruder." Rafe runs his hands up and down my bare arms before repositioning himself and working on the small of my back.

"This is not fair," I say, shaking my head.

"You can do me next," he says. "I don't mind. My calves are like rocks."

"Are they?" I lean forward and reach down to cup a hand behind each of his muscular calves to check. "They feel like normal calves to me," I say, losing my battle against arching my back as his hands work circles out toward my hips. I feel his calves flex beneath my fingers and squeeze, working the muscles rhythmically in time as he's working mine.

Oh, God, this feels good. Too good. I've got to focus. Focus on something else. Anything else. The podcast? What is Jackson saying on the podcast? It's still playing on the little speaker.

"This is the Second Chance episode," I say, "the one where Jackson was teasing Chelsea about having a crush on Dean Riley." And then it dawns on me. "Oh! Dean told you about the podcast?"

"Bingo." Rafe pauses a second, and I love the way he says the word, with just the slightest hint of an accent. "Here, let me put some sunscreen on you. You don't want to burn."

"What is that stuff?" I ask. The slick, fragrant oil is only making the sensation of his hands all over my body more intoxicating.

"It's oil, but it's got a pretty high SPF." He pours a generous amount into his palm. "We don't want to miss any spots." His hands skim my collarbones, and his fingers trace the ridges of my ribs with the lightest, most sensual touch, making me forget for a moment how "bony" and "awkward" I am. I don't care. I don't even care. He twirls a long finger around the tie of my bikini top, stretching the tightly tied bow looser, as if he means to take the top off. *Does he mean to? Should I let him?*

"Lioness." He pushes back my hair and rubs oil on my neck, along my breastbone, and into my cleavage and across the tops of my breasts. Yes. Yes I do want him to take my top off now. I want him to see me naked. The oil Rafe is rubbing on me is magical. It's making me sparkle like him. It's rearranging my DNA. It's—

"It's Xander," I say, spotting movement on the drive.

"What?" Rafe asks.

"Xander. I see his van." I point toward the vehicle on the horizon, slowly making its way toward us.

"Oh, shit!" Rafe stops. "Is it two o'clock already?"

"Almost," I sigh.

"Damn. Okay." Rafe stands, and I settle into his place on the lounge chair, not minding one bit that it's damp from his earlier dip. "Promise you won't go anywhere?" he says.

"Like where? The supermarket?" I laugh. "I think you forget that I don't even have a car that I can drive away from here at the moment."

"I'll take you out later and teach you."

I close my eyes and ask again. "Why are you being so nice to me, Rafe? You hardly know me."

He stands there a moment before answering, and I open my eyes to study him, watching a series of emotions flit across the screen of his totally open face. Concern. Confusion. A silly smile. And is that a blush?

It strikes me how little he looks like Titanium Man to me now. When did I stop seeing the character he plays when I look at him? Sometime yesterday?

"I don't know," Rafe says, simply. "I don't know why I feel like I *know* you. It isn't just because you look like Lorelei. There's something else. Something different. I don't know what it is. But I feel like we need to figure it out. Don't you?"

This is just a dream. Has to be.

"I thought you were afraid of things getting messy?" I murmur.

"Life is messy." Rafe smiles. "Although, to be honest, you have completely bewitched both my mother and my daughter. I feel bad for the real Lorelei. They're convinced you're her, only nicer."

And with that, he bends down to quickly brush his lips against mine, before pulling on a tee, grabbing his phone, and taking off, jogging toward the house. It's like the June bug all over again, only this time, I don't want to shake off the buzz.

As if on cue, Lorelei 1.0 chooses this moment to finally text me back.

> Sorry it's been so busy, but everything is GREAT. Talk later today?

There's so much to tell her, but I'm not sure where to start. With Rafe. I should probably start with Rafe. My stomach tenses up at the thought of this. I know she said there's nothing between them, but it's hard to fathom how that could be true? How can she not want him for herself? And even if she is telling the truth, how would she feel knowing that I want him for myself?

What a ridiculous thought. I can't have Rafe freaking Barzilay. I mean, maybe if I am lucky, I can have him for a night or two. But nothing beyond that.

Still, a night or two sounds better than nothing.

And to think that I was ready to demand we switch back immediately this morning.

> Xander just got here. Not sure when I will be free.

> No prob. Talk tonight?

> Sure.

Whatever Lorelei is up to in my life, I'm sure it will be fine. And if not, I'll just have to deal with it. Next week.

lorelei

. . .

I CRANK the music in Kenna's car on the way to Noah's place. Window down, alternative tunes wailing, wind in my hair, I follow Noah's army-gray Volvo down the freeway. I can't recall the last time I felt this free.

I trail my left hand out the window and let my hand surf on the side of the car, feeling the wind catch between my outstretched fingers. God, it all feels so good. No wig. No costume. No looking in the rearview mirror to check if I'm being followed.

Kenna's beat-up, old hatchback isn't nearly as luxurious as the cars I'm used to driving. There's a tatty, old aux cord I have to plug into my phone to play music on the car radio. But none of that bothers me. There's a sweet simplicity to being able to drive without your car demanding an answer to incoming texts.

. . .

Like the ones I'm pretty sure my mom will be sending tomorrow. *Happy Gotcha Day, Lorelei. Can't believe it's been twenty-seven years. Wish we could speak.*

Or something like that. The song that's playing is a remake of New Order's "Blue Monday," and the singer is pondering how it feels when your heart grows cold. *Good question. Numb?*

I don't hate my momager. I know she thought she was doing the right thing by me. But the issue is, she never asked. She never considered how I felt. My *feelings* weren't a consideration. They were whatever she told me they had to be. That was the deal. I changed my emotions like outfits. For her, for the director of the show, for the fans, and for the few friends I had. When wasn't I "putting on an act?"

Maybe when I hung out with Rafe? He really wasn't like anyone else I knew. He was older, smarter, and more *normal.* Rafe had been shocked by my teenaged efforts to seduce and corrupt him. Which was kind of the point. I'd wanted to shock him. I hadn't expected him to act so protective. Sure, he smoked the joint I scored for him. But he also forbade me from doing it again, with or without him. He'd let thirteen-year-old me get drunk on sweet kosher wine at his parents' Passover Seder, knowing full well I'd be sick as a dog and "learn my lesson." Afterward, he told me that he thought it was better for me to have that experience somewhere that was unlikely to result in anything truly terrible happening. He'd let me dig my own grave, and then he lent me a hand to get up out of it. He was like the big brother I never had.

. . .

I tap my fingers on my knee to the beat of the next song. Another classic oldie Lou Reed would like me to take a walk on the wild side. Doop-de-dooping my way along, I signal to get into the exit lane behind Noah. I feel a similar sense of ease with him as I do with Rafe. With the added fun of flirting. Maybe it's because Noah doesn't want or need anything from me? Maybe it's because I've been telling myself that it's all for Kenna, for her best interest.

But let's be honest. I don't want to jump his bones for Kenna. I want to do that for myself. I feel the same sort of naughty impulse I felt as a teenager when I was trying to get Rafe to misbehave.

I want to tempt Noah and see him crack. I want to push his buttons and drive him crazy. If he was standing next to a pool, I would not be able to resist pushing him in. *But why? And what would happen next?* I exhale and imagine his shocked face, watching his expression turn from shock to a focused desire. I picture him grabbing my hand at the last minute, pulling me in. And I've never wanted to get wet more.

Noah sticks a tanned arm out the window of his Volvo, giving me a thumbs-up and a wave as we come to a stop at the end of the exit ramp. He gestures that he's turning right, and I put on my blinker to follow.

New Order, Joy Division, The Cure, and INXS are the one thing that the momager gave me that stuck. This music is all hers. She grew up going to shows at tiny clubs in LA, working as a waitress while pursuing her dream of acting. It never happened for her. So she'd packed up her dreams and focused on mine. Which, conveniently, she had already chosen for me.

My therapist used to say that I probably had such a hard time accessing my own true feelings because of my early life in the orphanage. Feelings had no place in the orphanage. I learned at an early age that crying, in a room full of crying babies, was not a particularly effective way to get the limited staff to pay attention to me.

"She was just the calmest, most gorgeous toddler." The momager didn't talk about my having been adopted often. But when she did, it was always the same story. "She never cried. She just smiled and batted those long lashes, and who could resist her? Clever girl!"

"You learned that people would let you down," my therapist explained. "Your basic needs weren't met. So you figured out other ways to get what you needed."

In other words, I learned how to act. My momager couldn't have made a better decision when she accepted my dossier from the agency. Two years old. No significant health issues. Docile and never cries.

I don't remember the orphanage. Not really. But there's something. The smell of certain industrial soaps. The feeling of thin, cotton sheets threaded between my fingers.

.   .   .

Noah stops at the corner of a long residential street with massive pines and large lawns. There's about a dozen modest-size houses on the quiet block that are all well-spaced. Nothing at all like the overgrown and pot-bound houses in the Beverly Hills neighborhood where I grew up. I try to guess which one is Noah's and pick a cute, classic-looking home with a white picket fence at the end of the street. There's a perfectly mown lawn and two adorable garden gnomes beside the mailbox.

I'm sure I'm right and already dreaming about the ways I'll mess with the gnomes when he indicates he's turning left into the driveway of the house next door. The one with the rock garden and wood siding. There are two bird feeders hanging from the tree out front and a swing on the porch.

"Park in the driveway," Noah says, leaning his head out the window as he pulls his car into an immaculate garage.

This is when my heart starts pounding hard. I do a quick gut check. I know exactly how I, Lorelei, am feeling right now. *Excited. Anxious. Horny.*

It's always the nerdy English teachers.

———

"This is a much better idea than the cocoa." I hold up my wineglass and toast Noah.

. . .

We're sitting on his front porch. I'm sprawled in the swing, reading his campaign, and Noah is sitting at a nearby table, working on a map. From time to time, he points out the birds that are perched on the feeders, identifying the species.

"Well, I figure if you're telling me what you think about my gamification of a Shakespeare classic, it can't hurt to ply you with alcohol. Perhaps you'll go easier on it that way."

"I love what I've read so far," I say, honestly. No need to act. "So do you ever play *DND*, like … in person?"

Please say yes. Please say yes. I'm dying to get invited to participate in a session. Even if it means I'll have to reprise my Kenna role to do it.

"I do. My friends and I get together a couple of times a month," he says, smiling faintly. "Usually. Sometimes we go a little longer. But it's all on the DL. Please don't mention it to anyone at the diner?" He raises his eyebrows at me.

"Are there a lot of people in Ephron who play *DND*?" I ask.

"No. Most of the gang lives a half hour or more away. That's why we only get together once or twice a month. It's a whole production when we do."

"And do you, like, wear costumes?" I ask hopefully.

. . .

"Of course," Noah smiles. Naughtily.

Oh God.

"I do love a good costume." I bite my lip, fixating again on his swoopers.

"Oh, really." Noah arches a brow at me. "What do you imagine yourself dressed up as?"

I flash on an image of myself in my Ember costume. My latex bodysuits. Fishnet tights. Platform boots and talon nails.

"I dunno," I say. What would I like to dress up in for a session? "Maybe an elf? Or a princess?" Or *Ember.* I want to just come out and say it. Maybe with the character's accent. I want to shock him to see how he reacts when I do. Maybe it would turn him on. The Ember Enchantress has that effect on a lot of men. They want her. They want her to crack her snakeskin whip and tell them exactly what to do to her.

I know this for certain because there are whole subreddits. Scary ones. But Noah isn't scary. Noah is annoyingly calm and steady. I can't help myself. I want to rattle his cage.

. . .

"How about ... the Ember Enchantress?" I tip my head coyly and stare at him through the fringe of my lashes.

"Oh, please. You're nothing like Ember!" Noah bursts out laughing. "I'm sorry to tell you ... you can't pull that character off, Kenna." He shakes his head sadly.

"Excuse me? I think I do a perfect Ember impression," I huff. "Lorelei Dupont has nothing on me."

"Well, you're right about that." Noah stops drawing and glances up from his map. He looks me right in the eye. "I like you a hell of a lot more than Lorelei Dupont."

"You're telling me you'd kick Lorelei Dupont out of your bed?" I counter.

Push, push, push. Why can't I stop?

"I'm telling you I wouldn't kick *you* out of my bed." Noah reaches out and catches the porch swing, pulling it closer to him. The air is charged, and I wonder if he's going to lean forward, maybe try to kiss me. He's close enough. But at the last minute, he lets the swing go, giving it a shove. He turns back to his map.

Dammit.

. . .

"So what would you dress me up as?" I ask, trying to cover my disappointment. I set down the campaign and move to the table beside him, leaving the empty swing dangling and jerking awkwardly in my wake.

Noah looks up again and studies me.

"Not everyone dresses up for our sessions, Kenna. I wouldn't want to make you come as anything that made you uncomfortable. If you wanted to come, you could come as you are."

Come. Come. Come. Come now.

I can't take it anymore. I get up and lean forward on the table, lick my lips, and let him have it, guns blazing, all my desire on full display. "And when you say *come* as I am?"

And then we are kissing. Hard. Fast. Crazy. With tongue. Noah stands and drags me back to the swing, roughly pulling me onto his lap.

"You have no idea how much I've wanted to do this," I moan, straddling his obvious arousal and rocking.

"Don't I?" he asks, gripping my hips and repositioning me to make the most of the swaying motion.

. . .

"I might ... you know," I warn him.

"Might what?" he asks.

"Come. As I am."

I don't even care that we're sitting on his front porch, in plain sight of the world.

"No," Noah commands, stopping the swing from rocking. "Not here. Not now. And not like this."

He holds my hips still as I try to grind against him.

"I said no." He raises his eyebrows, speaking sternly. Now he sounds like an English teacher.

Is he freaking kidding me?

"Are you kidding me?" I pant.

"I'm totally serious," Noah says. "This isn't the time or the place. For one, we're in public, on display for all the world to watch. Which means we can't take our clothes off. And I'd want to take your clothes off. I'd want to rip them off. But not here."

. . .

"I mean, there's nobody watching. The houses are pretty spread out. We wouldn't have to take everything off," I cajole, running my fingers through his soft, fine hair.

"No," Noah insists. "Someone might be driving by, and I'd have to rip the throat out of anyone else who dared to look at you naked."

I swallow. Hard. This is doing nothing to cool me down.

"What's the second reason?" I ask.

"My mom is stopping by in a bit for dinner." He attempts to lift me off him, but I cling with my thighs. He gives me the stern teacher look again. "Come on, I don't think she signed up for dinner and a show."

"*Come* on? You're killing me, Noah." I grab a fistful of his shirt and continue grinding against him.

"No means no!" Noah snatches a handful of my hair with one hand, and wraps his other arm around my backside. Then he stands up, bad leg and all.

"And I'm saying no, Kenna."

. . .

Kenna.

He calls me Kenna, just before turning around and dropping me back on my ass on the swing.

His words hit me like a bucket of ice water. He means it. This is not happening. Not just because he doesn't want to do it. I don't want to anymore, either.

The ridiculousness of this folly kicks me in my overactive crotch. What the hell was I thinking? That I'd just sleep with this guy, and then what? That I'd swap back with the real Kenna and say, *"Don't mind the dude sliding into your DMs, Kenna. You're welcome. I went out and caught a good one for you."*

The thought of it makes me pulsate with toxic jealousy. I feel it in every extremity. It's pooling in my groin. If I can't have him, nobody can! The hell with all of this.

I jump up, shoving the campaign document back into my bag. Then I take it out again and toss it onto the table.

If I leave it, I'll never get to read how it ends. Shit. I shove it back in the bag.

"Well, thanks for the wine and cheese. I guess I'll leave you to it now."

. . .

"Hang on." Noah takes a tentative step toward his chair, pulls it out, and sits back down again. He runs his hands through his hair and smooths the map he was just working on, weighing down a corner with his phone before looking up. "Don't go yet? I just had an idea."

"An idea?" I freeze, desperately wanting to stay, but also wanting to go before I humiliate myself further.

Noah drums his fingers, seems to consider something, then takes a deep breath. He holds my eyes with his magical, melty gaze.

"Okay, here goes," he says. "It's kind of last minute, but would you be interested in attending my next *DND* session?"

"Possibly," I say, thinking that he'll tell me the session isn't till the following week, by which time Kenna and I will have switched back.

"Do you have plans this Sunday?"

"No," I say. I'm loving where this is going. And hating it.

"How would you like to be a part of my current adventure?"

. . .

"Really?" *Oh shit. I would like that. I would like that a LOT.* Like if there was only one thing I could wish for, this might be it.

"There's just one catch, and it's a really, really important one."

"Okay," I say. If he needs snacks, I'll bring them. Fog machine? No problem. Hell, I'll rent a venue if he needs it. "What is it?"

"You can't tell anyone. You can't blow my cover."

"Pardon?" I ask.

Noah looks up at me, and a small smile tugs at his lips. "I was going to have to tell you eventually if we started dating, Kenna, but I'm kind of a big deal in the gaming world. But nobody at school knows, and I'd like to keep it that way, if possible. It's nobody's business what I do in my free time, behind closed doors. There's nothing illegal or immoral about it, you know. It's just *DND*."

I can feel the flush starting. It's followed by that sweaty, dizzy-feeling palpitation and the urge to gulp air. I've seen it a million times before, at comic con and other fan events when I show up in costume. I've just never felt it firsthand. My palms feel slippery. He couldn't be ... could he?

"Holy shit, who are you?" I breathe out the question in a gasp.

"Still just Noah Greenberg," he says, but then his voice shifts to the velvety, mesmerizing tones of the Dungeon Master. "When I'm not sharing my notes on the number one *DND* show on Spotify and Apple podcasts."

"Oh, my God. I can't believe it's you. It's really you." My mouth makes the words, but it feels like a fish mouth making silent o's underwater. "I've never done this before, and you're like ... famous."

"Don't worry." Noah's voice vibrates straight through me on the porch. "Max Mercury is going to take care of you."

kenna

. . .

XANDER IS SITTING in the sunroom holding court with the Barzilay family. Princess is perched on his lap, clearly aware she is the center of attention and loving it. She's got on a pink, rhinestone-jeweled harness with a matching leash attached. I've been summoned to come over here from the pool to help out with the training session. I eye Xander warily. He's definitely up to something.

"It's very important we involve the whole family," Xander is saying. "And Rafe, if we want Princess to respond well to future relationships, it's essential that she gets comfortable seeing you with other women." Xander is speaking authoritatively, as if he's been a trainer for years, not just a groomer. "You don't mind, do you, *Lorelei*?" Xander winks at me boldly.

Okay, yep. Georgia and the real Lorelei have definitely filled him in on the farce.

But Naomi and Orly still seem none the wiser.

"I'm not sure I follow," Naomi says from behind the kitchen counter, where she is chopping parsley and squeezing lemon juice into a bowl of chickpeas. "What is it you want from Lorelei? She's not exactly a member of the *family*. She and Rafe are just friends."

Orly is sprawled on the floor, coloring on a roll of paper with chunky crayons. She doesn't even look up at the grown-ups, she is so engrossed in her work. I sit down next to her, idly doodling some flowers.

Xander nods sagely and strokes the dog. "Exactly, Mrs. Barzilay, but Princess here doesn't know that. She's a bit of a diva, and she wants your son all to herself." He gazes down at the dog, who looks up with adoration and licks his face excitedly.

"Really?" Naomi looks doubtful.

"Really." Xander nods confidently. "So it's important that we establish that while Princess holds rank in this house, she is not the *queen*."

"No problem, I can be the queen," Naomi says as she rinses and dries her hands. "I mean, I am Rafe's mother. And call me Naomi. Mrs. Barzilay was my mother-in-law."

"Of course, Naomi. You are the OG queen!" Xander replies. "But I was thinking about situations that Princess might interpret as more intimate. Dogs are very sensitive that way. I'd hate for her to get spooked and bolt in a fit of jealousy if, for example, she happened to see Rafe kissing someone else." He shoots me an obnoxiously smug glance. "I'm sure that Lorelei doesn't mind helping out, do you?"

"Do you maybe want her to change first?" Naomi asks, eyeing my sheer cover-up and bikini. She hasn't said anything about the fact that Rafe is wearing a pair of board shorts and a tee.

"Oh, Princess doesn't mind." Xander shakes his head. "If anything, it's better this way."

Wink. Wink. He has got to stop. I am going to kill him.

"What is it you'd like me to do, exactly?" I ask.

"Well, for starters, I'd like to see how Princess reacts to you and Rafe sitting together on the couch."

"What's that going to do?" Naomi asks. She walks over to the couch, glancing at my doodle as she passes. "Nice flowers, Lorelei, and with your left hand, no less. Are you drawing the peonies?"

"Ima," Rafe addresses his mother as he stands to pour himself a lemonade from the pitcher on the counter. "I think we need to pay attention to Xander. He is the expert here." He meets my eye and gestures to a second glass, questioning if I want some, too. I nod.

"Fine, fine. So what do you need me for?" Naomi asks impatiently.

"I need you to go outside," Xander says to Rafe's mom. "Go outside, and come back in five minutes. Ring the doorbell. Do you think you can do that? I just need five minutes."

"What about Orly?" Naomi asks, gesturing to her granddaughter.

"Hmm ..." Xander strokes his chin. "Good point. I think you should take her with you."

"So you gathered us all here just to tell us to go away?" Naomi looks offended.

"It's just for five minutes, Ima," Rafe says. "Maybe take Orly to feed the fishes in the koi pond?"

Hearing this, Orly jumps up, abandoning the crayons. "Feed fishies!"

"Fine." Naomi sighs and takes Orly by the hand. "Where's the food?"

"In the pantry," Rafe says. "Just don't feed them too much."

"I'm a Jewish mother." Naomi winks at her son before turning to go. "This is a tall order."

Xander jumps up the instant they are gone, but he doesn't put Princess down yet.

"Okay, you two. I'd like to see you on the couch together," Xander says, pointing at the upholstered sectional he's just vacated. He leans down to fluff a flowery pillow and pats the seat.

"Sure." Rafe hands me my glass of lemonade and a hand to help me up from the floor. "I take it you want us to act like we're a little more than just friends for this scenario?"

"This is a little awkward." I narrow my eyes at Xander. "Do you really need us to put on a show for you?"

"It's not for me!" Xander feigns shock at the very suggestion. "It's for *Princess*."

"Come on, Lorelei, *darling*." Rafe gently pulls me down next to him on the couch. "It's just acting. It's not like we've never had to do that."

"Perfect!" Xander squeaks slightly and claps, causing Princess to bark.

"How does this make you feel, *Princess*?" I stare down Xander while talking to the dog.

"I dunno. I think you two need to get closer." Xander grins back at me wickedly. "I don't think the dog's buying your act."

Rafe places both of our drinks on coasters on the coffee table before casually draping an arm around me and scooting closer. When my cover-up slips off my shoulder, he pulls it back up and toys with the trim, alternating between twirling a pompom and stroking my collarbone. His hair is still damp from the pool, and he smells delicious. Suntan oil, sunshine, earth, and that certain spice that's just him.

"Better," Xander says, nodding, pacing, and stroking his chin like a director setting up a scene. "But maybe—and I hate to be so forward—but maybe Rafe you could just kiss Lorelei?" He glances down at the dog and makes an apologetic face.

"Oh, for heaven's sake, Xander," I say, about to call his bluff and get him to fess up that he *knows*. But before I can get the words out, Rafe is leaning toward me and kissing me.

He places a hand on my neck and nibbles at my lower lip, pulling a low groan out of me that I really didn't mean to set free.

"Good. Good job, guys. I'm just going to put the dog down in the kitchen, and we'll see how she does." Out of the corner of my eye, I see Xander backing away, mumbling to the dog. "C'mon, girl, Uncle Xandy has some treats for you. Good girl."

Rafe's tongue is teasing mine, and I'm having flashbacks to the feeling of his hands all over my body by the pool.

I push him away, gasping a little. "Surely that's enough?"

Xander is standing in front of the fridge with the door open, helping himself to some berries straight out of the container. The dog is still tucked under his arm, eating treats out of his other hand.

"What?" he says absentmindedly, turning back to us.

"Come on, Xander!" I say. "You know it's me. Just admit it."

"Wait … you two know each other?" Rafe looks confused.

"Like family." Xander smirks. "Kenna's like my second big sister."

"And Xander's like my really annoying little brother." I sigh. "He's my best friend Georgia's brother. We volunteer together with the shelter pets."

"I fluff 'em up for her beauty shots." Xander shuts the fridge door. "Don't I, Princess?" He lets the dog lick his face again.

"So this was all some sort of joke?" Rafe removes his arm from around me. "You're punking me?"

"More likely, he's punking me," I say. "I'm so sorry, Rafe. Shame on you, Xander."

"Hey, you two put on a good show. Not just on the couch. Over by the pool earlier, too. Don't think I didn't see ya'll." Xander shifts the dog to the other arm and pours himself a glass of lemonade.

I can feel Rafe bristling beside me. "Do I need to remind you about the NDA you signed?"

"No, not at all. But I gotta say, you'd best not mess with my girls here." He sets the dog down and folds his hands across his chest. "Either of them."

Princess makes a beeline for us on the couch, barking up a storm. She then jumps up between us, effectively separating us with her furry self and looking at us both with what is frankly a very judgmental look.

"See," Xander says, tilting his head toward the dog. "I wasn't kidding. She doesn't like either one of you paying attention to anyone but her."

"Tough luck," Rafe says.

And then the doorbell rings, and Princess hits the ground running.

"Stay where you are. I'll get it. I want to see how she acts at the door," Xander says, taking off after the dog.

"I'm so sorry," I repeat the minute he's gone, bracing myself for Rafe's censure.

"Don't be silly." Rafe threads his fingers through mine and squeezes. "I knew he was full of shit, figured something was up."

"You knew?" I shake my head in disbelief. "Then why—"

"Because I wanted to kiss you," he says. "I want to kiss you. No acting required." He dips his head to kiss my neck quickly, pulling away just before Naomi and Orly come back in, followed by Xander and Princess. Orly leaps between us and curls into her father, sobbing.

"Abba!" She clings to Rafe.

Naomi is just standing there, arms folded.

"What happened?" I ask.

"She wanted to go in the pond," Naomi says.

"Abba! Savta wouldn't let me hug the fishies!" Orly knits her brows and stares angrily at her grandma. The front of her shirt is wet. I feel like I should get up, but she's curled one little arm under my elbow, and she's grabbed onto the pom-pom trim of my cover-up, which she is now rubbing against her snot and tear-filled face. This actually doesn't bother me at all. I'm used to being drooled on. But I do wonder if I'm going to have to get the garment dry cleaned for Lorelei.

"Savta just wants you to be safe, *hamuda*," Rafe says. "She doesn't want anything to mess up the trip to Disneyland tomorrow. Aren't you excited to go tomorrow?"

"Yes, but ..." Orly looks from me to her father. "I want Lie Lie to come."

Xander claps a hand over his mouth, taking it all in. Beside him, I notice Naomi watching us shrewdly. She's no longer looking at her granddaughter, in fact. She's looking at me.

"Lorelei is very busy, Orly. Why do you want Lorelei to come?" Naomi asks.

"Because she told me she's never been to Disneyland, either." Orly tugs on a pom-pom.

"Of course she has," Naomi says, looking at me suspiciously. "Lorelei grew up in LA."

"No, she's like me. She's never been." Orly's lip is quivering again.

Why had I let that information slip?

Naomi cocks her head. "I could have sworn that you and your mom had season passes."

"I think she just meant that she hasn't been there since they renovated," Rafe covers for me. "But it's not a terrible idea."

"I think it's a great idea!" Xander pipes up, reminding everyone that he's still there. Naomi looks questioningly at him, and he stands up straighter. "Even numbers and all that. You never want to go to theme parks with an odd number in your party. Then someone would have to sit on some of the rides alone."

"I don't want Abba to sit alone," Orly nods gravely. "Savta said I have to ride all the rides with her because Abba can take me to Disney any time."

Naomi considers this. Her eyes sweep curiously between me and Rafe, finally settling on her granddaughter's arms, wrapped around mine. "I do suppose it would make more sense to even out our numbers," she says. "It would be lovely if you wanted to join us, Lorelei."

"What do you say?" Rafe asks me. "You don't want me to sit alone, do you?"

Orly turns her little face toward me. "Pleeeeeeze?" she implores, letting go of the pom-poms and clutching my hand in her two tiny ones.

"Oof," Xander says. "How can you even consider refusing a request like that?"

"Fine," I say, biting back the smile that's threatening to split my face. Resistance is futile. "I guess I'm going to Disneyland."

"Yay! It's all settled!" Xander snaps. "What are you going to wear?"

"Excuse me, young man? What about the dog?" Naomi asks, suddenly remembering why Xander is there.

"Oh, she'll be fine. I know a guy who can come install an invisible perimeter tomorrow morning. That's probably the safest thing for now. And there are some great classes I can refer you to. Dog training's more about training the people than the pets." He shrugs apologetically. "Let me know if you need a pet sitter while you're at Disneyland."

lorelei

. . .

IS THERE SUCH a thing as lady blue balls?

I hit the drive-thru on the way home from Noah's. The plan is to cash in my Taco Bell v-card, drowning my sorrow in forbidden fast-food items while finishing reading his campaign module. I order one of everything on the dollar menu.

Damn, the chalupas are good. Does Chef Jose Andres know about chalupas? Chalupas and Cheetos. I have definitely been missing out all these years. No time like the present, though. I shove a Cheeto *into* a chalupa and wish I could tweet openly about it.

The other completely amazing thing is Noah's mind.

He has completely reimagined the story of *A Midsummer Night's Dream* in an almost virtual reality-esque world. I wish I was acting in a stage version of his vision, with audience participation and dice rolls shaking things up and adding an element of improv. Nothing against classic Shakespeare.

I'm dying to call Noah when I finally finish reading his notes at 1 a.m. I want to talk about it. I want to tell him how much I admire his mind. His vision. *His buns.* Then I start thinking about his sexy forearms and the way they looked, attached to his big, strong hands on my hips when he lifted me off him, saying, "This is not the time or the place."

That should have been the clue right there. I should have recognized that voice. Those words. It's pretty similar to the tagline to his show. "This is the time. You've come to the right place." I hear it every night in my bed.

"This is not the time or the place, *Kenna*." How many times have I fantasized about the Dungeon Master saying my name? But no. He'd called me Kenna. It was like I'd rolled myself a one. Critical failure.

When I can't sleep, I do the only sensible thing—I pull up one of my favorite episodes and take care of myself, with Dungeon Master Noah's growly voice echoing in my ear.

———

I wake up to the sound of my phone ringing at 7 a.m. There's a chalupa wrapper stuck to my face and a pile of used condiment packets on the floor next to the crumpled paper bag. The trash can in the kitchen is already overflowing from all the other delicious takeout I've consumed this week. I should take it out. Intellectually, I know that this is a thing people have to do. It involves trash bags and trash cans and trash days, and honestly, it seems so tedious. If there's one good thing about being a celebrity, it's never having to take the trash out.

"What? What? WHAT?" I flail, feeling around for my buzzing phone on the lumpy futon. There are two missed calls from Kenna. And six texts, not counting the one that comes in now from the momager. Short and sweet.

Happy Gotcha Day, Lorelei. Miss you so much. Xxoo Mom

Taco hangovers are bad. Almost as bad as booze. My head is swimming from all the salt, and I still think I have onion breath after double brushing my teeth. Coffee. Today, I might actually need some.

The phone rings again and I answer it this time. Kenna. She sounds as sleepy as I feel. "Lorelei, you gotta go to the diner. Carlos needs you there. The coffee machine is broken again."

"Isn't there a repair service you can call?" I ask.

"Already did. But he needs you to come in and help with the morning flow. The trainee called in sick, and the line's out the door. Plus, my uncles texted. There's a potential buyer stopping by the diner to have a look later. They're checking out our house, too. The realtor said we don't have to be there, but I dunno. I'd feel a lot better if someone could be there."

"Right." I splash cold water on my face. "I'm on it." At least I know I can get some coffee at the diner.

Before I leave, I call Carlos to let him know help is on the way.

"Is Noah there?" I ask.

"Who?" Carlos asks.

"Noah Greenberg? Walks with a slight limp? High school teacher?"

"Right ... let me check." I picture Carlos peeking out from the back room.

"No, he's not here, but half of Ephron is. How fast can you come?"

"Ten minutes," I assure him, reaching for the barista apron hanging over a chair.

———

Carlos was not exaggerating. The line is backed up past the Celestial Pets store. My "pal," the paparazzo, is standing in the line outside the door. He shakes his oversize camera at me as I pass, still clueless about who I really am.

"Nice tip about the cast trip to Vancouver," he snarls.

"Oh, they weren't there?" I feign innocence. "I must have heard wrong. Gosh, I'm so sorry. I hope you didn't go out of your way."

"It was fine," he grumbles. "I went whale watching. I got some great shots of a humpback."

"Good for you!" I laugh.

"I just wish I'd been able to bring my granddaughter. She's down in LA. I'm flying down for her birthday this weekend. But I'll be back. Don't you worry."

"Counting on it." I wave and head into the diner.

"Orders up!" the cook yells, placing more paper bags in the lineup in the window behind the counter.

"Oh, thank God you came," a beleaguered Carlos says. "I was ready to ask my wife to come help out."

"You could still ask her," I shrug.

"What's gotten into you, Kenna?" Carlos looks at me. "Does it have anything to do with the potential buyer coming in later?"

"Of course not," I reassure him, thinking that it *is* kind of sad that Kenna's uncles are planning to sell this place. It's grown on me.

Then I stand on a chair and do the New York cabbie whistle I learned for the *Moxie in Manhattan* spin-off movie.

"Oi! Everyone. Settle down. The espresso maker is out of order, so drip coffee is on the house this morning, and Carlos will write you an IOU for a free, fancy coffee drink if you were going to order one."

"Uh ... you sure about that, Kenna?" Carlos looks nervously at me, and in the moment, I see how old he is. Gotta be late seventies. Young in spirit, but not so much in the flesh. His hands have a slight tremor, and it's clear the problems this morning have been a strain for him.

"Don't worry," I say, patting him on the back. "I got this." *It's nothing a large check can't fix, and Lord knows, I can afford it.*

kenna

. . .

I FALL BACK ASLEEP after speaking with Lorelei, but not for long. Georgia's texts wake me back up.

Disneyland?

Kenna!

Answer me!

Where are you?

I shoot back a smiley face.

Why hadn't I? Mostly because I'd been waiting for the other Mickey Mitt to drop. I still can't believe it's really happening. And with so little notice. Most people I know spend months, if not years, planning a Disney trip.

I don't have enough patience to write in full sentences, so I bullet-point with plane, princess, and star emoji.

I'm pinching myself on your behalf. What are you going to wear?

No clue! Help!

Have you heard of Disneybounding?

???? What's Disneybounding?

It's when you theme outfits based on characters. Hold please. I'll pull images from Pinterest and call you back on FaceTime.

Thank goodness for Georgia. Hopefully, there's something in Lorelei's closet that will work.

———

Two hours later, I head over to the main house to grab some more food items. I'm still wearing the green, silk dress for the Tinkerbell-themed ensemble that Georgia and I have ruled out in favor of Aurora.

· · ·

As I near the house, I hear the hum of a motor, and I am surprised to find Rafe riding in very slow circles around the yard in an old-fashioned motorcycle. Orly is strapped into a harness in the side car, donning a helmet, and Princess is sitting on her lap, wearing her own tiny helmet and jeweled harness.

"Lorelei." Rafe waves, rolling to a stop near me. "We were just taking a break after playing croquet."

"I winned!" Orly reaches into the sidecar, producing a small, wooden mallet. She attempts to swing it over her head victoriously, but Rafe just reaches out one arm and snatches it away. "What did we talk about, Orly?"

"I Rey!" She screws up her face and tries to look ferocious.

"This is not a lightsaber." Rafe shakes his head. "Someone could get hurt." He tosses the tiny mallet onto the lawn and jumps off the bike. Quickly, he undoes Orly's harness and helmet. Next, he removes Princess from the side carrier and sets her down, careful to hold on to her leash.

"It's just about time for Orly's nap."

Orly rushes over to me, flinging herself at my legs. She grabs the hem of my silky, green dress and rubs the fabric on her face. "Pretty, Lie Lie!"

"Thanks, Lee Lee." I settle on a nickname for her. Two can play at that game.

"Lee Lee and Lie Lie!" Orly declares, patting my leg and shoving her thumb in her mouth. Her eyes are closing as she leans against me.

"Okay, I think it's time for Lee Lee to lie down. Someone looks sleepy." Rafe scoops both her and the dog up, then asks, "Can you stick around for lunch? My mom made bourekas."

"Okay," I answer tentatively. "You sure? I was just going to grab a few things and bring them back to the guesthouse."

"Don't be silly." Naomi comes out through the sliding doors, holding a tray full of flaky pastries. "I was just about to send someone over to come get you. I insist you join us."

"Give me a minute," Rafe says. "I'll be right back. I'm just going to grab the nanny and see if she can get Orly settled. Maybe after lunch, you and I can go for a drive."

"Okay," I say. "Can I help?"

. . .

"I think this is everything," Naomi says, leading me around the side of the house to a shady patio where a gorgeous table has been laid for three, with beautiful, floral linens, toile plates, and silver cutlery. It looks like something out of a magazine spread. But many of the items on the table are not familiar to me, starting with the tray of flaky pastries Naomi is setting down.

"These look a little like spanakopita," I say, "but with sesame seeds. Is that feta cheese?"

"Yes, the recipe is similar, and they have the same roots." Naomi looks impressed. "These have ricotta as well." She sets the tray on the table and rearranges some of the plates, moving pickles closer to the olives and setting nuts off to one side.

"What's this white stuff?" I ask, pointing at a bowl of what looks like pale, thinned peanut butter.

"Tahini," she says. And then she leads me on a virtual tour of the table. "We have some falafel and some pickles, some of my homemade hummus, egg salad, smoked fish, stuffed grape leaves, some eggplant, pita, and, of course, some yogurt."

"Where did you get all this?" I ask.

"I made most of it from scratch," she shrugs. "It's nothing. I'm used to cooking for a hundred people."

• • •

"May I taste it?" I point at the hummus. Naomi beams as she hands me a small spoon, waiting confidently for my reaction. "Wow. Oh, wow! This is incredible. This gives every other hummus I've ever eaten impostor syndrome," I say.

I've had hummus before, but never like this, with such bright notes of lemon, herby parsley, and olive oil. There's a tangy spice as well, sprinkled on top.

Naomi looks surprised. "Thank you, Lorelei. I thought you didn't eat chick peas. Are you no longer bean intolerant?"

Bean intolerant? Is that even a thing?

"Apparently not," I shrug. "What about that stuff?" I point at a block of something that looks like cheese. But not cheese. It's marbled and a little crumbly.

"Oh, that's the halvah from the market in Jerusalem. Close to the coffee bean shop. They grind their own sesame seeds to make the paste. My sister shipped some over."

"Can I try it?"

"Of course." Naomi cuts a small piece for me, and I pop the cube in my mouth. It reminds me of the filling of a Butterfinger bar, the way it is a little crunchy and crumbly and nutty. But it melts in my mouth more quickly.

"Yum!" I say. "I bet this stuff would go well with coffee."

"It does," she agrees, gesturing to the insulated carafe already on the table. "We'll have some with our dessert. Why don't we have a seat."

"Are you sure I can't do anything to help?" I hesitate before taking a seat.

"No, dear, you're my guest, and I'm my son's guest, and this house rental came with full-time staff, so we may as well both sit back and enjoy it, no?" Naomi pulls out a cushioned wicker chair for me, insisting I take a seat before she does. When she settles into her own chair, she pours herself a cup of coffee, sits back in her chair, and sighs, dramatically.

"I'm not used to doing nothing ... it makes me nervous," she says, sitting back up again to grab the honeypot. She scoops up some honey with a spoon and stirs it vigorously into the black coffee. "This was a good call. I think I might bring some of this local honey home with me."

I want to tell her about the uncles. How I picture them in Greece, equally fidgety and trying to relax. Despite the photo that Uncle Nick sent of Uncle Stavros, I can't picture the two of them lounging around for any significant length of time. Stavros probably popped up the minute after Nick took the photo and demanded to go check out the local markets. I have a feeling the uncles and Naomi would get along great.

"I have a hard time sitting still, too," I commiserate.

"Do you?" she asks. "That's new as well. I always admired your ability to sit and read for hours as a child. None of my own kids had that much focus. Especially Rafe. He's never been one to sit still."

I eye the door, wishing Rafe would hurry up and come back.

"That's an interesting dress," Naomi comments. "Is it silk?"

"I think so?" I glance down at my outfit, regretting my decision not to change back into shorts and a tee before coming over here. It seems like I'm always wildly over or underdressed around this woman.

"Have you ever heard of Disneybounding?" I ask.

"No." She hands me the cup of coffee that she's poured for me, along with another chunk of halvah. "Who says we can't have a little dessert before lunch? I won't tell if you don't." She winks as she pops a piece of the candy in her mouth. "Now tell me what Disneybounding is."

. . .

"Well, it involves theming your outfit to different Disney characters."

"Like a costume?"

"No, Disney doesn't allow adults to wear costumes, except on special theme days. They don't want any confusion with the official characters and employees," I explain, parroting what Georgia told me earlier. "But a lot of people come up with outfits inspired by characters. A sort of homage." I pull up a blog on my phone. "Here, let me show you."

"Wow!" Naomi leans in and pulls a pair of glasses out of her pocket so she can take a closer look. "Do you think I could go as ..." She pauses to think for a moment, then smiles as she comes to a decision. "The fairy godmother from Cinderella?"

"I don't see why not," I grin.

"Will you help me?" she asks.

"Sure," I nod.

"This is Tinkerbell?" She waves her hand at my outfit.

"Well, yeah, but I think I have something better to wear."

· · ·

"I was going to say I like it. I like you with blonde hair, too. Still getting used to it, but I like it."

"It's my natural color."

"Lucky you. I always wanted to be a blonde or a gingie. My husband was a gingie, but none of my children got his red hair, nor did any of my other grandkids." Naomi reaches out to touch one of my curls, smoothing it back. "It's really a shame that you and Rafe aren't a couple. Maybe then, we'd have red hair in the family again."

Before I can say anything, she turns in her chair, reaching for the throw blanket that's draped over the back. "This weather is crazy. I swear, it's freezing cold one minute and boiling hot the next."

"Maybe that's just your hot flashes, Ima," Rafe comments as he drops down into the empty chair beside me. "Now, tell me what you two were discussing while I was inside."

lorelei

. . .

THE MORNING RUSH isn't even over yet when a real estate agent named Ashley shows up with a potential buyer for the diner business. I hate her on sight.

For one, she's plastic from head to toe. Bleached blonde hair. Fake tan. Veneers. Acrylics. Boobs. Lip injections. Botox. The whole megillah, as the momager used to say. Ashley speaks in a nasal voice, adds extra syllables at the end of her words, and says "like" a LOT. "Like, oh my gawd-uh, this place is like, adorbs."

Seriously, sister? You're in your mid thirties and probably from Ohio. Stop talking like a teenager from the Valley.

The worst part is, I have to tune out most of what she is saying. I'm so terrified that her irritating tones will crawl into my mimic-prone mouth, and I'll have to wash them out with an hour of listening to BBC radio.

Her client isn't much better. He's a typical bro-hole, and every other word out of his mouth is stupid jargon.

"I think this is such a great spot for our concept. We can put the big-screen TVs up there and get those iPad things on every table so my dudes can order whatever they want, whenever they want it. The theme is bros and hos. We'll get the girls who bring the food to wear those French maid outfits."

"Cah-yute!" a half-checked-out Ashley enthuses, while checking herself out on her phone's front camera. "Hey, Kenna, is it? Has Rafe Barzilay been in here?" She leans in and whispers to me, "I hear he's here in town."

I ignore her question and turn back to the bro-hole.

"Why not dress them up like handmaids from *The Handmaid's Tale*?" I ask.

"Thanks for the suggestion, Kenna." He nods, in a patronizing fashion, as if he's doing me a favor by taking the suggestion seriously. He can't actually be taking it seriously, can he? "You know anything about applying for a liquor license?"

"Are you kidding me?" I reply.

"Right. Never mind. You're just a barista. Not your wheelhouse," he says dismissively.

Incredible. And here I thought that this brand of brain damage was confined to the LA area.

"Everything okay here?" Carlos catches me glaring at the idiot.

"We're fine," I say, trying to recall the bro-hole's name. I don't think we've been introduced yet, but I heard Ashley say it. *Dakota? Bowie? Brody?* I go with Brody. "Brody here was just discussing new ideas for theme eateries."

"What are you doing here, Cody?" Carlos asks, shooting me a protective look.

Uh-oh. Cody. This name I recall. Kenna's ex is Cody! The really, really shitty one who dumped her after making her life miserable for over five years. He doesn't disappoint. He's just as lousy as I thought he'd be. Slightly better looking. But that glamour wears thin the minute he opens his mouth. The douche fart won't shut up.

"My grandma kicked the can and left me some cash. I'm looking at some investment opportunities with my buddy Bryce Holm."

"Investment? Where? You don't think we'd want you here, do you?" Carlos asks. He's standing a little like a cowboy in a spaghetti western. Shoulders squared, hand on his arthritic hip, ready to defend me—or rather Kenna—from this asshole. He shifts his weight, and I notice that his orthopedic shoes are quite scuffed. Nevertheless, if he pulled out a six-shooter right now, I would not be surprised. Not in the least. He's frowning, hard. I don't think I've ever seen deeper lines on a man's face without the use of latex prosthetics.

I just want to hug him. I've decided I'm adopting Carlos when this is all over. He's going to be my honorary grandpa. The grandpa I never had. Maybe he'll even let me call him pops.

"Cody was just leaving," I say, walking demonstratively to the door and holding it open. "And why don't you take a break now, Carlos. The afternoon shift workers just arrived, and I think things are settling down. You've been here since opening at five."

"Aw, c'mon, Kenna. Aren't you even gonna offer me some of your famous coffee? I was hoping we could catch up," Cody says, lowering his hoodie to reveal more of his thin, greasy hair.

"How about you two kids catch up while we look at the house," Ashley says. She turns to Cody, "It's not officially on the market yet, but I'm sure I'll get the listing." She turns back to me, tipping her head back and looking down her pointy nose haughtily. "Nicky and Stavros said you were cool with me bringing my client by?"

"This? This is your client whom you're bringing to my house?" I gesture at the man-child in the doorway. He's got tufty patches of fuzz in a few areas on his face. He doesn't even know how to shave properly.

"Yeah, Kenna. Wouldn't it be sick if I bought your house?" Cody's hollow laugh gives me sociopath vibes. Like he's either super dumb or dead inside. Possibly both. "Pretty funny considering all the times I climbed in through the window."

"Nope," I say, shutting it down. "Not happening."

"Well, uh, I hate to say it," Ashley says, tapping her pink-and-white tips impatiently on the counter, "but I did get permission from the owners to show the property and I have the key, so ..." She does a little Baby Oopsie shrug #sorrynotsorry move that might have been cute on a tweenager, but makes me want to throat-punch her. I have a real WWGD moment, thinking about Georgia flipping Ashley onto her face in the back alley.

"Did they know you were showing the house to *him*?" I jerk a backward thumb at the dipshit. He's not good enough to lift an index finger for.

"Look, Kenna, I know this is a little awkward ... the optics are a little weird with me buying your house, but just to be clear, I don't want to get back together."

"Can we get going?" Ashley twangs through her nose. "I've got a really big appointment to get my extensions redone at four."

———

Kenna's uncles' house is a two-story, farmhouse-style home with white, clapboard siding, black shutters, and a steeply pitched roof. Nothing fancy, just a solid, semi-suburban home. There's a detached garage with a workshop over it, where I've been staying the last few days. But I haven't been inside the main house, and I'm not entirely prepared for the time warp within.

"Your old bedroom." Cody stands in the doorway to a bedroom with flowery wallpaper. He slaps the doorframe like he's patting a friend on the back. "Memories." Then he pulls out his electronic tape measure, steps into the room, and shoves a dresser aside. "Let me just get some measurements real quick here. I'm going to make this room a showcase for my sneaker collection."

"Can you hurry up?" I ask, tapping my foot. It cannot be healthy for me to roll my eyes this hard, this many times in rapid succession.

"Yeah, I guess I just need to measure all the walls and floor space in the living room. Say cheese, babe!" Cody snaps a quick photo with me in it, and I flinch, covering my face reflexively.

"Could you not?" I say.

"Oh, c'mon, Kenna. Your acne is looking a lot better. It hardly shows." He takes off down the stairs, smiling to himself.

"Just like your dick," I mumble.

I can't believe that I just felt my face before remembering that I do not, in fact, have acne. That's how he did it. What a gaslighting piece of shit.

"What'd you say, Kenna?" Cody whirls around at the foot of the stairs.

"Nothing." I clamp down on my urge to mess with him. The sooner he's out of here, the better. "Just finish up and get going?"

"Cool, cool."

I perch on the couch while Cody paces the living room and take a moment to review my messages. First up: Tabitha.

The genetics lab called and said that they sent the test

results to your inboxes. Just letting you know. I sent in

my final timesheet. Good luck finding another PA as

awesome as me.

You're staying in Ohio?

I'm in Kansas. Frowny Face. Oops, my bad.

So you're not coming back? Why not?

Talk to Rafe and your evil Twin. Blocking you now. Byeee.

I stare at the phone, stunned. What the hell is going on over there at the compound?

"Fuuuck," Cody curses. He's measured the same wall three times now, and he doesn't seem pleased. "This wall is like three inches too short for my equipment."

"Bummer," I look up from my phone to opine. "It sucks when your equipment is six inches too short."

"No, not my equipment, and I said three—" Understanding dawns on Cody's face, and his eyes narrow vindictively.

"I get it, Kenna. But bitter's not a good look on you. There's gotta be someone out there who's more like, on your level." He makes a face like he's just scraped poo off his shoe, then quickly amends that to an insultingly sympathetic expression.

"I guess what I'm saying is, isn't it time you moved on already?"

For Kenna's sake, I wish this dingleberry could see her hanging poolside with Rafe Barzilay right now.

"Guys! I gotta go. My stylist waits for no one." Ashley emerges from the kitchen, tottering on her dated stiletto heels and clutching her rhinestone-covered phone. It matches her over-size ring. Makes me wonder what sort of guy fell in her man trap. Clearly, a rich one.

She shakes her keys and turns to smile sweetly at Cody. "So what do you think? It's perf, right?"

"Nah. This place has bad vibes." Cody shakes his head. "It's not for me."

"Really?" Ashley looks disappointed for exactly two seconds before moving on. "Okay, well never mind. There are some lofts in my building that I'd love to show you."

———

I shut the door behind them and take myself back to the plaid couch. Comfortable, but hideous. Kenna's uncles are not living up to any of the gay-uncle stereotypes in the decor department. I text Kenna.

> The DNA results are back. Did you look at them yet?

> No. I was waiting to hear from you.
> Wouldn't it be wild if we were actually related?

It would be crazy, but who knows? We're from the same general part of Russia. We could be distant cousins. We should open the results together, right?

Sure. Want to do it when we swap back? Monday morning?

Ok.

Although I'm tempted to look sooner.

So ... Disneyland?

I change the subject. She doesn't respond right away.

I hope it's ok. I didn't know what to say. I've never been.

It's fine. I'm just surprised Rafe invited you. So I take it the two of you are getting along?

Actually, Naomi invited me.

Naomi?

My eyes bug out when I read this.

Well, Naomi suggested it first. And then Lee Lee.

Lee Lee?

Oh, sorry. I've been calling Orly that. She's so cute, isn't she?

Kenna texts me a picture of herself and Orly blowing bubbles.

I can totally see why Rafe is so protective.

Who took that picture?

Rafe.

I toss my phone on the couch. Holy fucking shit. Rafe is into Kenna. Like, for real. And she's into him. It gives me an idea.

Go for it. Enjoy Disney. There's nothing like a VIP Disney day.

Really? You're sure you don't mind? I mean, I'll wear the wig and everything. Whatever you want me to do.

Whatever you want to do is fine with me. So long as you don't get arrested. I just have one small request.

Shoot.

How would you feel about having a one-night stand with Noah?

Who?

Is she kidding me?

Noah Greenberg. He comes into the diner all the time. English teacher. Broken leg.

Oh, that Noah. You're kidding, right?

Not kidding.

Lorelei, I would never have a one-night stand with Noah Greenberg.

Well, technically, it wouldn't be you.

Smiley face emoji. Devil Emoji. Eggplant emoji.

But he would think it was me.

Yeah, but the good news is that as of yesterday, he really likes you a lot, and I think he'd be fine with that.

What did you do?

Eek face. Face plant.

Cool your jets. Nothing that requires a trip to planned parenthood.

She responds with three Easter Island guys. Whatever that means.

Listen, I think I'm being super cool about the Disney trip, so …

But that's different!

How so?

I drum my fingers on the plaid armrest.

Because Rafe knows I'm not you. Nobody is being deceived.

Do Naomi and Orly know? Have you thought about that?

…

The three dots come and go.

Why can't you just come clean? Tell Noah who you really are.

I'm afraid he won't like me. He's just so much cooler than me.

Noah Greenberg is cooler than you, Lorelei Dupont? A-list celeb, Ember Enchantress, and former kid detective w/a cult following?

Yeah, he is. Trust me. I have been around a lot of so-called cool people. None of them hold a candle to that guy.

...

Three dots again.

You don't give yourself nearly enough credit, Lorelei.

I met Cody, by the way. What a tool, Kenna. I'm so sorry…

My fingers hover over the send button, and then I delete the message.

Have fun in Disneyland. Wear a big hat or something. You guys should be fine.

I will. Please don't do anything I wouldn't do while I am away?

Praying hands.

Fine.

I throw my phone down and lean back into the plaid sofa. I'm still exhausted and tempted to take a nap. There's a certain reassuring quality about Kenna's uncles' living room. It's like time has stood still in this room. It's a very Y2K aesthetic with the television being the central focus of the room.

Once upon a time, this TV was probably a "big screen," but now, it seems old and small, crammed into the middle of a dark-wood console. There's also a DVD player, a stereo with a CD carousel, and a very dusty, old Nintendo Wii unit, which clearly has not been touched in years. *What, no TiVo?*

The bookshelves on either side are littered with framed photos and stacked albums. Curious, I stand to check them out. I lift a framed school photo of Kenna, probably age ten or so, and let out a slow whistle. She really did look a lot like my Moxie character. A little sweeter, more innocent, but damn.

There are several goofy photos of Nick and Stavros in the albums at assorted holiday and dinner parties, as well as numerous pictures taken in the diner. A particularly poignant framed photo of Kenna, and what I assume is her uncle Nick and her mom, graces the front of a combo album and frame. Nick and Kenna's mom both look a lot younger, and so excited. Kenna is just a little blob, wrapped up in way too much clothing for what looks like a warm day in Siberia.

The metal plate on the album reads 6/6. I do a double take. Today's date. Is it possible that Kenna and I have the same gotcha day? How?

I carry the album over to the couch and flip through the faded photos. It's clear that this album has been poured over plenty. Some of the plastic sleeves are cracked, and the individual photos are bent. Particularly the ones of Kenna's mom.

Kenna's mother and uncle took so many photos. The absolute opposite of my momager, who treated the journey to come get me more like a covert op than a core memory. I pore over the photos, sucking up the details like a sponge. There's the laundry lines and the feeding tables, a sort of group highchair with six seats. Indoor details include a high shelf with three dolls that appear to be on a prison break from the Island of Misfit Toys. Toothless caretakers in long aprons are posing, holding stacks of threadbare, folded blankets.

It all gives me goose bumps.

Everything looks vaguely familiar, which is probably because I've googled so many albums like this one over the years. Other people's memories. There's a certain sameness to them. Same institutional, cement-block buildings. Same pathetic, rusty, metal slide in the overgrown lot outside. Same sad-eyed babies in bare-bones cribs that resemble cages. And don't get me started on the toddlers. They look even more tragic.

I pause, seeing a photo of one such toddler in one of the shots from Kenna's album. Not all the shots are of Kenna and her new family. There are bits and pieces of other families in the photos. I can only assume that her mom and uncle traveled in a group like my mom did. An organized sort of group adoption tour that the agencies used to arrange to organize the court dates and logistics of becoming a family. It made sense to send people in batches.

This particular tiny, tufted-haired toddler is trying to climb into the stroller with a sleeping Kenna. It's hard to tell how old she is from behind. I'm just assuming she's a girl because she has a ridiculously fluffy, tulle tutu on over her lumpy orphanage clothes. It's just like something the momager would have put me in. I flip back a page to confirm it's Uncle Nick's arm on the stroller. Kenna's mom must have thought it was funny. It *is* kind of cute how she's trying to climb in there with her.

I turn the page. There's another photo of the same toddler and Kenna, but in this one, the stroller's been pushed aside. The serious toddler is sitting on Kenna's mom's lap, with a flailing Kenna sprawled on top of her. The toddler is cradling Kenna tightly, like she's her precious baby doll. You can see the toddler's face better in this one. Her head is tilted down over the baby, like she's sniffing its head. But her giant eyes are turned toward the camera, gazing intensely at the photographer. She looks like the solemn children from long ago eras when people didn't smile for the camera. And she appears malnourished. Her hair isn't just tufty. She has a bald patch and a really bad rash. There's someone sitting next to them—a woman, I think—but I can only see one leg and boot.

Kenna's mom looks so nice in these photos. It makes my heart break. I notice that there are a few more shots in the plastic sleeve that have been shoved behind this one. Carefully, I slide them out.

Outtakes. There's a blurry shot of Kenna in the stroller. Another one of Kenna's mom holding just her on the same bench but shot mid-blink, so it's not a flattering photo. And the last one is a curled and creased candid photo of Uncle Nick sitting on the same bench, talking to a woman who is seated next to him on the bench. The toddler is resting on his lap in this photo, and the tutu is gone. She appears to be eating a small box of cereal.

I'm so busy studying the details of Nick and the toddler that, at first, I don't register the woman he's talking with. She blends into the dark background in her all-black boots, tights, and a simple but chic sheath dress. Turned toward Nick, and leaning in, she's waving a hand, as if she was caught midsentence, trying to make a point. Her long, dark hair is hanging in a curtain, half-hiding her profile. All you can really see are her red lips and the tip of her nose.

A nose I'd know anywhere.

Carefully, I smooth out the photo. This is a photo of my mother in Russia. Adopting me.

The toddler holding Kenna is me.

The roaring in my ears is so loud, I'm afraid I'm going to pass out.

Quickly, I flip through the rest of the album, looking for more photos with me and my mother in them. But there's nothing —not a one—till the last page of the album, where I find a group shot of all five of the families that traveled together, along with the kids, outside the American Embassy in Moscow. Someone is holding a sign from the agency, and someone else is clutching a bottle of champagne. My mom is standing, holding me in the back. She is not smiling.

kenna

• • •

THE TOTAL TRAVEL time between Ephron and Disneyland by private jet and chauffeured limo is just over four hours. A short, comfortable trip. But as it's almost ten at night, we're still all tired. Orly is fast asleep in her car seat. Rafe sends the nanny into the hotel lobby to get our room keys and summon a bellman. We all sit silently, waiting for her to come back.

"I can't wait to go to bed," Naomi says. When she yawns, we all catch it, taking turns covering our mouths.

"It's supposed to be the happiest place on earth," Rafe admonishes, "not the sleepiest!"

"It's just the jet lag." Naomi waves his concerns away. "I'll be the first one in line tomorrow."

"There won't be any lines," Rafe says, shaking his head. "I booked a VIP experience."

The nanny taps on the window of the limo, and Rafe cracks the door.

"We're good to go," she says, passing the room keys in. "The bags are on their way up."

———

We follow a second bellhop through the lobby, heads down, hunkering behind the stroller and car seat-laden cart. With a baseball cap and sunglasses on, Rafe is still completely Rafe. There's no way he's not getting recognized. But it's me, in the brown wig, who gets tagged first. As we pass a family in the hallway, they stop dead in their tracks, doubling back to the elevator with their phones out and yelling "Ember!" as the door slides closed. Orly stirs on her father's shoulder, then resumes sucking her thumb as the elevator glides upward.

"Is it always like this traveling with you two?" Naomi asks. "How are we going to go on any rides tomorrow? Can you wear some kind of disguises?"

"That's why I booked the VIP experience," Rafe says, "that and the endless fast passes."

The elevator dings, letting us out into a blessedly empty hallway.

"What does that mean?" I ask, excitedly. I've heard rumors about celebs getting special treatment at Disneyland, but it seems to be cloaked in secrecy.

"Well, you know my friend Zara Jones?" Rafe asks.

I roll my eyes. "Yeah, I've heard of her."

"Weren't you all in the same films together?" Naomi glances back over her shoulder.

"Right," Rafe says. "Well, Zara is a huge Disney nerd. She comes here all the time. Has a Club 33 Membership. She helped me make plans. We'll have a cast member escorting us around for most of the day, and they will direct us to VIP entrances so we don't have to wait in line."

"No lines at all?" Naomi raises her eyebrows, looking impressed.

"Nope. And there are a few other things, but I don't want to ruin the surprises. I also made reservations for lunch and dinner."

The bellhop stops in front of a deluxe suite, with primitive masks flanking the doorway.

"This is it," he says, "the Adventureland Suite. Have you stayed with us here before?"

"No," Rafe says. "This is our first time."

"Okay, I guess I'll just check in with you guys in the morning, if you want to point me to my room," I say.

"Don't be silly, Lorelei. The suite sleeps five people. Rainey has her own room just down the hall. The four of us will fit in here just fine." Rafe hands his keycard to the bellhop, who swipes it to open the door.

"It's my favorite one of the themed suites," the bellhop says. "Let's start with the first bedroom."

He leads us into a bedroom that's been tented with white canvas. It's what I would call safari chic. There's a double bed and an en suite bathroom, and every last detail, from the dresser that looks like a steamer trunk, to the base, camp-style desk and mirror are perfect. The only thing missing are the elephants outside.

"It's styled to look like a 1930s' safari camp," the bellman tells us, then he notices the sleeping toddler on Rafe's shoulder and retrieves the porta-crib from the cart. "Looks like someone's ready to hit the hay. Where would you like me to set this up?"

"Hmm. Well, Mom, I assumed that you'd take the safari bedroom. We can put Orly in the living room or in my room."

"Don't be silly. Set up her bed in the room with me!" Naomi insists.

"Are you sure, Ima? She's likely to wake you up early," Rafe says.

"I'd love the company. I keep waking at 5 a.m." Naomi yawns again and turns to the bellman. "Just set it up in here."

"I'll wait while he sets it up. Hand her here." Rainey peels the slumbering child off her father.

"Thanks, Rainey. Be sure to tip the bellman before you go?" Rafe says quietly, slipping her a bill.

"Umm ... what about me? Where should I put my stuff?" I ask, as we walk back out to the spacious living room with Naomi. There's a large dining room table and a generous seating area, but unless this suite has a secret door to a third bedroom somewhere, I'm not exactly sure where I'm supposed to sleep.

"Well, there is a secret room in this suite." Rafe's eyes twinkle, as if he's read my mind. He presses on a bookcase, and it opens to reveal a small closet. Super cool, but no bed.

I blink, confused.

"I'm just messing with you. You're bunking in the master suite with me," says Rafe, his face impassive.

"Bunk as in bunk beds?"

"The master suite is pretty amazing, but I'm pretty sure it does not include bunk beds." Rafe chuckles. "Come, let's go check it out. I watched a video online, but I don't think it did this place justice."

I can feel my face growing hot. "Is that really appropriate? I mean ... maybe I can park myself on this couch?" I pat the tufted leather couch in front of the fireplace. *I've slept in worse places.* And then I notice that there's a daybed in an alcove, tucked off to one side.

"Oh, I'll just put my stuff here," I say.

"Are you nuts, Lorelei? You don't want to have to sleep in the middle of the living room. There's no privacy. And what if I want to come out here and play with Orly in the morning?" Naomi looks at me with raised eyebrows.

"Well, I mean, I don't want to—"

Naomi rolls her eyes and sits down on the couch. "Come on, Lorelei. You and Rafe are adults, and you've been friends since you were children. I'm not some Amish prude. I'm not doing bed checks."

"We can request a rollaway if you're afraid of getting cooties from me." Rafe's eyes are sparkling. "But if we do that, I'm not sure where I'd put the porta-crib if Orly decides she doesn't want to stay in the room with my mom. Just come see."

Rafe pulls me into the master suite, which is even more over the top than the other two rooms, if that's possible. There's a giant, four-poster bed with flowy, white curtains and luxurious, exotic, vintage details everywhere. Oriental carpets, zebra-print pillows, pith helmets, and faux antlers on the wall. It's like we've been transported to the veld.

"It's just two nights. And it's a really big bed. Bouncy." Rafe bounces on the edge of the bed to demonstrate.

"There's a tub in here!" I exclaim. "A proper slipper tub. My friend Georgia has one of these, and I have always been so jealous of her."

"The shower is so big, they call it a grotto!" Rafe comes over to examine the tub. He stands close behind me and leans forward, reaching for the tap and turning it on. "Can I run you a bath?"

"Jesus, Rafe." I turn to face him, and he doesn't budge. If anything, he leans closer. I notice the way his chest rises and falls with each breath. I feel the heat of his body in the charged space between us. It's electric. Like ... a bug zapper. And like a bug, I feel compelled to fling myself closer. Into his bright, bright light.

"What's happening here?" I whisper.

"Nothing, unless ..." he says, trailing a finger along my jawbone.

"Unless?" I breathe the question. His hand comes to rest on my chin, cupping it with the lightest pressure possible, like he's holding a soap bubble on the tip of his finger. I close my eyes, savoring his nearness with all my other senses.

"Unless you want it to." His answer sizzles and pops like static between us, waking all the butterflies in my stomach.

I raise my hand to his face, mirroring his actions. "Do you want it to?"

The spell is broken when the sound of a hundred tiki drums bursts from hidden speakers. We both jump at least six inches in the air. "That's the doorbell," Rafe lets me know. He closes his eyes and takes a breath before reaching for my hand and planting a kiss in my palm.

"Don't worry, it's just the luggage. I got it!" Naomi calls out. A moment later, she pokes her head in the door. She pauses when she notices the water in the tub still running.

"It's okay, you can come in," Rafe says. "We were just testing the water." He closes the tap.

"Do you want the good news or the bad news first?" Naomi asks.

"Good news," Rafe replies.

"The rest of the luggage is here," Naomi says, "so I was thinking I would go to bed."

"Okay, and the bad news?"

"Abba!" a tearful Orly runs into the room, trailed by the nanny. "I scared! I wanna sleep with you!"

"I can take her back to my room," Rainey says. "I'm sorry the doorbell woke her."

"No, Rainey, you get some sleep. It's going to be a long day tomorrow." Rafe scoops Orly up, and she looks around, her big eyes taking in all the details of the unfamiliar room. As sleepy as she was earlier, she is wide awake now.

"Ooooh! Abba! I take baff?" she asks, pointing at the tub.

lorelei

. . .

I SPEND the next few hours systematically going through all the photo albums in the console, hoping against hope that I'll find more pictures of our adoption journey. But other than the three photos I've laid out on the table, there's nothing. Birthday parties and Christmas trees. Missing teeth and chickenpox. Kenna's mom in a chemo cap. Awkward tweenager years in braces and some truly regrettable Halloween costume choices. *Was there really nobody to stop Kenna from dressing up as a human-size hot dog?*

Kenna's entire childhood is here, in these albums. And for the most part, it's so normal. So full of Girl Scout picnics and sleepovers and bake sales and all the sorts of things I never got to do.

It's a total invasion of privacy, but I go upstairs looking for more albums. I check closets and drawers. But there's nothing. When I notice the shoeboxes full of old drawings and other memories in the cabinets in the garage, I have to go through them, too. It takes hours to go through all the boxes. I can't be bothered to carry it all in, so I sit there, sorting, on the cold, cement garage floor. Christmas and holiday cards, postcards, and report cards dating back two and a half decades.

I read through the comments on Kenna's report cards, praising her character before recommending that she apply herself more to learning how to read, or seek a more remedial classroom. I'm angry again on her behalf. There's nothing slow about Kenna. So she has dyslexia? So many people do. I'm irked even more, reading the notes from her elementary school IEP plan that reads "possible delays due to early institutionalization in orphanage."

She was barely six months old when she was adopted. I wonder if her schools were using her history to cover up their inability to deal with a common learning difference.

I get so wrapped up in the school stuff that I almost miss the familiar holiday card sandwiched in one of the stacks. But it slips to the floor as I sift. I recognize the photo from my own childhood mantel. Up till now, I've thought of it as one of the very first photos of me, even though, now that I think of it, this photo was taken at least six months after the momager brought me home.

I bring the holiday card inside and lay it beside three other pictures on the coffee table, marveling at the transformation that took place in those six months. I don't even look like the same child as the one in the orphanage pictures. My skin is no longer sallow, and my rash is gone. My cheeks have filled out, and the bald patch has filled in. Hard to tell for sure because there's a giant bow on my head, but my hair looks thick and glossy, falling in strawberry-blonde ringlets. Just a little bit lighter than it is now.

Possibly the most striking difference, though, is that both my mother and I are smiling in the photo. Matching flash-bulb-,brilliant smiles.

Impulsively, I rip the photo in half, a decision that delivers remorse at the same lightning speed as the anger that made me do it. Too late, I notice there's a note on the back of the card.

Tears streaming down my face, I carry the card to the kitchen. I already know where the tape is, having found it while searching the drawers earlier.

Carefully, I piece the card back together, doing my best to mend the damage. Smoothing down the tape, I'm relieved to find that I am still able to make out most of the message on the back.

"We think of you still. Don't know how we would have made it through that week without you guys. Send love to your brother. Lorelei still eats Fruity Pebbles as a special treat. I hope your sweet baby brings you as much joy as my daughter brings me. Let's stay in touch."

Except they hadn't. Why hadn't they?

I clean up the mess I've made, locking the door behind me, and carry my treasure back to Kenna's apartment over the garage. I'm shocked to discover how late it is—almost 10 p.m. —but I'm not even hungry. I want to call someone and talk this through. But who to call?

I ponder this while I locate trash bags under the sink and clean up the evidence of my taco gluttony.

I can't call Georgia. I just don't know her well enough, and she's Kenna's friend.

Rafe is out. He's in Cali with Kenna. And Kenna? Bless her heart, she would probably insist on jumping on the next flight back here. Like me, she'd want to check the DNA results right now. Which actually might be better than sitting here, staring at all this new information alone.

But then I think of the photos of toothless Kenna in a Cinderella costume, and something tells me to wait. *Let her have this Disney trip.*

Calling Noah is also out of the question. I mean, boning him would definitely take my mind off this stuff, but visions of sweet, helpless, toothless, little Kenna float across my consciousness like a screensaver that's been set up by Jiminy fucking Cricket. I did sort of promise her there'd be no boning.

She better not be doing it with Rafe right now. It just seems unfair if I'm the only one suffering.

My phone lights up with a notification, and I snatch it up, hopeful that it will be a text from someone I can vent to. But it's just a coupon for alpaca socks from a brand that I love.

I delete the message, and the ones below it from Kenna and Tabitha. Then I come to the message I woke up to this morning.

Happy Gotcha Day, Lorelei.

I know who I need to call. The one and only person who can help me make sense of this.

There's a bottle of bourbon in the cabinet, and I pour myself a shot before I dial the number on the text. It's still familiar. The same number she had fifteen years ago. It hasn't changed. Before calling, I snap a photo of the pictures I've swiped and shoot them back to her in a text.

I drain my glass and punch in the number.

"Lorelei?" She picks up on the second ring, sounding breathless, "is that really you?"

"Did I wake you?"

"No, honey. I was just looking at some auditions," she says. My mother is still a manager, representing highly trained talent. Just not of the human variety. Now she's pushing poodles.

"Did you see my text?" I ask. I picture her sitting in her bed with a stack of folders beside her, a thick layer of anti-wrinkle cream on her face.

"No, I was working on the laptop. Let me check. I'll put you on speaker. God, it's so good to hear your voice. Don't hang up?" I hear her shut the laptop and wait patiently, trying to picture her face. Her reaction.

I am not disappointed. She gasps.

"Good Lord, Lorelei! Where did you find these photos?"

"So they are me," I reply.

"Of course they are. My God, I didn't think there were any photos like this out there."

"Well, surprise! You didn't manage to destroy all the evidence," I say bitterly. "Backstories have a way of bubbling up, you know."

"Destroy the evidence? What are you talking about?" she stammers.

"You know, until recently, I thought that stupid holiday card picture was the first photo you ever took of me," I say.

"What holiday card?" she asks.

"The one on the mantel? With the stupid bow? I was what, three?"

"I love that photo of you. You looked gorgeous in that shoot." My mother sounds hurt.

"I'm assuming that's why that photo made it into my portfolio, and these other ones didn't?"

"That's not it at all," my mom argues. I can picture her steeling herself to argue, then taking a deep breath before yelling at me. But she doesn't yell. She speaks quietly. "You're wrong, Lorelei."

"Then why aren't you smiling in the group shot? Did you have buyer's remorse once you got to Siberia? All these other people look happy, Mom. You look like you just choked on your fish oil capsules."

"Honestly, Lorelei." She sounds sad now. Sad and tired. "It was something kind of like that. I was freaking out. But not really because of you. Because of me. I was so seriously overwhelmed. In over my head. Totally convinced that they'd made a mistake in letting me take you home. You were *miserable* with me. Crying nonstop. Nobody prepared me for that. I don't know what I would have done without that nice lady and her brother. Honestly? I think you would have preferred to go home with them."

"Is that why you didn't take any photos of me? Because you weren't sure you were going to keep me?" I'm not certain when the tears started rolling down my face. "Did the agency give you a warranty on defective merchandise?"

"Lorelei, are you even *listening* to me? I felt like you didn't want to keep ME. You know, it wasn't that much of a shock to me when you emancipated yourself. It's like I'd been waiting for you to kick me to the curb and get on with your life already for all those years." Her voice cracks, and I can hear she is crying, too.

"I don't believe you," I say. "You were always ashamed of my being adopted. You didn't take any photos. You didn't want anyone to know. You were embarrassed. Just admit it."

"I wasn't embarrassed! I just didn't think it was anyone's business. You don't know how it was back then. There were all these news stories all the time about the effects of early institutionalization. Movies about possessed orphans. There was a stigma. Kids were discriminated against. I just wanted you to have a normal childhood."

"What about being a celebrity is normal?" I spit out.

"Do you have any idea how lucky you were?" my mom cries.

"Why, because you *saved* me? Is this where you tell me about how great you are because you plucked me out of obscurity and made me a star? Did it ever occur to you to ask me how I felt about any of it?"

"You have a huge talent, Lorelei. That's why you're lucky. Your luck has nothing to do with me and everything to do with you. It always has. You've always been driven, charismatic, and determined. And empathetic. Even as a baby. I watched you wrestle a bully twice your size to win back a toy that one of the babies in our group had dropped. Actually, I think it was that baby in the photo. You were so attached to her."

"Well, she was *my* baby," I say with primal certainty. I don't quite remember it, but the minute I looked at the photo, I just knew what I'd been feeling in that moment. I felt the hollow tearing at the threat of separation. The sense of *everything* being taken from me. If I'd been able to shoot fireballs out of my eyes, I would have. That baby was *mine*.

"Have you found her? I always wondered what happened to that family. I sent them Christmas cards every year, but after the first year, they always came back, return to sender," my mom says. "I sure would have loved to have had those photos. The few photos that I took were destroyed by the X-ray machines on the way home."

"Wait ... you took photos?" I ask. This is the first I've heard of it. "Why didn't you say?"

"No use crying over spilled milk. I really didn't take many, and they probably weren't very good. I thought it might have been some kind of divine intervention, saving us from reliving bad memories. I just wanted to get you home and start making better ones."

"I would have liked to have had those photos," I say quietly.

"Me, too." My mother sighs. "I know now that I was wrong. And not just about that stuff."

We both sit silently for a few seconds.

"I'd love to hear what you're up to, if you ever want to talk about it," my mom says, tentatively. Shyly. "I'm still your biggest fan, Lorelei. Literally. President of the Moxie McAllister Official Fan Club."

"That is so embarrassing, Mom," I groan. "Why? Why do you still do that stuff?"

"Because I'm proud of you. I was then, and I am now. Even more now, I think. I can't take any credit for your work these days, but I can still be proud. You are an artist."

I rock on the bed. This train has just crossed the border into Ugly Cry Country, and the snot trail agent is barreling down the aisle to check my papers. I don't have any Kleenex handy. Yesterday's tee is going to have to do. I offer up a silent apology to Kenna and vow to figure out the washing machine in the morning.

Noisily, I blow my nose. On the other end of the conversation, my mom is blowing hers. Probably into a tissue pulled from the decorator box on her nightstand. Or the packet in her purse. Band-Aids, tampons, Kleenex, tic tacs ... my mom was always prepared. If not to deal with emotional fallout, at least to clean up the mess.

"Mom," I say, once I've caught my breath. "Do you know if I have any siblings?"

"No way of knowing, really. As you know, you were abandoned on the church stairs," she says.

Like baby Moses in a basket. She doesn't say this now, but she always used to when I would ask her about my adoption story as a kid.

"Have you gotten any hits from the DNA sites you signed up for?" my mom asks. I brace for the lecture.

"Nothing yet. I know you don't think it's a good idea, but I'm not going to stop looking."

"I think it would be nice for you to have a little more information about your birth family."

"Who are you?" I'm tempted to say.

"I was just talking to Rafe's mom recently, and she was telling me about her daughter's research on the genetic components of Parkinson's, and we were both saying how it's not fair you don't have more to go on."

"Well, I'll be SOL if I ever need a kidney from a family member," I say.

"I'd give my kidney to you, Lorelei. Any time. Say the word."

"Hey Mom," I say, "would you have any interest in coming to the opening night of *A Midsummer Night's Dream* in Ephron next month? I think I can score you some free tickets. No need to donate a kidney."

"I'd love that so much," she says.

kenna

. . .

THE BEAUTIFUL HEAD on the pillow, nestled next to mine when I wake up the next morning, is Rafe Barzilay's. It is attached to his equally beautiful body, which is no less perfect in slumber. Yes, his hair's a little tousled and he's got some stubble. *Cue the loin clench*, but good Lord, he is perfect. Like, Greek-statue perfect. And nice to boot. All my adult life, I've been convinced that hot guys were kind of required to be dicks. And I'll be honest, sometimes it kind of turns me on when they are.

But apparently, it also turns me on when they aren't.

My sleepy mind wanders back to last night. Rafe running the bath. His answer when I asked what was happening. Nothing, unless *I* want it to. And I had wanted to. I mean, who wouldn't want to be naked in a tub with this man? Would he wash me with the same care and attention to detail that he'd summoned when he rubbed on the suntan oil?

A tiny toddler elbow pokes me in the ribs, and I feel Orly reaching for me, her fingers flossing my tee. I fell asleep fully clothed last night, listening to Rafe reading her bedtime stories. He did fantastic voices for every character in her book, of course. What a lucky, lucky little girl to have landed with him.

Except, she hasn't always been so lucky. She lost her mother, after all. Protectively, I curl an arm around her, and she snuggles into me. I inhale the strawberry scent of her fuzzy curls and sigh happily. My eyes are open. But this is a dream. This is like a movie. A Disney one.

I've made a decision to leave all my real life problems back in Ephron. Here in sunny Anaheim, California, they do not exist. I'm putting my worries on silent mode. Tomorrow morning, when I fly home alone on a commercial jet, using my own ID, and make the switch back with Lorelei, I will resume my normal life. But today, I plan to embrace everything about being a celebrity princess. And if that includes embracing my costar, so be it.

"Boker tov." Rafe's eyes flutter open, and he reaches an arm across to push the hair out of my face. I can't possibly look as good as he does in the morning, but the way he's gazing at me makes me feel like I do.

"Stop looking at me like that!" I say, quietly, "and what does Bokehtov mean?"

"Boker = morning, tov = good. And so far, my morning is looking pretty good." Rafe turns onto his side and props himself up on his elbow, still gazing at me and Orly. He pulls the covers up over his daughter a little.

"I thought you said 'bokeh,'" I muse, looking at the soft morning light filtering in from behind the windows.

"What's that?" Rafe asks.

"It's a camera term for when you get a shot with a sharp foreground and a blurry background," I say, thinking to myself that the morning light filtering in through the windows behind Rafe would make for one hell of a buttery background. If only I had my camera. I take a mental picture instead, zooming in on his face, framed by his tousled hair. His neck and shoulders are bare. He must have taken off his tee before he fell asleep. The taut muscles contrast with the wrinkled spill of white sheets.

"Speaking of cameras ..." Rafe turns away and reaches under the bed, pulling out a large, gold gift tote. "I got you a little something." I cannot move without waking Orly, so he tilts the tote forward to show me the contents.

I gasp.

It's not the Sony camera I wanted. It's the one that's two models up. At least twenty-five hundred dollars more, and that's not counting the two extra lenses that are also in the bag.

"Rafe, I don't know what to say. I can't accept that," I stammer.

"Kenna, I looked up all your work on the shelter's page, and I checked out your landing page as well. You are extremely talented. You have a way of capturing things so naturally and authentically. I know that's hard. Anyone can take a picture of people or flowers or a stunning view. It's a rare artist who really *sees* things in motion and 3D. More than that, your images show off the subjects' souls. They capture moments and tell stories. I want to invest in that, in *you*, and your work as a photographer. I believe in you."

I blink a few times. Rafe Barzilay looked at my site. He thinks these things about me?

He sits up and swings his legs over the side of the bed, turning his back to me as he stretches. I watch his back muscles ripple and tense, then unlock. My hands ache to reach out and touch them. I want to feel him moving under my palms. I want him to keep talking.

"Any chance I can hire you to write the copy for my site, Rafe?"

Rafe looks back over his shoulder at me and grins. "I am not ... what is the expression?" His forehead furrows as he thinks. "Blowing smoke up your butt?"

"Up your skirt!" I laugh.

"Oh, right. Well, I like butt better." He winks and stands up, walking a few feet to look out the window. "And I will admit, I have selfish motives. Today is going to be magical, and I want as many photos as possible, so you'll be doing me a favor. Orly will only have this 'first' once. You can never take too many photos of this stuff"—he pauses—"in my opinion."

"My mom felt the same way," I say. "She was always taking a million photos, most of them awful, but I am so glad that I have all the old albums now."

"I wish I had more photos from my childhood." Rafe stands and walks to look out the window. "The real ones. Not the posed family shots and press photos."

"What do you see out there?" I ask, watching him lean forward to look out the window.

"We have a great view of the pool. It's Mickey-shaped. Orly would love it."

"It's too bad there's not enough time to go swimming." I sigh.

"Next time," Rafe says. And then he pulls on a tee. "I'm going to go scare up some coffee for us and see who else is up. Can I get you anything else?"

"No, I'm good," I say, snuggling back down into the comfy bed with Orly, who now has a foot jammed into my tummy. "I'm good."

So good.

"To wig or not to wig?" I say, holding up the wig in front of me.

I'm standing with Naomi in the bathroom off her bedroom. We are both putting the final touches on our Disneybounding outfits. Our tour guide is due to meet us any minute now, and it's the moment of truth. I've got to decide. I've tried texting Lorelei for what she wants me to do, but she is not answering texts. I can see her phone is set to silent. I can only hope it's not because she's with Noah Greenberg.

Seriously. *Noah?*

I shake my curls in the mirror. I love what the stylist at the spa did with the trim and keratin. My curls are shinier and bouncier than I've ever seen them. And the facial I got seems to have worked some magic as well. My skin is perfectly clear and glowing. Even my eyes are sparkling. Perhaps it's spending so much time around Rafe. His glow is contagious.

"If you ask me, I think you should be yourself," Naomi says. "It's ridiculous for your agent and your manager to ask you to keep up this facade of being someone who, on your own time, you are clearly not, Lorelei. You need to put your foot down and quit living your life for other people."

Naomi somehow manages to look chic and pulled together, even when Disneybounding as the fairy godmother. She is wearing a simple, pale-blue, cotton trapeze top over a pair of capri-length, white leggings. A lightweight, lavender cardigan and hot-pink scarf, tied in a bow, complete the look.

"I say, leave the wig in the room and wear the hat and sunglasses without it. You'd be hot and uncomfortable all day in the wig. Plus, nobody is expecting you to be blonde."

She's right, of course. I glance at my phone one more time and make the executive decision to toss the wig back in its case. It wouldn't have gone with my Aurora ensemble anyway. I'm wearing a silky, pink minidress with a gold vest, matching pink trainers, and pink-and-gold sunglasses. A pink sleep mask as a makeshift headband, and I'm good to go.

"We're ready!" Naomi announces as she walks into the living room where Rafe, Rainey, and the plaid-vested tour guide are waiting. Her badge tells us she is Poppy from the UK, and when she greets us, she speaks in a posh accent, just like Mary Poppins.

"We're going to have a spectacular day," Poppy says, smiling. "I'm here to see to it that everything goes smoothly and that you have a magical experience. I'll be sharing tips, tricks, park history, and secrets throughout the day. Does anyone have any questions? Shall we do introductions first? Is this Princess Tiana?"

Orly, who is wearing a Tiana costume, smiles shyly. Her hair is brushed and in a simple ponytail, but Rafe has told me one of the first stops today will be at the Bibbidi Bobbidi Boutique salon where a stylist will offer to glam Orly up with some proper princess hair, complete with glitter.

Rafe is the most casual and the most surprising member of our party. He is wearing mirrored sunglasses and a Titanium Man baseball cap, along with a too-tight Titanium Man tee emblazoned with a plasticky image of the costumed hero. For added effect, he has on a tacky, silver chain with a large Titanium Man medallion. Even his belt buckle is self-branded.

"You're really going out like *that*?" his mother says. "You look like a cheesy walking ad. It's hardly inconspicuous."

"Yeah, I know it seems like that, but it's like click bait," Rafe says, smiling slyly. "You know how you tune it out and scroll by superfast? The more I lean into the brand, the less people see me. They just think I'm a super-annoying poser and paint me out. Trust me. Reverse psychology." He taps his head. "Works every time."

I have to laugh. "That is absolutely brilliant."

"You decided not to wear the wig?" Rafe asks.

"I did," I say.

"Good. I like your natural hair. Much better than a disguise." Rafe nods approvingly. "And I like your outfit, too." His eyes rake over me, giving me the distinct impression that he isn't only talking about my clothes.

"And what about me?" Naomi asks, doing a slow twirl.

"You make an excellent fairy godmother," Poppy says. "Did I get that right?"

"You got it," Naomi beams and waves her cell phone like a magic wand. "Now, let's go make some magic before we all turn back into pumpkins."

lorelei

. . .

I TRY on at least a dozen outfits, trying to get ready for the *DND* session at Noah's. I want to get it right. Of course, that's not easy when I have no idea what my character will be. All I know is that Noah is planning to assign one of the NPCS (non-player characters) from his story to me. These are characters that are already in the story, but don't have anyone acting them out. I hope I'm going to get a good one.

I decide to choose an outfit that's suitably Ren Faire without being too specifically elven or healer.

There's not a lot to choose from in Kenna's closet. Her clothes are all so *boring*. There are only so many ironic tees a girl can wear. I don't have much choice. I'm going to have to sacrifice some of her housewares for the cause. I get out the scissors and get to work transforming some black, plastic placemats and bootstrings into a lace-up corset that I try on over a cleverly draped and pinned bedsheet. Theater camp costume design class for the win!

I waffle over whether or not to make myself elf ears out of a vaguely flesh-toned silicone trivet. In the end, I put the trivet back in the drawer. I don't want to seem thirsty. I simply apply some deep-red lipstick and black eyeliner and call it a day.

———

There's a black Sprinter van with tinted windows parked in the driveway and a few cars parked on the street. But other than that, you'd never know that magic is about to happen inside Noah's house. I can't wait to see how he does it.

When I ring the doorbell, a techie answers the door. He takes the bag of muffins I'm clutching from me and leads me to the stairs to the basement.

"First time, huh?" he asks.

"Do I look like a total *DND* virgin? Does it show?" I ask anxiously.

"I meant on the show," he laughs.

Noah may be practical in his everyday life, but when it comes to Max Mercury's dungeon, no expense has been spared. This is next level. High-end, velvet curtains and realistic-looking, fake stone walls add to the production value. Expensive video cameras line the walls, ready to capture the action from every angle.

The intricately carved, wooden table needs its own zip code. It already has its own Instagram account. There's no other table like it. The base and sides are carved to look like the body and wings of a dragon. The tail snakes up and over the surface, holding an elaborate, crystal chandelier aloft. I don't think I've ever seen a table with a tail before!

And finally, the dragon's back is the playing surface. This is where the real action happens. It's a glossy, polished surface, covered with dozens of tiny, painted men and elaborately crafted pieces of fake battle terrain.

Chills.

I feel shy just standing here. At least a dozen people are rushing around, prepping for the session. Noah has traded the trekking pole for a wooden wizard's staff. He's wearing his black, velvet robes, which are imprinted with iridescent dragon scales, but he hasn't put on the dragon masque yet. He's standing at the head of the table beside a Lucite throne that is much taller than it is wide, actively chastising a girl in blue body paint. She has pointy ears and brightly colored eye contacts that give her the illusion of heterochromia. And she's inhaling cold-looking Pad Thai straight out of a Styrofoam container.

"I told you to eat before you came this time, Raven!"

"Not my fault—the delivery guy took forever!" she argues.

"You have sixty seconds to finish, and then it's going in the trash," Noah warns. I feel a thrill when he turns his head my way, noticing me. He waves and points me to a large, carved, wooden chair beside his throne before running off to have one last word with the techie.

I take my seat, shyly checking out the rest of the players, most of whom I recognize. Aside from Raven, the ravenous elf, there's Ira, the healer, and Perenthius, the bureaucrat. That dude's a total stickler for the rules. Rounding out the party, I spy Shagg, the horny bard. He keeps trying to get it on with tree nymphs, but rolling ones. This is a recurring theme every season. It never ends well for him.

"Kenna!" Noah's eyes light up when he comes over to give me a hug.

"What do you think?" he asks.

"I think I can't believe I'm here," I grin.

"It's almost time to start." Noah reaches under the table for a large, black, velvet box. "Are you ready to do this?" He opens the box, and I catch my first glimpse of the dragon masque. I'm blown away by how highly detailed and perfect it is!

"I think I'm ready," I nod.

"Buckle up!" he says, lowering the masque over his head. When he does this, everyone in the basement studio begins to clap.

When Noah turns toward me again, his catlike dragon eyes are flashing red at me. I can't help myself. I reach up to feel his scales but he leans away, smoke shooting out of his nostrils.

"No touching without consent," he warns loudly.

All the other players stare at me in shock.

"Did she just try to pet Max?" Raven asks Shagg.

"Yeah, I think she did," Shagg nods.

"He must really be into her," Raven says. "He never lets anyone drop in like this."

"You know everyone can hear you. Including Max and the new girl," says Ira. She reaches out to pat my hand.

Noah doesn't say anything. He just stares the players down, red eyes blazing. That's when I realize that Noah is not really Noah anymore.

I can feel the dragon's red eyes on me as I retrieve my glass dice from the velvet, amulet pouch resting in my cleavage. A virgin set. I've had them for years, but I have been saving them for my first time. My hands are shaking.

"Now is the time. And this is the place," Max growls at the players.

He passes me a character sheet describing my character's strengths and weaknesses. My mouth falls open in disbelief.

"Don't worry," Max purrs when he sees my alarmed expression. "I promise I'll be gentle with you today."

kenna

. . .

POPPY GOES over our list of "must do" experiences as we ride directly into the park in a private car in the monorail.

Rafe says he wants to go on all the rides that are not roller coasters, and Naomi, who follows the Disney Food Blog, is determined to taste as many famous treats as possible, starting with the churros.

For Orly, we check off Small World, Peter Pan, and a handful of character experiences. Most importantly, she wants to meet Rey.

"What about you, Ms. Dupont?" Poppy asks.

"I'm okay with whatever," I confess. "I'm just so happy to be here today."

I take out the new camera and snap a few photos of Orly looking out the monorail windows, and Naomi looking at her. When I lower the camera, I feel Rafe's eyes on me. He reaches out to squeeze my hand.

"Thank you," he mouths. The sunlight catches on his diamond-studded, Titanium Man medallion. He's right. It's like the cheap, plastic handles that signal a designer handbag is a fake. It's just awful. There's no way the REAL Rafe Barzilay would be caught dead in such a tacky necklace. Is there? I bite my lip.

"What?" Rafe smiles back at me and glances down over his sunglasses. "Do you have a problem with my ensemble?"

"Not at all, Titanium Man, not at all," I say and turn the camera on him, snapping several photos of him laughing before we pull into the station in Fantasyland.

By noon, we've ridden on every ride in Fantasyland except for the Matterhorn, Tea Cups, and Star Tours.

"The Matterhorn looks too fast," Rafe says, shaking his head. "And I don't want Orly to get dizzy."

"I don't believe it," I reply. "You're chicken!"

"I am not!" Rafe argues.

"He is." Naomi rolls her eyes. "He's always been super cautious. Such a goody-goody. You, of all people, know that, Lorelei."

"But he does do a lot of his own stunts," I say, defending him to his mother. I really don't like it when she picks on him.

"Well, there's usually a safety harness and a green screen involved. It's a matter of pride." Rafe puffs his chest out.

"A lot of our guests enjoy the Thunder Mountain roller coaster," Poppy mentions. "It's a smooth ride, and there aren't any loops. I think we have time for a couple more attractions before lunch. Maybe that one and Pirates of the Caribbean? We can swing by on our way to Blue Bayou. Your reservations are for one o'clock."

"I've always wanted to go on Big Thunder!" I admit. "I want to try to spot the goat!"

"So you've heard about the goat trick?" Poppy's eyes twinkle at me, and I feel like I just earned a gold star as she turns to explain to the group. "Billy the Goat is a beloved fixture at all the Disney parks. The rumor is that if you stare at Billy as you pass, it makes the ride feel much, much faster."

"Well, that sounds like fun," Naomi says. "I'd hate for Lorelei to miss it."

"Want to ride with me, Naomi?" I ask hopefully.

"Oh, I can't. Bad back. I'm so sorry." Naomi declines with a wave.

"I don't suppose Orly could ride that one with you?" Rafe suggests.

"I'm afraid not," Poppy says, shaking her head sadly. "There's a height requirement. We don't recommend it for our guests under five years of age."

"Rafe, you aren't going to make Lorelei ride alone, are you?" Naomi pokes her son in the ribs.

I can see Rafe's jaw clenching. "Of course not. I'll go."

"Are you sure?" I ask. "I can skip it. It's not a big deal."

"I'm sure," he nods gravely, flexing and unflexing his hands into fists. He inhales sharply, taking a long, deep breath. "How bad can a ride be if they let five-year-olds ride it?"

"You'll be fine," Poppy says cheerfully. "Just don't look at the goat."

———

"What happened?" Rainey asks when she and the rest of our group meet at the benches near the exit to the ride.

"I just need one more minute." Rafe holds up a finger. He has his head between his knees.

"He looked at the goat," I whisper. I also looked at the goat, but unlike Rafe, I didn't have a problem with it. I loved every second of that ride.

"Should I call for a medic?" Poppy is pale and looks worried.

"I thought she said *not* to look at the goat?" Naomi asks confusedly.

"I did," Poppy nods emphatically. "I most certainly said *not* to look at the goat if you are prone to motion sickness."

"Can I try something?" I ask, kneeling in front of him. He nods, and I place a finger on either side of his neck, just behind his ears, and press.

"This should just take two minutes," I say. "Want me to tell you a story while we wait?"

"How about I tell you one instead?" Rafe mumbles.

"Sure, go for it." I shift my weight to the balls of my feet and apply steady, firm pressure to the pressure points on either side of his neck, just below the ears.

"There once was a very foolish man, who wanted to impress a very beautiful woman," Rafe says. I feel him relax a bit, and he raises himself up slightly and sighs. "Thank you, I think that's working. Where did you learn that?"

"I used to do it for my mom when she was going through chemo. She got the spins really bad."

"Mmm," Rafe says. He's breathing more steadily.

"Are you going to finish that story?" I ask, giving a nod to Naomi, Rainey, and Poppy when they point at a nearby churro cart. I can smell the scent of cinnamon sugar surfing on the gentle, Cali breeze.

"Well," Rafe says, "this foolish man didn't want the woman to know he'd never been on a roller coaster before, due to his tendency to suffer from vertigo."

"*Never?*" I ask.

"Never." He nods slightly and sits up a little straighter.

"Wow." I marvel at this information. "But that doesn't explain why you looked at the goat."

"Well, *you* were looking at the goat." Rafe moves his head tentatively and straightens more. I have to scoot closer to keep up the pressure. I wobble, and he catches me by the shoulders, hunching forward toward me again.

"Don't stop just yet. That's magic, right there. Where were you when I had to do a scene on a zipline?"

"Making coffee at the diner, probably." I smile sympathetically, waiting another thirty seconds to release the pressure. "Better now?"

Rafe turns his head slowly from side to side before glancing back to look me in the eye. "Wow. Completely better. Thank you." He tugs at my shoulders, pulling me closer, and for a moment, I think he's going to kiss me.

Then I get the uncanny feeling that we're being filmed, and freeze.

"I think our cover may be blown here," I say, peering over my shoulder.

"Ten o'clock," Rafe nods in agreement.

Sure enough, there's a girl over by the churro cart, just a few feet away from the rest of our party, holding her phone up like she's taking a selfie. Except, I'm willing to bet she isn't. She's pretending poorly, and the phone is angled all wrong. It's pointed at us.

"The damage is probably already done, you know." Rafe is still staring intently at me.

I do wish he hadn't put it that way. *Damage.* As if something's been broken. But he's right. Things have shifted. The rules have changed. And it's getting harder and harder to pretend that's not the case. Especially when I'm already pretending to be someone I'm not.

"There's no going back," I agree.

"I don't want you to go back," Rafe says. And then he leans forward and kisses me in public.

Except Rafe isn't kissing *me*. Not really. In the eyes of anyone and everyone watching, the rumors about Titanium Man and his costar, Lorelei, have finally been confirmed.

That's a tomorrow problem, Kenna.

Naomi clears her throat, interrupting the kiss. She's not actually succeeding at suppressing her grin. "Well, well. This is quite a surprise. You seem to be doing much better, Rafe."

The rest of the morning flies by in a blur. Rainey takes Orly back to the hotel room for her lunch and a nap, while we head to our own meal.

Lunch at Blue Bayou transports us to a Southern plantation patio on a warm, summer evening. The sounds of glasses clinking and crickets chirping a serenade make it convincing. I have the hardest time choosing what I want off the menu, so

Rafe insists we order a couple of extra entrées to split and share, so we can all get to taste more items.

"I'm surprised you didn't tell us what to order," Naomi says as we rotate plates under the swaying lanterns. "You're usually so decisive with a menu."

"It doesn't hurt to try something new," Rafe says, as he slices a bit off a Monte Cristo sandwich and feeds it to me.

"Of course not. I like all this newness. In fact, I'd like to propose a toast to it." Naomi raises her glass.

After a leisurely lunch, we do some shopping in the boutiques, and Rafe has all the purchases sent directly back to the room, so there's nothing to carry.

When Rainey and Orly return, Poppy arranges for us to watch the parade in a special, roped-off, VIP viewing area. Afterward, Orly is treated to a unique, private, character meet and greet with all her favorite *Star Wars* characters. She suddenly becomes shy when she meets Rey. The photo op becomes a group shot when she refuses to get her picture taken unless Rafe and I flank her, holding her hands.

Throughout the day, I snap pictures—some posed, but mostly candids. Naomi clutching a bunch of balloons. Orly's hand trailing outside the stroller, catching bubbles. Rafe holding a massive, dripping ice cream outside the shop on Main Street. I only wish there was a way to capture the sweet, waffle-cone scent that lured us in.

We all get Mickey ears and decide that the Jungle Cruise will be our last attraction of the day.

"I could get used to this no-lines thing. I'm not sure how I'll ever come back here with your sisters," Naomi says, as Poppy escorts us to a private boat.

"You know who stands in line, Ima?" Rafe asks.

She looks blank for a second, then narrows her eyes, sensing the trap. "Who?" she says warily.

"Neurosurgeons and rocket scientists," Rafe tuts.

"Don't forget the philanthropists and climate change experts," I add.

Naomi smiles at her son. "You got me. I can see that your fame and fortune does have certain perks. But you know what fills my heart the most and makes me the most proud? Seeing how you've stepped up with Orly. Your father was right, Rafe. Of all my kids, you have the biggest heart."

She turns to look at me. "You should be careful with that."

———

We almost make it out of the park without any incidents. But then, we get cocky. We send Rainey back to the hotel and thank Poppy for her help curating and narrating what has genuinely been a magical day. We make one quick stop at the Starbucks on Main Street for some coffee before leaving the park.

Sitting on a bench near the railroad station, we rest our feet and indulge in some casual people-watching. A crowd has gathered to listen to the Dapper Dans singing an a cappella version of "We Don't Talk About Bruno" from the film *Encanto*. It's one of my favorites. I've made Georgia watch it with me three times!

Orly is dancing around in front of us, filling the air with teeny, tiny bubbles from a battery-powered bubble gun. I get some great shots of her, surrounded by clouds of the sparkling, iridescent orbs.

And then I see him. My eyes do their weird needle-in-a-haystack thing. There's no context at first. Just a sudden send of disruption as I unexpectedly register a familiar face while scanning the crowds. It takes my brain an additional six seconds for context to kick in while I sort out who it is, why they look familiar, and what I'm looking at now.

The same paparazzo that was hanging around the diner last week is here at Disneyland. I do a double take. It's definitely the same guy. And he's got a kid with him. *Why does he have a kid with him? Is she his cover? That seems totally wrong.*

Kid or not, he's clocked us. The big lens is pointed toward us, and it may as well be a laser pointer.

Giant lenses like that always attract attention. Particularly in a crowded area. People notice the lens. Then they notice it's pointed at something, and then they have to look. How can they not? It's only natural to be curious about whatever it is that's worth pointing such expensive optics at.

It happens quickly. So quickly, I don't even have time to say the words. Suddenly, the Dapper Dans are not the main attraction on this plaza. There's an atmospheric change. All around us, people start turning toward us. Phones are being raised. It happens in a wave. Slow and unstoppable. A tsunami.

"Guys ..." I jump up and stuff the camera into my tote, preparing to scoop up Orly and make a run for it, if necessary.

"Ember!" A man with a neck tattoo lunges at me and grabs my arm. "Take a selfie with me, babe." His cell camera is already rolling, streaming live footage to God only knows which platform.

"Get your fucking hands off her!" Rafe is on his feet for about two seconds before the man is down on the ground, clutching his kneecap. The dropped phone is still recording, but the screen is smashed. Rafe stomps his heel into it, cutting the feed.

"Dude, did you see Titanium Man take that guy out?"

"Holy shit! Is this being filmed? Like, are we in a movie right now?"

"Nah, bro, that's not the real Rafe. Or the real Lorelei. Look at her hair."

"Lorelei! Are you and Rafe a couple?"

Rafe puts his arm around me, protectively, and then we both look down at the empty bubble gun lying on the ground. *Orly.*

"Orly!" Naomi is also on her feet, screaming out her granddaughter's name, one hand on the empty stroller, the other shielding her eyes as she frantically scans the gathering crowd.

"Orly!" Rafe bellows, dropping my hand. He jumps up on the bench in an attempt to get a better view.

"Orly!" I call out, taking the stairs up to the train platform, two at a time. I have to get up there so that I can see the whole picture.

I notice the park employees closing in, working around the edges of the crowd, containing some people and redirecting others. The Dapper Dans are gone, and assorted people with walkie-talkies are coming out of the woodwork.

So many people.

My eyes sweep back and forth, searching for a tiny, brown-skinned girl with a sparkly updo in a Rey costume. I should be able to find her. *Quickly.* She has to be here, somewhere. But she isn't. She's not in front of the firehouse, and she's not by the bathrooms. I can't see all the way to the front gate from here, but I am gripped by a sudden wave of nausea, considering the possibility that someone might have grabbed her and made a beeline for the exit turnstiles.

"Do you see her?" Rafe joins me on the platform, frantic.

"No, where's your mom?"

"Speaking to security." Rafe's fists are clenched, and he looks like he's about to leap over the banister parkour style and rain wrath on the crowd till they produce his daughter. "We have to find her. If anyone lays a single finger on her ..."

I ignore him and focus my attention on scanning the crowd in sections, like there is an imaginary grid. I've cleared the three squares to the left and am almost done with the area in the center. I can see pretty far up Main Street, halfway to the castle. The street is blocked. They're not letting anyone pass there.

I move on to the section to the right. And then I see her, over by the hat shop. Not just her. Her and the paparazzo and the other kid. The paparazzo is carrying Orly in one arm and holding the other little girl by the hand, looking around anxiously, like he's not sure what to do.

"There! I point toward the hat shop and the paparazzo. She's there. She's with—"

But Rafe has already leaped over the railing. He's halfway across the plaza before I'm even halfway down the stairs.

————

"I want my bubbles!" Orly, who is now safely strapped in her stroller, is crying.

We're parked in a quiet area near the building by the front of the park, finally away from prying eyes. From what we can gather, Orly took off seconds before the man grabbed me. Her bubble gun had run out of soap, so she ran back toward the hat shop, hoping to get another one.

"It's okay, Hamuda. Savta is going to put more bubble juice in for you, see?" Naomi is holding the bubble gun that Orly dropped in one hand, shakily pouring more soap solution in with the other. "Everything is fine. Savta has your bubbles."

The little girl who was with the paparazzo is sitting on a bench in the shade near Naomi, eating ice cream, waiting while we get things ironed out. The man who grabbed me has been forcibly ejected from the park, and security is deciding what to do about the paparazzo.

"I'm just here for the day. It's my granddaughter's birthday." The paparazzo is explaining his side of the story to the security guard. "I saw the little girl wandering away from her family through my zoom lens. I watched her take off, and then that fight broke out." He shakes his head. "I didn't get any shots of it. I was too busy trying to keep the kid in focus. I almost lost her. But I saw where she was headed, and she was clearly lost. I didn't want anything bad to happen to her, so I followed her."

"Thank you so much for bringing her back," Rafe says, shaking his hand. "I cannot express how grateful I am."

"I get it," the paparazzo says, glancing back at his granddaughter on the bench. "I've been in your shoes, man. Don't beat yourself up. Impossible to have eyes in the back of your head, you know?"

My temper flares. I can't help but think that if the paparazzo hadn't been stalking us in the first place, none of this would have happened.

"This doesn't excuse why you thought it was okay to harass us," I jump in. "Don't you people ever give it a rest?"

"Any other day, you'd be right. I mean, I do like to take pictures of celebs here at Disneyland if I'm here already. The tabloids eat that shit up, and it's worth the price of admission. But not today. Today, I'm off duty. I'm just here for my Ellie. And you want to know what the funniest thing is?" The paparazzo shakes his head and laughs. "I didn't even know who you two were! I swear, I'm losing it. I wasn't taking a photo of you because you're Lorelei Dupont. I was taking a picture of you because you looked like a dead ringer for a friend of mine back up in Washington State. Girl who makes me my coffee by the name of Kenna. You should check out the Ephron Diner. I was trying to get a shot of you to show her." He holds out his camera and toggles through dozens of photos of his granddaughter on rides, ending with two shots of me sitting on the bench.

So basically, he's saying he was trying to get photos of me because I looked like … me.

"You were taking photos of me because I look like your barista?"

"You can check out my camera roll if you don't believe me."

"She must be one hell of a barista." Rafe raises a brow, and I can see a corner of his mouth twitching.

"Oh, yeah. She makes some excellent coffee, although she's been a little off her game for the last week or so. And she's not a fan of my profession. Sent me on a wild goose chase to Vancouver looking for you two."

The security guard raises his eyebrows at all of us and steps away to speak into his radio. He turns back a second later and waves at the paparazzo. "You're free to go, sir."

"Seriously, you didn't take any photos of Rafe?" I toggle back through his roll again, incredulous.

The paparazzo chuckles. "I gotta hand it to you, Rafe. This outfit's pure genius. I was sure you were some kind of weird superfan. Did you get the idea from Elvis? You know, he once lost an Elvis look-alike contest?"

———

Disney's most exclusive private dining experience, 21 Royal, is cloaked in secrecy. The details on the website are vague, which is probably deliberate. You need to call their concierge for more information and to make a booking. Rafe has reserved the experience that is for up to twelve people, but it looks like it will only be the two of us tonight.

"Are you sure you don't want to come with us, Ima?" Rafe asks Naomi again, back at the suite. "I would think this is right up your alley."

"I know. I've read all about it on the food blog. But I promised Orly I would take her to a character dinner, and to be honest, I'm a bit tired." Naomi, who is sitting at the dining table, sifts through her bag. She locates her lipstick, then applies it. It's a sparkling-pink color that we chose from Lorelei's stash. It really complements the fairy godmother vibe that she is still rocking. She has changed into a pale-blue dress that is shot through with silver threads, and she is still wearing the shocking-pink scarf. Orly has dressed for dinner in the brand-new Cinderella costume that we picked up at the shops. She models it for us, and we all clap as she does a little twirl and runs to sit in her grandmother's lap.

"I've got such a hot date tonight," Naomi declares as she squeezes Orly, who has two hands on her grandmother's face. They are staring into each other's eyes, smiling. "You two can keep your fancy dinner. Bring us back a slice of cake, if you remember."

"Do you want to get going?" Rainey has unfolded the stroller, and she tosses Orly's favorite blankie in the bottom, along with an iPad and a coloring book.

"Oh, yes." Naomi stands to go, carrying Orly over to the stroller. "We better get a move on if Orly and I are going to stay awake for this!" She pauses by the door. "We might watch the fireworks afterward, but don't wait on us for anything. Go —enjoy!"

There's a moment of charged awkwardness after Naomi, Rainey, and Orly leave. We're both standing there, achingly aware that, for the first time since we got here, we're alone in the suite. Totally alone.

"Well, we should get ready," Rafe says, unfastening the necklace and removing the gaudy belt buckle and dropping them on the dining room table. He rubs his chin. "I'm going to have to shave again if you don't want to go to the ball with the beast."

I wouldn't mind that one bit.

He leaves me alone in the master suite to get ready while he showers, shaves, and changes in Naomi's room. I'm happy that I packed the pale-gray, satin-and-tulle dress that I found in the back of Lorelei's closet. It's a proper ball gown, like something you would wear to an awards ceremony or a red-carpet event. Tiny, pink, embroidered ribbon roses twine their way across the bodice edging. As I slide the dress over my head, I almost feel like I'm stepping into a costume. I am a princess. The fabric skims over my hips and flows as I shift them side to side.

I clip two rhinestone barrettes in my hair, finger-combing the curls into glamorous, 1940s-style waves. Finally, I apply some mascara and a sheer lipstick. I blot my lips and survey the effect. I hardly recognize myself with makeup.

"I'm ready," Rafe calls out from the living room. "But take your time. We don't have to be there for another forty-five minutes."

"That's okay, I'm ready, too. Be right out!" I call back. Tucking the lipstick and my phone into a tiny, rhinestone bag, I take one last look at myself in the mirror before I go to meet Rafe. I may be impersonating royalty, but in my opinion, he's the real deal.

Rafe is sitting on a leather chair in the living room, scrolling through his phone, when I step out of the master suite. I stand there for a moment, waiting for him to notice me. Finally, he looks up and does a double take. He stands up and slides his phone into his pocket.

"Look at you ..." He stands there staring, marveling at me.

"I clean up okay, I guess," I say, smiling wryly and curtsying.

Rafe is wearing a tuxedo, with a fresh-cut rose in the pocket. Where did that even come from? My eyes drink him in. The black, satin trim on his jacket matches the subtle glow from his hair, which is curling thick and shiny against the collar of his shirt. I catch a whiff of his spicy aftershave and feel like swooning.

"Let me see you. Turn around," he says.

I'm tempted to twirl like Orly, picturing the skirt of my dress flaring and fanning out, but I'm not a little girl anymore, so I spin around more slowly.

"You are a princess," Rafe says. "Truly magnificent." He takes a step closer and holds out a hand. "I almost wish ..." and he lets his voice trail off.

"What?" I ask, feeling rather breathless as he takes my hand.

Rafe pulls me closer and kisses the side of my neck. "I almost wish we didn't have reservations. I'd be perfectly happy with room service right now."

"Well, I wouldn't." I shove him playfully. "I don't know when I'll ever get to dress up like this again, or have a world-famous chef prepare a dinner especially for me."

Rafe sighs.

"Well then, Princess, I suppose we better get going."

———

The atmosphere at 21 Royal is surprisingly mellow. It feels more like having dinner in someone's beautiful, private home than having dinner in a restaurant. A butler serves us classic cocktails in cut-crystal tumblers upon arrival. We wander out onto the balcony to enjoy the drinks and some light snacks while the chef puts the finishing touches on our custom-crafted meal.

"I hope you're hungry," Rafe says, poring over the menu. "There are a lot of courses."

"I'm starving," I say, thanking my lucky stars that I have been blessed with the ability to eat a lot and have an unusually fast metabolism. This is my lucky day. "Tonight, I want to taste everything."

"I love that you have an appetite." Rafe takes one of the hors d'oeuvres off the small plate on the table and feeds it to me, then pops a second one in his own mouth. I close my eyes at the flavor explosion.

"That was intense," I say, moaning a little. "Fig and I think ginger chutney? Sheep's milk cheese? So good."

Rafe swirls the ice in his cocktail. "The night is young. We're just getting started."

When the food arrives, it is served on gold-rimmed dishes at a table laid with sparkling-white linens. I can't help eating just past the point of being full, as well as drinking past the point of being sober. Each course comes with a perfect wine pairing. But it's a pleasant fullness. A delicious buzz. Decadently delicious. Every whimsical morsel seems to have been crafted to surprise and delight. I am a bit sad that Naomi isn't getting to experience it. But not terribly so. I love having Rafe all to myself. His attention is complete and unwavering. We dip effortlessly in and out of conversation, talking and tasting together.

Every so often, Rafe touches me. A brush with his knee. A playful dab with a napkin. A hand on my bare shoulder.

By the time dessert arrives, we have to ask them to pack it up to be taken back to the hotel. Our waiter asks us if we want to retire back to the balcony to view the light show over the water.

"I wish my mom was here to see this," I say, gazing out at the colorful explosion of lights, doubled in the reflections over the water. "She really would have loved this."

"My dad loved everything Disney, too," Rafe says with a smile. "The movies, the music, the parks. Every time we came to the US, he had to come. He was so excited when my sister moved to LA. It was perfect for him. I think he's probably having a great laugh that you got my mother to dress up for our visit."

"She wasn't a fan?" I ask.

"Not as much as he was. But I think she likes coming now because the park holds so many memories."

"I hope your dad and my mom are both watching," I say impulsively.

"Oh, for sure they are," Rafe nods, pointing at Tom Sawyer's Island. "I think that's them up in the tree over there. They have even better VIP seats than we do."

And then we both stop watching the show because we're making out.

———

The suite is silent and dark when we tiptoe our way back in. Naomi has hung a "Do Not Disturb" sign on her closed door.

Rafe backs me up to the table, dropping the bag of dessert on the surface. It falls over.

"Careful with that," I say. "I'll probably be starving again in a few hours."

Rafe nibbles on my earlobe. "Want to take that bath now?"

"Actually ..." I hesitate, slipping my fingers up his chest, undoing the top buttons of his shirt. "I was thinking about taking a shower in the grotto?"

The wine has made me bold. Or maybe it's this awareness that the clock is about to strike midnight. Or, more accurately, 6 a.m., which is when the driver is picking me up to take me back home to Ephron and my real life.

Rafe, Orly, and his mom won't be flying back till tomorrow night. They are spending a day visiting with his sister.

By then, Lorelei and I will have swapped back. *I only have tonight.*

"If the grotto is what you wish for, I think I can grant that wish." Rafe lifts me up in his arms as effortlessly as if he was lifting Orly and carries me back into the master suite, where he drops me on the bed and peels off his jacket. "Oh, I almost forgot!" He kneels to retrieve the jacket from the floor and pulls out the rose. "Kenna, will you accept this rose?"

"You goof!" I roll my eyes and take the rose from him, forgetting about it two seconds later when he pushes me back against the pillows. He's kissing me so much more urgently now and hiking my dress up my hips. His hands reach under, and his thumbs hook in my panties.

"These have to come off." He bends and tugs them down, raking a trail down my thighs with his fingertips and warm breath.

"Now you." I pull on the collar of his shirt, beckoning him back up the length of my body. He takes his time getting there, making slow but steady progress with kisses that travel up from my ankle, across my calves to my knees, then through more sensitive and dangerous territory—up my inner thigh to my hip bone. I groan and arch my back as he places a knee between my legs and sits up to remove his shirt. Not nearly fast enough.

"Let me help," I say, reaching to undo the buttons.

"What's your hurry, Kenna?" Rafe teases, batting my hands away.

How can I tell him that I don't want to waste any more time? I want to spend every moment I have left with him, without clothes on. No costumes, no barriers. Skin to skin.

"I just"—I blush at my own boldness—"I want to see you. All of you."

"Likewise." His eyes are shining, and he flings the shirt to the floor.

"Your turn," he says, raising an eyebrow.

"This is not a fair game," I say.

"Why not?"

"You have more clothes on than me." If this was strip poker, I'd be in trouble. I just have two items to go—the dress and a strapless bra.

"Okay, I'll even the score." Rafe undoes his trousers, and in an almost balletic movement, removes them completely. He is wearing nothing but his boxers and socks. "Now we are both two for two."

He's kissing me again, all along my neck and back to my lips, plundering my mouth. His tongue is a tease, seeking out my response and retreating, playing with me.

"Time for this to go." Rafe reaches under the silk bodice of my dress and tugs at my bra as he applies the wet-hot heat of his exquisite mouth to my breast, right through the fabric.

I try to reach around to undo the single hook, but he's already got it undone. He's snaking it out from under the dress and tossing it onto the growing pile of clothes.

"What next?" I walk my fingers along the waistband of his silky, boxer briefs, enjoying the way his now obvious arousal jumps as my hand flutters over it. The hard, lean lines of his stomach muscles form a V. And there is no missing the light dusting of dark hair that trails down from his belly button to the straining bulge below. I slide my hand lower and rest it there, feeling a bit like I'm petting a rather wild and unpredictable animal.

"Enough," Rafe groans. He unzips and yanks the dress over my head, then bends to suck my nipple. The dress hits the floor, and then he is standing beside the bed, peeling off his shorts and kicking off his socks. He makes no move to hide his enormous erection as he bends toward the bed and picks me up, sliding himself against me in the process.

I am throbbing with desire for him now. He could simply lift and shift me slightly, and he'd be inside me. But instead, he takes a step back, walking us toward the bathroom.

"Shower time," he says.

I wrap my legs around him, enjoying the friction of my sensitive nub rubbing against his treasure trail.

"We don't have to—" I moan.

"Oh, yes we do," he says, flicking on the steam and lowering the lights to a dim candle glow. "I'm still hungry, Kenna, and I intend to lick your plate clean. And after I do, I'm going to wash you by hand. Every last inch of you."

Oh, my God. Or rather, oh, my Titanium Man.

My brain ceases to function in words. It's regressed to the language of feeling and sensations as we slide against each other in the steamy grotto, hungrily seeking pleasure.

Rafe kneels between my legs, and I have to bite down on my hand to stop myself from crying out when the waves of pleasure crash over me. I'm almost embarrassed at how hard he's made me come. And without him. I feel selfish. Particularly when he stands up and I observe the obvious evidence of his unrelieved need. It doesn't seem fair.

"What about you?" I reach for him, thinking smugly to myself that I will never again wonder if he was "wearing a piece" in that skin-tight superhero costume. The answer to that question is right at my fingertips. On the tip of my tongue. Which I use to explore his tip, tasting him and trying out different rhythms to see how he reacts. I wrap my hand around the base of him and squeeze.

"Not yet." His hand cups the back of my head, gently pulling me away. "I'm going to wash you now, and then I'm going to tuck you in and put you to bed properly."

Rafe pulls me to my feet and rubs a bar of jasmine-scented soap between his hands, working up a handful of bubbles that he proceeds to apply to my body in a painterly fashion, drawing patterns in the frothy lather. On my belly, he draws a heart and writes, "Rafe + Kenna 4Ever," and then he kisses my belly button and offers to wash my hair.

Once we are both rinsed and wrapped in towels, Rafe carries me back to the bed and pulls back the duvet. We tumble in together, tossing the damp towels to the floor.

"Rafe," I say, "I think I'm hungry again."

"For dessert?" He strokes my bottom as I rock on top of him. "Do you want me to go get our dessert?"

"No," I say, teasing his earlobe with my tongue. "I'm hungry for you."

With this taunt, he flips me on my back and reaches for a condom in the nightstand.

"I'll show you what hungry is," he says, tearing the package open with his teeth.

"You look like you're pretty well fed to me." I raise an eyebrow at him, still impressed at the near perfection of him. His long, athletic limbs, his sooty eyelashes, his smooth, taut skin, and his incredible, muscular ass. I clench it. I need to feel these toned muscles moving, working under my hands as he thrusts.

"Help me with this?" He hands me the condom to roll onto him, which I do happily, but not before I've dropped a kiss on the underside of his manhood, near the tip.

"That sort of thing is not going to help me savor this," Rafe says. "And I want to savor it. I don't want to gobble you up just yet."

Savor away. I am savoring him. Even after being washed, his skin tastes of him, his own unique scent and flavor.

"I am starving, Kenna. Starving for you."

My body is thrumming, and burning, making me dizzy with wanting him. The orgasm in the shower was great. But hollow. I need to feel him inside of me. Even if this is only a one-night stand. I arch and writhe, pushing my hips toward him as if I mean to impale myself on his rock hardness. I do mean to. *I need to.*

"You've messed with my head, Kenna." Rafe shifts, rocking deeper into me, touching places that have never been touched before. Pleasure tension rockets to those places, raising the stakes for the orgasm that I know is waiting in the wings. I just hope it can wait for its cue.

"I have?" I gasp. He thrusts again. And again. And a third time, establishing a slow, steady beat like a drummer.

"Yes," he nods.

Thrust, thrust, thrust. The strokes are long, smooth, and confident. I settle into my own rhythm just as quickly, lifting my hips to meet him, tightening around him as if to hold him there longer, when he pulls away.

"But I'm not afraid of doing a little deep work."

He thrusts extra hard, extra deep with this proclamation, and I grip him, wrapping my legs, rolling my hips, needing this sense of fullness. But I cannot hold him there. He starts to move again, and this time, I know I am not going to last much longer. Sparkling bits of pleasure are starting to rain all around me, like the fireworks blooming in the sky outside our window.

"Your so fucking hot, Kenna," Rafe breathes in my ear. "But more than that, you're so kind," *stroke*, "so funny," *stroke*, "so talented," *stroke*, "so perfect." Rafe drives deep, deeper into my core, with one last powerful thrust that has us both disintegrating.

Afterward, I lie there, floating like a still-smoldering cinder on an updraft, as I watch Rafe sleep. He reaches for me, pulling me closer, and I fit myself against him, trying not to see the clock on the nightstand. Trying not to calculate the seconds till dawn, when I know I'll have to leave.

lorelei

. . .

"CAN I help you clean anything else up?" I ask Noah, after the tech crew and other players finally leave. We're standing in his kitchen, putting away leftovers, and I can tell all the trips up and down the stairs have been hard on his still-healing leg. The session went later than planned and got so emotional. I feel the exact same way I feel after a good improv class or therapy session. Wrung out. Wiped clean.

Also horny.

"That's okay." Noah shakes his head and snaps the lid on a Tupperware container. "We got all of the food and garbage. I like to leave the scene as it was for when we pick it back up next time. You were awesome, by the way."

"Was I? Really?" I find myself blushing. I am having such a hard time seeing Noah in the same light after witnessing him in his element during the session. It's a real Superman/Clark Kent situation, and nobody else in Ephron knows about it besides me. Does that make me Lois Lane? She does have good hair.

"Sorry to stick you with Dorcas, the orc," Noah says. "But holy shit, Kenna, the socials are blowing up. I almost can't believe that in one week, you've made her a fan fave." He pulls up the show's account on the phone and scrolls through page after page of positive comments.

I feel seen.

Normalize imperfection.

Dorcas, where have you been all my life?

Dorcas changes everything.

Noah shakes his head and shifts his weight to his good leg, doing a little hop as he lays the phone back on the counter. The dragon head is back in its box, but he's still wearing the velvet robe. I wonder what, if anything, he has on underneath.

"So you were okay with what I did with Dorcas?" I ask tentatively.

"I loved it. You were brilliant. So sensitive. I really think you tapped into something our followers were missing. Something elemental. Have you done any acting?" Noah asks, placing the Tupperware in his refrigerator.

"A bit," I say, biting my lip.

"Beer?" He pulls two bottles from the fridge, holding them up.

"Sure," I say. "Don't bother with a glass. You should get off that leg."

He looks dubious for a moment, as if he'd rather not drink straight out of the bottle, but then he shrugs, pulls out a bottle opener from a drawer, and pops the lids off.

Wisps of smoky mist curl up and out of the bottles, like steam, or a genie. Or dragon smoke.

I have to tell him. If I don't go for it now, I may never have another chance.

We go to sit outside on the porch swing again, swaying gently in the quiet night. It's like we're inside our own little pocket here. The distant sound of a neighbor's garage door closing, or a passing car, are the only sounds besides crickets. *Literal crickets.* I want to tell him who I really am, but I don't know where to start.

"Kenna—"

"Noah—"

We both blurt at the same time. Noah laughs. Then he takes my left hand in his right hand and we continue to rock.

"This beer is good," I say.

This beer is good? Really, Lorelei? Is that the best you can do?

I finish the rest of my bottle and set it aside, tucking my legs up under me and turning toward Noah. He's still holding my hand in his lap. I want to lay my head on his shoulder, but instead, I look into his eyes and ask a question.

"What do you have against Lorelei Dupont, Noah?"

"Lorelei Dupont?" He looks confused, like this is a totally unexpected non sequitur, which I suppose it is. "Why? What made you think of her?"

"I was just thinking about how you were talking about her in the diner when I met you the other day."

"When you met me?" He tilts his head. "I've been coming into that diner for ages," he says, shaking his head. "Though, I do suppose it was the first time we've talked at any length. I'm so glad we did."

The swing has come to a standstill, and he squeezes my hand again and pushes off with one foot, setting us adrift again.

"You seemed rather unimpressed with her. I was just curious why you hate her." His neck smells so nice. Like balsam and juniper. An old-fashioned men's cologne. Something classic and timeless. I cannot help myself. I lay my head on his shoulder, and once it's there, I can't be expected not to feather my lips against his neck, can I?

He lets go of my hand and puts his arm behind me, pulling me closer against him, but he doesn't make any other moves before answering my question.

"I don't hate her. She's a great actress. I grew up watching episodes of *Moxie*, and I guess I even had a crush on her. I mean, who didn't in the 2000s?" Noah says.

He had a crush? On me?

"But you know those celebrity types," Noah sighs. "Everything they say and do is calculated by their marketing managers and image consultants. They're about as real as an AI-generated portrait of an alligator winning a pie-eating contest. No wonder so many of them go batshit crazy. After a while, there's just no more there. I think we've all kind of been waiting for Lorelei Dupont to implode. Pity because she's obviously talented."

Ouch.

"That's pretty harsh, and arrogant, coming from a guy who has half a million followers." I sit up straighter. "One could argue that you have even more fans than Lorelei. So who's the celebrity now?" I cross my arms across my chest.

"Kenna," Noah says, stroking the side of my neck. "Why do you even care?"

"It just seems wrong of you to judge her like that. You don't even know her."

"You're probably right," he sighs. "I'm always telling my students that they shouldn't judge a book by its cover."

Another car drives by, windows down, rap music spilling out. The bass echoes in its wake.

"Exactly," I say. Still smelling him. Still horny. The bubbles from that beer are going straight to my …

"Come back here," Noah commands in that other voice of his. Deeper. Edgier. Needier. I can't refuse him.

"I am here," I say, resting my head against his chest.

"Not like that." He places a quick kiss on the top of my head and speaks quietly, confidently, and calmly. "I want you to sit on my lap."

It's like the barometer just dropped out from under me. I swear I can smell ozone. And then I do see a flash of lightning in the distance. I look up at the dark porch ceiling.

"You what?" I whisper, already unfurling my legs, shifting my weight onto my left hip. The humid air is charged, and so am I. Waves of wanting him are pounding against my shores of self-control.

"I want you"—he places a helpful hand on my hip—"to sit on my lap, like you did the other day."

"Like this?" I gather my sheet skirt up and press myself against him, legs parted, heat undeniable, and I grip the back of the floating bench.

"Yes," he nods. "Good. Now sit still. Let me rock you." Noah pushes the swing with his good leg, and I close my eyes, enjoying the sense of weightlessness.

"Are you going to say 'this isn't the time or the place' again?" I ask, as his hands begin to expertly unlace my placemat corset.

"No, I am not," he says, "because this *is* the time." He cups a breast in each hand and leans forward to plant a kiss on my breastbone. "And this *is* the place."

I gather a fistful of his hair, yanking his head back, and kiss him with wild abandon as we rock and grind, tongues thrusting, hips undulating, a tornado unleashing.

Another flash of lightning rips the sky open and lights up the porch like a strobe, followed by a sudden deluge of rain and hail, tiny balls of ice bouncing off the railing and pelting us.

"Christ, Kenna ..." Noah grips my hips again, pulling me closer against him, positioning me. The only thing keeping him out are the thin layers we are both straining against. "I think we need to go inside now."

It isn't the ice balls that do it. It's her name. The minute I hear it, I may as well be out on the front lawn, soaked and shivering and definitely not in the mood anymore. Once again, the image of toothless, little princess Kenna skips across my imagination.

Fuck. I promised. I cannot do this.

"Fuuuuck," I say, climbing off him and standing up.

"If you insist." Noah smiles. His large, brown eyes are shining, and his lips are a bit swollen, redder from the kissing. It softens the angular lines of his jaw. His floppy, brown hair is pushed back from my attention, and he looks wolfishly wild, beastly in the best way. Like he could devour me. And I want him to. I really do. But ...

"There's something I have to tell you," I say, "inside."

Noah sits on the couch, staring at me in disbelief as I tell him about the swap. I retrieve the spare, brown wig I've been saving for the swap back out of my bag. After quickly pulling my natural hair back into a pony, I tug it on. Along with the wig, I tug on my old public persona. The stony, resting bitch face. The distant stare.

"What. The. Fuck?" he says. "I mean, what the actual fuck?"

I shake my head apologetically.

"But ... you're Kenna. You look just like her." He is scrutinizing me now. "I mean, how do I even know you're telling me the truth and not just Kenna punking me?"

"The earth is a small place for fugitives." I recite the Kyrgysz proverb from the Titanium Man film that my character Ember is famous for, in Kyrgysz. Then I spit, dramatically, on the floor. It's way cooler in the movie because the CGI fireballs and my spit just instantly turn into steam. Kind of like dragon fire and steam.

"Did you just spit on my floor?" Noah asks, incredulous.

"I did. Would Kenna do that?" I put my hands on my hips, raising my brows. I'm pretty fucking certain she wouldn't.

"I have no idea what she would do."

"I know what she wouldn't do," I say.

"Do you?" Noah asks.

"Yeah," I assert. "You. She wouldn't do you. But I would." I take a step toward him.

"Look, Lorelei," Noah says, holding up a hand. "I'm not sure how I feel about this. You deceived me."

"I'm telling you the truth now."

"I invited you to sit at my table."

"And I came."

"I didn't know who you were."

"And I didn't know who you were, either. It's not as if you're sharing everything about yourself with the general public, is it *Dungeon Master Max*? We both have secrets."

"You knew who I was when you came here today."

"Yeah, and you made me be an orc!"

Noah's mouth twitches at this. "My bad. But you *were* insanely good." I can feel him starting to thaw.

"The advisory board is going to shit cinderblocks about it," I grin.

"Advisory board?"

"Manager, agent, lawyer … you know, my whole team?"

"You're actually going to tell people you were on my show?"

"Fuck it," I say. "I don't care who knows. I can't wait to see what happens at the next session."

"What makes you so sure I'll invite you back, Lorelei?"

He's speaking in the commanding voice of the Dungeon Master now, and it vibrates through me.

"Come on, Noah, you know you want me at your table." I place a hand on my hip, acting confident, but I'm actually desperately scared he's going to throw me out.

Noah stands and takes a step toward me, leaning on his wizard's staff for support. His robe's ties have come undone. The top is hanging open, exposing his hard, broad chest, which is lightly dusted with pale-brown fur. I follow his gaze to my chest, which is barely covered by the drooping sheet, now that my makeshift corset stays are unlaced.

The thunderstorm outside is growing closer. The flashes of lightning are becoming brighter, and the house-rattling booms are following them more closely.

"The Dungeon Master confesses that he actually wants to have you ON the table." He steps closer to me and pulls on the laces, undoing the stays entirely, then yanks the corset off, leaving my entire chest exposed.

I reach for the wig to pull it off, and he shakes his head. "Oh no, that stays on, and we'll be exploring suitable punishments for your character should you ever shout at me in Russian and spit on my floor again, Lorelei." His eyes flash and burn as he says my name. "It's your move," he says, handing me the di.

Lightning and thunder crack almost at the same time, and I fling myself at Noah, pressing my skin to his skin, lips to lips, teeth and tongues clashing. We both lean on his wooden staff for support.

"Just to be safe from the storm," I say, heart beating with anticipation, "we should probably go back down to the basement."

kenna

. . .

I TAKE one last look around the Adventureland Suite, trying to commit as much as possible to memory before I go. This really has been the adventure of a lifetime. And possibly exactly what I needed. Because even though I've managed to avoid thinking about the future all week, I woke up knowing exactly what I want to do next.

Rafe, Orly, and Naomi are all still fast asleep, and I don't want to wake them. I place the folded note for Rafe under the camera that I'm leaving in the middle of the dining room table. Much as I'd love to, I can't possibly keep it.

> Dear Rafe,
> Thanks for the most magical week and sharing your family with me. I'm a much better version of myself now that I know how to drive manually and make shakshuka—and homemade hummus!
> As much as I'd like to keep this camera, I think you really should keep it and use it to

I take one last peek out the window, glancing down at the empty, Mickey-shaped pool, wishing I had one more day to spend swimming with Orly, trading recipes with Naomi, and pushing back any time she suggests that her megawatt star is somehow less than because he didn't get a college degree from Harvard.

But the sun is leaking golden rays through the palm trees, and I suspect my driver will be here any moment. It's time to transition back to real life.

I slip out the door and into the elevator, still feeling like Lorelei Dupont, looking over my shoulder for fans and paparazzi. I won't miss that part. It's stressful. I can't imagine enduring years and years of that, particularly through the tender, awkward teenage years. Poor Lorelei.

I study myself in the mirrored interior of the elevator and twist my crazy, bedhead hair up into one of my signature messy buns. I untuck my souvenir Tiki Room tee that I am wearing and apply my usual banana-flavored lip balm.

By the time the elevator doors slide open in the lobby, I not only look like myself again, I feel like me, too. I stop at the coffee station and serve myself a cup of lobby coffee, doing my best to doctor it up with extra cream and sugar to fortify myself for reentry. It's only a moment or two before the driver comes into the lobby holding up an iPad with my name on it. My real name.

"You Kenna Papadopoulos?" he asks.

"Yes," I nod, "I am."

"Well, let's get a move on. There's a lot of traffic on the 405. I'd hate for you to miss your flight."

———

I enjoy one last bit of luxury in my business-class seat—Rafe insisted—eating breakfast and taking advantage of the free Wi-Fi to scroll through the course offerings in the Continuing Ed. Department at the small college just outside Ephron. There's a business management course starting in September. I put in my email address to be added to the mailing list for more information. It's time. If Georgia can run her own shop, and Naomi can run a culinary empire, there's no reason why I can't take over the management of the Ephron Diner.

I can't wait to tell Georgia. I tap on the messenger app on my phone.

Good Lord! That's a lot of messages!

My heart does a little flip-flop when I notice the unusually high number of messages that have piled up in my inbox since I switched my phone to silent almost forty-eight hours ago. Starting with the most recent one from Rafe. Short and sweet, the whole thing shows up in the preview. I don't even have to click on it to read it in its entirety.

It's not like any one person was blowing up my phone. It's just that so many people had tried to reach me, and a few more than once over the course of a day. But none of the messages are marked urgent. Any of them could have reached me, even on silent mode, in a real emergency by calling twice.

I scan down the rest of the list, sorted visually by the emoji I've chosen for everyone in my contact list. Just one more little dyslexic life hack that I've been happily using for years.

I open the messages from the uncles first.

Uncle Nick had texted first.

Five minutes later, Uncle Stavros had texted as well. I can picture them sitting on their terrace in Mykonos, realizing the flub at the same time and panicking.

Not too soon, though. The uncles are not due back for another three weeks, which is probably a good thing. I know things have slipped at the diner since the swap, and it's time for me to step up and show them I can do this.

I open the messages from Georgia next.

> Hope you're having fun at Disney, but I need you to get your ass back here. I mean, Lorelei is definitely a lot cooler than I expected, but I honestly can't take much more of this.

> Also, I wanted to keep my mouth shut, but I can't. You cannot let the uncles sell the diner. I cannot do this alone. Not just the shop. EVERYTHING.

There's a photo of my chair, back in its usual place, with a brand-new sign above it that says, "Reserved for Kenna."

> I'll find somewhere else for the bassinet. Or the kid can sleep in a stroller. Doesn't matter. You can never be replaced. You CANNOT LEAVE ME!!!!

I text her back a screenshot of the Continuing Ed. course.

> Wanna do this with me? I'm going to need all the support I can get if I want to convince the uncles to let me keep and run the diner.

> What? Are you serious? Yes!

Happy face emoji. Clapping hands. Confetti. Relieved guy with the sweat drop.

> I am serious.

I smile.

Next, I scroll down to the message from Xander, which is bracketed by several rows of flame, star, and heart eyes emoji.

The screenshot shows a post taken from the DILFSofDisney Instagram account. There's a whole carousel of shots, starting with Rafe carrying Orly on his shoulders and ending with him kissing me by the benches near the Thunder Mountain Railroad exit. The caption reads:

Titanium Man's her daddy! Rumors about the longtime relationship between Rafe Barzilay and costar Lorelei Dupont appear to be confirmed during this magical trip to the happiest place. Just looking at these makes us feel happy and other things. Lucky, lucky Lorelei. Really (heart emoji) *her new look, too.*

Well, shit. I hope that Lorelei is not too upset about that. And I also hope that whatever is going on between her and Noah Greenberg isn't going to come back to bite me in the butt.

Finally, I scroll down to Lorelei's messages. She'd agreed to pick me up at the airport this morning, in my car, so that I could drive her back to the guesthouse at the estate, and then head home to my own apartment. I'm going to miss the mister and the high-thread-count sheets.

Actually, I'd almost forgotten that we'd agreed to go over the DNA test results when we swap back, but now I am curious. Although the odds are pretty low that we're actually related, I'm curious to see what else the tests might have turned up. I've been reading that these tests can also show stuff like a genetic tendency toward dyslexia, fear of heights, and cilantro aversion.

There's another text from Lorelei, sent just a little while ago.

> On my way. Up since the ass crack of dawn, which is really saying something about how excited I am to see you and go over those test results. Last night was epic. You're driving home from the airport.

Epic as in?

> Please do not tell me I had a one-night stand with anyone that I was not physically present for.

A few minutes later, I finally get a response. It's the same photo of Rafe and I kissing that Xander sent.

> Hello, Pot.

> Not the sam thing! He knw who I rlly was. And he kissed me!

I misspell words in my haste to defend myself, but send the message anyway.

> Calm down. I told Noah the truth before anything serious happened. He knows I'm not you.

> Oh, thank God. And he was ok with that?

I'd bet he was more than OKAY with that. Not to be rude, but Noah Greenberg is kind of a nerd. Nice guy, but a little bookish and rough around the edges.

He didn't kick me to the curb.

Smiley face. Flames. Troll. Princess. Eggplant.

Ok then. I hope you had a nice time

We had a *dice* time.

???

I'll explain later. See you in two hours.

lorelei

. . .

I PARK in the cell phone lot at the airport and close my eyes for fifteen minutes, going back over the past twenty-four hours in my head.

My entire body is deliciously sore. I could probably skip my workout for three days. I won't, but I could. I've convinced Noah to start working out with me as soon as his doctor approves it. There may be dice involved. And lots of lunges. For sure, there will be lunges.

Noah and I lay awake till the wee small hours, talking about everything under the sun. What it was like to grow up on a TV show. His theories about artificial intelligence. The high school theater program. How he feels about his parents retiring to Washington State. Aliens.

I even told him a little bit about the conversation I had with my mom.

"I think you should give her another chance," he said, without hesitation.

"But she screwed up. She screwed me up."

"You seem pretty OKAY to me, actually," Noah argued.

"Yeah, well, years of therapy. That's how I originally got into gaming. My therapist suggested it as a way to track my own emotions."

"I get that." Noah had rolled on his side and looked at me. The rain had settled into a gentle pattern against the windows of his bedroom. He'd insisted I spend the night with him in his massive, four-poster bed. Honestly, I was grateful not to have to sleep on the futon. "The thing is, no parents are perfect. They all screw up. Yours did, mine did, and I'm sure we would if we were ever in that position."

"No thanks." I shook my head vehemently. "The buck stops here. I don't want to screw any more kids up."

"Me either." Noah pulled me closer and wrapped me in his arms. "Maybe I'm selfish. I already feel kind of like my students are all my kids, and that's enough. I like having my summers off to travel and do stuff, and having the extra cash to pay for it."

"I get that," I said, doing an internal fist pump. *Noah Greenberg is not going to ask me to settle down and play wifeymom with him? Could this get any better?*

"But the point is, you're only going to have so many people in your life who know you and share your history. And sometimes, you gotta take it from whence it comes. Accept that they are flawed, and so are you. Particularly when you're all adults. I say set some clear boundaries, but give her another chance. Seems like her heart is in the right place, and she'd really like to reconnect with you."

"I invited her to the opening of *A Midsummer Night's Dream*, and ..." I said, suddenly feeling a bit shy about inviting him, despite the fact that we are both stark naked, lying spent together.

"And?" He drew his fingers along the ridges of my ribs.

"And I'd love it if you were there, too," I breathed out.

"You couldn't keep me away."

We fell asleep shortly after that, but I hadn't slept for very long. I had to be out of there super early to make it to the airport in time to get Kenna.

Now that I'm here, ready to swap back, I can't stop thinking about the test results. I've already pulled up the DNA testing service's user portal in a browser on my phone. All I have to do is log in and I'll know. But I can't do that until I show Kenna the photos I've taken from her album.

The lot is getting busier and busier, and normally, I'd be worried about getting caught sleeping in a car in a public place —especially an old beater like Kenna's—but I don't feel like anyone is looking at me. And even if they are, I don't care. I don't have that hunted, haunted feeling anymore. I've made up my mind.

I'm done with wearing a wig and listening to the advisory board. If I want to play *DND* with a bunch of freaks and geeks, I will.

Then I get another idea. I pull up the invitation to the Nomad Games this fall and send a link to Noah.

Would you ever consider taking time off to travel?

Are you punking me? he replies immediately.

No, why?

I have always wanted to sleep in a yurt and watch the archers shooting bows with their feet while riding on horseback. Two

words: Bucket. List.

I smile and reply to the invite. It can't hurt to get more info.

My phone buzzes with incoming texts.

> Lorelei! What the hell. We're on the phone with Rafe's people and the studio, and we did not agree to any of this!

Took the advisory board a little longer than I expected. The photos from Disney have been out since last night. I delete the message and close the app, even though I am dying to text Rafe and pump him for more info. Rafe is into Kenna. Kenna is into Rafe. Is it weird for him that she looks so much like me? Is she really able to look past his disgusting troll toes and too-perfect lashes? And what about Naomi? Surely, she's not taking any of this sitting down.

I'm going to need all the deets. But not just yet.

> Flight 1229 from Santa Ana, CA has just landed.

My flight-tracking app pings me, and I swing out toward the white zone, wondering if I'll have any trouble recognizing Kenna in the crowd. Stupid.

When I see her waiting patiently on the curb for me, my heart races. Once again, I'm struck by the similarities between us, although I see plenty of differences as well. The angle of our eyes. The length of our fingers. It's the kind of stuff that the people who are closest to us might notice. But, as we both know from experience, the rest of the world sort of paints those things out. Sort of the way everyone accepts retouched photos and filters. We have internalized ideas about appearances that don't always match with what we see, and we're willing to excuse that.

After I pull over, I jump out of the car to give Kenna a big hug.

"God, I'm glad to see you," I say, throwing my arms around her and feeling tears come to my eyes. "I had no idea how hard you work and how awesome you are. And I know this is going to sound weird, but I really, really missed you."

"That's so funny," she says, hugging me back. "I was going to say pretty much the same thing."

————

"I don't understand." Kenna is looking from the photos to me, and back to the photos, her eyes wide. "Where did you get these?"

"I sort of stole them," I admit.

"From where?"

"From your uncles' house the other day when the realtor was showing it. Cody is a total fucking tool, by the way. Please tell me you're never getting back together with that guy."

"You met Cody? And he was in my house? What the fuck, Lorelei? What the hell is going on here?" Kenna's looking agitated now, and I can tell she is tired, too. There are dark circles under her eyes.

Oops. Probably not the best time to mention Cody.

"Well, you and Rafe didn't tell me you canned Tabitha," I say. "Who's going to mist me with ice water when I fall asleep at rehearsals now?"

"Tabitha was a psycho," Kenna says. "Rafe did you a favor. We didn't want to bug you with it."

"And I didn't think you needed to drop everything because your dumb ex, Cody, was the one the realtor was showing the house to. I watched him like a hawk, told him his junk was inadequate, and talked him out of making an offer, which"—I pause here—"your uncles never would have accepted anyway, right?"

"Right," she says. "I just *hate* the idea of him even being in the house."

"I get that," I agree. "We may want to go back there and burn some sage. But back to the photos." I tap the table, full of nervous excitement. "Recognize anyone?"

"Well, obviously, I recognize this one." Kenna picks up the photo of her mom holding both of us on her lap. "This is my mom, and this was another one of the kids in the adoption group when she came to get me. Their agency sent a whole group of Americans over together to pick up their kids at the same time. Apparently, according to my uncle Nick, this little girl wouldn't leave me alone. She was constantly trying to climb into my stroller and hold me and didn't want to go anywhere with her own mom." Kenna considers this for a moment. "That really must have sucked for her. Poor woman."

"Uh-huh," I nod, pointing at the pictures of myself, trying to climb into the stroller, and the other one of me sitting with her uncle Nick.

"Yeah, that's the same kid. And that's my uncle Nick. Remember I said he traveled with my mom to come get me? He must have been trying to help her mom out." Kenna leans back. "I'm not sure how I feel about you digging photos out of my family album, Lorelei. That's a little inappropriate, don't you think?"

I point at my mother. "And this lady here? What do you know about her?"

"Not much. My mom lost touch with most of the other families over the years."

"So you don't have any idea who this is?"

I'm not sure whether I'm savoring the drama or dreading the reveal. What if Kenna freaks out? What if she wants her photos back and doesn't want anything to do with me, ever again?

And we haven't even looked at the DNA test yet.

"No, Lorelei, I don't know who she is. Can you get to the point? Do you know who she is?" Kenna calls me on my BS.

"I do know who she is." I square my shoulders and sit taller in my seat at the coffee shop. This whole scene would probably have played off a little better if I wasn't still wearing two placemats and a bedsheet, but it is what it is. "This," I say, tapping the photo of my mother, "is my mother." And then I slide the other photo with the two of us on her mom's lap, the one where I am holding her so tightly, in front of her. I rotate it to face her. "And this little monster here? This is me."

Kenna doesn't say anything for at least ten seconds. I don't think she even breathes. She just stares at the photo. And then she takes a deep breath, opens her mouth as if she is about to talk, and then shuts it at me. She looks at me again and then picks up the photo, squinting at it, holding it in the air as if she is trying to find the similarities between me and the piebald toddler.

"How?" she finally asks.

"I spoke to my mom, and I guess both your mom and her used the same adoption agency. They were both on the West Coast and adopting as single moms. It's not that weird, actually."

"And we have the same gotcha day?"

"June 6th," I nod. "It just passed."

"I know," Kenna says. "The uncles forgot, but then they felt bad about missing it. They usually make me a cake."

"That is so sweet," I say. I haven't even met her uncles yet, but my eyes are filling with tears. "You're really lucky to have them."

"But wait, does this mean we're—" Kenna cuts herself off. "The DNA test results. Lorelei! What do the DNA test results say?"

"I don't know! I was *waiting for you to look*." I overemphasize my words, holding up my phone. "I have the site already loaded here. Do you want to check at the same time?"

"No. Open it." Kenna flaps her hand at me. "You do it. You'll be faster than me. Open, open, open!"

"Okay." I punch in my login credentials. There's a little number one over the messages icon in the navigation bar. I click on it.

You have one new relative.

I flip the phone around to show her the message subject.

"What does that mean?"

"It could mean nothing. It could mean we are fourth cousins, or it could be someone else entirely, some distant relative in Finland, for example," I say, speaking from experience. But my hands are shaking.

"You do the honors," I say, handing her the phone. "Either way, I think it's pretty significant that we share this much history. My mom didn't have any photos of the orphanage, and I've really struggled to find anyone I might be related to. No matter what this test says, I can't believe we found each other."

"Let's hold hands." Kenna reaches out her right hand and grips my left. The phone is sitting on the table between us. Her left pointer finger is poised above the screen. "On the count of three."

kenna

. . .

I HAVE A HALF SISTER.

Lorelei Dupont, my doppelgänger, isn't my twin. But she is my sister. We share the same biological mother.

"Why would the orphanage have separated us?" I wonder out loud, as I merge onto the freeway, headed back toward Ephron. It feels good to be back in a car I know how to drive.

"They couldn't have known," Lorelei explains, leaning all the way back in her seat and closing her eyes. "I was a foundling, abandoned on the church steps. Technically, I had no parents of record." She sits up for a moment, looking hopeful. "But maybe I can get some information about my, I mean *our*, birth mother after all now?"

"I don't think so." I sigh.

"Why not?" Lorelei frowns.

"I have a little bit of info—stuff like her name, age, and hair color—but she died when we were both pretty young," I say.

"How do you know?"

"The uncles hired a private investigator when I was a teenager, not long after my adoptive mom died. I didn't even care, but they wanted to know more. And Uncle Stavros thought I might want to know someday. He knew a guy who was doing a lot of business in Russia, and he knew a guy who was doing research for other adoptive families," I explain. "There's a letter, tucked behind one of the drawers in my old bedroom. They sent a copy of her death certificate."

"Well, crap," Lorelei sighs. A moment later she mumbles, "So much for the fantasy that we're secret descendants of the Romanov clan."

"You didn't really think that, did you?" I laugh.

"No, but I had a therapist who tried to convince me that I did." Lorelei smiles with her eyes closed. She reaches out and squeezes my arm. "We may not be bona fide princesses, but I think it's just as much of a magical miracle that we've found our way back to each other."

———

After I drop Lorelei back at the guesthouse, I go straight to the diner. As tired as I am, I need to be there. I need to inspect my espresso maker, check the stock, and make sure everything is okay.

I leave my suitcase at the apartment, which Lorelei has left spotlessly clean, and pull on my barista apron. I'm in such a hurry to get out the door and get to work that I almost don't notice all the new equipment on my desk out in the hallway. My old, sticker-covered iPad is still there, but it is leaning up against a large-screen Mac desktop. On the surface below it is a sleek, white box with a brand-new laptop. There's a sticky note on the box.

I didn't know which one you would want, so I just got you both. Also, I know you mentioned the camera you wanted, but then Noah printed out a comparison of all the different models and I wasn't sure if you might want to check it out before you order something. Look under the box.

I tip up the computer box and pull out a folder with a cost and feature comparison report. There's a generous gift card and another note,

Just get whatever damn camera you want.

I can't accept all this!

I shoot a photo and text to Lorelei.

The hell you can't. I'm not having my photo taken with the dog camera. Plus, a deal's a deal.

———

When I finally arrive at the diner, the lunch rush is over. It's the afternoon lull. There's nobody behind the counter. I assume Carlos has dashed off to use the restroom.

"I'm back!" I call out, reveling in all the familiar smells and more than a few familiar faces at the tables. In the back corner, at a round booth, I spy two-thirds of the *Lit Lovers'* podcast crew. Jackson Porter is sitting with his sister, Chelsea, and Emily Romano, as well as an unfamiliar-looking redhead. I duck behind the counter to grab a pot of freshly brewed coffee and head over to refill their cups.

"I didn't know you were away," Emily says, waving away my offer of coffee. "No thanks. I'm holding out for a London fog when the machine is fixed. I know you said to try the mocha macchiato the other day, but I'm afraid it just wasn't me."

Lorelei talked Emily into a macchiato? What had she been thinking?

"I can whip you up a London fog with the frother. I don't need to use the espresso maker for that," I say cheerily. "It's no problem, and it's on me."

"Oh, really? Well, then, I'd love one of your special drinks, too," says the redhead. She's got a British accent and warm, curious eyes. They are framed by hot-pink glasses that are further embellished by a colorfully beaded chain. "You must be Kenna. I've heard all about your magical, psychic, drink-matching abilities."

"Well, she isn't always right," Jackson points out. "Case in point—macchiato."

"Anyone can have an off day," the redhead chastises him. "I'm Isla, by the way. Emily and I met in Rome." She takes my hand and holds it, waiting dramatically. "Are you getting any kind of read on me?"

"Apricot tea with honey, frothed oat milk, and a ginger shot," I say confidently.

God, it feels good to be back. But a moment later, I see the waitress carrying a plate of fairy pancakes to another table, and my heart hurts. Hurts. How am I going to get over Rafe? And not just Rafe. Orly and Naomi, too. I miss them so much.

But they were never really mine.

"That is so uncanny!" Isla lets my hand go and claps her hands together. "Now I cannot think of anything I would rather drink more."

"Power of suggestion," smirks Jackson.

I give him a look. "Just for that, I'm not offering to make anything special for you, Dr. Spock. How's the dating app going?"

"Well, it's out on the market now." Jackson brushes some lint off his shirt. "Still testing, but we'll see. I can give you a code if you'd like to get in on the beta."

"Oh, Kenna doesn't need your app," Isla says, smiling. "Cupid's arrow has already struck this one." She grins knowingly, staring at me. Wait, how does she know?

And then I realize that the whole table is staring at me. At my neck. I can see the butterfly-shaped hickey reflected in the coffeepot.

Oh my God.

"I'll be right back with your drinks," I say, rushing back toward the kitchen, wondering whether I can use a cloth napkin as a neck kerchief, or if there's anything else in there I can use to mitigate the situation.

I'm so preoccupied that I barrel right into someone coming in through the back door of the kitchen.

"Kenna!" my uncle Nick calls out. He's accompanied by Uncle Stavros, and they are both holding suitcases.

———

"What are you doing here?" I ask incredulously.

"We got bored," Uncle Nick shrugs. "This one"—he points at Uncle Stavros—"decided he was the cheese police, the unelected island authority on feta. He started leaving reviews on Tripadvisor, ripping into most of the dockside cafés. I had to get him out of there before he made us both persona non grata."

"I don't care if it's just for the tourists," Stavros bursts out. "There's no excuse for serving such low-quality feta. I wouldn't feed that feta to my donkeys!"

"Stavros, do donkeys eat feta?" Uncle Nick asks.

I fling myself at them. "I missed you both so much!"

"We missed you, too, Kenna. And we're sorry. We shouldn't have blindsided you with our plans like we did. And forgetting gotcha day on top of that? I'm ashamed of us," Uncle Nick says.

"That's okay," I say. "You two deserve a break. Nobody's worked harder than the two of you. But if it's not too crazy an idea to consider," I say, taking a deep breath, "I'd like to keep the diner in the family. I'd like to continue to run it after you retire, and of course, you'd still be the majority owners."

"Well, thank you, Kenna." Uncle Nick looks at Uncle Stavros. "But that won't be necessary."

"What?" I look from one to the other, feeling the icy tendrils of panic coming for me. "Did you receive an offer on the place already? Is that why you came back early?"

"No, Kenna, no! What your uncle Nick is trying to say is that we are not selling the diner." Stavros hugs me again.

"We don't need you to run the diner just yet because we are not retiring. We changed our minds," Uncle Nick says. "This fool was in such a hurry to get back here to his beloved kitchen that he didn't even want to stop home and drop off the bags."

Stavros opens the refrigerator and pulls out a tub of locally made feta. "This," he says, shaking the fluid-filled tub, "is a FETA. Who would have thought I would have to go all the way to Mykonos to get supermarket cheese. Pre-crumbled. Feh!"

"What about the condo you got in Mykonos?" I ask.

"That's the best part," Uncle Nick says. "Income property. We can keep it rented out for most of the year, except for when we want to visit. It'll add to our nest egg for retirement. When we decide we actually do want to retire."

"Promise you'll give me a little more notice next time if you do?" I ask, wiping tears from my eyes.

"There's actually another reason we came to the diner before heading home," Nick confesses.

"What's that?" I ask.

"I wanted to bake your gotcha day cake."

"Oh wow," I smile. "You don't have to do that, Uncle Nick."

"Yes, I do!" he insists.

"But you must be tired from the trip," I protest.

"Tired, schmired. I've been napping for the last two weeks, and I slept the whole way home in those lay-flat business seats we used our miles for. If I wanna bake a cake, I'm gonna bake a cake!"

"Fine," I say. "But, in that case, you'd better make it a double. There's someone I need you both to meet."

lorelei

. . .

I'M NOT sure where I am for a moment when I wake up, alone in my bed at the guesthouse. The "phsssssst" of my ultrasonic mister and my preferred, high-thread-count, sateen sheets no longer feels familiar. It's too dark. Too quiet. I feel like there's somewhere I need to go when I wake, even though we aren't starting rehearsals until tomorrow.

It's the diner. I feel like I should be at the diner.

Rafe and I agreed that it's probably best for me to lay low until his mom leaves town tomorrow, so I pull on some leggings and a hoodie and head out to my patio with a cup of green tea and a slice of leftover gotcha day cake. I love the fresh, crisp, early morning air. All pine trees and mountain mist. Such a contrast to LA dust and pollution. I could see making the Pacific Northwest a base when I'm not traveling or working.

> I'm planning on doing some writing at the diner this morning. Are you free?

The text from Noah buzzes against my thigh. In my contacts, his name is framed with red and black heart emoji, plus a dragon and flames. I get a thrill every time I see it.

I smile. We both have so many ideas about storylines we'd like to explore for Dorcas—and each other—but that's a whole other kind of session.

The mountains are still fogged in a bit by mist this morning. It makes the forest at the edge of the property look magical, exactly like I imagine the forest from *A Midsummer Night's Dream* might look, with curtains of thick, lacy ferns and cushioned beds of moss. The sort of forest where you might meet an actual fairy, or an orc. I might go for a run later. I've got a lot of cake to work off, including the thick slice I've just finished.

I lick the delicious, pink frosting off the plate.

Last night, I finally got to meet Uncle Nick and Uncle Stavros, who were just as colorful as I imagined them to be. Warm, genial, and completely insisting that I was family. A member of their family. Whether I wanted to be or not.

Uncle Nick baked a whole separate cake for me. Three layers, with flecks of Fruity Pebbles in the batter! He hugged me so hard when he saw me, it took my breath away. I cried when he told me he remembered me from the orphanage. Then we all cried when we went through the adoption album together. Uncle Nick told the story of how he and Kenna's mom traveled to get her, an epic tale that's clearly been told many times before. But this year, he made sure to add lots of new details about me. Like how he gave my mom all the little Fruity

Pebbles cereal boxes he'd brought along for himself to snack on.

"It was you I was thinking of when I came up with these pancakes for the diner," Uncle Nick says, explaining the fairy pancakes on the Ephron Diner menu. "You were like this weird, intense, little fairy creature," he told me almost apologetically, "with your giant, fierce eyes and hedgehog hair."

"Or a baby orc," I mused.

I gave them their photos back, and Uncle Nick promised to have copies made. And then we called my mom on FaceTime, and everyone cried again. The uncles promised to make her an album, too, and take her to some local vineyards and fromageries when she visits.

I take the dishes back into the kitchenette and wash them. Why not meet Noah at the diner? I'm already missing Carlos and some of the regulars. I'd like a chance to see them again. This time as myself. No subterfuge. No making macchiatos. And no washing other people's dishes.

I check the key hook for my keys. Nothing. I rifle through the drawers. No car keys. Then I remember we agreed to keep all the keys over at the main house. Great. Laying low does not include barging in, unannounced, to get my keys.

Hey Rafe, I was thinking I'd head into town for the day. Can you get me my car keys?

No response.

While I'm waiting, I empty the trash. Four brown wigs are piled up like dead animals. I pull the drawstrings tight and take the bag outside. The sooner those things are out of my life, the better.

After ten minutes, I text again. Nothing. The big house looks quiet, like everyone is still asleep. I do know that Rafe, Naomi, and Orly didn't get back from LA till late last night. They weren't back yet when I got home at close to eleven. So they're probably still sleeping. If I'm quick and quiet, I can do this. I text Kenna again.

> Do you recall exactly where the keys are?

> There's a blue bowl on the kitchen counter.

Kitchen counter, blue bowl.

I avoid the driveway and creep down the hill, looping around toward the back of the house, passing the beautiful koi pond en route. Giant, spotted, colorful fish swarm to the side of the pond like reporters storming a red carpet, hopeful for a soundbite.

"I've got nothing for you guys right now, but someone will be back later," I promise them.

Finally, I reach the back door to the main house. I peer in through the glass and don't see anyone. They must all still be asleep. I can see the blue bowl on the counter right where Kenna said it would be. Easy-peasy, in and out.

Quietly, I unlatch the slider and let myself in, tiptoeing across the room in stealth mode. My hand is just inches from the bowl when I hear a little, squeaky voice.

"Who are you?"

Uh-oh.

A moment later, I hear dog claws skittering across the tile, and then my leg is getting humped by a small bundle of fur wearing a tutu. *Do not drop-kick the kid's dog.*

I reach down and peel the dog off my ankle as I answer the child, peeking around the back of a tufted wingback chair. She's holding a Cinderella doll in one fist and a Mermaid doll in the other.

"Oh hey, Orly. It's just me, Lorelei," I say.

"I Lee Lee," she says, narrowing her judgey, little toddler eyes at me. "And you Lie!"

"I am not lying," I defend myself, walking over and squatting down beside her chair. "It's really me, Lorelei. Do you want to see my driver's license?" I pat my pocket, feeling for my wallet.

"No, I hungee. You make me faycooks." Orly pokes me in the chest with a surprisingly bony finger. I take a moment to recover from the assault and to translate what she is saying. I think it is, "I am hungry. Will you make me ... pancakes?"

"Can you repeat that request?" I ask, eyeing the blue bowl. So close. Yet so far.

"Silly Lie! Poncooks!" Orly looks dubious. Am I going to have to make pancakes for this kid now? Isn't there anyone else here whose job it is to make pancakes for this child

I hear footsteps shuffling in. "Oh," Naomi says, looking me up and down. "It's *you*. I guess you're back?"

"I'm not the one who just got in from LA," I say. So much for Kenna warming her up for me. She's obviously still not my biggest fan.

"Is Rafe up yet?" Naomi asks. *Good question.*

"I dunno," I shrug. "I haven't seen him yet this morning. What time did you guys get in from California?"

"Late," she says, taking out the coffee press.

I stand up and retrieve a bottle of alkaline water from the refrigerator.

"Me so hunger." Orly shakes a princess doll over the back of the chair, making her talk like Cookie Monster. I have to admit, it's a little cute.

"Oh Lorelei, I almost forgot, but you were going to show me how to make the fairy pancakes Orly loves before I go, right?" Naomi hits the coffee grinder, pulverizing some beans. The sound makes me flinch.

"Right, I was," I nod. "But now that I think about it, I probably shouldn't share the recipe. It's a family secret." I edge closer to the counter. I can see my keys in the bowl.

"Don't be silly. I asked your mom about them the other day, and she told me that she never made anything like that."

"Weird," I say, swigging my water and considering my options for getting out of the kitchen. *Why hadn't I just waited for Rafe to wake up and bring me the keys?*

And then Rafe walks in. He's got circles under his eyes and bags. Actual bags. Like a normal human being.

When he sees me, his eyes light up for a fraction of a second, like a kid seeing his dream bike under the Christmas tree. But then something clicks, and he recognizes it's the real me, and it's like all his hopes and dreams have been dashed. *I* almost feel like crying.

"Oh hey, you're here," he observes in a monotone voice.

"Yes, I am," I nod, stiffly edging closer to the keys in the bowl on the counter. "But I was just about to get going. Talk later?"

"Don't be ridiculous, Lorelei," Naomi says. "You have to have breakfast with us. Today is my last day. I'm going back to Toronto tomorrow."

"Hungee!" Orly shakes another princess and does the voice again. Less cute, more possessed toddler this time.

"I'm sure Lorelei has better things to do." Rafe lowers himself slowly into a barstool. I've never seen him look more like a little, old man. His eyes are downright melancholy.

Naomi peers skeptically from Rafe to me. "What's with these sad faces?" She pours boiling-hot water from the kettle into the French press and pushes down the plunger. "You two were a regular pair of lovebirds two days ago in California. Aren't you even going to kiss hello?"

Rafe closes his eyes and sighs, mournfully.

"Well?" Naomi looks at me expectantly.

"Uh ... sure," I say and walk over to Rafe, holding my arms out. "So happy to see you again, sweetie."

He stands to deliver a perfunctory hug, and I kiss his cheek and pat his back. We are both leaning forward, as if to ensure as few body parts as possible are touching.

Naomi doesn't look like she's buying it. She rolls her eyes.

"Well, I better get a move on," I say, breezily reaching out for the keys. "I've got some errands to do in town today before we start rehearsals again."

"Aren't you going to take your camera?" Naomi intercepts me, shoving a big, ol' digital camera at me. "You left it at the hotel."

"Oh, this old thing? Of course," I say. "Silly me."

"What's old about it? Rafe said he just bought it for you for the trip?" Naomi's arms are folded in a challenge. "And I would really love it if you could edit the photos before I go. I'd like copies of them for me to show my friends back home. Especially the ones of my fairy godmother ensemble."

Naomi dressed up as a fairy godmother? This I have to see. I turn on the camera, flipping through and poring over the images on the LCD screen.

I click past pictures of Orly and Rafe on the monorail, and towel monkeys in their hotel room.

"Right," I say, smiling, holding up a photo of Naomi in a light-blue dress with a bright-pink scarf. She looks beneficent, standing beside Orly, holding a churro like it's a magic wand.

Damn, they all look like they had so much fun without me.

Quickly, I skip to the next photo in the queue. It's one of Rafe with Orly on his shoulders. It's similar to the one that was posted online, but this one is a close-up, so there is much more detail. This must be a really good camera. I can practically see every stubble pore on his face. Rafe looks so happy and relaxed, staring directly into the camera and smiling the hugest and goofiest grin. I've never seen him look that freaking happy. He's got his sunglasses on, kind of pushed down a little, and he's holding on to Orly's feet. She's got her little face all squinched up, hands in his hair. I zoom in a little closer on the screen to get a better look at his face, and that's when I see Kenna. Reflected perfectly in his sunglasses, holding the camera and smiling the *exact same goofy grin* back at him while she is taking the shot.

It's such a pure and unfiltered expression of love, there is no mistaking it. I'd try to arrange my own features into something similar, but I'm certain I couldn't do it. Some things can't be faked.

"Oh my God," I say, looking up from the camera and over at Rafe. "Oh my *God*. Oh. My. God."

Rafe is in *love*. Like, for real Disney movie in love. *With my little sister.*

"What is it?" Naomi looks concerned. She comes around the counter to look at the camera screen and freezes when she sees it, too. "Oh. Oh my," she says, and lays a hand on her heart.

"Can you believe this?" I ask, scratching my nose like I'm trying to hold back a sneeze and not like it's starting to run because it always does that when I am about to cry.

"I mean, if I hadn't seen it happening firsthand, with my own eyes, I would never have believed it." Naomi shakes her head, apparently agreeing with me, although I'm not sure what she's agreeing to.

"I mean, this kind of changes everything," I say.

"Absolutely," Naomi concurs. "You really can't fake that kind of thing, can you, *Lie Lie*?" She taps the screen and winks at me. "They say a picture is worth a thousand words."

Holy shit. She knows. I lunge toward the blue bowl, but Naomi smugly slides it away from me.

"For Christ's sake, what are the two of you looking at?" Rafe asks.

Naomi does the honors, flipping the camera around.

"We're looking at this photo of you and that girl you've been trying to pass off as Lorelei all week. The one whom you're in love with."

Precisely at this moment, a fairy princess Barbie comes sailing through the air and smacks me on the ass.

"HUNGEEEEE!" Orly yells, ducking back behind the chair when she sees my expression.

Meanwhile, Princess, the wonder mutt, helpfully dives after the Barbie, fetching and dropping it at my feet before resuming her post, ankle-side, at hump station zero. *I didn't even know female dogs were humpers.*

"Here's a thought," I say, finally managing to swipe my car keys and shake them. "How about we all go out for breakfast? I think I know where we can get some great fairy pancakes."

kenna

. . .

THE ESPRESSO MAKER is back up and running, and the sun is shining the next morning after my return to Ephron. Not a moment too soon. After three rainy days without "their regular" hits of caffeine, many of the towns-people are starting to show signs of withdrawal.

Xander pops into the diner for a matcha latte and claps when he spots me back at my regular station. "Thank the Lord," he says. "Our Legendary Lady of Latte is back."

"Yeah, Xander. I think everyone is glad old Bessie here is fixed," I say pointedly, patting the espresso maker.

"Righhhhht." Xander nods and takes a seat at a two-top near the door. "Any *celeb* sightings?"

"Nope," I say, busying myself with the steamer. I don't want to think about Rafe and how much I miss him. It's killing me, knowing he's still here in town, so close. I wish I'd made copies of all the photos I took in Disney with him. But would seeing those photos make it any easier? The only photo I do have is the one that Naomi took on my phone of a sleeping Rafe and

351

Orly. She hadn't deleted it, and neither have I, though I know I probably should. Why torture myself?

I had my fun. I'll have to be satisfied with the memories. I wonder if he likes the photos I took.

The thing about a fling with a celebrity is that you can't just get it on and get over it. There are reminders everywhere. On television and in magazines. On the Internet, and on that one kid's lunch box when he sits at the counter with his mom. I know I'm never going to be free from that.

But none of these stony-faced and steely-eyed Titanium Man images of Rafe are *my* Rafe. My Rafe is goofy and solicitous and incredibly kind. Able to leap over a railing with a six-foot drop in a single bound when he's concerned about his kid, but such a concerned citizen that he thinks tractors should have the right of way in farm territory. My Rafe Barzilay gives amazing back rubs and sings children's songs in Hebrew to his daughter with the well-trained voice of a former boy band member. My Rafe ...

Is not mine.

Mechanically, without thinking, I make drink after drink. I've got plans to hang with Georgia later today, after she gets back from her doctor's appointment. She's reached the point in her pregnancy where she's starting to slow down a bit, and I'm pretty sure there's no way she'll be able to complete the business management course with me. But she can follow along online, and just the fact that she's willing to do this in order to support me means everything.

"Morning, *Kenna*." Noah Greenberg winks at me as he takes a seat at the counter. I notice he's lost the cane and he's barely limping. In fact, he almost seems to have a new spring in his step.

"Noah," I nod. "How was your weekend?"

"My weekend was—"

He stops talking when he sees Lorelei. Her blonde curls are even crazier than mine, and she's wearing a *DND* sweatshirt with a pair of leggings and sheepskin boots. Car keys in hand, she throws open the door to the diner like she owns the place, spies Noah, and makes a beeline for him, all but jumping in his lap as she throws herself at him and kisses him passionately.

Everyone in the diner stops what they are doing to sit and watch the show the two of them are putting on. Including me. People start clapping. Xander wolf-whistles.

"God, I missed you," she says.

What's it been? One night? And then I realize how much I've missed Rafe in roughly the same amount of time.

"I missed you, too," Noah says. "And don't get me wrong, that was awesome, but uh, aren't you worried the paparazzi might be taking pics?"

"They better be. I just paid a guy fifteen hundred dollars to park himself on a bench out there in Holm Square and get a shot of me smooching you."

"Why would you do that?" Noah asks, still a bit breathless and distracted, which I'm guessing has everything to do with the way she's still stroking his chest.

"Because I don't have anything to hide. And also, I'm just setting the record straight. There have been some rumors flying around about me and another guy, and they are totally not true. There's only one man I'm into at the moment." Lorelei kisses Noah again, and I have to look away. The heat between those two. *Noah Greenberg! Who knew?*

I walk to the window and stare out, scanning the park across the street, looking for the paparazzi, but all I see is the old dude in the overalls—the same one I saw on Main Street when I was making the delivery to the theater, and who I saw again, delivering the milk and eggs at Rafe's place. Weirdly, he waves. He couldn't possibly have seen me looking out through the diner windows from that distance, could he?

I beckon Carlos over to have a look out the window. "Have you ever seen that guy out there on the bench before?"

But when I turn back to point the guy out, he's already gone.

"What guy?" Carlos looks confused. "There's nobody there."

"That's so weird. He was just there."

Carlos shrugs, then gestures at Lorelei and waggles his brows. "Should we make Lorelei her mocha macchiato?"

"You knew?" I laugh.

"Of course I knew. Every time she handed someone a drink, she splashed coffee on me and the cash register. With her right hand. You pass drinks with the left hand, and you don't spill."

"Was that the only tell?" I ask.

"No. When she didn't recognize Cody, that's when I knew for sure."

"I'm sorry, Carlos. I hope it wasn't too hard on you."

"Are you kidding? I can't believe I was working with a celebrity for a week. It's like one of those undercover reality shows. Secret Barista. Wait til I tell my wife."

"Carlos, there is no such show," I argue.

"But there should be!"

I excuse myself to refill the half-and-half carafes on the coffee bar. *Secret Barista. What a funny idea.*

"Oh good, the gang's all here." I hear the barstool squeaking as Lorelei swivels on it behind me.

When I turn around, I see Rafe, Naomi, and Orly coming in.

"Give her back the camera, Rafe. I bet it fits a hell of a lot better than a glass slipper."

———

I drop the creamer and bolt. Out the back door, into the alley. I don't know why I ran. I just saw them and panicked. Last week was supposed to be a dream. Not a recurring nightmare. What am I going to say to Naomi? She must know now that I deceived her. Rafe looked absolutely miserable. And Orly. Lee Lee. Sweet Orly.

I lean up against the wall, trying to catch my breath and gather my thoughts. It's ridiculous that I ran away, but the minute I saw them all standing there and knew that they knew who I really am, I just had to flee.

Rafe is in the diner. Waiting for me. Rafe Barzilay just walked into the diner with a camera.

"He's in love with you," Lorelei says, following me into the alley. She looks around and pats the wall. "Oh hey, this spot *is* kind of special, isn't it? It's where Georgia kicked the crap outta me."

"How? How can Rafe be in love with me? He's perfect!" I moan.

"Perfect? Seriously, have you seen his hairy big toes?" Lorelei leans against the brick wall.

"I couldn't care less about that," I admit.

"How about the snail speed at which he drives?" she asks.

"Who cares about that?" I say. "Better safe than sorry."

"And where do you stand with regard to his penchant for food that is loaded with beans and garlic?"

"I love both of those things, too. Especially his mom's hummus." I pace in circles.

"Okay. So while *I* don't think Rafe is perfect, I do think he might be perfect for you. And Kenna, I think you're perfect for Rafe, too. I've never seen him this miserable," Lorelei says.

"What?"

"I mean, he's just miserable because he thinks *you* aren't into him." Lorelei grins, like she thinks this is really funny.

"That's ridiculous! Why wouldn't I be into him?" I am offended on Rafe's behalf. Lorelei shouldn't be laughing at him, and obviously, I would be into him.

"Then what's your problem? Why'd you leave? And why didn't you keep the camera?" She looks exasperated.

"Because! We had to swap back. None of it was real. And I'm not good enough. I'm not you. It's messy. He's a dad!" I tick off all the reasons on my fingers. All the reasons I can't have Rafe Barzilay.

"Nobody asked you to actually be me, Kenna. Lord knows, Rafe doesn't want you to be me! And real? Shit just got *really real*! We're *sisters*. It's like your uncles said. We're family now, that's a fact. There's no going back." She pauses, kicking at the bricks, no longer making eye contact.

"Of course, you get to choose how much you want me in your life. But I'm kind of hoping you won't kick me to the curb."

There's just a hint of that toddler in her still. I see it now.

"Who hasn't secretly wished for a sister as cool and awesome as you?" I say. "But it's overwhelming. I'm not sure I can live up to your level of success. I don't fit into your world. I'm not smart, glamorous and ... shiny like you."

"Are you kidding me? You know that's all bullshit, right? There's nothing that makes celebrities better people than anybody else," Lorelei insists.

"I mean, it's not like you're a neurosurgeon." I imitate Naomi, and we both crack up.

"If anything, neither Rafe nor I are worthy of you, Kenna. You work tirelessly to make other people's lives better. And I know some bad dudes have taken advantage of you, but I'm here to tell you, Rafe is not that guy. I know Rafe like a brother, and that dude is crazy about you."

"If he's your brother and you're my sister ..."

"Stop. I said *like* a brother." Lorelei rolls her eyes. "Do you know how weird it was to find that photo of the two of you where you looked so much like me?" She shivers. "But here's the thing. It's so clearly not a picture of me because Rafe, my *buddy* Rafe, would never ever in a million years look at me the way he was looking at you in that photo."

"What photo?" *Is she talking about the ones on social media?*

"The one that you took."

"I didn't take a photo of me and Rafe."

"Oh yeah, you did." Lorelei holds out a hand. "Come back inside and see."

———

We cut through the kitchen when we head back in. Naomi is standing beside Uncle Nick and Uncle Stavros at the griddle.

"I suspected it, but I knew something was definitely up the minute I chatted with Lorelei's mom. She said Lorelei had found some photos, possible relatives here in Ephron. Plus, Lorelei can't make a grilled cheese sandwich, let alone pancakes."

"Oh, I've heard you make some excellent dishes with cheese at your restaurant," Uncle Stavros gushes.

"Oh yes. Come to my restaurant in Toronto, and I'll show you what I do with Halloumi," Naomi says, smiling.

Uncle Nick flips the last pancake onto the stack on the plate and slides it to me. Then he dusts the stack with a mixture of crushed Fruity Pebbles and powdered sugar. "Order up," he says, passing me the plate and jerking his head toward the seating area.

"You got this." Lorelei squeezes my hand.

I take a deep breath and head out into the diner where Rafe and Orly are sitting by themselves at one of the large, round booths. Orly is perched in a booster. Her dolls and crayons are spilled across the surface of the table where she is currently coloring and snacking on some fruit. She's stacked up all the jelly containers like blocks, and some of them have spilled onto the bench. Rafe is just sitting there, staring at the blank screen of the camera in front of him.

"Your pancakes, madam?" I set the plate in front of Orly. "We have strawberry syrup to go with them," I say, pointing at the cruet on the side of the plate. "I highly recommend you try it."

"LIE LIE!" Orly stands in the booth and flings herself at me, knocking her juice over in the process. Fortunately, there's a lid on it, and Rafe rights the cup and mops the spill before it travels. His eyes meet mine.

"Looks like we made a little bit of a mess after all," I say, sitting down in the booth with Orly still wrapped around me. "Are you going to eat these, or are they for me?" I tease, pretending that I'm going to eat one of her pancakes. She jumps off me, moving to guard her plate protectively.

"My poncooks!" she says.

"Better eat them while they're still warm then," I say, smiling.

"I wish you would keep the camera." Rafe looks up at me, pushing the camera toward me, hopefully.

"Show her the picture, Rafe," Lorelei hisses, sauntering by with a pot of coffee held aloft, like she works in the place and she's scouting for mugs to fill.

"Hi, Lorelei." Orly waves her Barbie at my sister without looking up from the plate of pancakes.

"Go away, Lorelei. I was getting to it." Rafe rolls his eyes and makes an annoyed face at her. Then he resumes blankly staring at the blank screen.

"So? Are you going to show me?" I hold out a hand.

Rafe flicks the power on the camera and begins to toggle through the photos. He can't help smiling a little as he scrolls past a few, and I wish I could see what he is looking at. I get a thrill at having taken photos he likes. Finally, he stops his scroll.

"My one regret is not taking the camera from you and taking more photos of *you*," he says. "But this one"—he stares at the image for a moment—"is my favorite from the whole weekend. And it just happens to be the only one that you're in."

I really don't remember taking any photos of myself.

"Let me see." I hold my hands out for the camera. Rafe turns it around and hands it to me.

Immediately, I recognize the picture. I stare down at the image of Rafe and Orly. Then I close my eyes, remembering the moment in my mind, reliving what I'd been thinking when I took the shot.

I'd been thinking how lucky Orly is to have such a loving and adoring father and family, and how beautiful and perfect the two of them are together, despite the bumps and bruises along the way, the imperfect circumstances and tragedies that got them here. And it was like the rainbow after the storm. Pure joy. That was what I had been feeling, basking in their glow.

Also, if I was being honest with myself, love. I was feeling my own pure, unadulterated love for both of them. Even if they weren't mine. I loved them, and I loved getting to be a part of their day.

"But this is just a picture of you and Orly," I say, not seeing myself anywhere in the photo. What is he talking about?

"Zoom in!" Lorelei makes a second pass with the coffeepot as a prop.

Is there even any coffee in that pot?

Rafe reaches out and pushes the button with the tiny + sign on it, zooming in closer, centering on his sunglasses. And that's when I see what Rafe is looking at in the photo. I see what's putting that incredible smile on *his* face.

I see myself.

Orly leans across and glances at the photo, too. She points. "Lee Lee and Lie Lie." She hugs me quickly and goes back to dipping her pancakes in the strawberry sauce, leaving a trail of sweet, sticky blobs on the table.

"We're making a mess," I whisper, feeling the tears starting to fill my eyes.

"A sweet, sweet, mess." Rafe slips out of his side of the booth and slides in next to me on mine.

"I wish you would keep the camera, but more importantly, I wish you would keep us." He glances sideways at Orly, who is wiping a hand on his shirt. "It's a sticky situation, but we're kind of a package deal. I love you, Kenna Papadopoulos," Rafe says, and then in front of his mom, my sister, the uncles, and everyone else in the diner, he kisses me.

epilogue: lorelei

"Is this the same yurt that Dean Riley and Chelsea Porter stayed in?" I ask Noah, turning down the latest episode of the *Lit Lovers'* podcast. Noah and I are sitting on the front porch outside a cozy, tan, canvas yurt, nestled in the mountains outside of Ephron, eating chocolate-covered strawberries provided by the Airbnb host. It's just dreamy.

I've got two days off, and Noah and I are holing up here, kicking back, planning our trip to the Nomad Games in Kyrgyzstan, and generally, relaxing. He pops a strawberry in my mouth and kisses me, rocking me back in my rocking chair. I nearly topple over.

"Noah Greenberg," I say. "You rock my world!"

"Mmmm," Noah says, reaching over to turn the podcast back on. "Hang on. I want to hear Jackson's big announcement."

"Congratulations, Jackson!" Emily is saying. "This is huge news!"

"Damn," I say. "Rewind a minute?"

Noah rewinds the podcast and repositions the tiny, portable speaker a little closer.

"... So, at first we were just going to sponsor the show with my matchmaking app, but then the producers asked me if I wanted to be on the show."

"As a member of the cast?" Alexis asks. "Like they are going to set you up with people?"

"No," Jackson says. "Don't be ridiculous. I would never."

"Then what? As a host?" Emily asks.

"No, not that, either," Chelsea chimes in. "They have some Italian stud hosting. Apparently, he's a real hottie who's on loads of book covers. Marco something."

"OMG!" Emily says. "I think I know that guy!"

"The show is part of a Summer of Love push at the network. Lots of new dating shows, but this one pits traditional matchmaking theories and techniques against modern compatibility tools and AI, like Jackson's app," Chelsea explains.

"Yeah. They asked me to participate as an expert. Me and Isla Fairfax, that crazy woo woman we had on the podcast last year. They want us to opine."

"Opining. Sounds right up Jackson's alley," Alexis chuckles.

"I would not describe Isla Fairfax as a crazy woo woman, Jackson," Emily argues. "We've discussed her novels on this show before. You yourself have said she is an excellent plotter."

"Yeah, but that was when we were discussing fiction, not trying to meddle in real people's lives. The couples in her books get set up by their spirit guides and shit."

"My brother doesn't believe in magic," Chelsea says. "Probably because he's never been in love himself. What's that phrase? 'Physician, heal thyself'?"

"What's the show called?" Alexis asks.

"Playing with Matches," Jackson sighs. "I know, so kitsch, right?"

"I love it," Emily says. "And it's being filmed at an all-inclusive resort in the Caribbean?"

"Yep," Jackson nods.

"Lucky you!"

"As long as we wrap before hurricane season. I've got my sunscreen, bug repellant, and allergy meds ready."

"You make it sound exotic in all the best ways, bro," Chelsea laughs. "But honestly, I am so excited for you. This all came together so quickly."

"They're still putting a lot of the details together. But I will be gone for a few weeks, so the podcast will have to go on hiatus in the meantime," Jackson says.

"Congratulations, Jackson! This is such huge news! I can't wait to follow along with you when the show airs this fall," Emily says.

I flip off the podcast and turn to Noah. "Are you sure you're okay taking time off from your show while we're at the Nomad Games?"

"It will be fine. We'll film a bonus episode before we go, so it won't break the flow."

"Have you thought about the thing we talked about?"

"I'd prefer to keep my professional identity as a teacher and my personal interests separate. You know that, Lorelei. It's just a lot to explain to the students and the school board, not to mention the parents. I don't want to quit my day job."

"I know that," I say, leaning over to kiss him again. "I love that you are so committed to all your kids. I just hate keeping secrets from my sister and the rest of the family."

"Maybe someday," Noah says. "After Rafe and Kenna get married."

"Oh, you think that they are getting married?" I ask, grinning goofily.

"I think they are essentially already married in their hearts," he says, smiling.

"And what about us?" I ask.

"We can do whatever we want, be whoever we want. If not in real life, then in our imaginations."

"I love your dirty imagination." I suck the chocolate off another strawberry and pour myself another glass of champagne. To be honest, I do kinda like being the only one who knows about Max. It's kind of hot. People keep asking me if I can reveal the identity of the Dungeon Master, and I just shrug my shoulders and play dumb, and it drives them crazy. The show's popularity has skyrocketed since I joined the cast. Top 100 on Twitch, and high up on the YouTube and Apple podcasts charts as well. The advisory board can't stop raving about my "brilliant decision to explore new, emerging platforms and try on new, inclusive personas."

Whatever, dudes.

"You know, people are bound to figure it out eventually," I sigh, pouring a second flute of champagne for Noah.

"Maybe," he says. "Probably. But that's a problem for *tomorrow* us. We'll cross that bridge when we get there. *Today* us just has to plan whether we want our yurt at the Nomad Games to have grassland or mountain views."

"I'm much more interested in the interior views." I glance back into the yurt behind us. *We could go in there any time. Now would be good.*

"I brought a double-silk sleep sack for us to share," Noah says, "and some mag-safe, rechargeable, light-up dice in case you want to roll with me."

"Oh, I want to roll with you," I nod. "I want to roll all over the world with you, Noah Greenberg." I hold up my glass to toast. "To us," I say.

"To us," Noah echoes. "The world is our oyster."

THE END

If you enjoyed this book, I hope you will take a moment to leave a review. Your reviews help other readers find what they are looking for, and they also mean the world to me!

acknowledgments

I've been writing this story in my head for over a decade. Along the way, I've discussed it with several people, including my brilliant, creative, and funny friend Geneva Wasserman. We batted notes back and forth, and at one point, we booked a hotel to hang out and work on a screenplay, but who were we kidding? We were a couple of exhausted moms who needed a break. Speaking of which, I'm still available for "working on the screenplay," Geneva! Maybe on a cruise this time?

I would not have been able to write all the Disney stuff without the insight and inspiration from my friend Heather Sievers, who has been a soul sister since our kiddos were small. I'm a long-term passholder and Disney fan, and have enjoyed plenty of insider perks via blogging and other connections over the years, but Heather is my VIP expert. Some of the details have been stretched because this is ultimately a work of fiction, but suffice it to say, the reality is just as magical, if not more so, than the story I have written.

Next, I need to mention the *Madmamas.*

When my husband and I adopted our oldest daughter from Russia, I joined all the online groups. That is how I became lifelong friends with a ragtag group of IRL superhero women who span the globe. Together, we have laughed and cried, celebrated and mourned, through every type of victory and challenge. I don't want to gloss over the adoption-related issues that many of us and our kids have faced. Those issues are real and devastating, in some cases. But I also don't wish to dwell

on or reinforce negative beliefs about our community. Stereotypes are unfair, and often wrong. We have proof.

While no one mom or child in the group inspired my characters, there are bits of all of us and our kids that inspired ideas
in this book. I thought about our early get-togethers and baby
Sadie trying to climb into my daughter's stroller with her. I
thought about Larissa, whose mom (one of our members)
passed away when she was a teenager, and how she is thriving
now, a mom herself. I thought about Valla hearing from her
long-lost sisters. I recalled everyone's travel stories. I hope this
book makes my adoption group friends and their families
smile a bit with recognition of the sweeter stuff. Maureen,
Rebecca, Eileen, Janet, Ellen, Roxanne, Lisa, Dede, Pam,
Donna, Wendy, Edita, Kathy, Susan, Jill, Denise, Kimberly,
Sally, Apryl, Mary, Cathie, Mimi, Lynn, Pat, Debbie—I am so
grateful that we are all still in touch on a near-daily basis.

To Sarah Peppel and all my fans who contributed such great
name ideas for Princess Von Floofy the wondermutt. In the
end she really was a Princess. As we all are!

To my kids:

Marly, thanks for being the oldest, the child of my heart, and
inspiring me. You are still the reigning champion of finding all
things lost, including Waldo, and I defy anyone to challenge
your title.

Fox, I really appreciate that you let me text you endless *DND*
questions. Your creativity inspires me.

Leo, thanks for letting me talk about my books in the car, a lot,
while driving you to school. You are so patient and
supportive.

Ani, thanks for always being sympathetic when I struggled on this. My goal in life is to write a book you think is cool because you are so cool.

To my husband, Brian, I'm not sure how you manage to be so supportive and steady as I have embarked on this midlife journey toward authorhood. It feels so selfish and self-indulgent at times, but your delight in the "dailies" and your willingness to dish about my characters over long breakfasts out makes me believe it's not a waste of everyone's time.

As usual, I am grateful for my editors. I could not have written this book without the excellent developmental help of Anya Kagan from Touchstone Editing and the copy editing/proofreading assistance from Joyce Mochrie, owner of One Last Look.

Finally, thanks, as usual, to my entire extended family and friend group for putting up with my crazy determination to finish five books in a year. I apologize in advance for next year's plans.

author's note

Thanks so much for coming along on this ride with me. This book was a labor of love and a true adventure! I'd love to hear what you thought of *The Princess and the Paparazzi*. You can email me any time: Author@CiaraBlume.com.

If you enjoyed this book, I sincerely hope you will take a moment to leave a review on Amazon, BookBub, Goodreads, or wherever you buy and/or share book recommendations. Your reviews help other readers find what they are looking for, and they also mean the world to me. Make sure to check out the other books in the Lit Lovers series as well.

I love hearing from readers on social media!

Here are all the places you can find me on online:

Facebook: https://www.facebook.com/ciarablumeauthor

Instagram: https://www.instagram.com/ciarablumeauthor

TikTok: https://www.TikTok.com/@ciarablumeauthor

Goodreads: https://www.goodreads.com/ciarablume

BookBub: https://www.bookbub.com/authors/ciara-blume

If you'd like to enjoy bonus chapters, fun giveaways, book "soundtracks," and a heads-up about the latest books in the Lit Lovers series, sign up for the Ciara Blume Playlist or visit www.ciarablume.com

xo,

Ciara Blume

bonus: playing with matches sneak peek

prologue: jackson

I'm sitting in the booth at the Ephron Diner, trying not to think about the call I just had with my investors. The app just "isn't performing" they said. They'd talked about the issues in the soberly hushed and clinical terms that doctors use when they discuss erectile dysfunction with a patient. Not that I've ever had that issue. But it's what I imagine.

"There are still things that can be done," the VC said. "Marketing. Although we don't have a lot of budget to put into a big campaign. But grassroots stuff. If you'd be willing. But we'd need to act fast."

"Hit me," I said. I'm not going to give up just yet. I've been working on my algorithm driven dating app for the better part of a decade. It's not about the money, I don't need more of that. It's about making a difference. It's about opening up new and enlightened ways for informed would-be couplers to make optimized matches. It's about preventing the kind of train wreck relationships that my parents had.

"Well..." My VC paused. "Have you ever considered being on a reality show about dating?"

"As what?" I asked.

You would think that as a data guy, reality TV would not be my thing. But I also host a podcast where we make fun of all the ridiculous things people do in the name of love and in that sense, it is SO my thing.

My sister and podcast co-hosts love to discuss what's happened on shows like The Bachelor and Love Island. In fact, studying the tropes and behavior patterns exhibited on these shows has really helped me train and perfect my algorithms. By the end of the third episode of most of these shows, I can predict who will end up together with greater than 67% accuracy - just by scraping public data from the contestants' Instagram profiles.

My podcast, "Lit Lovers," has gained a decent following over the last couple of years. Having celeb guests on the show, like Blaze Smith the popular relationship guru, and my old BFF Dean Riley the Oscar winning Art Director for the *Titanium Man* series, certainly hasn't hurt our ratings. I respect the powers of mainstream media.

"I'd definitely be up to *host* a dating show," I said. I could see myself providing wise counsel to the heartbroken contestants. Explaining to them that there's a better way.

"That's not what they were thinking, Jackson."

"Well I hope you weren't signing me up as a contestant," I balked, wrinkling my nose like I just smelled some bad milk. "There's no way. No way in hell."

Being a host is one thing, but I would never subject myself to being a contestant on one of those shows. I'm not looking for love in all the wrong places. I'm not looking for love at all! If I want to get laid there's a whole different kind of app for that. One that I have no problems tapping, or rather swiping, on occasion.

But I don't mix business and pleasure. Relationships, real ones, are complicated business affairs. And while I'm all for helping other people get what they want out of them? I am not interested in investing my own capital.

"Relax, Jackson," the VC said. "Nothing so demeaning. There's a new show filming at one of our partner properties next month and apparently they are looking for experts. It seems right up your alley. Matchmaking 2.0. They're pitting outdated methods of making matches against newer, better, data-driven models."

"Interesting," I considered this. "What's it called and where's it shooting?"

"It's called Playing with Matches," and it's shooting at the Peaches Luxury resort in the Caribbean. If you're free to fly down to LA tomorrow, we can get you in with the producer before lunch. They are anxious to meet with you. They want access to the algorithm for making the matches on the show."

"You really think this would be good for the app?" I asked. I'm kind of a bug magnet and not all that fond of hot weather. Plus I really don't like sharing proprietary data.

"I think that this is our best option. We can't afford to advertise but if the show is giving you a shout out every week? Dude this is a national primetime audience. Think of it as the blue pill."

"Fine," I'd finally capitulated. "I'll get my VA to book a flight, and I'll hear them out."

And then I'd rushed over to the Ephron Diner to meet my podcast cohost, Emily and her romance writer friend Isla who's in town visiting.

But two hours later I'm still wondering which blue kind of blue pill the VC was referring to.

According to my podcast host Emily we've discussed Isla's books on one of the past episodes of Lit Lovers but who can keep all these romance writers straight? I have the vague impression that there was something kooky about her stories, but perhaps it's her fluorescent yellow sweater, flaming red hair and hot pink glasses that are throwing me off. She's so bright and colorful I feel like I need sunglasses to look at her.

"I'm back!" announces a curly haired blond in a barista apron. Kenna, the barista who likes to call herself a "coffee witch", comes to our table to greet us.

"I didn't know you were away," Emily says, waving her offer of coffee, away. "No thanks. I'm holding out for a London Fog when the machine is fixed. I know you said to try the mocha macchiato the other day but I'm afraid it just wasn't *me*."

"I can whip you up a London Fog with the frother, I don't need to use the espresso maker for that," Kenna says cheerily. "It's no problem and it's on me."

"Oh really? Well then I'd love one of your special drinks too," says Isla. Her accent reminds me of Veruca Salt from *Charlie and the Chocolate Factory*. Sure she's polite, but I can totally picture her in a mini dress, mid-tantrum, stomping her foot and demanding "I want it NOW."

Bad idea. That mental image works faster than the fun kind of blue pill.

Too bad I have to be up so early tomorrow, no time to swipe right on a competitor's app tonight. I scowl. This is all my deadbeat father's fault. If he hadn't been such a horndog, and such a drunk. Well I probably wouldn't be here today. Lucky for me, I only inherited the horndog part. The app is a sort of penance for both of our sins.

If Isla notices my scowl she doesn't comment. Instead she turns to the woman holding the coffee pitcher. "You must be Kenna. I've heard all about your magical, psychic drink matching abilities."

Magical, psychic, drink matching abilities? I snort. More like magical upselling skills. "She isn't always right," I say. "Case in point - Emily's macchiato."

"Anyone can have an off day," Isla peers over her glasses, looking askance at me. A thick red strand of hair falls across her face and she puckers her hot pink lips to blow it away. Oh shit. Now there's a sexy punk rock librarian vibe happening. I cross and uncross my legs. She turns toward Kenna.

"I'm Isla, by the way, Emily and I met in Rome." She reaches out to grab Kenna's hand and holds it, staring at her wide eyed and expectantly. "Are you getting any kind of read on me?"

Kenna might not be getting a read on her, but I am. And it's full fruity nut cake. And yet, I am oddly tempted to lick her, like the kids licking the wallpaper in the *Charlie and the Chocolate Factory* film. Would her snozzberries taste like snozzberries?

"Apricot tea with honey, frothed oatmilk, and a ginger shot." Kenna grins as she makes her proclamation.

"That is so uncanny!" Isla lets her hand go and claps like a delighted child "Now I cannot think of anything I would rather drink more."

"Power of suggestion," I roll my eyes. I bet that's one of the priciest drinks on the menu.

"Just for that, I'm not offering to make anything special for you, Dr Spock." Kenna rolls her eyes. "How's the 'ol dating app going?" She looks at me with disdain, almost like she knows something. Which she couldn't. I remind myself that Kenna is known for dating Ephron's biggest losers. She's exactly the sort of person who needs my help.

"It's out on the market now," I say. "Still testing, but we'll see. I can give you a code if you'd like to get in on the beta."

"Oh Kenna doesn't need your app," Isla smiles mischievously and licks her lips. "Cupid's arrow has already struck this one." She winks at me, and as I follow her eyes to Kenna's face, I cannot help but spot the massive hickey on her neck. An actual hickey. Like junior high school style. What kind of loser is she spending her off hours with, now? I raise my brows, surprised?

Kenna sees my expression and you can see the moment that she figures out what we are all staring at - reflected in the shiny mirror-like surface of the coffee pot. Blushing red as a beet, and mumbling about fixing drinks she rushes off.

"Poor girl," Isla bites her lip. "I hope I didn't embarrass her. I can just tell she's in love. I definitely get the vibe that it's something serious."

"Let me guess, you read hickey shapes like entrails?" I smirk, stirring some sugar into my coffee.

"Pardon?" Isla blinks at me, her wide blue eyes doe-like and confused. "What is he talking about?" She turns toward Emily for clarification.

"I'm talking about the blue butterfly she was sporting on her neck flesh. The hickey. The leech marks. Dracula's love stamp. Whatever you wanna call it. Looks like our girl has reeled in a regular lamprey eel this time."

"Jeez, Jackson. That's so rude! Even for you." Emily exclaims, coloring.

"She had a hickey?" Isla cocks her head considering.

"Are you blind?" I ask. "Although, considering how bright your sweater is, I guess it is a possibility." I pull on my sunglasses to make a point. I was already in a bad mood because of the app. Now I can feel the tiny pulsing tap tap taps of a tension headache, beating a drum in the distance. I gotta cancel the episode we were planning to tape this evening. I'm not sure I can stand staring into the bright light that is Isla. I'm already seeing spots.

"I am not blind," Isla sticks out her chin and pushes up her glasses. "These are blue light glasses. I mostly wear them for reading and working on my laptop. And fashion, of course." She sits up straighter. "And I didn't notice her hickey but now that you mention it, it *is* interesting that it was butterfly shaped. Butterflies are powerful symbols of transformation, hope, and faith. They are a good omen, and portend love. Haven't you ever heard the term "butterflies in your stomach?"

"That butterfly flew the coop," I say. "And last time I had butterflies in my stomach was when a condom broke. I was scared shitless I was going to have to pay child support to my one night stand for the rest of my life."

I'm lying. I wasn't thrilled about the condom, which fortunately, didn't turn out to be an issue after all, but it had not given me butterflies. What gave me butterflies, in recent memory, was seeing my best friend, Dean Riley, kissing my little sister and *knowing*, without a doubt, that they were perfect for each other. What's worse is that I knew it before I ran their profiles through my system.

I chalk it up to knowing them both so well. I must have internalized the algorithm, and have already been "running the data" on a subconscious level.

"You are in rare form," Emily shakes her head disapprovingly at me. "Don't pay him any mind, Isla. He's always a grump, but he's not usually this bad. Did you wake up on the wrong side of the bed today?"

She's right. I know I'm being a dick, but I can't seem to make it stop.

"Maybe," I shake my head. "I'm working on a headache. Do you mind if we take a raincheck on recording that episode tonight? I've got some out of town meetings tomorrow, but maybe we can meet up later this week and discuss Isla's books? Or was it a blog?"

"I do both," Isla is staring at me. "But I'm afraid I'm leaving tomorrow. I'm visiting with my editor in California and I also have a few meetings and events to attend."

"But hopefully you'll be back in the fall?" Emily says. "It's glorious here when the leaves are changing."

"I'll try," Isla smiles warmly at Emily. "I'd love to see the leaves, but more importantly I'd love to see more of you and Blaze. I always knew you two were *destined* to be together."

"On that note," I toss a bill on the table, trying not to flinch as I glance back at Isla. "I hope you enjoy the rest of your travels stateside Isla. Meeting you has been - *illuminating*. Perhaps our paths will cross again." I slide to the edge of the circular booth and stand to go.

Isla holds out her hand, palm down, and I take it, a little reluctantly because I'd rather just get out of here. Is this a European thing? Palm down? I'm not sure whether she expects me to shake it or? Am I supposed to kiss it?

Fuck this is awkward.

She has hot pink fingernails and a large opal ring that's shooting iridescent sparks at me. Maybe I'm suppose to kiss the ring? No that's royalty. I close my eyes and try to imagine what Dean Riley would do. Dean has always been so effortlessly cool. Dean would definitely kiss her freckled little hand. I can picture it. No hesitation. So I do that. I bend forward, holding her hand firmly and confidently as I lift it to my lips. I hear Emily's sharp and sudden intake of breath as I do this. Not quite a gasp, but close.

Screw it. I'm still doing this.

Isla's eyes don't stray from mine. They bore into me like the blue beacons on top of a patrol car that's about to pull me over as I plant the lightest, most feathery kiss across her knuckles.

And that's when I feel them. Fucking blue butterflies. Not just in my stomach. I can feel them all the way down in my balls, too.